Diana Tempest

Diana Tempest
Mary Cholmondeley

MINT EDITIONS

Diana Tempest was first published in 1893.

This edition published by Mint Editions 2021.

ISBN 9781513291154 | E-ISBN 9781513294001

Published by Mint Editions®

 MINT
EDITIONS

minteditionbooks.com

Publishing Director: Jennifer Newens
Design & Production: Rachel Lopez Metzger
Project Manager: Micaela Clark
Typesetting: Westchester Publishing Services

VOLUME I

I

"La pire des mésalliances est celle du coeur."

Colonel Tempest and his miniature ten-year-old replica of himself had made themselves as comfortable as circumstances would permit in opposite corners of the smoking carriage. It was a chilly morning in April, and the boy had wrapped himself in his travelling rug, and turned up his little collar, and drawn his soft little travelling cap over his eyes in exact, though unconscious, imitation of his father. Colonel Tempest looked at him now and then with paternal complacency. It is certainly a satisfaction to see ourselves repeated in our children. We feel that the type will not be lost. Each new edition of ourselves lessens a natural fear lest a work of value and importance should lapse out of print.

Colonel Tempest at forty was still very handsome; and must, as a young man, have possessed great beauty before the character had had time to assert itself in the face; before selfishness had learned to look out of the clear grey eyes, and a weak self-indulgence and irresolution had loosened the well-cut lips.

Colonel Tempest, as a rule, took life very easily. If he had fits of uncontrolled passion now and then, they were quickly over. If his feelings were touched, that was quickly over too. But today his face was clouded. He had tried the usual antidotes for an impending attack of what he would have called "the blues," by which he meant any species of reflection calculated to give him that passing annoyance which was the deepest form of emotion of which he was capable. But *Punch* and the *Sporting Times*, and even the comic French paper which Archie might not look at, were powerless to distract him today. At last he tossed the latter out of the window to corrupt the morals of trespassers on the line, and, as it was, after all, less trouble to yield than to resist, settled himself in his corner, and gave way to a series of gloomy and anxious reflections.

He was bent on a mission of importance to his old home, to see his brother who was dying. His mind always recoiled instinctively from the thought of death, and turned quickly to something else. It was fourteen years since he had been at Overleigh, fourteen years since that event had taken place which had left a deadly enmity of silence and estrangement between his brother and himself ever since. And it had all been about a woman. It seemed extraordinary to Colonel Tempest, as he looked back, that a quarrel which had led to such serious consequences—which had, as he remembered, spoilt his own life—should have come from so slight a cause. It was like losing the sight of an eye because a fly had committed trespass in it. A man's mental rank may generally be determined by his estimate of woman. If he stands low he considers her—heaven help her—such an one as himself. If he climbs high he takes his ideal of her along with him, and, to keep it safe, places it above himself.

Colonel Tempest pursued the reflections suggested by an untaxed intellect of average calibre which he believed to be profound. A mere girl! How men threw up everything for women! What fools men were when they were young! After all, when he came to think of it, there had been some excuse for him. (There generally was.) How beautiful she had been with her pale exquisite face, and her innocent eyes, and a certain shy dignity and pride of bearing peculiar to herself. Yes, any other man would have done the same in his place. The latter argument had had great weight with Colonel Tempest through life. He could not help it if she were engaged to his brother. It was as much her fault as his own if they fell in love with each other. She was seventeen and he was seven and twenty, but it is always the woman who "has the greater sin."

He remembered, with something like complacency, the violent love-making of the fortnight that followed, her shy adoration of her beautiful eager lover. Then came the scruples, the flight, the white cottage by the Thames, the marriage at the local register office. What a fool he had been, he reflected, and how he had worshipped her at first, before he had been disappointed in her; disappointed in her as the boy is in the butterfly when he has it safe—and crushed—in his hand. She might have made anything of him, he reflected. But somehow there had been a hitch in her character. She had not taken him the right way. She had been unable to effect a radical change in him, to convert weakness and irresolution into strength and decision; and he had been quite ready to have anything of that sort done for him. During all those early weeks of married life, until she caught a heavy cold on her chest, he had believed existence had been easily and delightfully transformed for him. He was susceptible. His feelings were always easily touched. Everything influenced him, for a time; beautiful music, or a pathetic story for half an hour; his young wife for—nearly six months.

A play usually ends with the wedding, but there is generally an after-piece, ignored by lovers but expected by an experienced audience. The after-piece in Colonel Tempest's domestic drama began with tears, caused, I believe, in the first instance by a difference of opinion as to who was responsible for the earwigs in his bath sponge. In the white cottage there were many earwigs. But even after the earwig difficulty was settled by a move to London, other occasions seemed to crop up for the shedding of those tears which are known to be the common resource of women for obtaining their own way when other means fail; and others, many others, suggested by youth and inexperience and a devoted love had failed. If they are silent tears, or worse still, if the eyelids betray that they have been shed in secret, a man may with reason become much annoyed at what looks like a tacit reproach. Colonel Tempest became annoyed. It is the good fortune of shallow men so thoroughly to understand women, that they can see through even the noblest of them; though of course that deeper insight into the hypocrisy practised by the whole sex about their fancied ailments, and inconveniently wounded feelings for their own petty objects, is reserved for selfish men alone.

Matters have become very wrong indeed, when a caress is not enough to set all right at once; but things came to that shocking pass between Colonel and Mrs. Tempest, and went in the course of the next few years several steps further still, till they reached, on her part, that dreary dead level of emaciated semi-maternal tenderness, which is the only feeling some husbands allow their wives to entertain permanently for them; the only kind of love which some men believe a virtuous woman is capable of.

How he had suffered, he reflected, he who needed love so much. Even the advent of the child had only drawn them together for a time. He remembered how deeply touched he had been when it was first laid in his arms, how drawn towards its mother. But his smoking-room fire had been neglected during the following week, and he could not find any large envelopes, and the nurse made absurd restrictions about his seeing his wife at his own hours, and Di herself was feeble and languid, and made no attempt to enter into his feelings, or show him any sympathy, and—

Colonel Tempest sighed as he made this mournful retrospect of his married life. He had never cared to be much at home, he reflected. His home had not been made very pleasant to him; the poor meagre home in a dingy street, the wrong side of Oxford Street, which was all that a young man in the Guards, with expensive tastes, who had quarrelled with his elder brother, could afford. The last evening he had spent in that house came back to him with a feeling of bitter resentment at the recollection of his wife's unreasonable distress when a tradesman called after dinner for payment of a longstanding account which she had understood was settled. It was not a large bill he remembered wrathfully, and he had intended to keep his promise of paying it directly his money came in, but when it came he had needed it, and more, for his share of the spring fishing he had taken cheap with a friend. Naturally he would not see the man whose loud voice, asking repeatedly for him, could be heard in the hall, and who refused to go away. Colonel Tempest had a dislike to rows with tradespeople. At last his wife, prostrate, and in feeble health, rose languidly from her sofa, and went down to meet the recriminations of the unfortunate tradesman, who, after a long interval, retired, slamming the door. Colonel Tempest heard her slow step come up the stair again, and then, instead of stopping at the drawing-room door, it had gone toiling upwards to the room above. He was incensed by so distinct an evidence of temper. Surely, he said to himself with exasperation, she knew when she married him that she was marrying a poor man.

She did not return: and at last he blew out the lamp, and lighting the candle put ready for him, went upstairs, and opening the door of his wife's room, peered in. She was sitting in the dark by the black fireplace with her head in her hands. A great deal of darkness and cold seemed to have been compressed into that little room. She raised her head as he came in. Her wide eyes had a look in them of a dumb unreasoning animal distress which took him aback. There was no pride nor anger in her face. In his ignorance he supposed she would reproach him. He had not yet realized that the day of reproaches and appeals, very bitter while it lasted, was long past, years past. The silence of those who have loved us is sometimes eloquent as a tombstone of that which has been buried beneath it.

The room was very cold. A faint smell of warm india-rubber and a molehill in the middle of the bed showed that a hot bottle was found more economical than coal.

"Why on earth don't you have a fire?" he asked, still standing in the doorway, personally aggrieved at her economies. Di's economies had often been the subject of sore annoyance to him. An anxious housekeeper in her teens sometimes retrenches in the wrong place, namely where it is unpalatable to the husband. Di had cured herself of this fault of late years, but it cropped up now and again, especially when he returned home unexpectedly as today, and found only mutton chops for dinner.

"It was the coal bill that the man came about this evening," she said, apathetically, and then the peculiar distressed look giving place to a more human expression, as she suddenly became aware of the reproach her words implied, she added quickly, "but I am not the least cold, thanks."

Still he lingered; a sense of ill-usage generally needs expression.

"Why did not you come back to the drawing-room again?"

There was no answer.

"I must say you have a knack of making a man's home uncommonly pleasant for him."

Still no answer. Perhaps there were none left. One may come to an end of answers sometimes, like other things—money, for instance.

"Is my breakfast ordered for half-past seven, sharp?"

"Yes."

"Poached eggs?"

"Yes, and stewed kidneys. I hope they will be right this time. And I've told Martha to call you at seven punctually."

"All right. Good night."

"Good night."

That had been their parting in this world, Colonel Tempest remembered bitterly, for he had been too much hurried next morning to run up to say good-bye before starting for Scotland. Those had been the last words his wife had spoken to him, the woman for whom he had given up his liberty. So much for woman's love and tenderness.

And as the train went heavily on its way, he recalled, in spite of himself, the last home-coming after that month's fishing, and the fog that he shot into as he neared King's Cross on that dull April morning six years ago. He remembered his arrival at the house, and letting himself in and going upstairs. The house seemed strangely quiet. In the drawing-room a woman was sitting motionless in the gaslight. She looked up as he came in, and he recognized the drawn, haggard face of Mrs. Courtenay, his wife's mother, whom he had never seen in his house before, and who now spoke to him for the first time since her daughter's marriage.

"Is that you?" she said, quietly, her face twitching. "I did not know where you were. You have a daughter, Colonel Tempest, of a few hours old."

He raised his eyebrows.

"And Di?" he asked. "Pretty comfortable?"

The question was a concession to custom on Colonel Tempest's part, for, like others of his enlightened views, he was of course aware that the pains of childbirth are as nothing compared to the twinge of gout in the masculine toe.

"Diana," said the elder woman, with concentrated passion, as she passed him to leave the room—"Diana, thank God, is dead!"

He had never forgiven Mrs. Courtenay for that speech. He remembered even now with a shudder of acute self-pity all he had gone through during the days that followed, and the silent reproach of the face that even in death wore a look not of rest, but of a weariness stern and patient, and a courage that has looked to the end and can wait.

And when Mrs. Courtenay had written to offer to take the little Diana off his hands altogether provided he would lay no claim to her later on, he had refused with indignation. He would not be parted from his children. But the child was delicate and wailed perpetually, and he wanted to get rid of the house, and of all that reminded him of a past that it was distinctly uncomfortable to recall. He put the little yellow-haired boy to school, and, when Mrs. Courtenay repeated her offer, he accepted it; and Di, with her bassinette and the minute feather-stitched wardrobe that her mother had made for her packed inside her little tin bath, drove away one day in a four-wheeler straight out of Colonel Tempest's existence and very soon out of his memory.

His marriage had been the ruin of him, he said to himself, reviewing the last few years. It had done for him with his brother. He had been a fool to sacrifice so much for a pretty face, and she had not had a shilling. He had chucked away all his chances in marrying her. He might have married anybody; but he had never seen a woman before or since with a turn of the neck and shoulder to equal hers. Poor Di! She had spoilt his life, no doubt, but she had had her good points after all.

POOR DI! PERHAPS SHE TOO had had her dark hours. Perhaps she had given love to a man capable only of a passing passion. Perhaps she had sold her woman's birthright for red pottage, and had borne the penalty, not with an exceeding bitter cry, but in an exceeding bitter silence. Perhaps she had struggled against the disillusion and desecration of life, the despair and the self-loathing that go to make up an unhappy marriage. Perhaps in the deepening shadows of death she had heard her new-born child cry to her through the darkness, and had yearned over it, and yet—and yet had been glad to go.

MARY CHOLMONDELEY

However these things may have been, at any rate, she had a turn of the neck and shoulder which lived in her husband's memory. Poor Di!

Colonel Tempest shook himself free from a train of reflections which had led him to a death-bed, and suddenly remembered with a shudder of repugnance that he was on his way to another at this moment.

His brother had not sent for him. Colonel Tempest was hazarding an unsolicited visit. He had announced his intention of coming, but he had received no permission to do so. Nevertheless he had actually screwed up his weak and vacillating nature to the sticking point of putting himself and his son into the train when the morning arrived that he had fixed on for going to Overleigh.

"For the sake of the old name, and for the sake of the boy," he said to himself, looking at the delicate regular profile silhouetted against the window-pane. If Archie had had a pair of wings folded underneath his little great-coat, he would have made a perfect model for an angel, with his fair hair and face, and the sweet serious eyes that contemplated, without any change of expression, his choir book at chapel, or the last grappling contortions of a cockroach, ingeniously transfixed to the book-ledge with a pin, to relieve the monotony of the sermon.

"Overleigh! Overleigh! Overleigh!" called out a porter, as the train stopped. Colonel Tempest started. There already! How long it was since he had got out at that station! There was a new station-master, and the station itself had been altered. He looked at the little red tin shelter erected on the off-side with an alien eye. It had not been there in *his* time. There was no carriage to meet him, although he had mentioned the train by which he intended to arrive. His heart sank a little as he took Archie by the hand and set out to walk. The distance was nothing, for the station had been made specially for the convenience of the Tempests, and lay within a few hundred yards of the castle gates. But the omen was a bad one. Would his mission fail?

How unchanged everything was! He seemed to remember every stone upon the road. There was the turn up to the village, and the low tower of the church peering through the haze of the April trees. They passed through the old Italian gates—there was a new woman at the lodge to open them—and entered the park. Archie drew in his breath. He had never seen deer at large before. He supposed his uncle must keep a private zoological gardens on a large scale, and his awe of him increased.

"Are the lions and the tigers loose too?" he inquired, with grave interest, but without anxiety, as his eyes followed a little band of fallow deer skimming across the turf.

"There are no lions and tigers, Archie," said his father, tightening his clasp on the little hand. If Colonel Tempest had ever loved anything, it was his son.

They had come to a turn in the broad white road which he knew well. He stopped and looked. High on a rocky crag, looking out over its hanging woods and gardens, the old grey castle stood, its long walls and solemn towers outlined against the sky. The flag was flying.

"He is still alive," said Colonel Tempest, remembering a certain home-coming long ago, when, as he galloped up the steep winding drive, even as he rode, the flag dropped half-mast high before his eyes, and he knew his father was dead.

They had reached the ascent to the castle, and Colonel Tempest turned from the broad road, and struck into a little path that clambered upwards towards the gardens through the hanging woods. It was a short cut to the house. It was here he had first seen Diana, and he pondered over the fidelity of mind which, after fourteen years, could remember the exact spot. There was the wooden bridge over the stream where she had stood, her white gown reflected in the water below her, the heart of the summer woods enfolding her like the setting of a jewel. The seringa and the laburnum were out. The air was faint with perfume. She stood looking at him with lovely surprised eyes, in her exceeding youth and beauty. Involuntarily his mind turned from that first meeting to the last parting seven years later. The cold, dark, London bedroom, the bowed figure in the low chair, the fatigued smell of tepid india-rubber. What a gulf between the radiant young girl and the woman with the white exhausted face! Alas! for the many parts a woman may have to play in her time to one and the same man. Colonel Tempest laughed harshly to himself, and his powerful mind reverted to the old refrain, "What fools men are to marry."

It had been summer when he had seen her first, but now it was early spring. The woods were very silent. God was making a special revelation in their heart, was turning over one more page of His New Testament. He had walked once again in His garden, and at the touch of His feet, all young sheaths and spears of growing things were stirring and pressing up to do His will. The larch had hastened to hang out his pink tassels. The primroses had been the first among the

MARY CHOLMONDELEY

flowers to receive the Divine message, and were repeating it already in their own language to those that had ears to hear it. The folded buds of the anemones had heard the whisper *Ephphatha*, and were opening one after another their pure shy eyes. The arched neck of the young bracken was showing among the brown ancestors of last year. The marsh marigolds thronged the water's edge. Every battered dyke and rocky scar was transfigured. God was once again making all things new.

Only a mole, high on its funeral twig, held out tiny human hands, worn with honest toil, to its Maker, in mute protest against a steel death "that nature never made" for little agriculturists. Death was still in the world apparently, side by side with the resurrection of the flowers. Archie paused to glance contemptuously and shy a stick at the corpse as he passed. It looked as if it had not afforded much sport before it died. Colonel Tempest puffed a little, for the ascent was steep, and he was not so slim as he had once been. He sat down on a circular wooden seat round a yew tree by the path. He began to dislike the idea of going on. And, perhaps, after all, he would be told by the servants that his brother would not see him. Jack was quite capable of making himself disagreeable to the last. Really, on the whole, perhaps the best course would be to go down the hill again. It is always so much easier to go down than to go up; so much pleasanter at the moment to avoid what may be distasteful to a sensitive mind.

"Archie," said Colonel Tempest.

The boy did not hear him. He was looking intently at a little patch of ground near the garden seat, which had evidently been carefully laid out by a landscape-gardener of about his own age. Every hair of grass or weed had been scratched up within the irregular wall of fir cones that bounded the enclosure. Grey sand imported from a distance, possibly from the brook, marked winding paths therein, in course of completion. A sunk bucket with a squirt in it, indicated an intention, as yet unmatured, to add a fountain to the natural beauties of the site.

"You go in this way, father," said Archie, grasping the situation with becoming gravity, and pointing out the two oyster shells that flanked the main entrance, "then you walk round the lake. Look; he has got a duck ready. Oh, dear! and see, father, here is his name. I would have done it all in white stones if it had been me. J. O. H. N. John. Father, who is John?"

Colonel Tempest's temper was like a curate's gun. You could never tell when it might not go off, or in what direction. It went off now with an explosion. It had been at full cock all the morning.

"Who is John?" he repeated, fiercely kicking the letters on the ground to right and left. "You may well ask that. John is a confounded interloper. He has no right here. Damn John!"

Archie was following the parental boot with anxious eyes. The tin duck was dinted in on one side, and bulged out on the other in a manner painful to behold. It would certainly never swim again. The turn of the squirt might come any moment. But when his father began to say damn, Archie had always found it better not to interfere.

"Come along, Archie," said Colonel Tempest, furiously, "don't stand fooling there," and he began to mount the path with redoubled energy. All thought of turning back was forgotten.

Archie looked back ruefully at the devastated pleasure-grounds. The fir cone boundary was knocked over at one corner. All privacy was lost; anything might get in now, and the duck, if she recovered, could get out. It was much to be regretted.

"Poor damn John," said Archie, slipping his hand into that of the grown-up child whom he had for a father.

"Poor John!" echoed Colonel Tempest, his temper evaporating a little, "I only wish it *were* poor John; and not poor Archie. That was *your* garden, Archie, do you hear, my boy—yours, not his. And you shall have it, too, if I can get it for you."

"I don't want it now," said Archie, gravely; "you've spoilt it."

II

"And another dieth in the bitterness of his soul."

—Job xxi. 25

A profound knowledge of human nature enunciated the decree, "Thou shalt not covet thy neighbour's *house*," and relegated the neighbour's wife to a back seat among the servants and live stock.

The intense love of a house, passing the love even of prohibited women, is a passion which those who "nightly pitch their moving tents" in villas and hired dwellings, and look upon heaven as their home, can hardly imagine, and frequently regard with the amused contempt of ignorance. But where pride is a leading power the affections will be generally found immediately in its wake. In these days it is the fashion, especially of the vulgar-minded well-born, to decry birth as being of no account. Those who do so, apparently fail to perceive that, by the very fact of decrying it, they proclaim their own innate lack of appreciation of those very advantages of refinement, manners, and a certain distinction and freemasonry of feeling, which birth has evidently withheld from them personally, but which, nevertheless, birth alone can bestow. The strong hereditary pride of race which is as natural a result of time and fixed habitat as the forest oak—which is bred in the bone and comes out in the flesh from generation to generation—is accompanied, as a rule, by a passionate love, not of houses, but of *the* house, the home, the eyrie, the one sacred spot from which the race sprang.

Among the Tempests devotion to Overleigh had been an hereditary instinct from time immemorial. Other possessions, gifts of royalty, or dowers of heiresses came and went. Overleigh remained from generation to generation. Scapegrace Tempests squandered the family fortune, and mortgaged the family properties, but others rose up in their place, who, whatever else was lost, kept fast hold on Overleigh. The old castle on the crag had passed through many vicissitudes. It had been originally built in Edward II. 's time, and the remains of fortification, and the immense thickness of the outer walls, showed how fierce had been the inroads of Scot and Borderer which such strength was needed to repel. The massive arched doorway through which the yelling hordes of the Tempests and their retainers swooped down, with black lion on pennant flying, upon the enemy, was walled up in the time of the Tudors, and the vaulted basement with its acutely pointed chamfered arches became the dungeons of the later portion of the building; the cellars of the present day.

Overleigh had entertained royalty royally in its time, and had sheltered royalty more royally still. Cromwell's cannon had not prevailed against it. It had been partially burnt, it had been partially rebuilt. There it still stood, a glory, and a princely possession on the lands that had been meted in the Doomsday book to a certain Norman knight Ivo de Tempête, the founder of an iron race. And in the nineteenth century a Tempest held it still. Tempest had become a great name. Gradually wealth had gathered round Overleigh, as the lichen had gathered round its grey stones. There were coal-mines now among the marsh-lands of William the Conqueror's favourite, harbours and towns along the sea-coast. Tempest of Overleigh was a power, a name that might be felt, that had been felt. The name ranked high among the great commoners of England. Titles and honours of various kinds had been offered it from time to time. But for a Tempest, to be a Tempest was enough. And Overleigh Castle had remained their solitary dwelling-place. Houses were built for younger sons, but the head of the family made his home invariably at Overleigh itself. There were town houses in London and York, but country seats were not multiplied. To be a Tempest was enough. To live and die at Overleigh was enough.

Some one was dying at Overleigh now. Mr. Tempest had come to that pass, and was taking it very quietly, as he had taken everything so far, from the elopement of his betrothed with his brother fourteen years ago, to the death of his poor, pretty faithless wife in the room where he was now lying; the round oak-panelled room, which followed the outer wall of the western tower; the room in which he had been born, where Tempests had arrived and departed, and lain in state. And now after a solitary life he was dying, as he had lived, alone.

He had gone too far down the steep path which leads no man knows whither, to care much for anything that he was leaving behind. He had not read his brother's letter announcing his coming. It lay with a pile of others for some one hereafter to sort or burn. Mr. Tempest had done with letters, had done with everything except Death. The pressure of Death's hand was heavy on him, upon his eyes, upon his heart. He had been a punctual man all his life. He hoped he should not be kept waiting long.

Colonel Tempest followed the servant with inward trepidation across the white stone hall. He had been at once admitted, for it was known that Mr. Tempest was dying, and the only wonder in the minds of nurse and doctor and servants was that his only brother had not arrived before. The servant led the way along the picture-gallery. A child was playing at the further end of it under the Velasquez; or, to speak more correctly, was looking earnestly out of one of the low mullioned windows. The voice of the young year was calling him from without, as the spring calls only the young. But he might not go out today, though there were nests waiting for him, and holiday glories in wood and meadow that his soul longed after. He had been told he must stay in, in case that stern silent father who was dying should ask for him. John did not think he would want him, for when had he ever wanted him yet? but he remained at his post at the window, breathing his silent longing into a little mist on the pane.

He looked round as Colonel Tempest and Archie approached, and then came gravely forward, and put out a strong little brown hand.

Colonel Tempest just touched it without speaking, and turned his eyes away. He could not trust himself to look again at the erect dignified little figure with its square dark face. When had there ever been a dark Tempest?

The two boys, near of an age, looked each other straight in the eyes. Archie was the younger and the taller of the two.

"Are you John?" he asked at once.

"Yes."

"John what?"

"No. John Amyas Tempest."

"Archie," said Colonel Tempest, who had grown rather pale, "you can stay here with—, until I send for you." And with one backward glance at them, he followed the servant to an ante-room, where the doctor presently came to him.

"I am his only brother," said Colonel Tempest hoarsely. "Can I see him?"

"Certainly, my dear sir, certainly; but at the same time all agitation, all tendency to excitement, must be rigorously avoided."

"Is he really dying?" interrupted Colonel Tempest.

"He is."

"How long has he?" Colonel Tempest felt as if a hand were tightening round his throat. The doctor shrugged his shoulders.

"Three hours. Five hours. He might live through the night. I cannot say."

"There would be time," said Colonel Tempest to himself; and, not without a shuddering foreboding that his brother might die in his actual presence, without giving him time to bolt, he entered the sickroom, from which the doctor had beckoned the nurse, and closed the door.

The room was full of light, for the dying man had been oppressed by the darkness in which he lay, and a vain attempt had been made to alleviate it by the flood of April sunshine which had been let into the room. Through the open window came the rapture of the birds.

Mr. Tempest lay perfectly motionless with his eyes half closed. His worn face had a strong family resemblance to his brother's, with the beauty left out.

"Jack!" said Colonel Tempest.

Mr. Tempest heard from an immense distance, and came painfully back across long wastes and desert places of confused memories, came slowly back to the room, and the dim sunshine, and himself; and stopped short with a jarred sense as he saw his own long feeble hands laid upon the counterpane. He had forgotten them, though he recognized them now he saw them again. Why had he returned?

"Jack," said the voice again.

Mr. Tempest opened his eyes suddenly, and looked full at his brother—at the false, weak, handsome face of the man who had injured him.

It all came back, the passion and the despair; the intolerable agony of jealousy and baffled love; and the deadly, deadly hatred. Fourteen years ago was it since Diana had been taken from him? It returned upon him as though it were yesterday. A light flamed up in the dying eyes before which Colonel Tempest quailed.

All the sentences he had prepared beforehand seemed to fail him, as prepared sentences have a way of doing, being made to fit imaginary circumstances, and being consequently unsuited to any others. Mr. Tempest, who had not prepared anything, had the advantage.

"Curse you," he said, in his low, difficult whisper. "You damned scoundrel!"

Colonel Tempest was shocked. To bear a grudge after all these years! Jack had always been vindictive! And what an unchristian state of mind for one on the brink of that nightmare of horror, the grave! He was unable to articulate.

"What are you here for?" said Mr. Tempest, after a pause. "Who let you in? Why can't I be allowed to die in peace?"

"Oh, don't talk like that, Jack!" gasped Colonel Tempest, speaking extempore, after fumbling in all the empty pockets of his mind for something appropriate to say. "I am sure I am very sorry for—" A look warned him that even his tactful reference to a certain subject would be resented. "But, it's all past and gone now, and—it's a long time ago, and you're—"

"Dying," suggested Mr. Tempest.

". . . and," hurried on Colonel Tempest, glad of the lift, "it's not for my own sake I've come. But I've got a boy, Jack; he is here now. I have brought him with me. Such a fine, handsome boy—every inch a Tempest, and the image of our father. I don't want to speak for myself, but for the sake of the boy, and the place, and the old name."

Colonel Tempest hid his quivering face in his hands. He was really moved.

The sick man's mouth twitched; he evidently understood his brother's incoherent words.

"John succeeds," he said.

The two men looked away from each other.

"John is not a Tempest," said Colonel Tempest, in a choked voice. "You know it—everybody knows it!"

"He was born in wedlock."

"Yes; but he is not your son. You would have divorced her if she had lived. He is the legal heir, of course, if you countenance him; but something might be done still—it is not too late. I know the estate goes, failing you and your children, to me and mine. Don't bear a grudge, Jack. You can't have any feeling for the child—it's against nature. Remember the old name and the old place, that has never been out of the hands of a Tempest yet. Don't drag our honour in the dust and put it to open shame! Think how it would have grieved our father. Let me call in the doctor and the nurse, and disown him now before witnesses. Such things have been done before, and may be again. I can contest his claim then; I shall have something to go on. And you *must* have proofs of his illegitimacy if you will only give them. But there will be *no* chance if you uphold him to the last, and if—and if you—die— without speaking."

Mr. Tempest made no answer except to look his brother steadily in the face. The look was sufficient. It said plainly enough, "That is what I mean to do."

Colonel Tempest lost all hope, but despair made one final clutch—a last desperate appeal to his brother's feelings. It is one of the misfortunes of self-centred people that their otherwise convenient habit of disregarding what is passing in the minds of others, leads them to trample on their feelings at the very moment when most desirous of turning them to their own account. Colonel Tempest, with the best intentions of a pure self-interest, trampled heavily.

"Pass me over—cut me out," he said, with a vague inappreciation of points of law. "I'll sign anything you please; but let the little chap have it—let Archie have it—*Di's son*."

There was a silence that might be felt. Approaching death seemed to make a stride in those few breathless seconds; but it seemed also as if a determined will were holding him momentarily at arm's length. Mr. Tempest turned his fading face towards his brother. His eyes were unflinching, but his voice was almost inaudible.

"Leave me," he said. "John succeeds."

The blood rushed to Colonel Tempest's head, and then seemed to ebb away from his heart. A sudden horror took him of some subtle change that was going forward in the room, and, seeing all was lost, he hastily left it.

The two boys had fraternized meanwhile. Each, it appeared, was collecting coins, and Archie gave a glowing account of the cabinet his father had given him to put them in. John kept his in an old sock, which he solemnly produced, and the time was happily passed in licking the most important coins, to give them a momentary brightness, and in comparing notes upon them. John was sorry when Colonel Tempest came hurriedly down the gallery and carried Archie off before he had time to say good-bye, or to offer him his best coin, which he had hot in his hand with a view to presentation.

Before he had time to gather up his collection, the old doctor came to him, and told him, very gravely and kindly, that his father wished to see him.

John nodded, and put down the sock at once. He was a person of few words, and, though he longed to ask a question now, he asked it with his eyes only. John's deep-set eyes were very dark and melancholy. Could it be that his mother's remorse had left its trace in the young

MARY CHOLMONDELEY

unconscious eyes of her child? Their beauty somewhat redeemed the square ugliness of the rest of his face.

The doctor patted him on the head, and led him gently to Mr. Tempest's door.

"Go in and speak to him," he said. "Do not be afraid. I shall be in the next room all the time."

"I am not afraid," said John, drawing himself up, and he went quietly across the great oak-panelled room and stood at the bedside.

There was a look of tension in Mr. Tempest's face and hands, as if he were holding on tightly to something which, did he once let go, he would never be able to regain.

"John," he said, in an acute whisper.

"Yes, father." The child's face was pale and his eyes looked awed, but they met Mr. Tempest's bravely.

"Try and listen to what I am going to say, and remember it. You are a very little boy now, but you will hold a great position some day—when you are a man. You will be the head of the family. Tempest is one of the oldest names in England. Remember what I say"—the whisper seemed to break and ravel down under the intense strain put on it to a single quivering strand—"remember—you will understand it when you are older. It is a great trust put into your hands. When you grow into a man, much will be expected of you. Never disgrace your name; it stands high. Keep it up—keep it up." The whisper seemed to die altogether, but an iron will forced it momentarily back to the grey toiling lips. "You are the head of the family; do your duty by it. You will have no one much to help you. I shall not—be there. You must learn to be an upright, honourable gentleman by yourself. Do you understand?"

"Yes, father."

"And you will—*remember*?"

"Yes, father." If the lip quivered, the answer came nevertheless.

"That is all; you can go."

The child hesitated.

"Good night," he said gravely, advancing a step nearer. The sun was still streaming across the room, but it seemed to him, as he looked at the familiar, unfamiliar face, that it was night already.

"Don't kiss me," said the dying man. "Good night."

And the child went.

Mr. Tempest sighed heavily, and relaxed his hold on the consciousness that was ready to slip away from him, and wander feebly out he knew not whither. Hours and voices came and went. His own voice had gone down into silence before him. It was still broad daylight, but the casement was slowly growing "a glimmering square," and he observed it.

Presently it flickered—glimmered—and went out.

III

"As the foolish moth returning
To its Moloch, and its burning,
Wheeling nigh, and ever nigher,
Falls at last into the fire,
Flame in flame;
So the soul that doth begin
Making orbits round a sin,
Ends the same."

It was a sultry night in June rather more than a year after Mr. Tempest's death. An action had been brought by Colonel Tempest directly after his brother's death, when the will was proved in which Mr. Tempest bequeathed everything in his power to bequeath to his "son John." The action failed; no one except Colonel Tempest had ever been sanguine that it would succeed. Colonel Tempest was unable to support an assertion of which few did not recognize the probable truth. No proof of John's suspected illegitimacy was forthcoming. His mother had died when he was born; it was eleven years ago. The fact that Mr. Tempest had mentioned him by name as his son in his will was overwhelming evidence to the contrary. The long-delayed blow fell at last. A verdict was given in favour of the little schoolboy.

"I'm sorry for you, I am, indeed," said Mr. Swayne, composedly watching Colonel Tempest flinging himself about his little room, into which the latter had just rushed, nearly beside himself at the decision of a bribed and perjured court.

Mr. Swayne was a stout, florid-looking man between forty and fifty, with a heavy face like a grimace that some one else had made, who laboured under the delusion, unshared by any of his fellow-creatures, that he was a gentleman. In what class he had been born no one knew. What he was now any one could see for himself. He was generally considered by the men with whom he associated a good fellow for an ally in a disreputable pinch, and a blackguard when the pinch was over. Every one regarded Dandy Swayne with contempt, but for all that "The Snowdrop," as he was playfully called, might be seen in the chambers and at the dinners of men far above him in the social scale, who probably for very good reasons tolerated his presence, and for even better reviled him behind his back. He had a certain shrewdness and knowledge of the seamy side of human nature which stood him in good stead. He was a noted billiard player—a little too noted, perhaps. His short, thick ringed hands did not mind much what they fastened on. He was not troubled by conscientious scruples. The charm of Dandy Swayne's character was that he stuck at nothing. He would go down any sewer provided there was money in it, and money there always was somewhere in everything he took in hand. Dandy Swayne's career had had strange ups and downs. No one knew how he lived. The private fortune on which he was wont to enlarge of course existed only in his own imagination. Sometimes he disappeared entirely for longer or shorter periods—generally after money transactions of a nature that required privacy and foreign travel. But the same Providence which tempers the wind to the shorn lamb watches over the shearer also, and he always reappeared again, sooner or later, with his creased white waistcoat and yesterday's gardenia, and the old swagger that endeared him to his fellow-creatures.

He was up in the world just now, living "in style" in smart chambers strewn with photographs of actresses, and littered with cheap expensive furniture, and plush hangings redolent of smoke and stale scent, among which Colonel Tempest was knocking about in his disordered evening dress.

"I'm sorry for you, Colonel," repeated Mr. Swayne, slowly; "but I wish to— you'd sit down and not rush up and down like that. It's not a bit of good taking on in that way, though it's— luck all the same."

Mr. Swayne's conversation was devoid of that severe simplicity which society demands; indeed, it was so encrusted and enriched with ornamental gems of expression of a surprising and dubious character, that to present his conversation to the reader without the personal peculiarities of his choice of language is to do him an injustice which, however unavoidable, is much to be regretted. Mr. Swayne's conversation without his oaths might be compared to a bird without its feathers; the body is there, but all individuality and beauty of contour is gone.

Mr. Swayne filled his glass, and pushed the bottle across to his friend, whose flushed face and shaking hand showed that he had had enough already. Colonel Tempest sat down impatiently and filled his glass, too.

"It's the will that did it, I suppose," suggested Mr. Swayne; "that tipped it over."

"Yes," said Colonel Tempest, striking his clenched hand on the table. *"My son John* he called him in his will; there was no getting over that. He knew it when he put those words in. He knew I should contest the succession, and he hated me so that he perjured himself to keep me out of my own, and stuck to it even on his death-bed. John is no more his son than you are. A little dark Fane, that is what he is. They say he takes after his mother's family; he well may do,— him!"

Mr. Swayne sympathetically echoed the sentiment in a varied but not less forcible form of speech.

"And my son," continued Colonel Tempest, his fair weak face whitening with passion—"you know my boy; look at him—a Tempest to the backbone, down to his finger-nails. You can't look at him among the pictures in the gallery and not see he is bone of their bone and flesh of their flesh. He is as like the Vandyke of Amyas Tempest the cavalier as he can be. It drives me mad to think of him, cut out by a bastard!"

Mr. Swayne appeared to be in a meditative turn of mind. He watched the smoke of his cigar curl upwards from the unshaved crater of his lip into the air.

"You're in the tail, I suppose?" he remarked at last.

"Of course I am. If my brother John died without children, everything was to come to me and my heirs. My brother had only a life interest in the place."

"Then I don't see how he was to blame, doing as he did, if it was entailed all along on his son." Mr. Swayne spoke with a certain cautious interest.

"He never *had* a son. If he had disowned his wife's child, everything would have come to me."

"Lor!" said Mr. Swayne, "I did not understand it was so near as that. Then this little chap, this John, he's all that stands between you and the property, is he? Failing him, it still comes to you?"

Mr. Swayne's small tightly-wedged eyes, with the expression of dissipated boot-buttons, were beginning to show a gleam of professional interest.

"Yes, it would; but John won't fail," said Colonel Tempest, savagely. "He will keep us out. We shall be as poor as rats as long as we live, and shall see him chucking our money right and left!" and Colonel Tempest, who was by this time hardly responsible for what he said, ground his teeth and cursed his enemy in a paroxysm of rage and drink. Mr. Swayne observed him attentively.

"Don't take on so, Colonel," he remarked soothingly. "Dear me, what's a little boy?—What's a little boy here or there," he continued, meditatively, "one more or one less? There's a sight of little kids in the world; some wanted, some not. I've known cases, Colonel"—here he fixed his eyes on the ceiling—"cases with parents, maybe, singing up in heaven and takin' no notice, when little chaps that weren't wanted, that nobody took to, seemed to—meet with an accident, get snuffed out by mistake."

"John won't meet with an accident," said Colonel Tempest passionately. "I wish to—he would!"

"I look at it this way," said Mr. Swayne, philosophically. "There's things gentlemen can do, and there's things they can't. A gentleman is a party that can't do his dirty work for himself, though as often as not he has a deal on his hands that must be shoved through somehow. The thing is to find parties who'll take what I call a personal interest, if it's made worth their while. Now about this little boy, that no one wants, and is a comfort to nobody. It's quite curious the things little boys will do; out in boats alone, outriggers now, as dangerous as can be, or leaning out of railway carriages in tunnels. Lor! you never know what they won't be up to, little rascals. They're made of mischief. Forty thousand a year, is it, he is keeping you out of, and yours by right? Well, I don't say anything about that; but all I say is, I have friends I can find that are open to a bet. What's the harm of betting a thousand pounds to one sovereign that you never come into the property? It ain't likely, as you say. What's the harm of a bet, provided you don't mind risking your money? Let's say, just for the sake of—of argument, that there *was* ten bets—ten bets at a thousand to one that you never come in. Ten thousand pounds to pay, if you come in after all. What's ten thousand pounds to a man with forty thousand a year?" Mr. Swayne snapped his fingers. "And no trouble to nobody. Nothing to do but to pay up quietly when the time comes. It don't concern you who takes up the bets, and you don't know either. You know nothing at all about it. You lay your money, and, look here, Colonel, you mark my words, some way or somehow, some time or other, *that boy will disappear*."

The two men looked steadily at each other. Colonel Tempest's eyes were bloodshot, but Mr. Swayne had all his wits about him; he never became intoxicated, even at the expense of others, if there was money in keeping sober.

"Curse him!" said Colonel Tempest in a hoarse whisper. "He should not get in my light."

The child was to blame, naturally.

Mr. Swayne did not answer, but went to a side table, on which were pens, ink, and paper. Some things, if done at all, are best done quickly.

IV

"After the red pottage comes the exceeding bitter cry."

Fifteen years is a long time. What companies of trite reflections crowd the mind as it looks back across the marshes and the fens, and the highlands and the lowlands, and the weary desert places, to some point that catches the eye in the middle distance! We stood there once. Perhaps we go back in memory—all the way back—to that little town and spire in the green country, and pray once again in the cool vision-haunted church, and peer up once again at the window in the narrow street where Love lived and looked out, where patience and affection dwell together now. They were always friends, those two.

Or perhaps we look back to a parting of the ways which did not seem to be a parting at the time, and recall a "Good-bye" that was lightly uttered because it was only thought to be *Au revoir*. We see now, from where we stand, the point where the paths diverged.

Fifteen years!

They have not passed very smoothly over the head of Colonel Tempest. Whenever he looked back across the breezy uplands of his well-spent life, his eye avoided and yet was inevitably attracted with a loathing allurement to one dark spot in the middle distance, where—

Fifteen years ago or yesterday was it?

The old nightmare, with the shuddering horror of yesterday mingled with the heavy pressure of years, might come back at any moment—was always coming back.

That sultry night in June!

Everything was disjointed and fragmentary in his memory the morning after it; he could not see the whole. He had a confused recollection of an intense passionate hatred that was like a physical pain, and of Swayne's voice saying, "What's a little boy?" And then there were slips of paper. Swayne said a bet was a bet. He, Colonel Tempest, had had something to do with those slips of paper—*What?*—One had fallen on the floor, and Swayne had blotted it carefully. There was Swayne's voice again, "Your handwriting ain't up to much, Colonel." He had written something then. What was it? His own name? Memory failed. Who was that devil in the room, with Swayne's face and blurred watch-chain—two watch-chains—and the thick busy hands? And

MARY CHOLMONDELEY

then it was night, and he was in the streets again in the hot darkness, among the blinking lamps and stars that looked like eyes, and Swayne was seeing him home. And there was a horror over everything; horror leant over him at night, horror woke him in the morning and pursued him throughout the day, and the next day, and the next. What had he done? He tried to piece together the broken fragments that his groping memory could glean; but nothing came of it—at least, nothing he could believe. But Swayne knew. On the third day he could bear it no longer, and he went to find him; but Swayne had disappeared. Colonel Tempest went up to his chambers on the pretence of a letter— of something; he knew not what. They were swept and garnished in readiness for new arrivals, for if one choice spirit disappears, a good landlady knows what to expect.

Colonel Tempest looked once round the room, and then sat feebly down. It was as if for days he had been staring at a blank sheet, and now a dark slide had been suddenly taken from the magic lantern. The picture was before him in all its tawdry distinctness. *He knew what he had done.*

Colonel Tempest was not a radically bad man. Who is? But there was in him a kind of weakness of fibre which consists in being subservient to the impulse of the moment. The effects of a feeble yielding to impulse are sometimes hardly to be distinguished from those of the most deliberate and thorough-paced sin.

He was conscious of good in himself, of a refined dislike to coarseness and vice even when he dabbled in it, of vague longings after better things, of amiable, even chivalrous, inclinations towards others, especially towards women not of his own family. In his own family, where there had always been, even in his mother's time, some feminine weakness or imperfection for a manly nature to point out and ridicule, of course courtesy and tenderness could not be expected of him.

Thus at each juncture of his life he was obliged to justify what he would have called his failings, what some would have called sins, by laying the blame on others, and by this means to account for the glaring discrepancy between the inward and spiritual gracefulness of his feelings and the outward and visible signs of his actions.

A man with such good impulses, such an affectionate nature, cannot be a sinner. If there was one thing more than another that Colonel Tempest thoroughly believed in, it was in his affectionate nature. He might have his faults, he was wont to say, but his heart was in the right place. If things went amiss, the fault was in the circumstance, in the temptation, in the unfortunate character of those with whom his life was knit. Weakness has its superstition, and superstition its scapegoat. His father had spoilt him. His wife had not understood him. His brother had played him false. Swayne had tempted him.

What have not those to answer for who teach us in language, however spiritual, however orthodox, to lay our sins on others—on *any other* except ourselves!

After the first shock of panic, of terror lest he had done something for which he might eventually have to suffer, Colonel Tempest struggled back to the well-worn position, now clutched with both hands, that he had been betrayed in a moment of passion by a fiend in human shape, and that, if—anything happened, Swayne was the most to blame.

Still they were dreadful days at first—dreadful weeks in which he suffered for Swayne's sin. And Swayne seemed to have disappeared for good—or perhaps for evil.

And then—gradually—inasmuch as nothing had power to affect him for long together, the horror lightened.

The sun rose and set. The world went on. A year passed. Archie wrote for money from school. Things took their usual course. Colonel Tempest had his hair cut as usual; he observed with keen regret that it was thinning at the top. Life settled back into its old groove.

Nothing happened.

To persons gifted with imagination, what is more solemn, or more appalling, than the pause which follows on any decisive action which is perceived to have within it the seed of a result—a result which even now is germinating in darkness, is growing towards the light, foreseen, but unknown? With what body will they come, we ask ourselves—these slow results that spring from the dust of our spent actions? Faith sows and waits. Sin sows and trembles. The fool sows and forgets. Colonel Tempest was practically an Atheist. He did not believe in cause and effect; he believed in chance. He had sown, but perhaps nothing would come up. He had seen the lightning, but perhaps the thunder might not follow after all.

Suddenly, one winter morning, without warning, it growled on the horizon.

"That inconvenient little nephew of yours has precious nearly hooked it," said a man in the club to him as he came in. "His tutor must be a plucky chap. I should owe him a grudge if I were you."

The man held out the paper to him, and, turning away with a laugh, went out whistling. He meant no harm; but the smallest arrow of a refined pleasantry can prick if it happens to come between the joints of the harness.

Colonel Tempest felt sea-sick. The room was empty except for the waiter, who was arranging his breakfast on one of the tables by the window. The fire leapt and blazed; everything swayed. He sat down mechanically in his accustomed place, still clutching the paper. He tried to read it, to find the place, but he could see nothing. At last he poured out a cup of coffee and drank it, and then tried again. There it was: Narrow escape of Mr. Goodwin and Mr. Tempest on the Metropolitan Railway. Mr. Goodwin and his charge, Mr. Tempest, were returning by the last train from the Crystal Palace. Tremendous crowd on the platform. Struggle for the train as it came in. Mr. Tempest pushed down between the still moving train and the platform. Heroic devotion of Mr. Goodwin. Rescue of Mr. Tempest uninjured. Serious injuries of Mr. Goodwin.

Colonel Tempest read no more. He wiped his forehead.

Swayne's men were at their devil's work, then! Perhaps they had tried before and failed, and he had not heard of it? They would try again—presently. Perhaps next time they would succeed.

The old horror woke up again with an acuteness that for the moment seemed greater than he could bear. Weak men should abstain from wrong-doing. They cannot stand the brunt of their own actions; the kick of the gun is too much for them.

And from that time to this the horror never wholly left him; if it slumbered, it was only to reawaken. At long intervals incidents happened, sometimes of the most trifling description, and some of which he did not even hear of at the time, which roused it afresh. There seemed to be a fate against John at Eton which followed him to Oxford. Archie, who was at Eton and Oxford with him, occasionally let things drop by chance which made Colonel Tempest's blood run cold.

"They have failed so far," he would say to himself; "but they will do it yet. I know they will do it in the end!"

At last he made a desperate attempt to find Swayne, and cancel the bet; but perhaps Swayne knew the man he had to deal with, and had foreseen a movement of that kind. At any rate, he was not to be discovered. Colonel Tempest found himself helpless.

Was there no anodyne for this recurring agony? He dared not drown it in drink. What might he not say under its influence? The consolations of religion, or rather of the Church, which he had always understood to be a sort of mental chloroform for uneasy consciences, did not seem to meet his case. The thought of John's danger never troubled him—John's possible death. The superstitious terror was for himself alone. He wanted a religion which would adhere to him of its own accord, and be in the way when needed; and he tried various kinds recommended for the purpose, but—without effect.

Perhaps a religion for self-centred people remains to be invented. Even religiosity (the patent medicine of the spiritual life of the age—the universal pain-killer)—even religiosity, though it meets almost all requirements, does not quite fill that gap.

Colonel Tempest became subject to long attacks of nervous irritation and depression. He ceased to be a good, and consequently a popular, companion. His health, never strong, always abused, began to waver. At fifty-five he looked thin and aged. He had come before his time to the evil days and the years which have no pleasure in them.

As he turned out of St. George's Church, Hanover Square, on this particular spring afternoon, whither he had gone to assist at a certain fashionable wedding at which his daughter Diana had officiated as bridesmaid, he looked broken down and feeble beyond his years.

A broad-shouldered, dark man elbowed his way through the throng of footmen and spectators, and came up with him.

"Are not you going back to the house?" he asked.

"No," said Colonel Tempest—"I hate weddings! I hate the whole thing. I only went to have a look at my child, who was bridesmaid. Di is my only daughter, but I don't see much of her; others take care of that." His tone was pathetic. He had gradually come to believe that his child had been wrested from him by Mrs. Courtenay, and that he was a defrauded parent.

"I am not going to the house, either," said John Tempest, for it was he. "I don't hate weddings, but I detest that one. Do you mind coming down to my club? I have not seen you really to speak to since I came back. I want to have a talk with you about Archie; he seems to have been improving the shining hours during these three years I have been away."

Colonel Tempest winced jealously. He knew John had paid the considerable debts that Archie had contrived to amass, not only during

MARY CHOLMONDELEY

the short time he was at Oxford, before he left to cram for the army, but also at Sandhurst. But Colonel Tempest had felt no gratitude on that score. Was not all John's wealth Archie's by right? and John must know it. Men do not grow up in ignorance of such a fact as a slur on their parentage. What was a dole of a few hundred pounds now and again, when a man was wrongfully keeping possession of many thousands?

"Young men are all alike," said Colonel Tempest, testily. "Archie is no worse than the rest. Poor fellow, it's very little I can do for him! It's deuced expensive living in the Guards; I found it so myself."

John might have asked, except that these are precisely the questions that make enmity between relations, why Colonel Tempest had put him in the Guards, considering that it was an idle life, and Archie was absolutely without expectations of any description. He and his sister Di had not even the modest fortune of a younger son eventually to divide between them. One of the beauties of Colonel Tempest's romantic clandestine marriage had been the lack of settlements, which, though it had prevented his wife bringing him anything owing to the rupture with her family, had at any rate enabled him to whittle away his own private fortune at will, and to inveigh at the same time against the miserliness of the Courtenays, who ought, of course, to have provided for his children.

How Colonel Tempest kept going at all no one knew. How Archie was kept going most people knew, or rather guessed without difficulty. John and Archie had held firmly together at Eton, and afterwards at Oxford. John had untied a very uncomfortable knot that had arranged itself round the innocent Archibald at Sandhurst. It could hardly be said that there was friendship between the two, but John, though only one year his cousin's senior, had taken the position of elder brother from the first, and had stood by Archie on occasions when that choice, but expensive, spirit needed a good deal of standing by. Archie had inherited other things from his father besides his perfect profile, and knew as well as most men which side his bread was buttered. They were friends in the ordinary acceptance of that misused term. John had just returned from three years' absence at the Russian and Austrian Courts, and Archie, who had begun to feel his absence irksome in the extreme, had welcomed him back with effusion.

"Come into the Carlton and let us talk things over," said John.

In spite of himself, Colonel Tempest occasionally almost liked John, even while he kicked against the pricks of a certain respect which he could not entirely smother for this grave quiet man of few words. When he was not for the moment jealous of him—and there were such moments—he could afford to indulge a sentiment almost of regret for him. At times he still hated him with the perfect hatred of the injurer for the injured; but nothing to stir that latent superstitious horror, and consequent detestation of the cause of the horror, had occurred of late years. They had walked slowly down Bond Street and St. James's Street, and had reached the Carlton. Close by the steps a man was lounging. Colonel Tempest saw him look attentively at John as they came up, and the blood left his heart. It was Swayne.

In a moment the horror was awake again—wide awake, hydra-headed, close at hand, insupportable.

Swayne stared for a moment full at Colonel Tempest, and then turned away and sauntered slowly along Pall Mall.

"Won't you come in?" said John, as his companion hesitated.

"Not today. Another time," said Colonel Tempest, and incoherently making he knew not what excuse, he left John to join another man who was entering at that moment, and hurried after Swayne. He overtook him as he passed through the gates into St. James's Park. It was a dull, foggy afternoon, and there were not many people about.

Swayne nodded carelessly to him as he joined him. He evidently did not mind being overtaken.

"Well, Colonel," he said, in the half insolent manner that in men like Swayne implies a knowledge that they have got the whip hand. Swayne was not to be outshone in the art of grovelling by any of his own species of fellow-worm, but he did not grovel unnecessarily. His higher nature was that of a bully.

"—you, Swayne, where have you been all these years?" said Colonel Tempest, hurriedly. "I've tried to find you over and over again."

"I've been busy, Colonel," returned Mr. Swayne, swaying himself on tight light-checked legs, and pushing back his grey high hat. "Business before pleasure. That's my motto. And I've been mortal sick, too. Thought I should have gone up this time last year. I did indeed. You look the worse for wear too; but I must not be standing talking here, pleasant as it is to meet old friends."

"Look here, Swayne," said Colonel Tempest, in great agitation, laying a spasmodic clutch on Swayne's arm, "I can't stand it any longer. I can't indeed. It's wearing me into my grave. I want you—to cancel the bet. You must cancel it. I won't bear it. If you won't cancel it, I won't pay up when the—if the time comes."

"Won't you?" said Swayne, with contempt. "I know better."

"I must get out of it. It's killing me," repeated Colonel Tempest, ignoring Swayne's last remark.

"Pay up, then," said Swayne. "If you won't bear it, pay up."

Colonel Tempest was staggered.

"I have not a thousand pounds I could lay my hands on," he said hoarsely, "much less ten. I've been broke these last five years. You know that."

"Raise it," said Swayne. "I ain't against that; quite the reverse. There's been a deal of time and money wasted already. All the parties will be glad to have the money down. He's in England again now, thank the Lord. That's a saving of expense. I was waiting to have a look at him myself when you came up. I've never set eyes on him before."

"I can't raise it," said Colonel Tempest with the despairing remembrance of repeated failures in that direction. "I can't give security for five hundred."

"If you can't pay it, and you can't raise it," said Swayne, shaking off Colonel Tempest's hand, and thrusting his own into his pockets, "what's the good of talking? Sorry not to part friends, Colonel; but what's done is done. You can't send back shoes to the maker that have come to pinch on wearing 'em. You should have thought of that before. Business is business, and a bet's a bet."

V

"Alas! the love of women! It is known
To be a lovely and a fearful thing."

—Byron

Rooms seldom represent their inmates faithfully, any more than photographs their originals, and a poorly-furnished room, like a bad photograph, is, as a rule, a caricature. But there are fortunate persons who can weave for themselves out of apparently incongruous odds and ends of *bric-à-brac*, and china, and cretonne, a habitation which is as peculiar to them as the moss cocoon is to the long-tailed tit, or as the spillikins, in which she coldly cherishes the domestic affections, are to the water-hen.

Madeleine Thesinger's little boudoir looking over Park Lane was as like her as a translation is to the original. Madeleine was one of the many young souls who mistake eccentricity for originality. It was therefore to be expected that a life-sized china monkey should be suspended from the ceiling by a gilt chain, not even holding a lamp as an excuse for its presence. Her artistic tendencies required that scarlet pampas grass should stand in a high yellow jar on the piano, and that the piano itself should be festooned with terra-cotta Liberty silk. A little palm near had its one slender leg draped in an *impromptu* Turkish trouser, made out of an amber handkerchief. Even the flowers are leaving their garden of Eden now. They require clothing, just as chrysanthemums must have their hair curled. We shall put the lily into corsets next!

There was a faint scent of incense in the room. A low couch, covered with striped Oriental rugs and cushions, was drawn near the fire. Beside it was a small carved table—everything was small—with a few devotional books upon it, an open Bible, and a hyacinth in water. A frame, on which some elaborate Church embroidery was stretched, kept the Bible in countenance. The walls were draped as only young ladies, defiant of all laws of taste or common sense, but determined on originality, can drape them. The *portière* alone fell all its length to the ground. The other curtains were caught up or tweaked across, or furled like flags against the walls above chromos and engravings, over which it was quite unnecessary that they should ever be lowered. The pictures themselves were mostly sentimental or religious. Leighton's "Wedded" hung as a pendant to "The Light of the World." The small room was crowded with tiny ornaments and brittle conceits, and mirrors placed at convenient angles. There was no room to put anything down anywhere.

Sir Henry Verelst, when he was ushered in, large and stout and expectant, instantly knocked over a white china mandarin whose tongue dropped out on the carpet as he picked it up. He replaced it with awe, tongue and all, and then, taking refuge on the hearth-rug, promenaded his pale prawn-like eyes round the apartment to see where he could put down his hat. But apparently there was no vacant place, for he continued to clutch it in a tightly-gloved hand, and to stare absently in front of him, sniffing the unmodulated sniff of solitary nervousness.

Sir Henry had a vacant face. The only change of which it was capable was a change of colour. Under the influence of great emotion he could become very red, instead of red, but that was all. He was a stout man, and his feelings never got as far as the surface; they probably gave up the attempt half way. He was feeling a great deal—for him—at this moment, but his face was as stolid as a doll's. He had fallen suddenly and desperately in love, bald head over red ears in love, with Madeleine, after his own fashion, since she had shown him so decidedly that he was dear to her on that evening a fortnight ago when he had hovered round her in his usual "fancy free" and easy manner, merely because she was the prettiest girl in the room. He now thought her the most wonderful and beautiful and religious person in the world. He had been counting the hours till he should see her again. He did not know how to bear being kept waiting in this way; but he did not turn a hair, possibly because there were not many to turn. He stood as if he were stuffed. At last, after a long interval, there was a step in the passage. He sighed copiously through his nose, and changed legs; his dull eyes turned to the *portière*.

A French maid entered, who in broken English explained that mademoiselle could not see monsieur. Mademoiselle had a headache. Would monsieur call again at five o'clock?

Sir Henry started, and became his reddest, face, and ears, and neck; but, after a momentary pause, he merely nodded to the woman and went out, knocking over the same china figure from the same table as he did so, but this time without perceiving it.

As soon as he was gone, the maid replaced the piece of china now permanently tongueless, and then raised her eyes and hands.

"Mon Dieu!" she said below her breath, as she left the room. "Quel fiancé!"

A few moments later Madeleine came in her headache appeared to be sufficiently relieved to allow of her coming down now that her betrothed had departed. She pulled down the rose-coloured blinds, and then flung herself with a little shiver on to the couch beside the fire. She was very pretty, very fair, very small, very feminine in dress and manner. That she was seven and twenty it would have been impossible to believe, except by daylight, but for a certain tinge of laboured youthfulness in her demeanour.

She put up two of the dearest little hands to her small curled head, and then held them to the fire with a gesture of annoyance. Her eyes—they were pretty appealing eyes, with delicately-bistred eyelashes—fell upon her diamond engagement-ring as she did so, and she turned her left hand from side to side to make the stones catch the light.

She was still looking at her ring when the door opened, and "Miss Tempest" was announced.

"Well, Madeleine?" said a fresh clear voice.

"*Dear* Di!" said Madeleine, rising and throwing herself into her friend's arms. "How good of you to come, and so early, too! I have been so longing to see you, so longing to tell you about everything!" She drew her visitor down beside her on the couch, and took possession of her hand.

"I am very anxious to hear," said Di, disengaging her hand after a moment, and pulling off her furred gloves and boa.

"Let me help you, you dear thing," said Madeleine, unfastening her friend's coat, in which action the engagement-ring took a good deal of exercise. "Is it very cold out? What a colour you have! I never saw you looking so well."

"Really?" said Di, remembering how Madeleine had made the same remark on her return last year from fishing in Scotland with her face burnt brick red. "One does not generally look one's best after being out in a wind like a knife; but I am glad you think so. And now tell me all about *it*."

Di's long, rather large, white hand was taken into both Madeleine's small ones again, and fondled in silence for a few moments.

Di looked at her with an expression half puzzled, half benevolent, as a Newfoundland might look at a toy terrier. She was in reality five or six years younger than Madeleine, but her height and a certain natural dignity of carriage and manner gave her the appearance of being much older—by a rose-coloured light.

"It was very sudden," said Madeleine in a shy whisper, evidently enjoying the situation.

"How sudden? Do you mean it was a sudden idea on his part?"

"No, you tiresome thing, of course not; but it came upon *me* very suddenly."

"Oh!"

After all a bite may with truth be called sudden by the angler who has long and persistently cast over that and every other rise within reach.

"You see," said Madeline, "I had not seen him for a long time, and somehow his being so much older and—and everything, and—"

Di recalled the outward presentment of Sir Henry—elderly, gouty, the worse for town wear.

"I see," she said gravely.

There was a pause.

"I knew you would feel with me about it," said Madeleine, affectionately. "I always think you are so sympathetic."

"But you *did* think it over—it did occur to you before he asked you?" said the sympathizer in rather a low voice.

"Oh yes! The night before I thought of it."

"The night before?" echoed Di.

"Yes, that last evening at Narbury. I don't know how it was; there were some much prettier girls there than me, but I was quite monopolized by the men—Lord Algy and Captain Graham in particular; it was really most embarrassing. I have such a dislike to being made conspicuous. One on each side of the piano, you know; and, as I told them, they ought not to leave the other girls in the way they were doing. There were two girls who had no one to speak to all the evening. I begged them to go and talk to them, but they would not listen; and Sir Henry stood about near, and would insist on turning over, and somehow suddenly I thought he meant something, but I never thought it would be so quick. Men are so strange. I sometimes think they look at things *quite* differently from a woman. It's such a solemn thought to me that we have got to influence them, and draw them up."

"Or draw them on," said Di gravely—"one or the other, or both at the same time. Yes, it's very solemn. When did you say Sir Henry became sudden?"

"Next morning—the very next morning, after breakfast, in the orchid-house. I just wandered in there to read my letters. It took me entirely by surprise. It is such a comfort to talk to you, dear Di. I know you do enter into it all so."

"Not into the orchid-house," said Di, looking straight in front of her.

"You naughty thing!" said Madeleine, delightedly. "I shall shake you if you tease like that."

To threaten to shake any one was Madeleine's sheet-anchor in the form of repartee. Di knit her white brows.

"And though the idea had never so much as crossed your mind till a few hours before, still you accepted him?" she asked.

"No," said Madeleine, withdrawing her hand with dignity; "of course I did not. I don't know what other girls feel about it, but with me there is something too solemn, too sacred, in an engagement of that kind to rush into it all in a moment. I told him so, and that I must think it over, and that I could not answer him anything at once."

"And how long did you think it over?"

"All that morning. I stayed by myself in my own room. I did not go out, though the others all went to a steeplechase on Lord Algy's drag, and I had a new gown on purpose. I suppose most girls would have gone, but I felt I could not. I can't take things lightly like some people. I dare say it is a mistake, but I always have felt anything of that kind very deeply."

"I suppose he did not go either?"

"N—no, he didn't."

"That would have been awkward if you had not intended to accept him."

Madeleine looked into the fire.

"It was a very painful time," she went on, after a pause. "And it was so embarrassing at luncheon—only him and me, and that old General Hanbury. Every one else had gone."

"Even your mother?"

"Yes; she was the chaperone of the party, as Mrs. Mildmay had a headache. But I did not want her to stay. She did not know till it was all settled. I could not have talked about it to her; mamma and I feel so differently. You know she always remembers how much she cared for poor papa. I was dreadfully perplexed what I ought to do, but"—in a lowered voice—"I took it where I take all my troubles, Di. I prayed over it; I laid it all before—"

Madeleine stopped short as Di suddenly hid her face in her hands. The white nape of her neck was crimson.

"And then?" she asked, after a moment's silence, with her face still hidden.

"Then it all seemed to become clear," murmured Madeleine, gratified by Di's evident envy. "And I saw it was *meant*. You know, Di, I believe those things are decided for one. And I felt quite peaceful, and I went out for a little bit in the garden, and the sun was setting—I always care so much for sunsets, they mean so much to me, and it was all so beautiful and calm; and—I suppose he had seen me go out—and—"

Di uttered a sound between a laugh and a sob, which resulted in something like a croak. Her fair face was red with—*was* it envy?—as she raised her head. Two large tears stood in her indignant wistful eyes. She looked hard at Madeleine, and the latter avoided her direct glance.

"Madeleine," she said, "do you care for this man?"

Madeleine gave a little pout which would have appealed to a masculine heart, but which had no effect on Di.

"I was very much surprised when you wrote to tell me," continued Di, rather hurriedly. "I never should have thought—when I remember what he is—I can't believe that you can really care about him."

"I have a great influence over him—an influence for good," said Madeleine. "He would promise anything I asked; he has already about smoking. I know he has not been always— But you know a woman's influence. I always mention him in my prayers, Di."

Madeleine had been long in the habit of presenting the names of her most eligible acquaintances of the opposite sex to the favourable consideration of the Almighty, without whose co-operation she was aware that nothing matrimonially advantageous could be effected, and in whose powers as a chaperon she placed more confidence than in the feeble finite efforts of a kind but unworldly mother. She had never so far felt impelled to draw His attention to the spiritual needs of younger sons.

"Every woman has an enormous influence for the time over a man who is in love with her," said Di, who seemed to have frozen perceptibly. "It is nothing peculiar. It is one of the common stock feelings on such occasions. The question is, Do you really care for him?"

Madeleine shivered a little, and then suddenly burst into uncontrollable weeping. Di was touched to the quick. Loss of self-control sometimes moves reserved people profoundly. They know that only an overwhelming onslaught of emotion would be able to wrest their own self-control from them; and when they witness the loss of it in another, they think that it must have been caused by the same amount of suffering.

"I think you are very unkind, Di," Madeleine said, between her sobs. "And I always thought you would be the one to sympathize with me when I was engaged. And I have chosen the bridesmaids' gowns on purpose to suit you, though I know Sir Henry's niece, that little fat Dalrymple with her waist under her arms, will look simply hideous in it. And I wrote to you the *very* first! I think you are very unkind!"

"Am I?" said Di, gently, as if she were speaking to a child; and she knelt down by the little sobbing figure and put her arms round her. "Never mind about the bridesmaids' gowns, dear. It was very nice of you to think how they would suit me. Never mind about anything but just this one thing: Do you think you will be happy if you marry Sir Henry Verelst?"

"Others do it," sobbed Madeleine. "Look at Maud Lister, and she hated Lord Lentham—and he was such a dreadful little man, with a mole, worse than— But she got not to mind. And I've been out nine years. You are only twenty-one, Di. It's all very well for you to talk like that; I felt just the same when I was your age. But I shall be twenty-eight this year; and you don't know what it feels like to be getting on, and one's fringe not what it was; and always having to pretend to be glad when one is bridesmaid to girls younger than one's self, and seeing other girls have *trousseaux*, and thinking, perhaps, one will never have one at all. I don't know how I could bear to live if I was thirty and was not married!"

Di was silent for a moment from sheer astonishment at a real declaration of feeling from one who felt, and lived, and talked, and dressed according to a social code fixed as the laws of the Medes and Persians.

Her low voice had a certain tremor of repressed emotion in it as she said: "But think of Sir Henry. The bridegroom is part of the wedding, after all; think of what he is. What can you care for in him? Nothing. I don't see how you could. And he is twice your age. Be a brave girl, and break it off."

Di felt as she said the last words that the courage of being able to break off the engagement was as nothing to that of continuing to keep it. She did not realize that an entire lack of imagination wears, under certain circumstances, the appearance of the most stoical fortitude.

The brave girl sobbed again, and pressed a little frilled square of cambric to her eyes.

MARY CHOLMONDELEY

"No," she gasped; "I can't—I can't! It has been in all the papers. Half my things are ordered; I have asked the bridesmaids. I can't go back now. It is wicked to break off an engagement. God would be very angry with me."

It is difficult to argue with any one who can make a Jorkins of the Almighty. Every word Madeleine spoke showed her friend how unavailing any further remonstrance would be. Di saw that she had gone through that common phase of imagination which a shallow nature feels to be prophetic. Madeleine had, in what stood proxy for her imagination, already regarded herself as a bride, as the recipient, not of diamonds in general, but of the Verelst diamonds in particular. Already in maiden meditation she had seen herself arrive at certain houses on bridal visits—had contemplated herself opening a county hunt ball as the bride of the year—until she looked upon the wedding as a settled event, the husband as a necessary adjunct, the *trousseaux* as a certainty.

"And you must see my under-things when they come, because we have always been such friends," continued Madeleine, as Di remained silent. She dried her eyes with little dabs, for even in emotion she remembered the danger of wiping them, while she favoured Di with minute details respecting those complete sets of under-clothing which so mysteriously enhance and dignify the holy estate of matrimony in the feminine mind. But Di was not listening. The image of Sir Henry, who had besought herself to marry him a year ago, reverted to her mind with a remembrance of her own repulsion towards the Moloch to which Madeleine was preparing to offer herself up.

"Madeleine," she said suddenly, "I am sure from what I have seen that marriage is too difficult if you don't care for your husband. The married people who did not marry for love tell one so by their faces. I am sure there are some hard times to be lived through even when you care very much. Nothing but a great love, granny says, will float one over some of the rocks ahead. But to marry without love is like undertaking to sew without a needle, or dig without a spade—attempting difficult work without the tool provided for it. Oh, Madeleine, don't do it! Break it off—break it off!"

Madeleine clung closer to the girl kneeling beside her. It almost seemed as if the urgent eager voice were not speaking in vain.

A tap came at the door.

Di, always shy of betraying emotion, was on her feet in a moment. Madeleine drew the screen hastily between herself and the light as she said, "Come in."

It was the French maid, who explained that the dressmaker had sent the two rolls of brocade as she had promised, so that mademoiselle might judge of them in the piece. She brought them in with her, and spread them in artistic folds on two chairs.

Madeleine sat up and gave a little sigh.

"If she gives them up, she will give him up, too," thought Di. "This is the turning-point."

"Di," she said earnestly, "which would you advise, the mauve or the white and gold? I always think you have such taste."

Di started and turned a shade pale. She saw by that one sentence that the die had been thrown, though Madeleine was not herself aware of it. The moments of our most important decisions are often precisely those in which nothing seems to have been decided; and only long afterwards, when we perceive with astonishment that the Rubicon has been crossed, do we realize that in that half-forgotten instant of hesitation as to some apparently unimportant side issue, in that unconscious movement that betrayed a feeling of which we were not aware, our choice was made. The crises of life come, like the Kingdom of Heaven, without observation. Our characters, and not our deliberate actions, decide for us; and even when the moment of crisis is apprehended at the time by the troubling of the water, action is generally a little late. Character, as a rule, steps down first. It was so with Madeleine.

Sir Henry owed his bride to the exactly timed appearance of a mauve brocade sprinkled with silver *fleur-de-lys*. The maid turned it lightly, and the silver threads gleamed through the rich pale material.

"It is perfect," said Madeleine in a hushed voice; "absolutely perfect. Don't you think so, Di? And she says she will do it for forty guineas, as she is making me other things. The front is to be a silver gauze over plain mauve satin to match, and the train of the brocade. The white and gold is nothing to it."

"It is very beautiful," said Di, looking at it with a kind of horror. It seemed to her at the moment as if every one had their price.

Madeleine smiled faintly. She felt that Di must envy her. It was of course only natural that she should do so. A thought strayed across her mind that in the future many gowns of this description, hitherto unobtainable and unsuitable, might sweeten existence; and she would be kind to Di. She would press an old one, before it was really old, on her occasionally.

Madeleine gave the sigh that accompanies relaxation from intense mental strain.

"I will decide on the mauve," she said.

VI

*"Ready money of affection
Pay, whoever drew the bill."*

—Clough

"Put not your trust in brothers," said Di, coming in from a balcony after the departure of the bride and bridegroom, and looking round the crowded drawing-room, where the fictitious gaiety of a wedding was more or less dismally stamped on every face. "I do believe Archie has deserted me."

"I know he has," said her companion. "He told me half an hour ago that he was going to bolt."

"Did he? The deceiver! He gave me a solemn promise that he would see me home. I believe young men are the root of all evil. Don't pin your faith to them, Lord Hemsworth, or you will live to rue it, like me."

"I won't."

"And why, pray, did not you mention the fact that he was going when I was laboriously explaining all the presents to you, and exhausting myself in pointing out watches in bracelets or concealed in the handles of umbrellas, which you were quite unable to see for yourself? One good turn deserves another. Ah! now the people are really beginning to go. Is not that Lady Breakwater in the inner drawing-room? Poor woman—I mean, happy mother! I will try and get near her to say good-bye. Look at her smiling; I think I should know a wedding smile anywhere."

"No, you need not see me home," she added a few minutes later, as she stood in the hall. "Have I not a hired brougham? One throws expense to the winds on an occasion of this kind. There comes your hansom behind it. What a lovely chestnut! How I do envy you it! The blessings of this world are very unevenly distributed. Good-bye."

"I am going to see you home," said Lord Hemsworth, with decision. "It is the duty of the best man to make himself generally useful to the chief bridesmaid. I've read it in my little etiquette book; and, however painful my duty may be made to me, I shall perform it."

"You have performed it thoroughly already. No, you are not coming in. Don't shut the door on my gown, please. Thanks. Home, coachman."

"Are you going to the Speaker's tonight?" said Lord Hemsworth, with his arms on the carriage-door, perfectly regardless of the string of carriages behind him.

"I am."

"Good luck; so am I."

"That's not in the etiquette book," said Di, with mischief in her eyes. "In the meantime you are stopping the whole procession. We have shaken hands once already. Good-bye again."

Mrs. Courtenay was sitting in her armchair with her back to the light in the long sunny drawing-room of her little house in Kensington, waiting for the return of her granddaughter from the wedding to which at the last moment she had been unable to escort her herself. Her headache was better now, and she had taken up her work, the fine elaborate lace work in imitation of an old design which she had copied in some Italian church.

Mrs. Courtenay had been one of the four beautiful Miss Digbys of Ebberstone about whom society had gone wild fifty years ago; and in her old age she was beautiful still, with the dignified and gracious manner of one who has been worshipped in her day. Her calm keen face bore the marks of much suffering, but of suffering that had been outlived. Perhaps next to the death of her husband, who had left her in her early youth to struggle with life alone, the blow which she had felt most keenly had been the clandestine and most miserable marriage of her only daughter with Colonel Tempest; but it was all past now. People while they are undergoing the strain of the ordinary ills that flesh is heir to, the bitterness of inadequately returned love, the loss or alienation of children, the grind of poverty or the hydra-headed wants of insufficient wealth, are not as a rule pleasant or sympathetic companions. The lessons of life are coming too quickly upon them to allow of it. They are preoccupied. But *tout passe*. Mrs. Courtenay had loved and had suffered, and had presented a brave front to the world, and had known wealth, as she now knew poverty. The pain was past; the experience remained; therein lay the secret of her power and her popularity, for she had both. She seemed to have reached a little quiet backwater in the river of life where the pressure of the current could no longer reach her, would never reach her again. She sometimes said that nothing could affect her very deeply now, except, perhaps, what affected her granddaughter. But that was a large exception. Mrs. Courtenay loved her granddaughter with some of the stern tender affection which she had once lavished on her own daughter—which she had buried in her grave. The elder Diana had taken two hearts down to the grave with her—her mother's and Mr. Tempest's.

Mrs. Courtenay had that rarest gift—

> "A heart at leisure from itself
> To soothe and sympathize."

To that little house in Kensington many came, long before her beautiful granddaughter was of an age to be its principal attraction, as she had now become. Mrs. Courtenay's house had gained the magic name of being agreeable, possibly because she made it so to one and all alike. None but the pushing and the dictatorial were ever overlooked. Country relations with the loud voices and the abusive political views peculiar to rural life were her worst bugbears, but even they had a pleasing suspicion that they had distinguished themselves in conversation, and departed with the gratified feeling akin to that depicted on a plain woman's face when she has come out well in a photograph.

In talking with the young Mrs. Courtenay remembered her own far-away youth, its romantic passions, its watchful nights, its splendour of sunrise illusions. She remembered, too, its great ignorance, and was not, like so many elders, exasperated with the young for having omitted to learn, before they came into the world, what they themselves only learned by living half a century in it.

She had sympathy with old and young alike, but perhaps she felt most deeply for those who were struggling in the meshes of middle age, no longer interesting to others or even to themselves. Many came to Mrs. Courtenay for comfort and sympathy in the servitude with hard labour of middle age, and none came in vain.

Mrs. Courtenay lifted her calm clear eyes to the Louis Quatorze clock on the old Venetian cabinet near her.

"Di is late," she said half aloud.

The low sun was thinking better of it, and was shining in through the tracery of the bare branches of the trees outside. If there was ever a ray of sunshine anywhere, it was in that little Kensington drawing-room. The sun never forgot to seek it out, to come and have a look at the little possessions which in spite of her narrow means Mrs. Courtenay had gradually gathered round her. It came now, and touched the white *Capo di Monte* figures on the mantelpiece, and brought into momentary prominence the inlaid ivory dolphins on the ebony cabinet; those dolphins with curly tails which two Dianas had loved at the age when permission to drive dolphins and sit on waves was not a final impossibility though denied for the moment. It lighted up the groups of Lowestoft china, and the tall Oriental jars which Mrs. Courtenay suffered no one to dust but herself. The little bits of old silver and enamel on the black polished table caught the light. So did the daffodils in the green Vallauris tripod. They blazed against the shadowed pictured wall. The quiet room was full of light.

Presently a carriage stopped at the door, the bell rang, and a moment later a swift light step mounted the stair, and Di came in, tall and radiant in her flowing white and yellow draperies, her bouquet of mimosa in her hand.

She was beautiful, with the beauty that is recognized at once. Beauty is so rare nowadays and prettiness so common, that the terms are often confused and misapplied, and the most ordinary good looks usurp the name of beauty. But between prettiness and beauty there is nevertheless a great gulf fixed. No one had ever called Di a pretty girl. At one and twenty she was a beautiful woman, with that nameless air of distinction which can ennoble the plainest face and figure.

She had a right to beauty from both parents, and resembled both of them to a certain degree. She had the tall splendid figure of the Tempests with their fair skin and pale golden hair, waving back thick and burnished from her low white forehead. But she had her mother's dark unfathomable eyes with the long dark eyelashes, and her mother's features with their inherent nobility and strength, which were so entirely lacking in the Tempests—at least, in the present generation of them. Some people, women mostly, said there was too much contrast between her dark eyes and eyebrows and the extreme fairness of her complexion and hair. Men, however, did not think so. They saw that she was beautiful, and that was enough. Indeed, it was too much for some of them. Women said, also, that her features were too large, that she was on too large a scale altogether. No doubt that accounted for the fact that she was seldom overlooked.

"Well, Granny, and how is the headache?" she asked gaily, pulling off her long gloves and instantly beginning to unwire the mimosa in her bouquet with rapid, capable white hands.

"Oh! the headache is gone," said Mrs. Courtenay, watching her granddaughter. "And how did it all go off?"

"Perfectly," said Di, in her clear gay voice. "Madeleine looked beautiful, and often as I have been bridesmaid I never stood behind a bride with a better fitting back. I suppose the survival of the best fitted is what we are coming to in these days. Anyhow, Madeleine attained to it. It was a well done thing altogether. The altar one mass of white peonies! White peonies at Easter! Sir Henry was the only red one there. And eight of us all youth and innocence in white and amber to bear her company. We bridesmaids were all waiting for her for some time before she arrived or he either; but Lord Hemsworth marched him in at last, just when I was beginning to hope he would not turn up. I have seen him look worse, Granny. He did not look so very bald until he knelt down, and I have known his nose redder. To a friend I dare say it only looked like a blush that had lost its way. He is a stout man to outline himself in a white waistcoat, but I thought on the whole he looked well."

"Di," said Mrs. Courtenay, with her little inward laugh, "you should not say such things."

"Oh yes, I can say anything I like to you," said Di. "Dear me, I am sitting on my new amber sash! What extravagance! It will be long enough before I have another. It was really good of Lady Breakwater to give me the whole turn-out. We never could have afforded it."

"Did Madeleine look unhappy?"

"No; she was pale, but perfectly collected, and she walked quite firmly to the chancel steps where the security for fifteen thousand a year and two diamond tiaras and a pendant was awaiting her. The security looked a little nervous."

"Di," said Mrs. Courtenay, with an effort after severity, "never again let me hear you laugh at the man who once did you the honour to ask you to marry him. You show great want of feeling."

Di's face changed. It became several degrees sterner than her grandmother's. That peculiar concentrated light came into her soft lovely eyes which is a life-long puzzle to those who can see only one aspect of a character, and whose ideas are consequently thrown into the wildest confusion by a change of expression. There was at times an appearance of intensity of feeling about Di which sometimes gleamed up into her eyes and gave a certain tremor to her low voice, that surprised and almost frightened those who regarded her only as a charming but somewhat eccentric woman. Di's best friends said they did not understand her. The little foot-rule by which they measured others did not seem to apply to her. She was grave or gay, cynical or tender, frivolous or sympathetic, according to the mood of the hour, or according as her quick intuition and sense of mischief showed her the exact opposite was expected of her. But behind the various moods which naturally high spirits led her into for the moment, keener eyes could see that there was always something kept back—something not suffered to be discussed and commented on by the crowd—namely, herself. Her frank, cordial manner might deceive the many, but others who knew her better were conscious of a great reserve—of a barrier beyond which they might not pass; of locked rooms in that sunny, hospitable house into which no one was invited, into which she had, perhaps, as yet rarely penetrated herself.

Mrs. Courtenay possibly understood her better than any one, but Di took her by surprise now. She laid down her flowers and came and stood before her grandmother.

"Do I show want of feeling?" she said, in her low, even voice. "I know I have none for that man; but why should I have any? If he wanted to marry me, why did he want it? He knew I did not like him—I made that sufficiently plain. Did he care one single straw for anything about me except my looks? If he had liked me ever so little, it would have been different; but why am I to be grateful because he wanted me to sit at the head of his table, and wear his diamonds?"

"You talk as young and silly girls with romantic ideas do talk," replied Mrs. Courtenay, piqued into making assertions exactly contrary to her real opinions. "I fancied you had more sense! Madeleine did a wise thing in accepting him. She has made a very prudent marriage."

"Yes," said Di, moving slowly away and sitting down by the window—"that is just it. I wonder if there is anything in the whole wide world so recklessly imprudent as a prudent marriage? But what am I talking about?" she added, lightly. "It is not a marriage; it is merely a social contract. I can't see why they went to church myself, or what the peonies and that nice little newly-ironed Bishop were for. They were quite unnecessary. A register-office and a clerk would have done just as well, and have been more in keeping. But how silly it is of me to be wasting my time in holding forth when your cap is not even trimmed for this evening. The price of a virtuous woman is above rubies nowadays. Nothing but diamonds and settlements will secure a first-rate article. And now, to come back to more serious subjects, will you wear your diamond stars, G"—("G" was the irreverent pet name by which Di sometimes called her grandmother)—"or shall I fasten that little marabou feather with your pearl clasp into the point-lace cap? It wants something at the side."

"I think I will wear the diamonds," said Mrs. Courtenay, thoughtfully. "People are beginning to wear their jewels again now. Only sew them in firmly, Di."

"You should have seen the array of jewellery today," said Di, still in the same tone, arranging the mimosa in clusters about the room. "Other people's diamonds seem to take all the starch out of me. A kind of limpness comes over me when I look at tiaras. And there was such a *rivière* and pendant! And a little hansom cab and horse in diamonds as a brooch. I should like to be tempted by a brooch like that. Sir Henry has his good points, after all. I see it now that it is too late. And why do people sprinkle themselves all over with watches nowadays, Granny, in unexpected places? Lord Hemsworth counted five—was it, or six?—set in different presents. There were two, I think, in bracelets, one in a fan, and one in the handle of an umbrella. What can be the use of a watch in the handle of an umbrella? Then there was a very little one in—what was it?—a paper-knife, set round with large diamonds. It made me feel quite unwell to look at it when I thought how what had been spent on that silly thing would have dressed you and me, Granny, for a year. That reminds me—I shall tear off this amber sash and put it on my white *miroitant* dinner-gown. You must not give me any more white gowns; they are done for directly."

"I like to see you in white."

"Oh! so do I—just as much as I like to see you, Granny, in brocade; but it can't be done. I won't have you spending so much on me. If I am a pauper, I don't mind looking like one."

She looked very unlike one as she gathered up her gloves and lace handkerchief and bouquet holder, and left the room. And yet they were very poor. No one knew on how small a number of hundreds that little home was kept together, how narrow was the margin which allowed of those occasional little dinner-parties of eight to which people were so glad to come. Who was likely to divine that the two black satin chairs had been covered by Di's strong hands—that the pale Oriental coverings on the settees and sofas that harmonized so well with the subdued colouring of the room were the result of her powers of upholstery—that it was Di who mounted boldly on high steps and painted her own room and her grandmother's an elegant pink distemper, inciting the servants to go and do likewise for themselves?

MARY CHOLMONDELEY

It was easy to see they were poor, but it was generally supposed that they had the species of limited means which wealth is so often kind enough to envy, with its old formula that the truly rich are those who have nothing to keep up. This is true if the narrow means have not caused the wants to become so circumscribed that nothing further remains that can *be put down*. The rich, one would imagine, are those who, whatever their income may be, have it in their power to put down an unnecessary expense. But probably all expenses are essentially necessary to the wealthy.

Mrs. Courtenay and her granddaughter lived very quietly, and went without effort, and, indeed, as a matter of course, into that society which is labelled, whether rightly or wrongly, as "good."

Persons of narrow means too often slip out of the class to which they naturally belong, because they can give nothing in return for what they receive. They may have a thousand virtues, and be far superior in their domestic relations to those who forget them, but they *are* forgotten, all the same. Society is rigorous, and gives nothing for nothing.

But others there are whose poverty makes no difference to them, who are welcomed with cordiality, and have reserved seats everywhere because, though they cannot pay in kind, they have other means at their disposal. Their very presence is an overpayment. Every one who goes into society must, in some form or other, as Mrs. Lynn Linton expresses it, "pay their shot." All the doors were open to Mrs. Courtenay and her granddaughter, not because they were handsomer than other people, not because they belonged by birth to "good" society, and were only to be seen at the "best" houses, but because, wherever they went, they were felt to be an acquisition, and one not invariably to be obtained.

Madeleine had been glad to book Di at once as one of her bridesmaids. Indeed, she had long professed a great affection for the younger girl, with whom she had nothing in common, but whose beauty rendered it probable that she might eventually make a brilliant match.

As the bridesmaid sat down rather wearily in her own room, and unfastened the diamond monogram brooch—"the gift of the bridegroom"—the tears that had been in her heart all day came into her eyes; Di's slow, difficult tears.

What a mass of illusions are torn from us by the first applauded mercenary marriage that comes very near to us in our youth! Death, when he draws nigh for the first time, at least leaves us our illusions; but this voluntary death in life, from which there is no resurrection, filled Di's soul with loathing compassion. She bowed her fair head on her hands and wept over the girl who had never been her friend, but whose fate might at one time have been her own.

VII

"Broad his shoulders are and strong;
And his eye is scornful,
Threatening and young."

—Emerson

There was the usual crush at the Speaker's, the usual sprinkling of stars and orders, and splendid uniforms. If it made Di feel limp to look at other people's diamonds, she would be very limp tonight.

Two men with their backs to the wall, somewhat withdrawn from the moving pressure of the crowd, were commenting in the absolute privacy of a large gathering on the stream of arrivals.

"Who is that old parchment face and the eyeglass?" asked the younger man, whose bleached eyes and moustache betokened foreign service.

"Which?"

"Coming in now; looks as if he had seen a thing or two. There—he is talking to one of the Arden twins."

"That man? That is Lord Frederick Fane, an old reprobate. See, he has buttonholed Hemsworth. I should like to hear what he is saying to him. Look how his eye twinkles. He is one of our instructors of youth."

"Hemsworth has been standing there for the last half-hour."

"He is waiting; anybody can see that. So am I, though not for the same person."

"Whom are you looking out for?"

"Do you see that dark man with the high nose, talking to the Post Office? There—the Duchess of Southark has just spoken to him, and is introducing her daughter."

"Do you mean that ugly beggar with the clean-shaved face and heavy jaw?"

"I don't see that he is so ugly. He has got a head on his shoulders, and his face means something, which is more than you can say of many. There is no lack of ability there. He is one of the men of the future, and people are beginning to find it out. He has not taken any line in politics yet, but he is bound to soon. Both sides want him, of course. He is one of our most promising Commoners, Tempest of Overleigh."

The younger man glanced at the square-shouldered erect figure and strong dark face with deep interest.

"Is he the man about whom there was a lawsuit when his father died?"

"Yes; Colonel Tempest brought an action, but he lost it. There was no evidence forthcoming, though there was very little doubt how matters really stood."

"He is not like the Tempests."

"No; if you want a Tempest pure and simple, look at the man with tow-coloured hair in the further doorway, making running with the little soda-water heiress. That is the regular Tempest style."

"He is too beautiful; he has overdone it," said the other. "If he were less handsome, he would be better looking, and his hair looks like a wig. He has the face of a fool on him."

"The last two generations have had no grit in them. Jack Tempest, the last man, might have done something, but he never came to the fore. He was a trustworthy Conservative, but not an energetic man like his father, the old minister, who lies in Westminster Abbey."

"Perhaps the present man will come to the fore."

"Perhaps! I know he will; you can see it in his face, and he has the *prestige* of his name and wealth to back him. But I don't know which side he will take. I know that he voted right at the last election, but so did half the Liberals. I incline to think he has Liberal leanings, but he refused to stand three years ago for the family constituency, which is an absolute certainty whatever he professes himself, and he has been secretary to the Embassy at St. Petersburg for the last three years."

"He is very like his mother's family, except that the Fanes are not so ugly."

"Of course he is like his mother's family; it's an open secret. Look at him now; he is speaking to Lord Frederick Fane, his mother's— first cousin. There's a family resemblance for you! I wonder they stand together."

His companion drew in his breath. The likeness between the elder man and the young one was unmistakable.

"Does he know, do you think?" he asked after a moment.

"Of course he must know that there is a 'but' about himself. People don't grow up in ignorance of such things; but I should think he does *not* know that it is more than a suspicion, that it is a moral certainty, and that Lord Frederick— But it is seven and twenty years ago, and it is half forgotten now. He is not the only heir with a doubt about him. He will

MARY CHOLMONDELEY

be a credit to the Tempests, anyhow. If the property had fallen into the hands of those two thieves, Colonel Tempest and his son, there would not have been much left of it for the next generation."

"It's frightfully hot!" said the younger man. "I shall bolt."

"Just home from Africa, and find it hot!" said the other. "Ah!"—with sudden interest, looking back to the doorway—"I thought so. Hemsworth was not waiting for nothing. By—she *is* handsome, and what a figure! She is the tallest woman in the room except Lady Delmour's two yards of unmarriageable maypole. Look how she moves, and the way her head is set on her shoulders. If I had not a wife and seven children, I should make a fool of myself. I remember her mother, just as handsome twenty years ago, but not so brilliant, and with an unhappy look about her. Hang Tempest! I won't wait any longer for him. I must go and speak to her before Hemsworth takes possession of her."

"You take my advice, John," said Lord Frederick Fane confidentially to his kinsman; "don't tie yourself to a party any more than you would to a woman. Leave that for fools like Hemsworth. Just go your own way, and give no one a claim on you."

"I intend to go my own way when I have decided where I want to go."

"Well, in the meanwhile don't commit yourself. Always leave yourself a loop-hole."

"I don't see the use of worrying about loop-holes if I don't want to back out of anything. I shall never consciously put myself anywhere where it might be necessary to wriggle out on all fours."

"Oh! I dare say. I thought all that in my salad days, but you'll grow out of it as you get older. You'll chip your shell, John, like the rest of us, he! he! and not be above a shift. There's not a man who won't stoop to a shift on a pinch, provided the pinch is sharp enough, any more than there is a woman, bespoken or otherwise, who does not like being made love to, provided it is done the right way. That is my experience."

Lord Frederick's experience was that of most men of his stamp, the crown of whose maturer years, earned by a youth of strenuous self-indulgence, is a disbelief in human nature. Secret contempt of women, coupled with a smooth and adulatory manner towards them, show only too plainly the school in which these opinions have been formed.

"Look at Hemsworth," continued Lord Frederick, as Mrs. Courtenay and Di, and Lord Hemsworth in close attendance, were being gradually drifted towards the room in which they were standing. "If Hemsworth goes on giving that girl a hold over him, he will find himself deuced uncomfortable one of these days. He had better hold hard while he can. Discretion is the better part of valour. I've been telling him so."

"Why should he hold hard?" said John, rather absently. "After all, none but the brave deserve the fair."

"And none but the brave can live with some of them. He, he!" said Lord Frederick, chuckling. "There are cheaper ways of getting out of love than by marriage; but she is a fine woman. Hemsworth has got eyes in his head, I must own. I remember being dreadfully in love with her mother, nearly thirty years ago, and she with me. She had that sort of stand-off manner which takes some men more than anything; it did me. I wonder more women don't adopt it. I very nearly married her. He, he! But Tempest, your uncle, made a fool of himself while I hesitated, and was wretched with her, poor devil! I have never had such a shave since. Upon my word" putting up his eyeglass—"if I were a young man, I think I'd marry Di Tempest. Those large women wear well, John; they don't shrivel up to nothing like Mrs. Graham, or expand like Lady Torrington, that emblem of plenty without waist. He, he! Look at Mrs. Courtenay, too. There's a fine old pelican with an eye to the main chance. Always look at the mother and the grandmother if you can. But she is on too large a scale for you."

"Not in the least," said John, calmly. "I cherish thoughts of Miss Delmour, who is quite three inches taller."

"Don't marry a Delmour! They are too thin. Those girls have neither mind, body, nor estate. I have seen two generations of them. They have a sort of prettiness when they are quite new; but look at her married sisters. They all look as if they had shrunk in the wash."

"I must go and speak to Mrs. Courtenay," said John, from whose impenetrable face it would have been difficult to judge whether his companion's style of conversation amused or disgusted him. "Three years' absence blunts the recollection of one's friends." And he moved away towards the next room. The recollection of a good many people, however, had apparently not become blunted, and it was some time before he could make his way to Mrs. Courtenay, who was talking with a Turkish Ambassador and revolutionizing his ideas of English women.

She was genuinely glad to see John, having known him from a boy.

"You know your cousin Diana, of course?" she said, as Di came towards them.

"Indeed I do not," said John. "I asked who she was at the Thesinger wedding today, and found myself in the ludicrous position of not knowing my own first cousin."

"Not recognizing her, you mean?" said Mrs. Courtenay. "Surely you must have seen her often in my house before you went abroad; but I suppose she was in a chrysalis school-room state then, and has emerged into young ladyhood since. Here is your cousin saying he does not know you," continued Mrs. Courtenay, turning to Di. "John, this is Di. Di, this is your first cousin, John Tempest."

Both bowed, and then thought better of it and shook hands. Their eyes met on the exact level of equal height, and the steady keen glance that passed between was like the meeting of two formidable powers. Each was taken by surprise. It was as if, instead of shaking hands, they had suddenly measured swords.

"If you don't know each other you ought to," continued Mrs. Courtenay. "Lord Hemsworth, what is that unwholesome-looking compound you have got hold of?"

"Lemonade for Miss Tempest."

"Kindly fetch me some too." And Mrs. Courtenay turned away to continue her conversation with the Turk, who was still hovering near, and whose bead-like eyes under his red fez showed a decided envy of John.

He and Di were standing in the doorway that led into the last room where the refreshments were, and a stream of people beginning at that moment to press out again, pressed them back into the room they had just been leaving.

"I shall upset this down some one's back in another minute and make an enemy for life," said Di, holding her glass as best she could. She would have given anything at that instant to say something unusually frivolous in order to shake off the impression of the moment before; but her frivolity had temporarily departed with Lord Hemsworth.

"Don't oppose the stream; subside into this backwater," said John, placing his square shoulders between the throng and herself, and nodding to a recess by one of the high arched windows.

Having reached it, Di sipped the highwater mark off her lemonade.

"It's safe now," she said. "I don't know why I took it; I don't want it now I've got it. Have you seen Archie since you came back? You know *him*, of course? He often talks about you."

"Yes, I saw him at the Thesinger wedding today."

"Were you there?"

"Yes, but only at the church. I did not go on to the house; I disliked the whole affair too much. Many marriages, half the marriages one sees, are only irrevocable flirtations; but the ceremony of today was not even that."

Di looked away through the mullioned window out across the river and its gliding shimmer to the lights beyond. She did not know how long it was before she spoke.

"I think it was a great sin," she said, at last, in a low voice, unconscious of a pause that to her companion was full of meaning.

"Or a great mistake," he said, gently.

"No, not a mistake," said Di, still looking out. "The others, the irrevocable flirtations, are the mistakes. There was no mistake today. But it was a dull wedding," she added, with sudden self-recollection and a change of manner. "Not like one I was at last autumn in the country. I was staying in the same house as the bridegroom, and he and the best man, a Mr. Lumley, got up at an early hour, woke some of the other men, and paraded the house with an *impromptu* band of music. I remember the bridegroom performed piercingly upon the comb. I wonder people ever play the comb; it is so plaintive. But perhaps it is your favourite instrument, perfected in the course of foreign travel, and I am trampling on your feelings unawares."

"I used to play upon it," said John, "but not of late years. I left it off because it tickled and increased the natural melancholy of my disposition. What were the other instruments?"

"Let me see, Lord Hemsworth murmured upon a gong, and Mr. Lumley uttered his dark speech upon a tray. The whole was very effective. He told me afterwards that it was a relief to his feelings, which had been much lacerated by the misplaced affections of the bride."

Di's laughing mischievous eyes met John's fixed upon her with a grave attention that took her aback. She had an uncomfortable sense that he was regarding her with secret amusement. A moment before she had been sorry that she had inadvertently spoken with a force that was unusual to her. Now she was equally vexed that she had been flippant.

"Here you are," said Lord Hemsworth, elbowing his way up to them. "I have been looking for you everywhere. Mrs. Courtenay is going, and is asking for you."

VIII

"Psyché-papillon, un jour
Puisses-tu trouver l'amour
Et perdre tes ailes!"

"Di," said Mrs. Courtenay, as they drove away at last, after the usual half-hour's waiting for the carriage, the tedium of which Lord Hemsworth had exerted himself to relieve, "do you usually talk quite so much nonsense to Lord Hemsworth as you did tonight?"

"Generally, granny. Yes, I think it was about the usual quantity. Sometimes it is rather more, a good deal more, when you are not there."

Mrs. Courtenay was silent for a few minutes.

"You are making a mistake, Di," she said at last.

"How, granny?"

"In your manner to Lord Hemsworth. You make yourself cheap to him. A woman should never do that!"

Di did not answer.

"When I was young," said Mrs. Courtenay, "I should have been proud to have been admired by a man of his stamp."

"So should I," said Di, quietly, "if I did not like him so much."

"You do like him, then?"

"I do, and I mean to act on the square by him!"

"I don't know what you mean."

"Yes, you do, granny, perfectly! I have known him too long to alter my manner to him. I know him by heart. If I once begin to be serious and reserved with him, if I once fail to keep him at arm's length, which talking nonsense does, his feeling towards me, which only amuses him now, will become serious too. Lord Hemsworth is not so superficial as he seems. He would have been in earnest before now if I would have let him, and he is the kind of man who could be very much in earnest. I can't help his playing with edged tools, but I *can* prevent his cutting himself."

"My dear, he is in love with you now, and has been for the last six months."

"Yes," said Di, "he is in a way; but he would be much worse if he had had encouragement."

"And what do you call allowing him to talk to you for half an hour on the stairs, if it is not encouragement? You may be certain there was not a creature there who did not think you were encouraging him."

"I don't mind what creatures think, as long as I don't *do* the thing. And he knows well enough I don't!"

"Why *not* do it, if you like him?"

"Well, granny," said Di, after a pause, "the way I look at it is this. I don't mean only about Lord Hemsworth, but about any one who, well, who is interested in me—really interested in me, I mean; not one of the sham ones who want to pass the time. I never consider them. I say something like this to myself. 'Di, do you observe that man?' 'Yes,' I say, 'my eye is upon him.' 'Are you aware that he will come and speak to you the first instant he can?' 'Yes, I know that.' 'Look at him well.' Then I look at him. 'What do you think of him?' 'He is rather nice-looking,' I say, 'and he is pleasant to talk to, and he has the right kind of collars. I like him.' 'Di,' I say to myself very solemnly—you have no idea how solemn I am on these occasions—'are you willing to prefer him to the rest of the whole universe, to listen to his conversation for the remainder of your natural life, to knock under to him entirely; in short, to take him and his collars for better for worse?' 'No, of course not,' I say indignantly; 'I should not think of such a thing!' 'Then,' I reply, 'you have no earthly right to let him think you might be persuaded to; or to allow him to take a single one of the preliminary steps in that direction, however gratifying it may be to your vanity to see him do it, or however sorry you may be to lose him. He is paying you the highest compliment a man can pay a woman. One good turn deserves another. He has seen you looking at him. Here he comes to try the first rung of the ladder. Stop him at once, before he has climbed high enough for a fall. He will soon go away if he thinks you are heartless and frivolous. Well, then, he is a good fellow. He deserves it at your hands. Let him think you heartless, and send him away none the worse.' That is something of what I feel about men—I mean the nice ones, granny."

Mrs. Courtenay raised her eyes to the ceiling of the carriage, and her two hands made a simultaneous upheaval under her voluminous wraps. Her hopes for Lord Hemsworth had suffered a severe shock during the last few minutes, and words were a relief.

"Of all the egregious folly I have heard in the course of a long life," she remarked, "I think that takes the palm. How do you suppose any woman in the whole world, or man either, would marry if they looked at marriage like that? Things come gradually."

"Not with me, granny," said Di, promptly. "Either I see them or I don't see them; and at the beginning I always look on to the end, just as one does in a novel to see whether it is worth reading. I can't pretend to myself when I walk in the direction of church bells that I don't know I shall arrive at the church in the end, however pleasant the walk may be."

"You will never marry, so you may as well make up your mind to it," said Mrs. Courtenay, who was already revolving an entirely new idea in her mind, which cast Lord Hemsworth completely into the shade. "If you are so fond of looking at the future, you had better amuse yourself by picturing yourself as a penniless old maid."

"I wish there was something one could be between an old maid and a married woman," said Di. "I think if I had my choice I would be a widow."

Mrs. Courtenay, somewhat propitiated by her new idea, gave her silent but visible laugh, and Di went on—

"What do you think of John Tempest, granny? He is so black that talking of widows reminded me of him."

Mrs. Courtenay sustained a slight nervous shock.

"I had not much conversation with him," she said, stifling a slight yawn. "I am glad to see him back in England. Remind me to ask him next time we have a dinner-party."

"He looks clever," said Di. "Ugly men sometimes do. It is a way they have."

"It does not matter how ugly a man is if he looks like a gentleman."

"Not a bit," said Di. "I am only sorry he looks as if he had been cut out with a blunt pair of scissors because he is a Tempest, and Tempests ought to be handsome to keep up the family traditions. Look at the old man in Westminster Abbey. I am proud of his nose whenever I look at it. I wish the present head of the family had kept a firmer hold on that feature, that is all; and, it being a hook, I should have thought he might easily have done so. I think it is a want of good taste to bring the Fane features so prominently to Overleigh, don't you? Archie represents the looks of the family certainly, and so do I, granny, though I believe you fondly imagine I am not aware of it. But it does not matter so much what we look like, as it does with the head of the family."

"The family has got a head to it for the first time for two generations," remarked Mrs. Courtenay, closing the conversation by putting on her respirator.

As Lord Hemsworth turned away from putting Mrs. Courtenay and Di into their carriage he saw John coming down the steps.

"Still here?" he said. "I thought you had gone hours ago."

"It is a fine night," said John, who did not think it necessary to say that he *was* still there; "I think I shall walk."

"So will I," replied Lord Hemsworth, and they went out together.

John and Lord Hemsworth had known each other since the Eton days, and had that sort of quiet liking for each other which has the germ of friendship in it, which circumstances may eventually quicken or destroy.

As they turned into Whitehall a hansom, one of many, passed them at a foot's pace, with its usual civil interrogatory, "Cab, sir?"

"That cab horse with the white stocking reminds me," said Lord Hemsworth, "that I was looking at a bay mare at Tattersall's today for my team. I wish you would come and see her, Tempest. I like her looks, and she is a good match to the other bay, but she has a white stocking."

"I don't see any harm in one," said John, with interest; "but it rather depends on the rest of the team."

"That is just it," said Lord Hemsworth. "I drive a scratch team this year, two greys and two bays with black points. She is right height, good action, not too high, and has been driven as a wheeler, which is what I want her for; but I don't like the idea of a white stocking among them."

And talking of one of the subjects that most Englishmen have in common, they proceeded slowly past the Horse Guards and into Trafalgar Square.

"Tempest," said Lord Hemsworth, after a time, "do you know it strikes me very forcibly that we are being followed?"

"Not likely," said John.

"Not at all likely, but the fact all the same. Look there, that is the same hansom waiting at the corner that hailed us as we came out of the gates. I know him by the white stocking."

"I should imagine there might be about five hundred and one cab horses with white stockings in London."

"I dare say, but I know a horse again when I see him just as much as I know a face. I bet you anything you like that is the same horse."

"I dare say it is," said John absently.

Lord Hemsworth said nothing more. They walked up St. James's Street in silence.

"I have taken rooms here for the moment," said John, stopping at the corner of King Street. "I will come round to Tattersall's about two tomorrow. Good night."

MARY CHOLMONDELEY

Lord Hemsworth bade him good night, and then walked on up St. James's Street. There were a few hansoms on the stand. The last, which was in the act of drawing up behind the others, had a horse with a white stocking.

"Now," said Lord Hemsworth to himself, "we will see whether it is Tempest or me he is after, for I am certain it is one of us."

He stopped short near the cab-stand, and, striking a light, lit a cigarette, holding the match so that his face was plainly visible. Then he proceeded leisurely on his way and turned down Piccadilly. There were a good many people in the street and a certain number of carriages.

Presently he stopped under a somewhat dark archway, and threw away his cigarette.

"No," he said, after carefully watching for some time the cabs and carriages which passed; "nothing more to be seen of our friend. I wonder what's up! It's Tempest he was after, not me."

IX

"Is it well with the child?"

—2 KINGS iv. 26

A happy childhood is one of the best gifts that parents have it in their power to bestow; second only to implanting the habit of obedience, which puts the child in training for the habit of obeying himself later on.

A happy childhood is like a welcome into the world. This welcome John never had. No one had been glad to see him when he arrived. No little ring of downy hair had been cut off and treasured. No one came to look at him when he was asleep. No wedded hands were clasped the closer for his coming. The love and awe and pride which sometimes meet over the cradle of a first child were absent from his nursery. The old nurse who had been his mother's nurse took him and loved him, and gave herself for him, as is the marvellous way of some women with other people's children. I believe the under-housemaid occasionally came to see him in his bath, and I think the butler, who was a family man himself, gave him a woolly lamb on his first birthday. But excepting the servants and the village people, no one took much notice of John. It is not even on record whether he ever crept, or what the first word he could say was. It was all chronicled on Mitty's faithful heart, but nowhere else. Mitty was proud when he began to sway and reel on unsteady legs. Mitty walked up and down with him in her arms night after night when teeth were coming, crooning little sympathetic songs. Mitty dressed him every afternoon in his best frock with blue sash and ribboned socks, just like the other children who go downstairs. But John never went downstairs at teatime; never gnawed a lump of sugar with solemn glutinous joy under a parent's eye; or sucked the stiffness out of a rusk before admiring friends. No one sent for John; he was never wanted.

Mitty had had troubles. She had buried Mr. Mitty many years ago, and, after keeping a cow of her own, had returned to the service of the Fanes, with whom she had lived before her marriage. But I do not think she ever felt anything so acutely as the neglect of her "lamb."

When Mr. Tempest was expected home John was put through tearful and elaborate toilets. His hair, dark and straight, the despair of

Mitty's heart, was worked up till it rose like a crest on the top of his head; his bronze shoes (which succeeded the knitted socks) were put on. But after these great efforts Mitty always cried bitterly, and kissed John till he cried too for company, and then his smart things would be torn off, and they would go down to tea together in the housekeeper's room. That was a treat. There was society in the housekeeper's room. Mrs. Alcock was very large, spread over with black silk which had a rich aroma of desserts and sweet biscuits. There were in her keeping certain macaroons John knew of, for she was a person of vast responsibilities. He sat on her knee sometimes, but not often, for she breathed and rose and fell all over, and creaked underneath her buttons. She was kind, but she was billowy, and the geography of her figure was uncertain, and she could never think of anything to interest him but macaroons, and she was enigmatical as to how the almond was fastened into the top. The butler, Mr. Parker, was estimable, but Mr. Parker, like Mrs. Alcock, was averse to answering questions, even when John inquired, "Why his head was coming through his hair?" Charles the footman was more amusing, but he never came into the housekeeper's room. It was difficult to see as much of Charles as could be wished. He was really funny when Mitty was not there. He could dance a hornpipe in the pantry. John had seen him do it; and Charles was always ready to pull off his coat and give John a ride. What kickings and neighings and prancings there were going upstairs on these occasions. How John clutched round his horse's neck urging him not to spare himself, till he pressed his charger's shirtstud into his throat. Once on a wet day they went out hunting in the garret gallery, but only once, when Mitty was out: and the housemaid with the red cheeks was the fox. Ah! what an afternoon that was. But it came to an end all too soon. Charles wiped his forehead at last, and said the fox was "gone to ground," though John knew she was only in the housemaid's closet, giggling among the brooms. That was an afternoon not to be forgotten, not even to be spoilt by the fact that when Mitty and a bag of bull's-eyes came home she was very angry, and called the fox an "impudent hussy." Perhaps that event was the first that remained distinctly in his memory. Certainly afterwards people and incidents detached themselves more clearly from the haze of confused memories that preceded it.

The following day as it seemed to John—perhaps, in reality many weeks later—he had a vague recollection of a stir in the house, and of seeing various kinds of candles laid out on a table near the storeroom; and then he was in a new black velvet suit with a collar that tickled, and they were in the picture-gallery, he and Mitty, and there were lamps, and all the white sheets were gone from the furniture, and it was all very solemn; and Mitty held his hand tight and told him to be a good boy, and blew his nose for him with a handkerchief of her own that had crumbs in it, and then wiped her eyes and gave him a flower to hold, telling him to be very careful of it; and John was *very* careful. Years later he could see that flower still. It was a white orchis with maidenhair; and then suddenly a door at the further end of the gallery opened, and a tall man, whom John had seen before, came out.

Mitty loosed John's hand and gave him a little push, whispering, "Go and speak to your papa, and give him the pretty flower." But John stood stock still and looked at the advancing figure.

And the tall gentleman came down the gallery, and stopped short rather suddenly when he saw them, and said, "Well, nurse, all flourishing, I hope? Well, John," and passed on.

And Mitty and John were much depressed, and went upstairs again the back way; and Mrs. Alcock met them at the swing door and said *she never did*, and Mitty cried all the time she undressed him, and he pulled the orchis to pieces, and found on investigation that it had wire inside; and experienced the same difficulty in putting it together again next morning that he had previously found in readjusting the toilet of a dead robin after he had carefully undressed it the night before. After that "Papa" became not a familiar but a distinct figure in John's recollection. "Papa" was seen from the nursery windows to walk up and down the bowling-green on the wide plateau in front of the castle, where the fountain was, with Neptune reining in his dolphins in the middle. John was taught by Mitty to kiss his hand to papa, but papa, who seldom looked up, was apparently unconscious of these blandishments. He was seen to arrive and to depart. Sometimes other men came back with him who met John in the gardens and made delightful jokes, and were almost equal to Charles, only they did not wear livery.

One event followed close upon another.

A lady came to Overleigh. Mitty and Mrs. Alcock agreed that no lady had ever stayed at Overleigh since—and then they stopped: and that very evening John was actually sent for to come down to dessert. Charles, who had run up to the nursery during dinner to say so, remarked with a prefatory "Lawks" that wonders would never cease. John was quite ready at the time the message came, sitting in his black velvet suit and his silk stockings and his buckled shoes in his own chair by the fire. He had grown out of several suits whilst he waited. It was one of the many inexplicable things that he took in wondering silence at the time, that when he wore those particular garments a certain red cushion was always put on the seat of his little cane-bottomed chair. Mitty told him when he inquired into it that was because of the pattern coming off on his velvets, "blesh" him, and John did not understand, but turned it over in his mind together with everything he heard, and pondered long beside the nursery fire over many things, and was a very solemn, richly-dressed, lonely little boy.

He had always been ready, always waiting when Mr. Tempest was at home. Now at last he was sent for. He took it with a stoic calm. Mitty and Charles were much more excited than he was. Even Mrs. Alcock, who had seen too much of the ways of scullery and dairymaids to be capable of being surprised at anything in this world—even she was taken aback. Mitty and he went together down the grand staircase; and the carved figures on the banisters had lamps in their hands, so many lamps that they made him wink, and in the great stone hall there was a blazing log fire, and among the statues there were tall palms and growing things.

John was still looking at the white fur rugs upon the stone floor, and counting the claws of the outstretched bear's paws when Charles came to tell them that dinner was over. The moment had come. Mitty took him to the door, opened it, and pushed him gently in.

The dining-hall looked very large and very empty. John had never been in it at night before. A long way off at a little table in the bay window two people were sitting. A glow of shaded light fell on the table. Mr. Parker was not there. Even Charles, whom John had always considered indispensable in the highest circles, was absent. John walked very slowly across the room and stopped short in the middle, his strong little hands tightly clasped behind his back on the clean folded pocket handkerchief that Mitty had thrust into them at the last moment. He was not afraid, but he did not know what was going to happen next.

The lady turned and looked towards him.

She was pale, with white hair, and a sad, beautiful face as if she had often been very, very sorry. She was older than Mitty and Mrs. Alcock, and Mrs. Evans of the shop, and quite different, very awful to look upon.

John wondered whether she was Queen Victoria, and whether he ought to kneel down.

"Come here, John," said Mr. Tempest, but John did not stir.

"So this is John," said the lady, and she put out her wonderful jewelled hand with a very gentle smile, and John went straight up to her at once and stood close beside her, on her gown, in fact; and it was not Queen Victoria. It was Mrs. Courtenay.

After that night a change came over John's life. He was not forgotten any more. Mrs. Courtenay during the few days that she remained at Overleigh came up several times to the nursery, and had long conversations with Mitty. John, arrayed in the stiffest of white sailor suits with anchors at the corners, came down to see her in the sunny morning-room where his mother's picture hung, and showed her at her request his Noah's Ark which Mitty had given him, and afterwards conversed with her on many topics. He repeated to her the hymn Mitty had taught him,

"When little Samiwell awoke,"

and mentioned Charles to her with high esteem. She was very gentle with him, very courteous. She gave him her whole attention, looking at him with a certain pained compassion. Gradually John unfolded his mind to her. He confided to her his intention of marrying Mitty at a future date, and of presenting Charles at the same time with a set of studs like Mr. Parker's. He was very grave and sedate, and every morning shrank back afresh from going to see her, and then forgot his fears in the kind feminine presence and the welcome that was so new and strange and sweet. Once she took him in her arms and held him closely to her. Her eyes were stern through her tears.

"Poor little fatherless, motherless child!" she said, half to herself, and she put him down and went to the window and looked out—looked out across the forest to the valley and over the stretching woods to the long lines of the moors against the sky. Perhaps she was thinking that it would all belong to that little child some day; the home where she had once hoped to see her own daughter live happily with children growing up about her.

Mr. Tempest came into the room at that moment.

"What, John here?" he said.

"Yes," she replied, and was silent. There was a great indignation in her face.

"Mr. Tempest," she said at last, "evil has been done to you, not once, but twice. You have suffered heavily at the hands of others. Be careful that some one does not suffer at *your* hands!"

"Who?"

"Your," Mrs. Courtenay hesitated, "your *heir*."

"He *is* my heir," said Mr. Tempest, sternly; "that is enough!"

"Then do your duty by him," said Mrs. Courtenay. "You do it to others; do it also to him." And thenceforward, and until the day of his death, Mr. Tempest did his duty as he conceived it! never a fraction more, but never a fraction less.

JOHN WAS PUT EARLY TO school. No one went down to see the place before he came to it. No one wrote anxiously about him beforehand, describing his health and his attainments in the Latin grammar. Mr. Goodwin, who was afterwards his tutor, long remembered the arrival of the little, square, bullet-headed boy with a servant, with whom he gravely shook hands on the platform. Mr. Goodwin had come to meet him, and Charles, the last link to home, was parted from in silence. The small luggage was handed over. Once as they left the station, John looked back, and Mr. Goodwin saw the little brown hands clench tightly. John had a trick of clenching his hands as a child, which clung to him throughout life, but he walked on in silence. He was seven years old, and in trousers. *Pantalon oblige.* Mr. Goodwin, a good-natured under-master fresh from college, with small brothers at home, respected his silence. Perhaps he divined something of the struggle that was going on under that brand new little great-coat of many pockets. Presently John swallowed ominously several times.

Mr. Goodwin supposed the usual tears were coming.

"Those are very large puddles," said John suddenly, with a quaver in his voice, "larger than—" The voice, though not the courage, failed.

"They are, Tempest," said Mr. Goodwin, "uncommonly large!"

And that was the beginning of a lasting friendship between the two. That friendship took a long time to grow. John was reserved with the reticence that in a child speaks volumes of what the home-life had been. He had not the habit of talking to anyone. He listened and obeyed. At first he held aloof from the other boys. Mr. Goodwin advised him to make friends, and John listened in silence. He had never been with boys before. He did not know how. The first half he was very lonely. He would have been bullied more than he actually was had he not been so strong and so impossible to convince of defeat. As it was, he took his share with a sort of doggedness, and would have started on the high road to unpopularity in his new little world if he had not turned out good at games. That saved him, and before many weeks were over long blotted accounts of football and cricket and racquets were written to Mitty and Charles. Mr. Goodwin noticed that the weekly letter to his father never contained any particulars of this kind.

There had been a difficulty at first about his correspondence, which—after long pondering upon the same—John had brought to Mr. Goodwin for advice.

"I want to send a letter to some one," he said one day, when Mr. Goodwin had asked him into his study. "Not father."

"To whom, then?"

"To Mitty. I said I would write; I promised." And he produced a very much blotted paper and spread it before Mr. Goodwin.

"It's a long letter." It was indeed; the writing had been so severe and the paper so thin, that it had worked through to the other side.

"For Mitty," said John. "That is the person it's for; and another for Charles, with a picture in it." And a second sheet, suggestive of severe manual labour, was produced.

"I see," said Mr. Goodwin, his hand laid carelessly over his mouth, "but—yes, I see. This for Charles, and this for—ahem!—Mitty. And you want them to go today?"

"Yes." John was evidently relieved. He extracted from his trousers pocket two envelopes, not much the worse for seclusion, and laid one by each letter. One envelope was stamped. "I had two stamps," he explained; "one I put on, and the other I ate in a mistake. I licked it, and then I could not find it."

"Well, we will put on another," said Mr. Goodwin, who was a person of resources. "Now, what next? Shall we put them into their envelopes?"

John cautiously assented.

"And perhaps you would like me to direct them for you?"

"Yes." John certainly had a nice smile.

"Well, here goes; we will do Charles first. Who is Charles?"

"He lives with us. He brought me in the train."

"Really! Well, what is his name? Charles what?"

"He is not Charles anything," said John, anxiously. "That's just it; he's only Charles."

Mr. Goodwin laid down the pen. He saw the difficulty.

"He must have another name, Tempest," he said. "Try and think."

"I *have* thought," said John. "Before I came to you I thought. I thought in bed last night."

"And don't you know Mitty's name either?"

"No." John's voice was almost inaudible.

"Dear me!" said Mr. Goodwin, smiling, and not realizing the gravity of the situation. "We can't put 'Mitty' on one letter, and 'Charles' on the other. That would never do, would it?"

There was a moment's silence, in which hope went straight out of John's heart. If Mr. Goodwin could not see his way out of the difficulty, who could? He turned red, and then white. His harsh-featured, little face took an ugly look of acute distress.

"I said I would write," he said, in a strangled voice. "I promised Charles in the pantry; it was a faithful promise."

Mr. Goodwin looked up in surprise, and his manner changed.

"Wait a minute," he said, eagerly; "the letters shall go. We will manage it somehow. Is Charles the butler at home?"

"No; that is Mr. Parker."

"What is he, then?"

"He does things for Mr. Parker. Mr. Parker points, and Charles hands the plates."

"Footman, perhaps?"

"Yes," said John, with relief, "that's Charles."

"Now," said Mr. Goodwin, with interest, "shall we put, 'The footman, Overleigh Castle,' on the envelope? Then it will be sure to reach him."

"There's Francis; he's a footman, too," suggested John, but with dawning hope. "Francis might get it then. He took a kidney once!"

"We will put 'Charles, the footman,' then," said Mr. Goodwin, writing it. "'Overleigh Castle,' Yorkshire. Now then, for the other."

"When I write to father, what do I put at the end?" said John, his eyes still riveted on the envelope. "'J. Tempest,' and then something else."

"Esquire?" suggested Mr. Goodwin.

"Yes," said John. "I think I should like Charles to be the same as father, please."

Mr. Goodwin added a large esquire after the word footman.

"Now for Mitty," he said. "I suppose Mitty is the housekeeper?"

"Why, the housekeeper is Mrs. Alcock!" said John, with a smile at Mr. Goodwin's ignorance.

"There seem to be a good many servants at Overleigh."

"Yes," replied John, "it is a nice party. We are company to each other. You see, father is always away almost, and he does not play anything when he is at home. Now, Charles always does his concertina in the evenings, and Francis is learning the flute."

After the direction of the second letter had been finally settled, John licked them carefully up, and looked at them with triumph.

"You must go now," said Mr. Goodwin. "I'm busy."

John retreated to the door, and then paused.

"Me and Mitty and Charles are much obliged," he said, with dignity.

"Don't mention it," said Mr. Goodwin.

But the incident remained in his mind.

X

"Whoso would be a man must be a Nonconformist."

—EMERSON

John was eleven years old when, during a memorable Easter holidays, his father died, and lay in state in the round room in the western tower, and was buried at midnight by torchlight in the little Norman church at Overleigh, as had been the custom of the Tempests from time immemorial.

His father's death made very little difference to John, except that his holidays were spent with Miss Fane, an aunt in London: and Charles left to become a butler with a footman under him; and the other servants, too, seemed to melt away, leaving only Mitty, and Mr. Parker, and Mrs. Alcock, in the old shuttered home. Mr. Goodwin was John's tutor during the holidays. It was he who saved John's life at the railway station, at the risk of his own.

No one had been aware, till the accident happened, that John had been particularly attached to his tutor. He evidently got on with him, and was conveniently pleased with his society, but he had, to a peculiar degree, the stolid indifferent manner of most schoolboys. He was absolutely undemonstrative, and he tacitly resented his aunt's occasional demonstrative affection to himself. When will unmarried elder people learn that children are not to be deceived? John was very courteous, even as a boy, but his best friends could not say of him, at that or at any later period of his life, that he was engaging. He had, through life, a cold manner. No one had supposed, what really was the case, namely, that he would have given his body to be burned for the sake of the kind, cheerful young man who had taken an easy fancy to him on his arrival at school, and had subsequently become sufficiently fond of him to prefer being his tutor to that of any one else. He guessed John's absolute devotion to himself as little as any one. John's boyish thoughts, and feelings, and affections, were of that shy yet fierce kind, which shrink equally from expression and detection. No one had so far found them hard to deal with, because no one had thought of dealing with them.

Yet John sat for two days on the stairs outside the sick man's room, after the accident, unnoticed and unreprimanded. He was never seen to cry, but he was, nevertheless, almost unable to see out of his eyes. His aunt, Miss Fane, at whose house in London he was spending his Christmas holidays, had gone down to the country to nurse a sister, and the house was empty, but for the servants and the trained nurse. The doctor, who came several times a day, always found him sitting on the stairs, or appearing stealthily from an upper landing, working himself down by the balusters. He said very little, but the doctor seemed to understand the situation, and always had a kind and encouraging word for him, and gave him Mr. Goodwin's love, and took messages and offers of his best books from John to the invalid. But during those two long days, he always had some excellent reason for John's not visiting his tutor. He was invariably, at that moment, tired, or asleep, or resting, or— A deep anxiety settled on John's mind. Something was being kept from him.

Christmas Day came and passed. Mitty's present, and a Christmas card from a friend, the Latin master's youngest daughter, came for John, but they were unopened. The next day brought three doctors who stayed a long time in the drawing-room after they had been in the sick-room.

John sat on the stairs with clenched hands. At last he got up deliberately and went into the drawing-room. Two of the doctors were sitting down. One was standing on the hearth-rug looking into the fire.

"It can't be done," he was saying emphatically. "Both must go."

All three men turned in surprise as John entered the room. He came up to the fire, unaware of the enormity of the crime he was committing in interrupting a consultation. He tried to speak. He had got ready what he wished to ask. But his lips only moved; no words came out.

The consultation was evidently finished, for the man on the hearth-rug, who seemed anxious to get away, was buttoning his fur coat, and holding his hands to the fire for a last warm. They were very kind. They were not jocose with him, as is the horrible way of some elder persons with childhood's troubles. The old doctor who came daily put his hand on his shoulder and told him Mr. Goodwin had been very ill, but that he was going to get better, going to be quite well and strong again presently.

John said nothing. He was convinced there was something in the background.

"Twelve o'clock tomorrow, then," said the man who was in a hurry, and he took up his hat and went out.

"I have two boys about the same age as you," said the old doctor, patting John's shoulder. "Tom and Edward. They are making a little model steam-engine. I expect you are fond of engines, aren't you?"

"Not just now, thank you," said John. "I am sometimes."

"I wish you would come and see it tomorrow," continued the doctor. "They would like to show it you, I know. I could send you back in the carriage when it has set me down here about—shall we say twelve? Do come and see it."

"Thank you," said John almost inaudibly, "you are very kind, but—I am engaged."

Miss Fane always said she was engaged when she did not want to accept an invitation, and John supposed it was a polite way of saying he would rather not go. The other doctor laughed, but not unkindly, and the father of Tom and Edward absently drew on his gloves, as if turning over something in his mind.

"Have you seen the new lion, and the birds that fly under water at the Zoo?" he inquired slowly, "and the snakes being fed?"

"No," said John.

"Ah! That's the thing to see," he said thoughtfully. "Tom and Edward have been. Dear me! How they enjoyed it! They went at feeding time, mid-day. And my nephew, Harry Austin, who is twenty-one and at college, went with them, and said he would not have missed it for anything. You go and see that, with that nice man who answers the bell. I will send you two tickets tonight."

"Thank you," said John.

The two doctors shook hands with him and departed.

"You may as well keep your tickets," said the younger one as they went downstairs. "He does not mean going."

"He is a queer little devil," said Tom's and Edward's father. "But I like him. There's grit in him, and he watches outside that room like a dog. I wish I could have got him out of the house tomorrow, poor little beggar."

John stood quite still in the middle of the long, empty drawing-room when they were gone. A nameless foreboding of some horrible calamity was upon him. And yet—and yet—they had said he was going to get better, to be quite strong again. He waylaid the trained nurse for the twentieth time, and she said the same.

He suffered himself to be taken out for a walk, after hearing from her that Mr. Goodwin wished it; and in the afternoon he consented to go with George, Miss Fane's cheerful, good-natured young footman, to the "Christian Minstrels." But he lay awake all night, and in the morning after breakfast he crept noiselessly back to the stairs. It was a foggy morning, and the gas was lit. Jessie, the stout, silly housemaid, always in a perspiration or tears, was sweeping the landing just above him, sniffing audibly as she did so.

"Poor young gentleman," she was saying below her breath to her colleague. "I can't a-bear the thought of the operation. It seems to turn my inside clean upside down."

John clutched hold of the banisters. His heart gave one throb, and then stood quite still.

"Coleman says as both 'is 'ands must go," said the other maid also in a whisper. "She told me herself. She says she's never seen such a case all her born days. They've been trying all along to save one, but they can't. They're to be took hoff today."

John understood at last.

He slipped downstairs again, and stood a moment in hesitation where to go: not to the little back-room on the ground-floor, which had been set apart for his use by his aunt. He might be found there. George might come in to see if he would fancy a game of battledore and shuttle-cock, or the cook might step up with a little cake, or the butler himself might bring him a comic paper. The servants were always kind. But he felt that he could not bear any kindness just now. He must be somewhere alone by himself.

The drawing-room door was locked, but the key was on the outside. He turned it cautiously and went in. The room was dark and fiercely cold. Bands of yellow fog peered in over the tops of the shutters. The room had been prepared the day before for the consultation, but now it had returned to its former shuttered, muffled state. John took the key from the outside and locked himself in.

Then he flung himself on his face on to one of the muffled settees and stuffed the dust-sheet into his mouth. Anything not to scream—a low strangled cry was wrenched out of him; another and another, and another, but the dust sheet told no tales. He dragged it down with him on to the floor and bit into the wet, cobwebby material. And by degrees the paroxysm passed. The power to keep silence returned. At last John sat up and looked round him, breathing hard. A clock ticked in the darkness, and presently struck a single chime. Half-past something— half-past eleven it must be—and they were coming at twelve.

Was there no help?

MARY CHOLMONDELEY

"God," said John suddenly, in a low, distinct voice in the darkness. "Do something. If you don't stop it nobody else will. You know you can if you like. You divided the Red Sea. Remember all your plagues. Oh, God! God! make something happen. There's half an hour still. Think of him. Both hands. And all the clever books he was going to write, and all the things he was going to do. Oh, God! God! and *such* a cricketer!"

There was a short silence. John felt absolutely certain God would answer. He waited a long time, but no one spoke. The fog deepened outside. The quarter struck faintly from the church in the next street.

"I give up one hand," said John, stretching out both of his. "I only ask for one now. Let him keep one—the other one. He is so clever, he could soon learn to write with his left, and perhaps hooks don't hurt after the first. Oh, God! I dare say he could manage with one, but not both, not both."

John repeated the last words over and over again in an agony of supplication. He would *make* God hear.

It was growing very dark. The link-boys were crying in the streets: a carriage stopped at the door.

"Oh, God! They're coming. Not both; not both!" gasped John, and the sweat broke from his forehead.

Two more carriages—lowered voices in the passage, and quiet footfalls going upstairs. John prayed without ceasing. The house had become very silent. At last the silence awed him, and an overmastering longing to know seized upon him. He stole out of the drawing-room, and sped swiftly upstairs. On the landing opposite Mr. Goodwin's room the butler was standing listening. Everything was quite still. John could hear the gas burning. There was a can of hot water just outside the door. The steam curled upwards out of the spout. As he reached the landing the door was softly opened, and the nurse raised the heavy can and lifted it into the room.

Through the open door came a hoarse inarticulate sound, which seemed to pierce into John's brain.

"Courage," said a gentle voice, and the door was closed again. The butler breathed heavily, and there was a whimper from the upper landing. Trembling from head to foot John fled down the stairs again unperceived into the drawing-room, and crouched down on the floor near the open door, turning his face to the wall. Every now and then a strong shudder passed over him, and he beat his little black head dumbly against the wall. But he did not move until at last the doctors came down. He let the first two pass, he could not speak to them; and it was a long time before the father of Tom and Edward appeared. John came suddenly out upon him at the turn of the stairs.

"Is it both?" he said, clutching his coat.

"Both what, my boy?" said the doctor, puzzled by the sudden onslaught, and looking down at the blackened convulsed face and shaggy hair.

"Both *hands*."

The doctor hesitated.

"Yes," he said gravely. "I am grieved to say it is." John flung up his arms.

"I will never pray to God again as long as I live," he said passionately.

"John," said the doctor sternly, and then suddenly putting out his hand to catch him as he reeled backwards. "What? Good gracious! The child has fainted."

JOHN WENT BACK TO SCHOOL before the holidays were over, for Miss Fane on her return found it difficult to know what to do with him. Mr. Goodwin came back no more. He slowly regained a certain degree of health, a ruined man, without private means, at seven and twenty. John wrote constantly to him, and wrote also long urgent letters in a large cramped hand to his trustees. And something inadequate was done. When he came of age his first action was to alter that something, and to induce Mr. Goodwin and the sister who lived with him to take up their abode in the chaplain's house, in the park at Overleigh, where they had now been established nearly seven years. Whether John's was an affectionate nature or not it would be hard to say, for affection had so far intermeddled little with his life; but he had a kind of faithfulness, and a memory of the heart as well as of the head. John never forgot a kindness, never wholly forgot an injury. He might forgive one, for he showed as he grew towards man's estate, and passed through the various vicissitudes of school and college life, a certain stern generosity of temper, and contempt for small retaliations. He was certainly not revengeful, but—he remembered. His mind was as tenacious of impression as engraved steel. That very tenacity of impression had given Mr. Goodwin an unbounded influence over him in his early youth. John had believed absolutely in Mr. Goodwin; and Mr. Goodwin, hurried by a bitter short cut of suffering from youth to responsible middle age, had devoted himself with the religious fervour of entire self-abnegation to the boy for whom he had risked his life. John's intense attachment to him had after his recovery come as a surprise to him, yoked with a sense of responsibility; for to be loved in any fashion is to incur a great responsibility.

Mr. Goodwin acted according to his lights. But the good intentions of others cannot pave the way to heaven for us. In the manner of many well-meaning teachers, Mr. Goodwin used his influence over John to impress upon him the stamp of his own narrow religious convictions. He honestly believed it was the best thing he could do for the young, strong, earnest nature which sat at his feet. But John did not sit long. Mr. Goodwin was aghast at the way in which the little chains and check-strings of his scheme of salvation were snapped like thread when John began to rise to his feet. An influence misused, if once shaken, is lost for ever. John went away like a young Samson, taking the poor weaver's inadequate beam with him; and never came back. Mr. Goodwin's teaching had done its work. John never leaned again "on one mind overmuch." Mr. Goodwin pushed him early into scepticism, into which narrow teaching pushes all independent natures, and regarded his success with bitter disappointment. John left him, and Mr. Goodwin's office others took. Mr. Goodwin suffered horribly.

John had not, of course, reached seven and twenty without passing through many phases, each more painful to Mr. Goodwin than the last. He had spoken fiercely at Oxford on one occasion in favour of community of goods, to the surprise and amusement of his friends; and on one other single occasion in support of the philosophy of Kant, with which he did not agree, but whose side he could not bear to see inefficiently taken up only for the sake of refutation. When the spirit moved him John could be suddenly eloquent, but the spirit very seldom did. As a rule he saw both sides with equal clearness, and could be forced into partisanship on neither. Those who expected he would make a brilliant speaker in the House of Commons would probably be disappointed in him. It was remarkable, considering he had apparently no special talent or aptitude for any one line of study, and had never particularly distinguished himself either at school or college, that nevertheless he had unconsciously raised in the minds of those who knew him best, and many who knew him not at all, a more or less vague expectation that he would make his mark, that in some fashion or other he would come to the fore.

The abilities of persons with square jaws are usually taken for granted by the crowd, and certainly John's was square enough to suggest any amount of reserved force. But general expectation rarely falls on those who have sufficient strength not only to resist its baneful influence, but also to realize its hopes. The effect of the expectation of others on many minds is to draw into greater activity that personal conceit which, once indulged, saps the roots of individual life, and gradually vitiates the powers. Conceit is only mediocrity in the bud. Like a blight in Spring it stunts the autumn fruit.

On some natures again the expectation of others acts as a stimulus, the force of which is quite incalculable. It spurs a natural humility into fixed resolution and self-reliance; turns sloth into energy, earnestness into action, and goads diffidence up the hill of achievement. It has been truly said, that "those who trust us educate us." Perhaps it might be added that those who believe in us make or destroy us.

If John, who was perfectly aware of the enthusiastic or grudging expectations that others had formed of him, had not as yet fallen into either of these two extremes, it was probably because what others might happen to think or not think concerning him was of little moment to him, and had no power to sway him either way.

The thing of all others that puzzled John's staunchest adherents was their inability to fix him in any one set of opinions, social, political, or religious. Many after Mr. Goodwin tried and failed. For John's great wealth and position, besides the native force of character of which even as a very young man he gave signs, and an openness of mind which encouraged while it ought to have disheartened proselytism, all these attributes had made him an object of interest and importance, which would have ruined a more self-conscious man. As it was, he listened, got to the bottom of the subject, whatever it might be, never left it till he had probed it to the uttermost, and then went his way. He marched out of every mental prison he could be temporarily lured into. He would go boldly into any that interested him, but locks and bars would not hold him directly he did not wish to stay there any longer.

Mr. Goodwin hoped against hope that John would see the error of his ways, and "come back"; that, according to his mode of expressing himself, the pride of the intellect might be broken, and John might one day be moved to return from the desert and husks and the sw— philosophy of free thought to his father's home. He said something of the kind one day to John, and was astonished at the sudden flame that leapt into the young man's eyes as he silently took up his hat and went out.

The one thing of all others which the Mr. Goodwins of this world are incapable of discerning, is that to leave an outgrown form of faith is in itself an act of faith almost beyond the strength of shrinking human frailty. To bury a dead belief is hard. They regard it invariably as a voluntary desertion, not of their form of religion, but of religion itself for private ends, or from a sense of irksomeness. Mr. Goodwin had reproachfully suggested that John had got into "a bad set" at Oxford, and was in the habit of mixing in "doubtful society" in London. Those whose surroundings have moulded them attribute all mental changes in others to a superficial and generally an entirely inadequate influence such as would have had power to affect themselves.

John left the house white with anger. He had been anxious and humble half an hour before. He had listened sadly enough to Mr. Goodwin's counsels, the old, old counsels that fortunately always come too late—that are worse than none, because they appeal to motives of self-interest, safety, peace of mind, etc.; the pharisaical reasoning that what has been good enough for our fathers is good enough for us.

But now his anger was fierce against his teacher, who was so quick to believe evil of any development not of his own fostering.

"He calls good evil, and evil good," he said to himself. "It seems to me I have only got to lose hold of the best in me, and lead a cheap goody-goody sort of life, and I should please everybody all round, Mr. Goodwin included. He wants me to remain a child always. He would break my mind to pieces now if he could, and would offer up the little bits to God. He thinks the voice of God in the heart is a temptation of the devil. I will not silence it and crush it down, as he wants me to do. I will love, honour, and cherish it from this day forward, for better for worse, for richer for poorer, in sickness and in health."

THERE SEEMS TO BE IN life a call which comes to a few only who, like the young man in the Gospel, have great possessions. From youth up the life may have been carefully lived in certain well-worn grooves traced by the finger of God—grooves in which many are allowed to pass their whole existence. But to some among those many, to some few with great mental possessions, the voice comes sooner or later: "Forsake all, leave all, and follow Me." How many turn away sorrowful? They cannot believe in the New Testament of the present day. They ponder instead what God whispered eighteen hundred years ago in the ear of a listening Son, but they shrink from recognizing the same voice speaking in their hearts now, completing all that has gone before. And so the point of life is missed. The individual life, namely, the life of Christ—obedient not to Scripture, but to the Giver of the Scripture— is not lived. The life Christ led—at variance with the recognized faiths and fashionable opinions of the day, at variance just because it did not conform to a dead ritual, just because it was obedient throughout to a personal prompting—that life is not more tolerated today than it was eighteen hundred years ago. The Church will have none of it—treats the first spark of it as an infidelity to Christ Himself. Against every young and ardent listening and questioning soul the Church and the world combine, as in Our Lord's day, to crucify once again the Christ— life which is not of their kindling, which is indeed an infidelity, but an infidelity only to them. So the crucifix is raised high. The sign of our great rejection of Him is deified; the Mediator, the Saviour, the Redeemer is honoured. The instrument of His death is honoured; but the thought for the sake of which He was content to stretch His nailed hands upon it, His thought is without honour.

POOR MR. GOODWIN! POOR JOHN! AFFECTION had to struggle on as best it could as the years widened the gulf between them, and was reduced to find a meagre subsistence in cordial words and sympathy for neuralgia on John's part, and interest in John's shooting and hunting on Mr. Goodwin's. Affectionate and easy terms were gradually re-established between them, and a guarded sympathy on general subjects returned; but Mr. Goodwin knew that, from being "the friend of the inner, he had become only the companion of the outer life" of the person he cared for most in the world, and the ways of Providence appeared to him inscrutable. And now Mr. Goodwin understood John even less at seven and twenty than at twenty-one. The conception of the possibility of a mind that after being strongly influenced by a succession of the most "dangerous" teachers and books, gives final allegiance to none, and can at last elect to stand alone, was impossible to Mr. Goodwin. And yet John arrived at that simple and natural result at which those who have sincerely and humbly searched for a law and an authority outside themselves do arrive. An external authority is soon seen to be too good to be true. There is no court of appeal against the verdict of the inexorable judge who dwells within.

How many rush hither and thither and wear down the patience of earnest counsellors, and whittle away all the best years of their lives to nothingness, in fretting and scratching among ruins for the law by which they may live! They look for it in Bibles, in the minds of anxious friends who turn over everything to help them, in the face of Nature, who betrays the knowledge of the secret in her eyes, but who utters it not. And last of all a remnant of the many look in their own hearts, where the great law of life has been hidden from the beginning. David says: "Yea, Thy law is within my heart." A greater than David said the same. But it is buried deep, and few there be that find it.

XI

*"Still as of old
Man by himself is priced.
For thirty pieces Judas sold
Himself, not Christ."*

—H.C.C.

L ent gave way to Easter, and Easter melted into the season, and Mrs. Courtenay gave a little dinner-party, at which John was one of the guests; and Madeleine was presented on her marriage; and Di had two new gowns, and renovated an old one, and nearly broke Lord Hemsworth's heart by refusing the box-seat on his drag at the meeting of the Four-in-hand; and Lord Hemsworth did not invest in the bay mare with the white stocking, but turned heaven and earth to find another with black points, and succeeded, only to drive in lonely bitterness to the meet. And John was to have been there also, but he had been so severely injured in a fire which broke out at his lodgings, in the room below his, three weeks before, that he was still lying helpless at the house in Park Lane, which he had lent to his aunt, Miss Fane, and whither he was at once taken, after the accident, to struggle slowly back to life and painful convalescence.

For the last three weeks, since the fire, hardly any one had seen Colonel Tempest. The old horror had laid hold upon him like a mortal sickness. Sleep had left him. Remorse looked at him out of the eyes of the passers in the street. There was no refuge. He avoided his club. What might he not hear there! What might not have happened in the night! He could trust himself to go nowhere for fear of his face betraying him. He wandered aimlessly out in the evenings in the lonelier portions of the Park. Sometimes he would stop his loitering, to follow with momentary interest the children sailing their boats on the Round Pond, and then look up and see the veiled London sunset watching him from behind Kensington Palace, and turn away with a guilty sense of detection. The aimless days and waking ghosts of nights came and went, came and went, until his misery became greater than he could bear. The resolutions of the weak are as much the result of the period of feeble, apathetic inertia that precedes them, as the resolutions of the strong are the outcome of earnest reflection and mental travail.

"It will kill me if it goes on," he said to himself. There was one way, and one only, by means of which this intolerable weight might be shifted from his shoulders. He hung back many days. He said he could not do *that*, anything but *that*—and then he did it.

His heart beat painfully as he turned his steps towards Park Lane, and he hesitated many minutes before he mounted the steps and rang the bell at the familiar door of the Tempest town-house, where his father had lived during the session, where his mother had spent the last years of her life after his death.

It was an old-fashioned house. The iron rings into which the links used to be thrust still flanked the ponderous doorway, together with the massive extinguisher.

The servant informed him that Mr. Tempest had been out of danger for some days, but was not seeing any one at present.

"Ask if he will see me," said Colonel Tempest, hoarsely. "Say I am waiting."

The man left him in the white stone hall where he and his brother Jack had played as boys. The dappled rocking-horse used to stand under the staircase, but it was no longer there: given away, no doubt, or broken up for firewood. John might have kept the poor old rocking-horse. Recollections that took the form of personal grievances were never far from Colonel Tempest's mind.

In a few minutes the man returned, and said that Mr. Tempest would see him, and led the way upstairs. A solemn, melancholy-looking valet was waiting for him, who respectfully informed him that the doctor's orders were that his master should be kept very quiet, and should not be excited in any way. Colonel Tempest nodded unheeding, and was conscious of a door being opened, and his name announced.

He went forward hesitatingly into a half-darkened room.

"Pull up the further blind, Marshall," said John's voice. The servant did so, and noiselessly left the room.

Colonel Tempest's heart smote him.

The young man lay quite motionless, his dark head hardly raised, his swathed hands stretched out beside him. His unshaved face had the tension of protracted suffering, and the grave steady eyes which met Colonel Tempest's were bright with suppressed pain. The eyes were the only things that moved. It seemed to Colonel Tempest that if they were closed—. He shuddered involuntarily. In his morbid fancy the prostrate figure seemed to have already taken the rigid lines of death, the winding-sheet to be even now drawn up round the young haggard face.

Colonel Tempest was not gifted with imagination where he himself was not concerned. He was under the impression that the influenza, from which he occasionally suffered, was the most excruciating form of mortal illness known to mankind. He never believed people were really ill until they were dead. Now he realized for the first time that John had been at death's door; that is to say, he realized what being at death's door was like, and he was fairly staggered!

"Good God, John!" he said with a sort of groan. "I did not know it had been as bad as this."

"Sit down," said John, as the nurse brought forward a chair to the bedside, and then withdrew, eyeing the new-comer suspiciously. "It is much better now. I receive callers. Hemsworth was here yesterday. I can shake hands a little; only be very gentle with me. I cry like a girl if I am more than touched."

John feebly raised and held out a bandaged hand, of which the end of three fingers only were visible. Colonel Tempest, whose own feelings were invariably too deep to admit of his remembering those of others, pressed it spasmodically in his.

"It goes to my heart to see you like this, John," he said with a break in his voice.

John withdrew his hand. His face twitched a little, and he bit his lip, but in a few moments he spoke again firmly enough.

"It is very good of you to come. Now that I have got round the corner, I shall be about again in no time."

"Yes, yes," said Colonel Tempest, as if reassuring himself. "You will be all right again soon."

"You look knocked up," said John, considering him attentively with his dark earnest gaze.

"Do I?" said Colonel Tempest. "I dare say I do. Yes, people may not notice it as a rule. I keep things to myself, always have done all my life, but—it will drag me into my grave if it goes on much longer, I know that."

"If what goes on?"

It is all very well for a nervous rider to look boldly at a hedge two fields away, but when he comes up with it, and feels his horse quicken his pace under him, he begins to wonder what the landing on the invisible other side will be like. There was a long silence, broken only by Lindo, John's Spanish poodle, who, ensconced in an armchair by the bedside, was putting an aristocratic and extended hind leg through an afternoon toilet by means of searching and sustained suction.

"I don't suppose there is a more wretched man in the world than I am, John," said Colonel Tempest at last.

"There is something on your mind, perhaps."

"Night and day," said Colonel Tempest, wishing John would not watch him so closely. "I have not a moment's peace."

"You are in money difficulties," said John, justly divining the only cause that was likely to permanently interfere with his uncle's peace of mind.

"Yes," said Colonel Tempest. "I am at my wit's end, and that is the truth."

John's lips tightened a little, and he remained silent. That was why his uncle had come to see him then. His pride revolted against Colonel Tempest's want of it, against Archie's sponge-like absorption of all John would give him. He felt (and it was no idle fancy of a wealthy man) that he would have died rather than have asked for a shilling. A Tempest should be above begging, should scorn to run in debt. John's pride of race resented what was in his eyes a want of honour in the other members of the family of which he was the head.

Colonel Tempest was in a position of too much delicacy not to feel hurt by John's silence. He reflected on the invariable meanness of rich men, with a momentary retrospect of how open-handed he had been himself in his youth, and even after his crippling marriage.

"I do not know the circumstances," said John at last.

"No one does," said Colonel Tempest.

"Neither have I any wish to know them," said John, with a touch of haughtiness, "except in so far as I can be of use to you."

Colonel Tempest found himself very disagreeably placed. He would have instantly lost his temper if he had been a few weeks younger, but the memory of those last few weeks recurred to him like a douche of cold water. Self-interest would not allow him to throw away his last chance of escaping out of Swayne's clutches, and he had a secret conviction that no storming or passion of any kind would have any effect on that prostrate figure, with the stern feeble voice, and intense fixity of gaze.

John had always felt a secret repulsion towards his uncle, though he invariably met him with grave, if distant civility. He had borne in a proud silence the gradual realization, as he grew old enough to understand it, that there was a slur upon his name, a shadow on his mother's memory. He believed, as did some others, that his uncle had originated the slanders, impossible to substantiate, in order to wrest his inheritance from him. How could this man, after trying to strip him of everything, even of his name, come to him now for money?

John had a certain rigidity and tenacity of mind, an uprightness and severity, which come of an intense love of justice and rectitude, but which in an extreme degree, if not counterbalanced by other qualities, make a hard and unlovable character.

His clear-eyed judgment made him look at Colonel Tempest with secret indignation and contempt. But with the harshness of youth other qualities, rarely joined, went hand in hand. A little knowledge of others is a dangerous thing. It shows itself in sweeping condemnations and severe judgments, and a complacent holding up to the light of the poor foibles and peccadilloes of humanity, which all who will can find. A greater knowledge shows itself in a greater tenderness towards others, the tenderness, as some suppose, of wilful ignorance of evil. When or how John had learnt it I know not, but certainly he had a rapid intuition of the feelings of others; he could put himself in their place, and to do that is to be not harsh.

He looked again at Colonel Tempest, and was ashamed of his passing, though righteous, anger. He realized how hard it must be for an older man to be obliged to ask a young one for money, and he had no wish to make it any harder. He looked at the weak, wretched face, with its tortured selfishness, and understood a little; perhaps only in part, but enough to make him speak again in a different tone.

"Do not tell me anything you do not wish; but I see something is troubling you very much. Sometimes things don't look so black when one has talked them over."

"I can't talk it over, John," said Colonel Tempest, with incontestable veracity, softened by the kindness of his tone, "but the truth is," nervousness was shutting its eyes and making a rush, "I want—*ten thousand pounds and no questions asked.*"

John was startled. Colonel Tempest clutched his hat, and stared out of the window. He felt benumbed. He had actually done it, actually brought himself to ask for it. As his faculties slowly returned to him in the long silence which followed, he became conscious, that if John was

MARY CHOLMONDELEY

too niggardly to pay his own ransom, he, Colonel Tempest, would not be the most to blame, if any casualty should hereafter occur.

At last John spoke.

"You say you don't want any questions asked, but I *must* ask one or two. You want this money secretly. Would the want of it bring disgrace upon your—children?" He had nearly said your "daughter."

"If it was found out it would," said Colonel Tempest, in a choked voice. The detection, which he always told himself was an impossibility, had, nevertheless, a horrible way of masquerading before him at intervals as an accomplished fact.

John knit his brows.

"I can't pretend not to know what it is," he said. "It is a debt of honour. You have been betting."

"Yes," said Colonel Tempest, faintly.

"I suppose you can't touch your capital. That is settled on your children."

"No," said Colonel Tempest. "There were no settlements when I married. I had to do the best I could. I had twenty thousand pounds from my father, and my wife brought me a few thousands after her uncle's death; a very few, which her relations could not prevent her having. But there were the children, and one thing with another, and women are extravagant, and must have everything to their liking; and by the time I had settled up and sold everything after the break-up, it was all I could do to put Archie to school."

(Oh! Di, Di, cold in your grave these two and twenty years! Do you remember the little pile of account books that you wound up, and put in your writing-table drawer, that last morning in April, thinking that if anything happened, he would find them there—afterwards. He had always inveighed against the meanness of your economy before the servants, and against your extravagance in private. Do you remember the butcher's book, with thin blotting paper, that blotted tears as badly as ink sometimes, for meat was dear; and the milk bills? You were always proud of the milk bills, with the space for cream left blank, except when he was there. And the little book of sundries, where those quarter pounds of fresh butter and French rolls, were entered, which Anne ran out to get if he came home suddenly, because he did not like the cheap butter from the Stores. Do you remember these things? He never knew, he never looked at the dumb reproach of that little row of books: but I cannot think, wherever you are, that you have quite forgotten them.)

John was silent again. How could he deal with this man who roused in him such a vehement indignation? For several minutes he could not trust himself to speak.

"I think I had better go," said Colonel Tempest at last.

John started violently.

"No, no," he said. "Wait. Let me think."

The nurse and his aunt came into the room at that moment.

"Are not you feeling tired, sir?" the nurse inquired, warningly.

"Yes, John," said Miss Fane, grunting as her manner was. "Mustn't get tired."

"I am not," he replied. "Colonel Tempest and I are discussing business matters which won't wait—which it would trouble me to leave unsettled. We have not quite finished, but he is more tired than I am. It is the hottest day we have had. Will you give him a cup of tea, Aunt Flo, and bring him back in half an hour."

When he was left alone John turned his head painfully on the pillow, and slowly opened and shut one of the bandaged hands. This not altogether satisfactory form of exercise was the only substitute he had within his power for the old habit of pacing up and down while he thought.

Ought he to give the money? He had no right to make a bad use of anything because he happened to have a good deal of it. This ten thousand would follow the previous twenty thousand, as a matter of course.

Giving it did not affect himself, inasmuch as he would hardly miss it. It was a generous action only in appearance, for he was very wealthy; even among the rich he was very rich. His long minority, and various legacies of younger branches, which had shown the Tempest peculiarity of dying out, and leaving their substance to the head of the family, had added to an already imposing income. In his present mode of life he did not spend a third of it.

The thought flashed across his mind that if he had died three weeks ago, if the hinges of the door had held as firmly as the shot lock, and he had perished in that room in King Street like a rat in a trap, Colonel Tempest would at this very moment have been in possession of everything. He looked at his own death, and all it would have entailed, dispassionately.

That improvident selfish man had been within an ace of immense wealth. And yet—John's heart smote him—his uncle had been genuinely grieved to see him so ill: had been really thankful to think he was out of danger. He had almost immediately afterwards reverted to himself and his own affairs; but that was natural to the man. He had nevertheless been unaffectedly overcome the moment before. The emotion had been genuine.

John struggled hard against his strong personal dislike.

Perhaps Colonel Tempest had become entangled in the money difficulty at the very time his—John's—life hung in the balance, when he took for granted he was about to inherit all. The speculation was heartless, perhaps, but pardonable. John saw no reason why Colonel Tempest should not have counted on his death. For ten days it had been more than probable; and now he might live to a hundred. Perhaps the probability of his reaching old age was slenderer than he supposed.

He lay a little while longer and then rang the bell near his hand, and directed his servant to bring him a locked feminine elegancy from a side-table which, until he could replace his burnt possessions, had evidently been lent him by his aunt to use as a despatch-box. He got out a cheque-book, and with clumsy fingers filled in and signed a cheque. Then he lay back panting and exhausted. The will was strong in him, but the suffering body was desperately weak.

When Colonel Tempest returned, John held the cheque towards him in silence with a feeble smile.

Colonel Tempest took it without speaking. His lips shook. He was more moved than he had been for years.

"God bless you, John," he said at last. "You are a good fellow, and I don't deserve it from you."

"Good-bye," said John, in a more natural tone of voice than he had yet used towards him. "If you are at the polo match on Thursday, will you look in and tell me how it has gone? It would be a kindness to me. I know Archie and Hemsworth are playing." Colonel Tempest murmured something unintelligible, and went out.

He did not go back at once to his rooms in Brook Street. Almost involuntarily his steps turned towards the Park. The world was changed for him. The weary ceaseless beat of the horses' hoofs on the wood pavement had a cheerful exhilarating ring. All the people looked glad. There was a confused rejoicing in the rustle of the trees, in the flying voices of the children playing and rolling in the grass. He wandered down towards the Serpentine. Dogs were rushing in and out of the water. An elastic cockeared retriever, undepressed by its doubtful ancestry, was leaping and waving a wet tail at its master, giving the short sharp barks of youth and a light heart. An aristocratic pug in a belled collar was delicately sniffing the evening breeze across the water, watching the antics of the lower orders with protruding eyes like pieces of toffy rounded and glazed by suction. An equally aristocratic black poodle—Lindo out for a stroll with the valet—with more social tendencies, was hurrying up and down on the extreme verge, beckoning rapidly with its short tufted tail to the athletes in the water. The ducks bobbed on the ripples. The children sprawled and shouted and clambered. The low sun had laid a dancing, glancing pathway across the water. How glad it all was, how exceeding glad! Colonel Tempest patted one of the children on the head and felt benevolent.

As he turned away at last and sauntered homewards, he passed a little knot of people gathered round a gesticulating open-air preacher. Two girls, arm in arm, just in front of him, were lounging near, talking earnestly together.

"Sin no more lest a worse thing come unto thee," bawled the strident fanatic voice.

"I shall have mine trimmed with tulle, and a flower on the crown," said one of the girls.

Colonel Tempest walked slowly on. Yes, yes; that was it. *Sin no more lest a worse thing come unto thee.* He had always dreaded that worse thing, and now that fear was all over. He translated the cry of the preacher into a message to himself, his first personal transaction with the Almighty. He felt awed. It was like a voice from another world. Religion was becoming a reality to him at last. There are still persons for whom the Law and the Prophets are not enough—who require that one should rise from the dead to galvanize their superstition into momentary activity. Sin no more. No—never any more. He had done with sin. He would make a fresh start from today, and life would become easy and unembarrassed and enjoyable once again; no more nightmares and wakeful nights and nervous haunting terrors. They were all finished and put away. The tears came into his eyes. He regretted that he had not enjoyed these comfortable feelings earlier in life. The load was lifted from his heart, and the removal of the pain was like a solemn joy.

MARY CHOLMONDELEY

XII

"On entre, on crie,
C'est la vie.
On crie, on sort,
C'est la mort."

O n the paths of self-interest the grass is seldom allowed to grow under the feet. Colonel Tempest hurried. It would be tedious to follow the various steps feverishly taken which led to his finally unearthing the home address of Mr. Swayne. He procured it at last, not without expense, from an impoverished client of that gentleman who had lately been in correspondence with him. Mr. Swayne had always shown a decided reticence with regard to the locality of his domestic roof. Colonel Tempest was of course in possession of several addresses where letters would find him, but his experience of such addresses had been that, unless strictly connected with pecuniary advantage to Mr. Swayne, the letters did not seem to reach their destination. But now, even when Colonel Tempest wrote to say he would pay up, no answer came. Swayne did not rise even to that bait. Colonel Tempest, who was aware that Mr. Swayne's faith in human nature had in the course of his career sustained several severe shocks, came to the conclusion that Mr. Swayne did not attach importance to his statement—that indeed he regarded it only as a "blind" in order to obtain another interview.

It was on a burning day in June that Colonel Tempest set forth to search out his tempter at Rosemont Villa, Iron Ferry, in the manufacturing town of Bilgewater. The dirty smudged address was in his pocket-book, as was also the notice of his banker that ten thousand pounds had been placed to his credit a few days before.

The London train took him to Worcester, and from thence the local line, after meandering through a desert of grime and chimneys, and after innumerable stoppages at one hideous nigger station after another, finally deposited him on the platform of Bilgewater Junction. Colonel Tempest got out and looked about him. It was not a rural scene. Heaps of refuse and slag lay upon the blistered land thick as the good resolutions that pave a certain road. Low cottages crowded each other in knots near the high smoking factories. Black wheels turned slowly against the grey of the sky, which whitened upwards towards the ghost of the midsummer sun high in heaven. We are told that the sun shines equally on the just and on the unjust; but that was said before the first factory was built. At Bilgewater it is no longer so.

Colonel Tempest inquired his way to Iron Ferry, and, vaguely surprised at Mr. Swayne's choice of locality for his country residence, set out along the baked wrinkles of the black high-road, winding between wastes of cottages, some inhabited and showing dreary signs of life, some empty and decrepit, some fallen down dead. The heat was intense. The steam and the smoke rose together into the air like some evil sacrifice. The pulses of the factories throbbed feverishly as he passed. The steam curled upwards from the surface of the livid pools and canals at their base. The very water seemed to sweat.

Colonel Tempest reached Iron Ferry, being guided thither by the spire of the little tin church, which pointed unheeded towards the low steel sky, shut down over the battered convulsed country like a coffin lid over one who has died in torment.

At Iron Ferry, which had a bridge and a wharf and a canal, and was everything except a ferry, he inquired again concerning Rosemont Villa, and was presently picking his way across a little patch of common towards a string of what had once been red brick houses, but which had long since embraced the universal colour of their surroundings. They were rather better looking houses if a sort of shabby gentility can be called anything except the worst. They were semi-detached. From out of one of them the strains were issuing faintly and continuously of the inevitable accordion, which for some occult reason is always found to consort with poverty and oyster-shells.

At the open door of another a girl was standing tearing pieces with her teeth out of a chunk of something she held in her hand. She was surrounded by a meagre family of poultry who fought and pecked and trod each other down with almost human eagerness for the occasional morsels she threw to them. Something in her appearance and in the way she seemed to enjoy the greed and mutual revilings of her little dependents reminded Colonel Tempest—he hardly knew why—of Mr. Swayne.

Another glance made the supposition a certainty. There were the small boot-buttons of eyes, the heavy mottled expressionless face, which Colonel Tempest had until now considered to be the exclusive property of Mr. Swayne. This slouching, tawdry down-at-heel arrow was no doubt one of that gentleman's quiverful.

Mr. Swayne had always worn such very unmarried waistcoats and button holes that it was a shock to Colonel Tempest to regard him as a domestic character.

"Is Mr. Swayne at home?" he asked, amid the cackling and flouncing of the poultry.

The "arrow," her cheek "bulged with the unchewed piece," looked at him doubtfully for a moment, and then called over her shoulder—

"Mother!"

The voice as of a female who had never been held in subjection answered shrilly from within—"Well?"

"Here's a gent as wants to see father."

There was a sound of some heavy vessel being set down, and a woman, large and swarthy, came to the door. She might have been good-looking once. She might perhaps have been "a fine figure of a woman" in the days when Swayne wooed and won her, and no doubt her savings, for his own. But possibly the society of Mr. Swayne may not in the long run have exerted an ennobling or even a soothing influence upon her. Her complexion was a fiery red, and her whole appearance bespoke a temperament to which the artificial stimulus of alcohol, though evidently unnecessary, was evidently not denied.

"Swayne's sick," she said, eyeing Colonel Tempest with distrust. "He can't see no one, and if he could, there's not a shilling in the house if you was to scrape the walls with a knife—so that's all about it. It's no manner of use coming pestering here for money."

"I don't want money," said Colonel Tempest. "I want to pay, not to be paid."

The woman shook her head incredulously, and put out her under lip, uttering the mystic word, "Walker!" It did not seem to bear upon the subject, but somebody, probably the accordion next door, laughed.

"I must see him!" said Colonel Tempest, vehemently. "I've had dealings with him which I want to settle and have done with. It's my own interest to pay up. He would see me directly if he knew I was here."

The woman hesitated.

"Swayne is uncommon sick," she said, slowly. "If it's business I doubt he could scarce fettle at it now."

"Do you mean he is not sober?"

"He's sober enough, poor fellow," said Mrs. Swayne, with momentary sympathy; "but he's mortal bad. He hasn't done nobbut but dithered with a bit of toast since Tuesday, and taking it out of hisself all the time with flouncing and swearing like a brute beast."

"Is he—do you mean to say he is *dying*?" demanded Colonel Tempest in sudden panic.

"Doctor says he won't hang on above a day or two," said the girl nonchalantly. "Doctor says his works is clean wore out."

"Let me go to him at once," said Colonel Tempest. "It is of great importance; I must see him at once."

The women stared at each other undecidedly, and the girl nudged her mother.

"Lor, mother, what does it signify? If the gentleman 'ull make it worth while, show him up."

Colonel Tempest hastily produced a sovereign, and in a few minutes was stumbling up the rickety stairs behind Mrs. Swayne. She pushed open a half-closed door, and noisily pulled back a bit of curtain which shaded the light—what poor dim light there was—from the bed, knocking over as she did so a tallow candle in the window-sill bent double by the heat.

Colonel Tempest had followed her into the room and into an atmosphere resembling that of the monkey-house at the Zoo, stiffened with brandy.

"Oh, good gracious!" he exclaimed, as Mrs. Swayne drew back the curtain. "Oh dear, Mrs. Swayne! I ought to have been prepared. I had no idea— What's the matter with him? What is he writing on the wall?"

For Mr. Swayne was changed. He was within a measurable distance of being unrecognizable. That evidently would be the next alteration not for the better in him. Already he was slow to recognize others. He was sitting up in bed, swearing and scratching tearfully at the wall-paper. He looked stouter than ever, but as if he might collapse altogether at a pin prick, and shrivel down to a wrinkled nothing among the creases of his tumbled bedding.

Mrs. Swayne regarded her prostrate lord with arms akimbo. Possibly she considered that her part of the agreement, to love and to cherish Mr. Swayne, and honour and obey Mr. Swayne, was now at an end, as death was so plainly about to part them. At any rate, she appeared indisposed to add any finishing touches to her part of the contract. Mr. Swayne had, in all probability, put in his finishing touches with such vigour, that possibly a remembrance of them accounted for a certain absence of solicitude on the part of his helpmeet.

　　　　　　　　　　　　　　　　MARY CHOLMONDELEY

"Who's this? Who's this? Who's this?" said Mr. Swayne in a rapid whisper, perceiving his visitor, and peering out of the gloom with a bloodshot furtive eye. "Dear, dear, dear! . . . Mary. . . I'm busy. . . I'm pressed for time. Take him away. Quite away; quite away."

Mr. Swayne had been a man of few and evil words when in health. His recording angel would now need a knowledge of shorthand. This sudden flow of language fairly staggered Colonel Tempest.

"I must have out those bonds," he went on, forgetting his visitor again instantly. "I can't lay my hand on 'em, but I've got 'em somewhere. Top left-hand drawer of the walnut escritoire. I know I have 'em. I'll make him bleed. Top left-hand. No, no, no. Where was it, then? Lock's stiff;—the lock. Break it. I say I will have 'em."

As he spoke he tore from under the pillow a little footstool, having the remnant of a frayed dog, in blue beads, worked upon it, a conjugal attention no doubt on the part of Mrs. Swayne, to raise the sick man's head.

And Mr. Swayne, after endeavouring to unlock the dog's tail, smote savagely upon it, and sank back with chattering teeth.

"That's the way he goes on," said Mrs. Swayne. "Mornin', noon, and night. Never a bit of peace, except when he gets into his prayin' fits. I expect he'll go off in one of them tantrums."

It did not appear unlikely that he would "go off" then and there, but after a few moments a sort of ghastly life seemed to return. Even death did not appear to take to him. He opened his eyes, and looked round bewildered. Then his head fell forward.

"Now's yer time," said the woman. "Before he gets up steam for another of them rages. Parson comes and twitters a bit when he's in this way; and he'll pray very heavy while he recollects hisself, until he goes off again. He'll be better now for a spell," and she left the room, and creaked ponderously downstairs again. Colonel Tempest advanced a step nearer the lair on which poor Swayne was taking his last rest but one, and said faintly:

"Swayne. I say, Swayne. Rouse up."

The only things that roused up were Swayne's eyelids. These certainly trembled a little.

In the next house the accordion was beginning a new tune, was designating Jerusalem as its ha-appy home.

Apprehensive terror for himself as usual overcame other feelings. It overcame in this instance the unspeakable repugnance Colonel

Tempest felt to approaching any nearer. He touched the prostrate man on the shoulder with the slender white hand which had served him so exclusively from boyhood upwards, which had never wavered in its fidelity to him to do a hand's turn for others, which shrinkingly did his bidding now.

"Wake up, Swayne," repeated Colonel Tempest, actually stooping over him. "Wake up, for—," he was going to add "heaven's sake;" but the thought of heaven in connection with Swayne seemed inappropriate; and he altered it to "for mercy's sake," which sounded just as well.

"Is it the parson?" asked Swayne feebly, in a more natural voice.

"No, no," said Colonel Tempest reassuringly. "It's only me, a friend. It's Colonel Tempest."

"I wish it *was* the parson," repeated Swayne, seeming to emerge somewhat from his torpor. "He might have come and let off a few more prayers for me. He says it's all right if I repent, and I suppose he knows; but it don't seem likely. Don't seem as if God *could* be greened quite as easy as parson makes out. I should have liked to throw off a few more prayers so as to be on the safe side," and he began to mutter incoherently.

As a man lives so, it is said, he generally dies. Swayne seemed to remain true to his own interests, only his aspect of those interests had altered. He felt the awkwardness of going into court absolutely unprepared. Prayer was cheap if it could do what he wanted, and he had had professional advice as to its efficacy. A man who all his life can grovel before his fellow-creatures, may as well do a little grovelling before his Creator at the last, if anything is to be got by it.

It is to the credit of human nature that, as a rule, men even of the lowest type feel the uselessness, the degradation, of trying to annul their past on their deathbeds. But to Swayne, who had never shone as a credit to human nature, a chance remained a chance. He was a gambler and a swindler, a man who had risked long odds, and had been made rich and poor by the drugging of a horse, or the forcing of a card. If, in his strict attention to never losing a chance, he had inadvertently mislaid his soul, he was not likely to be aware of it. But a *chance* was a thing he had never so far failed to take advantage of. He was taking his last now.

Colonel Tempest looked at him in horror. The interests of the two men clashed, and at a vital moment.

"For God's sake don't pray now, Swayne," said Colonel Tempest, appealingly, as Swayne began to mutter something more. "I've come to

MARY CHOLMONDELEY

set wrong right, and that will be a great deal better than any prayers; do you more good in the end."

Swayne did not seem to understand. He looked in a perplexed manner at Colonel Tempest.

"I don't appear to fetch it out right," he said. "But it's in the Prayer-book on the mantelpiece. That's what our parson reads out of. You get it, colonel; just get it quick, and pray 'em off one after another. It don't matter much which. They're all good."

"Swayne," said Colonel Tempest, in utter desperation, "I'll do anything; I'll—pray as much as you like afterwards, if you will only give me up those papers you have against me—those bets."

"What?" said Swayne, a gleam of the old professional interest flickering into his face. "You han't got the money?"

"Yes. Here, here!" and Colonel Tempest tore the banker's note out of his pocket-book, and held it before Swayne's eyes.

"I was to have had twenty-five per cent. commission," said Swayne, rallying perceptibly at the thought. "Twenty-five per cent on each. I wouldn't let 'em go at less. Two thousand five hundred I should have made. But"—with a sudden restless relapse—"it's no use thinking of that now. Get down the book, colonel."

But for once Colonel Tempest was firm.

Perhaps his indignation against Swayne's egotism enabled him to be so. He made Swayne understand that business must in this instance come first, and prayers afterwards. It was a compact; not the first between the two.

"The papers," he repeated over and over again, frantic at the speed with which the last links of Swayne's memory seemed falling from him. "Where are they? You have them with you, of course? Tell me where they are?" and he grasped the dying man by the shoulder.

Swayne was frightened back to some semblance of effort.

"I haven't got 'em," he gasped. "The—the—the chaps engaged in the business have 'em."

"But you know who have got them?"

"Yes, of course. It's all written down somewhere."

"Where?"

But Swayne "did not rightly know." He had the addresses in cipher somewhere, but he could not put his hand upon them. Half wild with fear, Colonel Tempest searched the pockets of the clothes that lay about the room, holding up their contents for Swayne to look at. It was like some hideous game of hide-and-seek. But the latter only shook his head.

"I have 'em somewhere," he repeated, "and there was a change not so long ago. When was it? May. There's one of 'em written down in cipher in my pocket-book in May, I know that."

"Here. This one?" said Colonel Tempest, holding out a greasy pocket-book.

"That's it," said Swayne. "Some time in May."

Colonel Tempest turned to the month, and actually found a page with a faint pencil scrawl in cipher across it.

"That's him," said Swayne. "James Larkin," and he read out a complicated address without difficulty.

"Will that find him?" asked Colonel Tempest, his hand shaking so much that he could hardly write down Swayne's words.

"If it's to his advantage it will."

"For certain?"

"Certain."

"And the others?"

"There's one dead," said Swayne, his voice waxing feebler and feebler as the momentary galvanism of Colonel Tempest's terror lost its effect. "And there's two I had back the papers from; they were sick of it, and they said he had a charmed life. And one of 'em went to America, and married, and set up respectable. I have his paper too. And one of 'em's in quod, but he'll be out soon, I reckon, and he's good for another try. He precious near brought it off last time. There's a few left that's still biding their time! There! And now I won't hear nothin' more about it. Get to the prayers, Colonel, and be quick. Parson might have come again, damn him."

"Stop a minute. Can I get at the others through Larkin?"

Swayne had sunk back spent and livid. He looked at Colonel Tempest with fixed and glassy eyes.

"Yes," he said, with the ghost of an oath; "get to the prayers."

Colonel Tempest was still trembling with the relief from that horrible nightmare of suspense as he opened the shiny new Prayer-book which the clergyman had left. He held the first link. He had now only to draw the whole chain through his hand, and break it to atoms; the chain that was dragging him down to hell. He hastily began to read.

God has heard many prayers, but, perhaps, not many like those which ascended from that hideous tumbled death-bed, where kneeling self-interest halted through the supplication, and prostrate self-interest gasped out Amen.

Oh! did He who first taught us how to pray, did He, raised high upon the cross of an apparent failure, look down the ages that were yet to come, and see how we should abuse that gift of prayer? Was that bitter cry which has echoed through eighteen hundred years wrung from Him even for our sakes also as well as those who stood around Him—"Father, forgive them, for they know not what they do"?

Colonel Tempest was still on his knees when the door was softly opened, and a young, a very young, clergyman came in and knelt down beside him, clasping his thin hands over the collapsed felt *soufflée* which did duty for a hat. After stumbling to the end of the prayer he was reading, Colonel Tempest put the book into his hand and escaped.

He stole down the stairs and past the little sitting-room unobserved. He was out again in the open air, the live free air, which seemed freshness itself after the atmosphere of that sick-room. He held the clue. He had it, he held it, he was safe. God was on his side now, and was helping him to make restitution. At one despairing moment when he had been tearing even the linings out of the pockets of Swayne's check trousers he had feared that Providence had deserted him. Now that he had the pocket-book he regretted his want of faith. I do not think his mind reverted once to Swayne, for Swayne was no longer of any interest to him now that he was out of Swayne's power. Colonel Tempest did not exactly forget people, but his mind was so constituted that everything with which it came in contact was wiped out the moment it had ceased to affect or group itself round himself. His imagination did not follow his colleague's last faltering steps upon that steep brink where each must one day stand. His mind turned instinctively to the most frivolous subjects, was back in London wondering what he would have had for dinner if he had dined with Archie as he had intended; was anxious to know how many cigarettes of that new brand he had put into his case before he left London that morning. Colonel Tempest stopped, and got out his cigarette-case and counted them.

Those who had known Colonel Tempest best, those few who had misunderstood and loved him, had often pondered with grave anxiety, or with the wistful perplexity of wounded affection, as to what it was in him that being so impressionable was yet incapable of any real impression. His wife may or may not have mastered that expensive secret. At any rate, she had had opportunities of studying it. When first, a few weeks after her marriage, she had fallen ill, she, poor fool, had suffered agonies from the fear that because he hardly came into her sick-room after the first day, he had ceased to care for her. But when after a few days more she was feeling better and was pretty and interesting again in a pink wrapper on the sofa, she had found that he was as devoted to her as ever, and had confided her foolish dread to him with happy tears. Possibly she discovered at last that the secret lay not so much in the selfishness and self-indulgence of a character moth-eaten by idleness, as in the instant and invariable recoil of the mind from any subject that threatened to prove disagreeable, the determination to avoid everything irksome, wearisome, or reproachful. For a moment, while it was quite new, a sentiment might be indulged in. But as soon as a certain novelty and pleasure in emotion ceased the feeling itself was shirked, at whatever expense to others. Those who shirk are ill to live with, and lay up for themselves an increasing loneliness as life goes on.

Colonel Tempest found it unpleasant to think about Swayne, so he thought of something else. He could always do that unless he himself was concerned. Then, indeed, as we have seen, it was a different thing. He was annoyed when, after slowly picking his way back to the station, he found the last passenger train had just gone; that even if he drove fifteen miles in to Worcester he should be too late to catch the last express to London; in fact, that there was nothing for it but a bed at the station inn. He found, however, that by making a very early start from Bilgewater the following morning he could reach London by noon, and so resigned himself to his lot with composure. He had hardly expected he should be able to go and return in one day.

It was indeed early when he walked across to the station next morning, so early that there was a suspicion of freshness in the air, of colour in the eastern sky.

On a heap of slag a motionless figure was sitting, black against the sky line, looking towards the east. It was the curate, who when he perceived Colonel Tempest, came crunching and flapping in his long coat tails down to the road below, raised his hat from a meagre clerical brow, and held out his hand. His face was thin and poor, suggestive of a starved mind and cold mutton and Pearson on the Creed, but the smile redeemed it.

"It is all over," he said; "half an hour ago. Quite quietly at the last. I stayed with him through the night. I never left him. We prayed together without ceasing."

MARY CHOLMONDELEY

Colonel Tempest did not know what to say.

"It was too late to go to bed," continued the young man impulsively, his face working. "So I came here. I often come and sit on that ash heap to see the sun rise. I'm so glad just to have seen you again. I longed to thank you for those prayers by poor Mr. Crosbie's bed. You know the Scripture: 'Where two or three are gathered together.' I felt it was so true. I have lost heart so of late. No one seems to care or think about these things down here. But your coming and praying like that has been such a help, such a reproach to me for my want of faith when I think that the seed falls on the rock. I shall take courage again now. Ah! You are going by this train? Good-bye, God bless you! Thank you again."

XIII

"Every man's progress is through a succession of teachers."

—EMERSON

As John slowly climbed the hill of convalescence many visitors came to relieve his solitude, and one of those who came the oftenest was Lord Frederick Fane.

Lord Frederick was a square-shouldered, well-preserved, well set up, carefully-padded man of close on sixty, with a thin-lipped, bloodless face, and faded eyes, divided by a high nose.

"Do you like that man?" said Lord Hemsworth to John one day when he was sitting with him, and Lord Frederick sent up to know whether the latter would see him.

"No," said John.

"But you seem to see a good deal of him."

"He is civil to me, and I am not rude to him. He is a relation, you know."

"I can't stand him," said Lord Hemsworth. "If he is coming up I shall bolt;" and Lord Frederick entering at that moment, Lord Hemsworth took his departure.

"You're better, John," said Lord Frederick, looking at him through his half-closed eyes, and settling himself gently in a high chair, his hat and one glove and crutch-handled stick held before him in his broad lean hand.

"I feel more human," said John, "now that I'm shaved and dressed. When I saw myself in the glass yesterday for the first time, I thought I was Darwin's missing link."

"You look more human," said Lord Frederick, crossing one leg over the other, and then contemplating his white spats for a change. "Able to attend to business again yet?"

"Not yet. I have tried, but I am as weak as a worm that can't turn."

"Pity," said Lord Frederick, glancing at a sheaf of letters and some opened telegrams on the table at John's elbow. "Things always happen at inconvenient times," he went on. "Old Charlesworth might have chosen a more opportune moment to die and leave Marchamley vacant again."

"He is not dead yet."

"I suppose both sides have been at you already to stand for it yourself," hazarded Lord Frederick.

"Yes."

"I thought so."

Silence.

"Are you going to stand?"

"What is your opinion on the subject? I see you have one."

"Well," said Lord Frederick, "I look at it this way. I have often said 'Don't tie yourself.' I am all for young men keeping their hands free, and seeing the ins and outs of life, before they settle down. But you are not so very young, and a time comes when a sort of annoyance attaches to freedom itself. It's a bore. Now as to this seat. Indecision is all very well for a time; it enhances a man's value. You were quite right not to stand three years ago; it has made you of more importance. But that won't do much longer. You are bound to come to a decision for your own advantage. Neutral ground is sometimes between two fires. I should say 'stand,' if you ask me. Throw in your lot with the side on which you are most likely to come to the front, and stand."

"And private opinions? How about them if they don't happen to fit? Throw them overboard?"

"Yes," said Lord Frederick. "It has got to be done sooner or later. Why not sooner? A free-lance is no manner of use. There's a hitch somewhere in you, John, that if you don't look out will damn your career as a public man. I don't know what your politics are. My own opinion, between ourselves, is that you have not got any, but you are bound to have some, and you may as well join forces with what will bring you forward most, and start young. That's my advice."

"Thanks."

"There is not a man in the world with an ounce of brains who has not high-flown ideas at your age," continued Lord Frederick. "I have had them. Everybody has them. You buy them with your first razors. People generally sicken with them just when they could make a push for themselves, and while they are getting better, youth and opportunity pass and don't come back. I've seen it over and over again. Every young fool with a ginger moustache, when he first starts in public life, is going to be a patriot, and do his d—d thinking for himself. He might as well make his own clothes, and expect society to receive him in them. By the time he is bald he has learnt better, and he's a party man, but he has lost time in the meanwhile. You may depend upon it, a strong party man is what is wanted. The country doesn't want individuals with brains; they are mostly kicked out in the end. If you don't want to go with the crowd, don't go against it, but throw yourself into it heart and soul, and get in front of it on its own road. It's no good coming to the fore unless you have a following."

"Thanks," said John again. His face was as expressionless as a mask. He looked, as he lay back in his low couch, a strange mixture of feebleness and power. It was as if a strong man armed kept watch within a house tottering to its fall.

He put out his muscular, powerless hand, and took up one of the telegrams.

"Charlesworth is not dead yet," he said.

Lord Frederick could take a hint.

"His death will put the Moretons in mourning again," he remarked. "Mrs. Moreton's ball is doomed. I am sorry for that woman. She is cumbered with much time-serving, and her ball fell through last year; this is the second time it has happened. I have been asking her young men for her. I put down your cousin in the Guards, the Apollo with the tow wig. What's-his-name, Tempest?"

"Archibald."

"Yes. That would be a dangerous man, if he were not such a fool, but the same placard that says he is to let says he is unfurnished, and it's poor work taking an empty house, when it comes to living in it. Women know that. He has let the soda water heiress slip through his fingers. She is going to marry young Topham. I thought Apollo seemed rather down on his luck when it was first given out, but he has consoled himself since. Apparently he has a mission to married women. He is always with Lady Verelst now; I saw him riding with her again this morning. I don't know who mounts him, but he was on the best horse I've seen this season. You are not such a f—, such a philanthropist as to lend him horses, are you?"

"When I can't use them myself I have that amount of generosity."

"H'm! Well, he makes good use of his opportunities to cheer up Lady Verelst. I wish you would flirt more with married women, John. You would find your account in it. I did at your age. You see you are too eligible to go on much with girls, and that's the truth. You would be watched. But you don't pay enough attention to women, and three-quarters of the world is made up of them. You are too much of a Puritan, but you may remember human nature is like a short-footed stocking. If you darn it up at the heel it will come out at the toe. It's no manner of use to ignore women. People who do always come the worst croppers in the end. A flirtation with a fast, married woman would peel your illusions off you like the skin off an orange. All young men believe in women—till they know them. He! He! If I were a rabbit I should take a personal interest in the habits of birds of prey. I told Hemsworth something of the kind the other day, but he is bent on making a fool of himself."

"He knows his own affairs best."

"I fancy I know them better than he does. Miss Di is young, but she is uncommonly well aware of her own value, and she is looking higher. I should not wonder if she tried to marry you. She'll take him in five years' time, if he is still willing, and she outstands her market: but in the mean time she keeps him dangling. I told him so, and that I admired her for it. She holds her head high, but she is a splendid creature, and no mistake. She has not that expectant anxious look about her that you see in other girls, and she is not made up. It's sterling good looks in her case. If you are interested in that quarter, you may take my word for it, it is all genuine, even to her hair. That is why her frank manner is so telling; it's of a piece with the rest. She knows how to play her cards. The old woman has taught her a thing or two."

"What a knowledge you have of—human nature."

"I have looked about," said Lord Frederick, rising as gently as he had sat down, and pulling up his shirt collar. "I had my eyes opened pretty young, and I have kept them open ever since. Glad you're better. That black devil in tights of a poodle wants shaving as much as you did last time I saw you. No, don't ring for that melancholy valet. I will let myself out. I dare say I shall be in again in the course of a day or two. Ta, ta."

John crushed the telegram he was still holding into a hard ball as soon as his self-constituted guide, philosopher, and friend had left the room.

Cynicism was not new to him. It is cheap enough to be universally appropriated by the poor in spirit, for whom generosity and tolerance are commodities too expensive to be indulged in. Our belief in human nature is a foot rule, by which we may be accurately measured ourselves. There are those in whose enlightened eyes, purity herself is only a courtesan in fancy dress. John had already had many teachers, for he was a man who was being educated regardless of expense; but perhaps to no two persons did he owe so much as to Mr. Goodwin and Lord Frederick Fane. Our elders act as danger-signals oftener than they know.

John's room looked out across the Park. His couch had been drawn near the open window, and to lie and watch the passing crowd of carriages and pedestrians was almost as much excitement as he could bear after the darkened rooms and enforced quiet of the last few weeks. John, with Lindo erect on the vacant chair beside him, saw Lord Frederick's hansom, with his pale profile inside it, turn down Park Lane below his windows. Pain had burned all John's energy out of him for the time, and he had soon forgotten his annoyance in watching the people attempting to cross the thoroughfare, and in counting the omnibuses that passed. It was all he was up to. It was about five in the afternoon, and carriage after carriage turned into the Park at the gates opposite his window. There went Lady Delmour with her brand new daughter, a sweet, wild rose from the country, that must be perfected by London smuts and gaslight. John pointed her out to Lindo, but he only yawned and looked the other way. There was Mrs. Barker walking with her husband. Those two white parasols he had danced with somewhere, but he could not put a name to them. Neither could Lindo when asked. Another red omnibus. That was the tenth red one within the last half-hour. Royalty went flashing by, bowing and bowed to. John obliged Lindo, whom he suspected of democratic tendencies, to make a bow also. He hoped his nurse would not come in and send him back to bed yet. It was really very interesting watching the passers-by. Was that—no, it was not—yes, it was Lady Verelst with red parasol and husband to match, in the victoria with the greys. There was actually Duchess, his old polo pony whom he had not seen since he sold her three years ago, looking as spry as ever. John craned his neck to see the last of the bob-tail of his old favourite whisk round the corner. A moment later Mrs. Courtenay and Di, erect and fair beside her, spun past in the opposite direction. Before he had time to realize that he had seen her, almost before he had recognized her, the momentary glimpse struck him like a blow. His head swam, his heart, so languid the moment before, leapt up and struggled like a maddened caged animal. She had passed some time before he was conscious of anything but the one fact that he had seen her.

He stumbled to his feet and walked unsteadily across the room, clutching at the furniture. He seemed to have left his legs behind.

"What am I doing?" he said to himself half aloud, holding on to and swaying against a table. "What has happened? Why did I get up?"

MARY CHOLMONDELEY

He dragged himself back to his couch again, and sank down exhausted. The excursion had been too much for him. He had not walked so far before. He was bewildered.

Through the open window came the jingle, and the "clip-clop" and the hum. Another red omnibus passed. But there was a loud knocking at the door of John's heart that deafened him to all beside; the peremptory knocking as of one armed with a claim, who stood without and would not be denied.

END OF VOLUME I

VOLUME II

I

"The fact is, I have never loved any one well enough to put myself into a noose for them. It is a noose, you know."

—George Eliot

It was the middle of July. The season had reached the climax which precedes a collapse. The heat was intense. The pace had been too great to last. The rich sane were already on their way to Scotch moor or Norwegian river; the rich insane and the poor remained, and people with daughters—assiduously entertaining the dwindling numbers of the "uncertain, coy, and hard to please" *jeunesse dorée* of the present day. There were some great weddings fixed for the end of July, proving that marriage was not extinct,—prospective weddings which, like iron rivets, held the crumbling fabric of the season together.

If the unusual heat had driven away half the world, still the greater part of the little world mentioned in these pages remained. Not quite all, for Sir Henry and Lady Verelst had departed rather suddenly for Norway, and Lord Frederick was drinking the water at Homburg or Aix; and thriving on a beverage which never passed his lips without admixture in his own country, except in connection with the toothbrush.

But John and his aunt Miss Fane were still in the large cool house in Park Lane. Lord Hemsworth was still baking himself for no apparent reason in his rooms over his club. Mrs. Courtenay and Di were still in town, because they could not afford to go until their country visits began.

"Oh, granny," said Di one afternoon as they sat together in the darkened drawing-room, "let us cut everything. Do be ill, and let me write round to say we have been obliged to leave town."

Mrs. Courtenay shook her head.

"We can't go till we have somewhere to go to, and we are not due at Archelot till the first of August."

"Could not we afford a week, just one week, at the sea first?"

"No, Di," said Mrs. Courtenay, "I have thought it over. Only the rich can have their cake and eat it. We had a victoria for a fortnight in June. That meant no seaside this year."

There was a pause.

"I wish I were married," said Di, looking affectionately at Mrs. Courtenay's pale face. "I wish I had a rich, kind husband. I would not mind if he parted his hair down the middle, or even if he came down to breakfast in slippers, if only he would give me everything I wanted. And he should stay up in London, and we would run down to the seaside together, G., first-class; I am not sure I should not take a *coupé* for you; and you should go out on the sands in the donkey-chairs that your soul loves; and have ice on the butter and cream in the tea; and in the evening we would sit on a first-floor balcony (no more second-floors if I were rich) and watch a cool moon rising over a cool sea. I wish moonlight on the sea were not so expensive. The beauties of nature are very dear, granny. Sunsets cost money nowadays."

"Everything costs money," said Mrs. Courtenay.

Di was silent a little while; it was too hot to talk except at intervals.

"I don't think I mind being poor," she said at last. "For myself, I mean. I have looked at being poor in the face, and it is not half so bad as rich people seem to think. I mean our kind of poorness; of course, not the poverty of nothing a year and ten children to educate, who ought never to have been born. But some people think that the kind of means (like ours) which narrow down pleasures, and check one at every turn, and want a sharp tug to meet at the end of the year, are a dreadful misfortune. Really I don't see it. Of course it is annoying being less well off than any of our friends, and now I come to think of it, all the people we know are richer than ourselves. I wonder how it happens. But there is something rather interesting after all in combating small means. Look at that screen I made you last year, and think of the gnawing envy it has awakened in the hearts of friends. It was a clothes-horse once, but genius was brought to bear upon it, and it is a very imposing object now. And then my dear Emersons, all eleven of them, I don't think I could have valued them so much, or have been so furious with Jane for spilling water on one of them, if they had not emerged one by one out of my glove and shoe money."

"Oh, my dear, poverty does not matter, nothing matters while you are young and strong. But it presses hard when one is growing old. Money eases everything."

"I feel that; and sometimes when I see you working a sovereign out of the neck of that horrid little woollen jug in the writing-table drawer, I simply long for money for your sake, that you may never be worried about it any more. And sometimes I should like it for the sake of all

MARY CHOLMONDELEY

the lovely places in the world that other people go to (people who only remember the *table d'hôte* dinners when they come back), and the books that I cannot afford, and the pictures that seem my very own, only they belong to some one else; and the kind things one could do to poor people who could not return them, which rich people don't seem to think of: rich people's kindnesses are always so expensive. Yes, I long for money sometimes, but all the time I know I don't really care about it. There seems to be no pleasure in having anything if there is no difficulty in getting it. I would rather marry a poor man with brains and do my best with his small income, and help him up, than spend a rich man's money. Any one can do that. I fear I shall never take you to the seaside, my own G., or send you pre-paid hampers of hothouse flowers, or game, after Mr. Di's *battues*, for I am certain Providence intends me to be a poor man's wife, if I enter the holy estate at all, because—I should make such a good one."

"You would make a good wife, Di, but I sometimes think you will never marry," said Mrs. Courtenay, sadly. She felt the heat.

"Well, granny, I won't say I feel sure I shall never marry, because all girls say that, and it generally means nothing. But still that is what I feel without saying it. Do you remember poor old Aunt Belle when she was dying, and how nothing pleased her, and how she said at last: 'I want—I want—I don't know what I want'? Well, when I come to think of it, I really don't know what *I* want. I know what I *don't* want. I don't want a kind, indulgent husband, and a large income, and good horses, and pretty little frilled children with their mother's eyes, that one shows to people and is proud of. It is all very nice. I am glad when I see other people happy like that. I should like to see you pleased; but for myself—really—I think I should find them rather in the way. I dare say I might make a good wife, as you say. I believe I could be rather a cheerful companion, and affectionate if it was not exacted of me. But somehow all that does not hit the mark. The men who have cared for me have never seemed to like me for myself, or to understand the something behind the chatter and the fun which is the real part of me—which, if I married one of them, would never be brought into play, and would die of starvation. The only kind of marriage I have ever had a chance of seems to me like a sort of suicide—seems as if it would be one's best self that would be killed, while the other self, the well-dressed, society-loving, ball-going, easy-going self, would be all that was left of me, and would dance upon my grave."

Mrs. Courtenay was silent. She never ridiculed any thought, however crude and young, if it were genuine. She was one of the few people who knew whether Di was in fun or in earnest, and she knew she was in earnest now.

"There are such things as happy marriages," she said.

"Yes, granny; but I think it is the *happy* marriages I see which make me afraid of marrying. I know it is foolish to expect to meet with anything better than the ordinary happy marriage, and one ought to be thankful if one met with that, for half the world does not. But when I see what is *called* a happy marriage I always think, is that all? Somebody who believes everything I do is right, however silly it is, and knows how many lumps of sugar I take in my tea—like Arnold and Lily—people point at that marriage as such a model, because they have been married two years and are still as silly as they were. But whenever I stay with them, and she talks nonsense, and he thinks it is all the wisdom of Solomon; and she gives him a blotting-pad, and he gives her a fan; and then they look at each other, and then run races in the garden, and each waits for the other, and they come in hand-in-hand as if they had done something clever—whenever I behold these things it all seems to me a sort of game that I should be ashamed to play at, and I feel, if that is all, at least all I ought to expect, that it is a kind of happiness I don't care to have. Must love be always a sort of pretence, granny, and such a blind, silly, unreasoning feeling when it does exist? If ever I fall in love, shall I set up an assortment of lamentable, ludicrous illusions about some commonplace young man, as Lily does about that pink Arnold? Can't love be real, like hate? Can't people ever look at each other, and see each other as they *are*, and love each other for *what* they are?"

"The Lilies and the Arnolds would not marry if they saw each other as they are, my dear, and they would miss a great deal of happiness in consequence. There would be very few marriages if there were no illusions."

Di was silent.

Mrs. Courtenay stitched a resolution into her lace-work concerning a man whom no one could call commonplace, and presently spoke again.

"You are confusing 'being in love' with love itself," she said. "The one is common to vulgarity, the other rare, at least between men and women. It is the best thing life has to offer. But I have noticed that those who believe in it, and hope for it, and refuse the commoner love for it, generally—remain unmarried. And now, my dear, send down

Evans with my black lace mantilla, and my new bonnet, for Mrs. Darcy said she would lend us her carriage for the afternoon, and it comes at five. Put on a white gown, and make yourself look cool. I must call on Miss Fane, and afterwards we will go down and see the pony races at Hurlingham. Lord Hemsworth sent us tickets for today. He is riding, I think."

II

"The little waves make the large ones, and are of the same pattern."

—GEORGE ELIOT

John was dragging himself feebly across the hall to the smoking-room, after a dutiful cup of tea with his aunt, who was prostrate with a headache, when the door-bell rang, and he saw the champing profiles of a pair of horses through one of the windows. Following his masculine instincts, he hurried across the hall with all the celerity he could muster, and had just got safe under cover when the footman answered the bell. His ear caught the name of Mrs. Courtenay through the open door of the smoking-room, and presently, though he knew Miss Fane did not consider herself well enough to see visitors, there was a slow rustling across the hall, and up the stairs, accompanied by a light firm footfall that could hardly belong to James, whose elephantine rush had so often disturbed him when he was ill.

As James came down again, John looked out of the smoking-room door.

"Who is with Miss Fane?"

"Mrs. Courtenay, sir."

"Any one else?"

"No, sir. Miss Fane could only see Mrs. Courtenay. Miss Tempest, as come with her, is in the gold drawing-room."

John shut the smoking-room door and went and looked out of the window. It was not a cheerful prospect, but that did not matter much, as he happened to be looking at it without seeing it. Lindo got up on a chair and looked solemnly out too, rolling the whites of his eyes occasionally at his master from under his bushy brows, and yawning long tongue-curling yawns of sheer *ennui*. The cowls on the chimney-pots twirled. The dead plants on the leads were still dead. The cook's canary was going up and down on its two perches like a machine. John reflected that it was rather a waste of canary power; but, perhaps, there was nothing to hold back for in its bachelor existence. It would stand still enough presently when it was stuffed.

Could he get upstairs by himself? That was the question. He could come down, but that was not of much interest to him just now. Could he get up again? Only the first floor. Shallow stairs. Sit down half way. Awkward to be found sitting there, certainly. One thing was certain: that he was not going to be conveyed up in Marshall's solemn embrace as heretofore. John reflected that he must begin to walk by himself some time. Why not now? Very slowly, of course. Why not now?

It certainly was slow. But the stairs were shallow. There were balusters. It was done at last. If that alpine summit—the upper mat—was finally reached on hands and knees, who was the wiser?

John was breathless but triumphant. His hands were a trifle black; but what of that? The door of the gold drawing-room was open. It was a historic room, the decoration of which had been left untouched since the days when the witty Mrs. Tempest, whom Gainsborough painted, held her salon there. It was a long pillared room. Curtains of some old-fashioned pale gold brocade, not made now, hung from the white pillars and windows. The gold-coloured walls were closely lined with dim pictures from the ceiling to the old Venetian leather of the dado. Tall, gilt eastern figures, life size, meant to hold lamps, stood here and there, raising their empty hands, hideous, but peculiar to the room, with its bygone stately taste, and stiff white and gilt chairs and settees. John drew aside the curtain, and then hesitated. A family of tall white lilies in pots were gathered together in one of the further windows. Di was standing by them, turned towards him, but without perceiving him. She had evidently introduced herself to the lilies as a friend of the family, and was touching the heads of those nearest to her very gently, very tenderly with one finger. She stood in the full light, like some tall splendid lily herself, against the golden background.

John drew in his breath. It was *his* house; they were *his* lilies. The empty setting which seemed to claim her for its own, to group itself so naturally round her, was all his. There was a tremor of prophesy in the air. His brain seemed to turn slowly round in his head. He had come upstairs too quickly. His hand clutched the curtain. He felt momentarily incapable of stirring or speaking. The old physical pain, which only loosed him at intervals, tightened its thongs. But he dreaded to see her look up and find him watching her. He went forward and held out his hand in silence.

Di looked up and her expression changed instantly. A lovely colour came into her face, and her eyes shone. She advanced quickly towards him.

"Oh, John!" she said. "Is it really you? I was afraid we should not see you before we left town. But you ought not to stand." (John's complexion was passing from white to ashen grey, to pale green.) "Sit down." She held both his passive hands in hers. She would not for worlds have let him see that she thought he was going to faint. "This is a nice chair by the window," drawing him gently to it. "I was just admiring your lilies. You will let me ring for a cup of tea, I know. I am so thirsty." It was done in a moment, and she was back again beside him, only a voice now, a voice among the lilies, which appeared and disappeared at intervals. One tall furled lily head came and went with astonishing celerity, and the voice spoke gently and cheerfully from time to time. It was like a wonderful dream in a golden dusk. And then there was a little clink and clatter, and a cup of tea suddenly appeared close to him out of the darkness; and there was Di's voice again, and a momentary glimpse of Di's earnest eyes, which did not match her tranquil unconcerned voice.

He drank the tea mechanically without troubling to hold the cup, which seemed to take the initiative with a precision and an independence of support, which would have surprised him at any other time. The tea, what little there was of it, was the nastiest he had ever tasted. It might have been made in a brandy bottle. But it certainly cleared the air. Gradually the room came back. The light came back. He came back himself. It was all hardly credible. There was Di sitting opposite him, evidently quite unaware that he had been momentarily overcome, and assiduously engaged in pouring out another cup of tea. She had taken off her gloves, and he watched her cool slender hands give herself a lump of sugar. (Only one *small* lump, John observed. He must remember that.) Then she filled up the teapot from the little gurgling silver kettle. What forethought. Wonderful! and yet all apparently so natural. She seemed to do it as a matter of course. He ought to be helping her, but somehow he was not. Would she take bread and butter, or one of those little round things? She took a piece of bread and butter. Perhaps it would be as well to listen to what she was saying. He lost the first part of the sentence because she began to stir her tea at the moment, and he could not attend to two things at once. But presently he heard her say—

"Mrs. Courtenay thinks young people ought not to mind missing tea altogether. But I do mind; don't you? I think it is the pleasantest meal in the day."

John cautiously assented that it was. He felt that he must be very careful, or a slight dizziness which was now rapidly passing off might be noticed.

Di went on talking unconcernedly, bending her burnished golden head in its little white bonnet over the teacups. She seemed to take a great interest in the tea-things, and the date of the apostle spoons. Presently she looked at him again, and a relieved smile came into her face.

"Are you ready for another cup?" she said. And it was not a dream any longer, but all quite real and true, and he was real too.

"No, thanks," said John, taking his cup with extreme deliberation from a table at his elbow, where he supposed he had set it down. "There is something wrong about the tea, I think. Do send yours away and have some more. It has a very odd taste."

"Has it?" said Di, meeting his eye firmly, but with an effort. "I don't notice it. On the contrary, I think it is rather good. Try another cup."

"Perhaps the water did not boil," suggested John feebly, reflecting that his temporary indisposition might have been the cause of his dislike, but anxious to conceal the fact.

"That is a direct reflection on my tea-making," said Di. "You had better be more careful what you say." And she quickly pushed a stumpy little liqueur-bottle behind the silver tea-caddy.

"I beg pardon, and ask humbly for another cup," said John, smiling. The pain had left him again, as it generally did after he had remained quiet for a time, and in the relief from it he had a vague impression that the present moment was too good to last. He did not know that it was usual to wash out a cup so carefully as Di did his, but she seemed to think it the right thing, and she probably knew. Anyhow, the second cup was capital. John was not allowed to drink tea. The doctors who were knitting firmly together again the slender threads that had so far bound him to this world, believed he was imbibing an emulsion of something or other strengthening and nauseous at that moment.

"Oh! There is a tea-cake," said Di, discovering another dish behind the kettle. "Why did not I see it before?"

"It is not too late, I hope," said John, anxiously. The stupidity of James in putting a tea-cake (which might have been preferred to bread and butter) out of sight behind an opaque kettle, caused him profound annoyance.

But Di could not take a personal interest in the tea-cake. She looked back at the lilies.

"Don't you long to be in the country?" she said. "I find myself dreaming about green fields and flowers gratis. I have not seen a country lane since

Easter, and then it rained all the time. It is three years since I have found a hedge-sparrow's nest with eggs in it. Don't you long to get away?"

"I long to get back to Overleigh," said John. "I went there for a few days in the spring on my return from Russia. The place was looking lovely; but," he added, as if it were a matter of course, "naturally Overleigh always looks beautiful to me."

Di did not answer.

"You know the wood below the house," he went on. "When I saw it last all the rhododendrons were out."

"I have never seen Overleigh," said Di, looking at the lilies again, and trying to speak unconcernedly. She knew Lord Hemsworth's tiresome old Border castle. She had visited at many historic houses. She and Mrs. Courtenay were going to some shortly. But her own family place, the one house of all others in the whole world which she would have cared to see, she had never seen. She had often heard about it from acquaintances, had looked wistfully at drawings of it in illustrated magazines, had questioned Mrs. Courtenay and Archie about it, had wandered in imagination in its long gallery, and down the lichened steps from the postern in the wall, that every artist vignetted, to the stone-flagged Italian gardens below. But with her bodily eyes she had never beheld it, and the longing returned at intervals. It had returned now.

"Will you come and see it?" said John, looking away from her. It seemed to him that he was playing a game in which he had staked heavily, against some one who had staked nothing, who was not even conscious of playing, and might inadvertently knock over the board at any moment. He felt as if he had noiselessly pushed forward his piece, and as if everything depended on the withdrawal of his hand from it unobserved.

"I have wished to see Overleigh from a child," said Di, flushing a little. "Think what you feel about it, and my father, and our grandfather. Well—I am a Tempest too."

John was vaguely relieved. He glanced from her to the Gainsborough in the feathered hat that hung behind her. There was just a touch of resemblance under the unlikeness, a look in the pose of the head, in its curled and powdered wig that had reminded him of Di before. It reminded him of her more than ever now.

"Archie has been to Overleigh so constantly that I had not realized you had never seen it," said John. "But I suppose you were not grown up in those days; and since you grew up I have been abroad."

"Shall you go abroad again?"

"No. I have given up my secretaryship. I have come back to England for good."

"I am glad of that."

"I have been away too long as it is."

"Yes," said Di. "I have often thought so."

"Why?"

There was a pause.

"We are not represented," said Di proudly. She was speaking to one of her own family, and consequently she was not careful to choose her words. She had evidently no fear of being misunderstood by John. "We have always taken a place," she went on. "Not a particularly high one, but one of some kind. There was Amyas Tempest the cavalier general, and John who was with Charles of Bourbon at the sacking of Rome; and there were judges and admirals. Not that that is much when one looks at other families, the Cecils, for instance, but still they were always among the men of the day. And then our great-grandfather who lies in Westminster Abbey really was a great man. I was reading his life over again the other day. I suppose his son only passed muster because he was his son, and owing to his wife's ability. She amused old George IV., and made herself a power, and pushed her husband."

"My father never did anything," said John.

"No. I have always heard he had brains, but that he let things go because he was unhappy. Just the reason for holding on to them all the tighter, I should have thought, wouldn't you?"

"Not with some people. Some people can't do anything if there is no one to be glad when they have done it. I partly understand the feeling."

"I don't," said Di. "I mean, I do, but I don't understand giving in to it, and letting a little bit of personal unhappiness, which will die with one, prevent one's being a good useful link in a chain. One owes that to the chain."

"Yes," said John. "And yet I know he had a very strong feeling of responsibility from what he said to me on his death-bed. I have often thought about him since, and tried to piece together all the little fragments I can remember of him; but I think there is no one I can understand less than my own father. He seemed a hard cold man, and yet that face is neither hard nor cold."

John pointed to a picture behind her, and Di rose and turned to look at it.

It was an interesting refined face, destitute of any kind of good looks, except those of high breeding. The eyes had a certain thoughtful challenge in them. The lips were thin and firm.

Both gazed in silence for a moment.

"He looks as if he might have been one of those quiet equable people who may be pushed into a corner," said Di, "and then become rather dangerous. I can imagine his being a harsh man, and an unforgiving one if life went wrong."

"I am afraid he did become that," said John. "As he could not find room for forgiveness, there was naturally no room for happiness either."

"Was there some one whom he could not forgive?" asked Di, turning her keen glance upon him. She evidently knew nothing of the feud of the last generation.

At this moment the rush of James the elephant-footed was heard, and he announced that Mrs. Courtenay was getting into the carriage, and had sent for Miss Tempest.

"Good-bye," said Di, cordially, gathering up her gloves and parasol. "Go to Overleigh and get strong. And—you will have so many other things to think of—try not to forget about asking us."

"I will remember," said John, as if he would make a point of burdening his memory.

He was holding aside the curtain for her to pass.

"You see," said Di, looking back, "when we are on the move we can do things, but once we get back to London we cannot go north again till next year. We can't afford it."

"I will be sure to remember," said John again. He was a little crestfallen, and yet relieved that she should think he might forget. He felt that he could trust his memory.

She smiled gratefully and was gone. She had forgotten to shake hands with him. He knew she had not been aware of the omission. She had been thinking of something else at the moment. But it remained a grievous fact all the same.

He walked back absently into the drawing-room and stopped opposite the tea-table.

"Vinegar," he said to himself. "What can James have been about? I draw the line at vinegar at five o'clock tea. I hope she did not see it."

He took out the glass stopper.

Not vinegar. No. There is but one name for that familiar, that searching smell.

MARY CHOLMONDELEY

"It's brandy," said John aloud, speaking to himself, while the past unrolled itself like a map before his eyes. "Yes, look at it. Would you like to smell it again? There is no need to be so surprised. You had some of it not ten minutes ago, you poor deluded, blinded, bandaged idiot."

"WHOM DO YOU THINK *I* have seen?" said Di, as they drove away.

Mrs. Courtenay made no attempt to guess, which was the more remarkable because, when Miss Fane had ordered a cup of tea for Di, James had volunteered the information that he had already taken tea to Mr. and Miss Tempest.

"Whom but John himself," continued Di.

"I thought he was still invisible."

"I am sure he ought to be. I never saw any one look so ill. We had tea together. I really thought you were never going away at all, but I was glad you were such a long time, because it was so pleasant seeing him again. I like John; don't you? I have liked him from the first."

"He is a sensible man, but I prefer people with easier manners myself."

"He is more than sensible, I think."

"We shall be too late for the pony races," said Mrs. Courtenay. "It is nearly six now, and I told Lord Hemsworth we would be at the entrance at half-past five."

"He will survive it," said Di, archly. "And, granny, John is going to ask us to Overleigh. I told him I had never seen it."

"Good gracious!" exclaimed Mrs. Courtenay, and there was no doubt about her interest this time. "You did not *suggest* our going, did you?"

"I am not sure I did not," said Di, unfurling her parasol. "Look, granny, there is Mrs. Buller nodding to you, and you won't look at her. Yes, I rather think I did. I can't remember exactly what I said, but he promised he would not forget, and I told him we could only come when we were on the move. I impressed that upon him."

"Really, Di," said Mrs. Courtenay with asperity, "I wish you would prevent your parasol catching in my bonnet, and not offer visits without consulting me. It would have been quite time enough to have gone when he had asked us."

"He might not have asked us."

Mrs. Courtenay, who had seen a good deal of John in the weeks that preceded his accident, was perhaps of a different opinion; but she did not express it. Neither did she mention her own previously fixed intention of going to Overleigh somehow or other during the course of her summer visits.

"What is the use of near relations," continued Di, "if you can't tell them anything of that kind? I believe John will be quite pleased to have us now that he knows we wish to come; if only he remembers. Come, granny, if I take you to Archelot to please you, you ought to take me to Overleigh to please me. That's fair now, isn't it?"

"It may be extremely inconvenient," said Mrs. Courtenay, still ruffled. "And I had rheumatism last time I was there."

"Think what rheumatism you always have at Archelot, which sits up to its knees in mist every night in the middle of its moat; and yet you would insist on going again. There is that nice Mr. Sinclair taking off his hat. Won't you recognize him? You thought him so improved, you said, since his elder brother's death."

"My dear," said Mrs. Courtenay, "I am not so perpetually on the look out for young men as you appear to be. All the same, you may put up my parasol, for I can see nothing with the sun in my eyes."

MARY CHOLMONDELEY

III

"The moving Finger writes; and having writ,
Moves on: nor all your Piety nor Wit
Shall lure it back to cancel half a line,
Nor all your tears wash out a Word of it."

—OMAR KHAYYÁM

W hat thou doest do quickly," has been advice which, in its melancholy sarcasm, has been followed for eighteen hundred years when any special evil has been afoot in the dark. And yet surely the words apply still more urgently when the doing that is premeditated is good. What thou doest do quickly, for even while we speak those to whom we feel tenderly grow old and grey, and slip beyond the reach of human comfort. Even while we dream of love, those whom we love are parted from us in an early hour when we think not, without so much as a rose to take with them, out of the garden of roses that were planted and fostered for them alone. And even while we tardily forgive our friend, lo! the page is turned and we see that there was no injury, as now there is no compensation for our lack of trust.

Colonel Tempest acted with promptitude, but though he was as expeditious as he knew how to be, that was not saying much. His continual dread was that others might be beforehand with him. He had at this time a dream that recurred, or seemed to recur, over and over again—that he was running blindly at night, and that unknown adversaries were coming swiftly up behind him, were breathing close, and passing him in the darkness, unseen, but felt. It haunted him in the daytime like a reality.

Superstition would not be superstition if it were amenable to reason. Punishment hung over him like a sword in mid-air—it might fall at any moment—what form of punishment it would be hard to say—something evil to himself. If he struck down another might not the Almighty strike him down? It seemed to him that God's hand was raised.

"Sin no more." Wipe it out. Obliterate it. Expiate it. Quick, quick.

He set to work in feverish haste to find out Larkin. But although he had a certain knowledge of how to approach gentlemen of Swayne's class, he could not at first unearth Larkin. The habitation of the wren is not more secluded than that of some of our fellow-creatures. Colonel Tempest went very quietly to work. He never went near the address given him; he wrote anonymous letters repeatedly, suggesting a personal interview which would be found greatly to Mr. Larkin's advantage. Mr. Larkin, however, appeared to take a different view of his own advantage. It was in vain that Colonel Tempest said he should be walking on the Thames Embankment the following evening, and would be found at a given point at a certain hour. No one found him there, or at any other of the places he mentioned. He took a good deal of unnecessary exercise, or what appeared so at the time. Still he persisted. While the quarry remained in London, the hunter would probably remain there also. John had not gone yet. Colonel Tempest went on every few days making appointments for meeting, and keeping them rigorously himself.

A fortnight passed. Larkin made no sign.

At last Colonel Tempest heard that John was leaving town. He went to see him, and came away heavy at heart. John was out; and the servant informed him that Mr. Tempest was going to Overleigh the following morning. Colonel Tempest had a presentiment that a stone would be dropped between the points of the Great Northern. The train would come to grief, somehow. It would all happen in a moment. There would be one fierce thrust in the dark which he should not be able to parry. And if John got safe to Overleigh he would be followed there. The shooting season was coming on, and some one would load for him, and there would be an *accident*.

Colonel Tempest went back to his rooms in Brook Street, and stared at the carpet. He did not know how long it was before he caught sight of a batch of letters on the table. He looked carelessly at them; the uppermost was from his tailor. The address of the next was written in printed letters; he knew in an instant that it was from Larkin, without the further confirmation of the heavy seal with its shilling impression. His hands shook so much that he opened it with difficulty. The sheet contained a somewhat guarded communication also written in laboriously printed capitals.

Yours of the 14th to hand. All right. Place and time you say.

L.

MARY CHOLMONDELEY

The writer had been so very desirous to avoid publicity that he had even taken the trouble to tear off the left inner side of the envelope on which the maker's name is printed.

That significant precaution gave Colonel Tempest a sickening qualm. It suggested networks of other precautions in the background, snares which he might not perceive till too late, subtleties for which he was no match. He began to feel that it was physically impossible for him to meet this man; that he must get out of the interview at any cost. The maddening sense of being lured into a trap came upon him, and he flung in the opposite direction.

But the facts came and looked him in the face. He seldom allowed them to do so, but they did it now in spite of him. Eyes that have been once avoided are ever after difficult to meet. Nevertheless, he had to meet them—the cold inexorable eyes of facts come up to the surface of his mind to have justice done them, grimy but redoubtable, like miners on strike. Cost what it might, he saw that he must capitulate; that he must take this, his one—his last chance, or—hateful alternative—take instead the consequences of neglecting it.

He went over the old well-worn ground once again. Detection was impossible. That nightmare of a murder, and of a voice that cried aloud, while all the world stood still to hear: "*Thou art the man:*" was only a nightmare after all. And this was the best way, the only way to get rid of it.

He tried to recall the time and place of meeting, but it was gone from him. There had been so many. No, he had scrawled it down on the fly-leaf of his pocket-book. Six o'clock. It was nearly five now. He had had the money in readiness for the last fortnight. He had drawn one thousand of the ten which John had placed to his credit. He got out the ten crisp hundred pound notes, and put them carefully into his breast pocket. Then he sat down and waited. When the half-hour chimed he went out.

THERE IS A STRAIGHT AND quiet path behind Kensington Palace which the lovers and nursery-maids of Kensington Gardens frequent but little. A line of low-growing knotted trees separates it from the Broad Walk at a little distance. A hedge and fence on the other side divides the Gardens from a strip of meadow not yet covered by buildings.

The public esteem this particular walk but lightly. Invalids in bath-chairs toil down it sometimes; nurses with grown-up children, who are children still, go there occasionally, where the uncouth gambols and vacant bearded laugh of forty-five will not attract attention.

But as a rule it is deserted.

Colonel Tempest had it almost to himself for the first ten minutes, except for a covey of little boys who fought and clambered and jumped on some stacked timber at one end. He had not chosen the place without forethought. It would be presumed that he would have a large sum of money with him, and he had taken care on each occasion to select a rendezvous where foul play would not be possible. He was within reach of numbers of persons merely by raising his voice.

An old man on the arm of a young one passed him slowly, absorbed in earnest conversation. A girl in mourning sat down on one of the benches. There was privacy enough for business, and not too much for safety.

Colonel Tempest paced up and down, giving each face that passed a furtive glance. He did not know what to expect.

The three quarters struck. The girl got up and turned away. A stout, shabby-looking man, whose approach Colonel Tempest had not noticed, was sitting on one of the benches under a gnarled yew, staring vacantly in front of him. The old man and the young one were coming down the walk again. A check suit with six depressed, amber-eyed dachshunds in a leash passed among the trees.

A few more turns.

The clock began to strike six.

Colonel Tempest's pulse quickened. As he turned once more at the end of the walk, he could see that the hunched-up figure, with the hat over the eyes, was still sitting under the yew at the further end. He walked slowly towards it. How should they recognize each other? Who would speak first?

A quietly-dressed man, walking rapidly in the opposite direction, touched his hat respectfully as he passed him. Colonel Tempest recognized John's valet, and slackened his pace, for he was approaching the bench under the yew tree, and he did not care to be addressed while any one was within earshot. He was opposite it now, and he looked hard at the occupant. The latter stared vacantly, if not sleepily, back at him, and made no sign.

"He is shamming," said Colonel Tempest to himself. "Or else he is not sure of me." And he took yet another turn.

The man had moved a little when he came towards him again. He was leaning back in the corner of the bench, with his head on his chest, and his legs stretched out. An elderly lady, with curls, and an umbrella clutched like a defensive weapon, was passing him with evident distrust, calling to her side a fleecy little toy dog, which seemed to have left its stand and wheels at home, and to be rather at a loss without them. Colonel Tempest looked hard a second time at the figure on the bench, when he came opposite him, and then stopped short.

The man was sleeping the sleep of the just, or, to speak more correctly, of the just inebriated. His under lip was thrust out. He breathed stertorously. If it was a sham, it was very well done.

Colonel Tempest stood a moment in perplexity, looking fixedly at him. Should he wake him? Was he, perhaps, waiting to be waked? Was he really asleep? He half put out his hand.

"I think, sir," said a respectful voice behind him, "begging your pardon, sir, the party is very intoxicated. Sometimes if woke sudden they're vicious."

Colonel Tempest wheeled round.

It was Marshall, John's valet, who had spoken to him, and who was now regarding the slumbering rough with the resigned melancholy of an undertaker.

The quarter struck.

"Sorry to have kept you waiting, sir," said Marshall, after a pause, in which Colonel Tempest wondered why he did not go.

And then, at last, Colonel Tempest understood.

He put his hand feebly to his head.

"Oh, my God!" he said below his breath, and was silent.

Marshall cleared his throat.

There are situations in which, as Johnson has observed respecting the routine of married life, little can be said, but much must be done.

The slumbering backslider slid a little further back in his seat, and gurgled something very low down about "jolly good fellows," until, his voice suddenly going upstairs in the middle, he added in a high quaver, "daylight does appear."

The musical outburst recalled Colonel Tempest somewhat to himself. He turned his eyes carefully away from Marshall, after that first long look of mutual understanding.

The man's apparent respectability, his smooth shaved face and quiet dress, from his well-brushed hat and black silk cravat to the dark dog-skin glove that held his irreproachable umbrella, set Colonel Tempest's teeth on edge.

He had not known what to expect, but—*this*!

In a flash of memory he recalled the several occasions on which he had seen Marshall in attendance on John, his attentive manner, and noiseless tread. Once before John could move he had seen Marshall lift him carefully into a more upright position. The remembrance of that helpless figure in Marshall's arms came back to him with a shudder that could not be repressed. Marshall, whose expressionless face had undergone no change whatever, cleared his throat again and looked at his watch.

"Begging your pardon, sir," he said, "it's nearly half-past six, and Mr. Tempest dines early tonight."

"Did you receive my other letters?" said Colonel Tempest, pulling himself together, and beginning to walk slowly down the path.

"Yes, sir. I'm sorry to have put you to the inconvenience of going to so many places, 'specially as I saw for myself how regular you turned up at 'em. But I wanted to make sure you were in earnest before I showed. My character is my livelihood, sir. There was a time when I was in trouble and got into Mr. Johnson's hands, but before that I'd been in service in 'igh families, very 'igh, sir. Mr. Tempest took me on the recommendation of the Earl of Carmian. I was with him two year."

"Mr. Johnson," said Colonel Tempest, stopping short, and turning a shade whiter than he had been before. "By— I don't know anything about a Mr. Johnson. What do you mean?"

The two men eyed each other as if each suspected treachery.

"Did you write this?" said Marshall, producing Colonel Tempest's last letter.

"Yes."

"Then it's all right," said Marshall, who had forgotten the *sir*. "He had a sight of names. Johnson he was when he found I'd took up your— your bet. But I wrote to him, I remember, at one place as Crosbie."

Colonel Tempest recalled the curate's mention of Swayne under the name of Crosbie.

"Swayne, or Crosbie, or Johnson, it's all one," he said hastily. "I want a certain bit of paper you have in your possession, and I have ten Bank of England notes, of a hundred each, in my pocket now to give you in exchange. I suppose we understand each other. Have you got it on you?"

"Yes."

"Produce it."

"Show up the notes, too, then."

Unnoticed by either, the manner of both, as between gentleman and servant, had merged into that of perfect equality. Love is not the only leveller of disparities of rank and position.

They were walking together side by side. There was not a soul in sight. Each cautiously showed what he had brought. The dirty half-sheet of common note-paper, with Colonel Tempest's signature, seemed hardly worth the crisp notes, each one of which Colonel Tempest turned slowly over.

"Ten," said Marshall. "All right."

"Stop," said Colonel Tempest, hoarsely, the date on the ragged sheet he had just seen suggesting a new idea. "You're too young. You're not five and thirty. By— it's nearly sixteen years ago. You weren't in it. You couldn't have been in it. How did you come by that? Whom did you have it from?"

"From one who'll tell no tales," returned Marshall. "He was sick of it. He had tried twice, and he was near his end, and I took it off him just before he died."

"Did he die?" said Colonel Tempest. "I am not so sure of that."

"I am," said the man; "or I'd never have had nothing to do with the business."

"How long have you been with Mr. Tempest?"

"A matter of three months. He engaged me when he came back from Russia in the spring."

"You will leave at once. That, of course, is understood."

"Yes. I will give warning tonight if—" and the man glanced at the packet in Colonel Tempest's hand.

Without another word they exchanged papers. Colonel Tempest did not tear the document that had cost him so much into a thousand pieces. He looked at it, recognized that it was genuine, put it in his pocket, and buttoned his coat over it. Then he got out a note-book and pencil.

"And now," he said, "the others. How am I to get at them?"

The man stared. "The others?" he repeated. "What others?"

"You were one," said Colonel Tempest. "Now about the rest. I mean to pay them all off. There were ten in it. Where are the nine?"

Marshall stood stock still, as if he were realizing something unperceived till now. Then he shook his fist.

"That Johnson lied to me. I might have known. He took me in from first to last. I never thought but that I was the—*the only one*. And all I've spent, and the work I've been put to, when I might just as well have let one of them others risk it. He never acted square. Damn him."

Colonel Tempest looked at him horror-struck. The man's anger was genuine.

"Do you mean to say you don't *know*?" he said, in a harsh whisper, all that was left of his voice. "Swayne, Johnson said you did. On his death-bed he said so."

"Know," retorted the man, his expressionless face having some meaning in it at last. "Do you suppose if I'd *known*, I'd have— But that's been the line he has gone on from the first, you may depend upon it. He's let each one think he was alone at the job to bring it round quicker; a double-tongued, double-dealing devil. Each of them others is working for himself now, single-handed. I wonder they haven't brought it off before. Why *that fire*! We was both nearly done for that night. I slept just above 'im, and it was precious near. If he had not run up hisself and woke me—that fire—"

Marshall stopped short. His mouth fell ajar. His mind was gradually putting two and two together. There was no horror in his face, only a malignant sense of having been duped.

"By—," he said fiercely. "I see it all."

A cold hand seemed to be laid on Colonel Tempest's heart, to press closer and closer. The sweat burst from his brow. Swayne had been an economizer of truth to the last. He had deliberately lied even on his death-bed, in order to thrust away the distasteful subject to which Colonel Tempest had so pertinaciously nailed him. The two men stood staring at each other. A governess and three little girls, evidently out for a stroll after tea, were coming towards them. The sight of the four advancing figures seemed to shake the two men back in a moment, with a gasp, to their former relations.

Marshall drew himself up, and touched his hat.

"I ought to be going, sir," he said, almost in his usual ordered tones. "Mr. Tempest dines early tonight."

Colonel Tempest nodded. He had forgotten for the moment how to speak.

"And it's all right, sir, about—about me," rather anxiously.

Colonel Tempest perceived that Marshall had not realized the possible hold he might obtain over him by the mere fact of his knowledge of this last revelation. He had been obtuse before. He was obtuse now.

MARY CHOLMONDELEY

"As long as you are silent and leave at once," said Colonel Tempest, commanding his tongue to articulate, "I will be silent too. Not a moment longer."

Marshall touched his hat again, and went.

Colonel Tempest walked unsteadily to a bench under a twisted yew, a little way from the path, and sat down heavily upon it.

How cold it was, how bitterly cold! He shivered, and drew his hand across his damp forehead. The tinkling of voices reached him at intervals. Foolish birds were making choruses of small jokes in the branches above his head. Some one laughed at a little distance.

He alone was wretched beyond endurance. Perhaps he did not know what endurance meant. Panic shook him like a leaf.

And there was no refuge. He did not know how to live. Dared he die? die, and struggle up the other side only to find an angry judge waiting on the brink to strike him down to hell even while he put up supplicating hands? But his hands were red with John's blood, so that even his prayers convicted him of sin—were turned into sin.

A feeling as near despair as his nature could approach to overwhelmed him.

One of the most fatal results of evil is that in the same measure that it exists in ourselves, we imply it in others, and not less in God Himself. Poor Colonel Tempest saw in his Creator only an omniscient detective, an avenger, an executioner who had mocked at his endeavours to propitiate Him, to escape out of His hand, who held him as in a pillory, and would presently break him upon the wheel.

Superstition has its uses, but, like most imitations, it does not wear well—not much better, perhaps, than the brown paper boots in which the English soldier goes forth to war.

A cheap faith is an expensive experience. I believe Colonel Tempest suffered horribly as he sat alone under that yew tree; underwent all the throes which self-centred people do undergo, who, in saving their life, see it slipping through their fingers; who in clutching at their own interest and pleasure, find themselves sliding into a gulf; who in sacrificing the happiness and welfare of those that love them to their whim, their caprice, their shifting temper of the moment, find themselves at last—alone—unloved.

Are there many sorrows like this sorrow? There is perhaps only one worse—namely, to realize what onlookers have seen from the first, what has brought it about. This is hard. But Colonel Tempest was spared this pain. Those for whom others can feel least compassion are, as a rule, fortunately able to bestow most upon themselves. Colonel Tempest belonged to the self-pitying class, and with him to suffer was to begin at once to be sorry for himself. The tears ran slowly down his cheeks and his lip quivered. Perhaps there is nothing quite so heartbreaking as the tears of middle-age for itself.

He saw himself sitting there, so lonely, so miserable, without a creature in the world to turn to for comfort; entrapped into evil as all are at times, for he was but human, he had never set up to be better than his fellows; but to have striven so hard against evil—to have tried, as not many would have done, to repair what had been wrong (and the greatest wrong had not been with him) and yet to have been repulsed by God Himself! Everybody had turned against him. And now God had turned against him too. His last hope was gone. He should never find those other men, never buy back those other bets. John would be killed sooner or later, and he himself would *suffer*.

That was the refrain, the key-note to which he always returned. *He should suffer.*

Natures like Colonel Tempest's go through the same paroxysms of blind despairing grief as do those of children. They see only the present. The maturer mind is sustained in its deeper anguish by the power of looking beyond its pain. It has bought, perhaps dear, the chill experience that all things pass, that sorrow endures but for a night, even as the joy that comes in the morning endures but for a morning. But as a child weeps and is disconsolate, and dries its eyes and forgets, so Colonel Tempest would presently forget again—for a time.

Indeed, he soon took the best means within his reach of doing so. He felt that he was too wretched to remain in England. It was therefore imperative that he should go abroad. Persons of his temperament have a delightful confidence in the benign influences of the Continent. He wrote to John, returning him £8,500 of the £10,000, saying that the object for which it had been given had become so altered as to prevent the application of the money. He did not mention that he had found a use for one thousand, and that pressing personal expenses had obliged him to retain another five hundred, but he was vaguely conscious of doing an honourable action in returning the remainder.

John wrote back at once, saying that he had given him the money, and that as his uncle did not wish to keep it, he should invest it in his name, and settle it on his daughter, while the interest at four per cent. would be paid to Colonel Tempest during his lifetime.

"Well," said Colonel Tempest to himself, after reading this letter, "beggars can't be choosers, but if *I* had been in John's place I *hope* I should not have shown such a grudging spirit. Eight thousand five hundred! Out of all his wealth he might have made it ten thousand for my poor penniless girl. No wonder he does not wish her to know about it."

And having a little ready money about him, Colonel Tempest took his penniless girl, much to her surprise, a lapis-lazuli necklace when he went to say good-bye to her.

On the last evening before he left England he got out the paper Marshall had given him, and having locked the door, spread it on the table before him. He had done this secretly many times a day since he had obtained possession of it.

There it was, unmistakable in black and grime that had once been white. The one thing of all others in this world that Colonel Tempest loathed was to be obliged to face anything. Like Peer Gynt, he went round, or if like Balaam he came to a narrow place where there was no turning room, he struck furiously at the nearest sentient body. But a widower has no beast of burden at hand to strike, and there was no power of going round, no power of backing either, from before that sheet of crumpled paper. When he first looked at it he had a kind of recollection that was no recollection of having seen it before.

The words were as distinct as a death-warrant. Perhaps they were one. Colonel Tempest read them over once again.

"I, Edward Tempest, lay one thousand pounds to one sovereign that I do never inherit the property of Overleigh in Yorkshire."

There was his own undeniable scrawling signature beneath Swayne's crab-like characters. There below his own was the signature of that obscure speculator, since dead, who had taken up the bet.

If anything is forced upon the notice, which yet it is distasteful to contemplate, the only remedy for avoiding present discomfort is to close the eyes.

Colonel Tempest struck a match, lit the paper, and dropped it into the black July grate. It would not burn at first, but after a moment it flared up and turned over. He watched it writhe under the little chuckling flame. The word Overleigh came out distinctly for a second, and then the flame went out, leaving a charred curled nothing behind. One solitary spark flew swiftly up like a little soul released from an evil body. Colonel Tempest rubbed the ashes with his foot, and once again—closed his eyes.

IV

"I give thee sixpence! I will see thee d—d first."

—Canning

Some one rejoiced exceedingly when, in those burning August days, John came back to Overleigh. Mitty loved him. She was the only woman who as yet had shown him any love at all, and his nature was not an unthankful one. Mitty was bound up with all the little meagre happiness of his childhood. She had given him his only glimpse of woman's tenderness. There had never been a time when he had not read aloud to Mitty during the holidays—when he had forgotten to write to her periodically from school. When she had been discharged with the other servants at his father's death, he had gone in person to one of his guardians to request that she might remain, and had offered half his pocket-money annually for that purpose, and a sum down in the shape of a collection of foreign coins in a sock. Perhaps his guardian had a little boy of his own in Eton jackets who collected coins. At any rate, something was arranged. Mitty remained in the long low nurseries in the attic gallery. She was waiting for him on the steps on that sultry August evening when he returned. John saw her white cap twinkling under the stone archway as he drove along the straight wide drive between the double rows of beeches which approached the castle by the northern side.

Some houses have the soothing influence of the presence of a friend. Once established in the cool familiar rooms and strong air of his native home, he regained his health by a succession of strides, which contrasted curiously with the stumbling ups and downs and constant relapses which in the earlier part of his recovery had puzzled his doctors.

For the first few days just to live was enough. John had no desire beyond sitting in the shadow of the castle with Mitty, and feeling the fresh heather-scented air from the moors upon his face and hands. Then came the day when he went on Mr. Goodwin's arm down the grey lichened steps to the Italian garden, and took one turn among the stone-edged beds, under the high south wall. Gradually as the languor of weakness passed he wandered further and further into the woods, and lay for hours under the trees among the ling and fern. The irritation of weakness had left him, the enforced inaction of slowly returning strength had not yet begun to chafe. His mind urged nothing on him, required no decisions of him, but, like a dear companion instead of a taskmaster, rested and let him rest. He watched for hours the sunlight on the bracken, listened for hours to the tiny dissensions and confabulations of little creatures that crept in and out.

There had been days and nights in London when the lamp of life had burned exceeding low, when he had never thought to lie in his own dear woods again, to see the squirrel swinging and chiding against the sky, to hear the cry of the water-hen to its mate from the reeded pools below. He had loved these things always, but to see them again after toiling up from the gates of death is to find them transfigured. "The light that never was on sea or land" gleams for a moment on wood and wold for eyes that have looked but now into the darkness of the grave. Almost it seems in such hours as if God had passed by that way, as if the forest had knowledge of Him, as if the awed pines kept Him ever in remembrance. Almost. Almost.

Di was never absent from John's thoughts for long together. His dawning love for her had as yet no pain in it. It wandered still in glades of hyacinth and asphodel. Truly—

"Love is bonny, a little while, while it is new."

Its feet had not yet reached the stony desert places and the lands of fierce heat and fiercer frost, through which all human love which does not die in infancy must one day travel. The strain and stress were not yet.

John was coming back one evening from a longer expedition than usual. The violet dusk had gathered over the gardens. The massive flank and towers of the castle were hardly visible against the sky. As he came near he saw a light in the arched windows of the chapel, and through the open lattice came the sound of the organ. Some one was playing within, and the night listened from without; John stood and listened too. The organ, so long dumb, was speaking in an audible voice—was telling of many things that had lain long in its heart, and that now at last trembled into speech. Some unknown touch was bringing all its pure passionate soul to its lips. Its voice rose and fell, and the listening night sighed in the ivy.

MARY CHOLMONDELEY

John went noiselessly indoors by the postern, and up the short spiral staircase in the thickness of the wall, into the chapel, an arched Elizabethan chamber leading out of the dining-hall. He stopped short in the doorway.

The light of a solitary candle at the further end gave shadows to the darkness. As by an artistic instinct, it just touched the nearest of the pipes, and passing entirely over the prosaic footman, blowing in his shirt-sleeves, lit up every feature of the fair exquisite face of the player. Beauty remains beauty, when all has been said and done to detract from it. Archie was very good to look upon. Even the footman, who had been ruthlessly torn away from his supper to blow, thought so. John thought so as he stood and looked at his cousin, who nodded to him, and went on playing. The contrast between the two was rather a cruel one, though John was unconscious of it. It was Archie who mentally made the comparison whenever they were together. Ugliness would be no disadvantage, and beauty would have no power, if they did not appear to be the outward and visible signs of the inner and spiritual man.

Archie was so fair-haired, he had such a perfect profile, such a clear complexion, and such tender faithful eyes, that it was impossible to believe that the virtues which clear complexions and lovely eyes so plainly represent were not all packed with sardine-like regularity in his heart. His very hair looked good. It was parted so beautifully, and it had a little innocent wave on the temple which carried conviction with it—to the young of the opposite sex. It was not because he was so handsome that he was the object of a tender solicitude in many young girls' hearts—at least, so they told themselves repeatedly—but because there was so much good in him, because he was so misunderstood by elders, so interesting, so unlike other young men. In short, Archie was his father over again.

Nature had been hard on John. Some ugly men look well, and their ugliness does not matter. John's was not of that type dear to fiction. His features were irregular and rough, his deep-set eyes did not redeem the rest of his face. Nothing did. A certain gleam of nobility shining dimly through its harsh setting would make him better-looking later in life, when expression gets the mastery over features. But it was not so yet. John looked hard and cold and forbidding, and though his face awoke a certain interest by its very force, the interest itself was without attraction. It must be inferred that John had hair, as he was not bald, but no one had ever noticed it except his hair-cutter. It was short and dark. In fact, it was hair, and that was all. Mitty was the only other person who had any of it, in a lozenge-box; but who shall say in what lockets and jewel-cases one of Archie's flaxen rings might not be treasured? Archie was a collector of hair himself, and there is a give-and-take in these things. He had a cigar-box full of locks of different colours, which were occasionally spread out before his more intimate friends, with little anecdotes respecting the acquisition of each. A vain man has no reticence except on the subject of his rebuffs. Bets were freely exchanged on the respective chances of the donors of these samples of devotion, and their probable identity commented on. "Three to one on the black." "Ten to one on the dyed amber." "Forty to one on the lank and sandy, it's an heiress."

Archie would listen in silence, and smile his small saintly smile. Archie's smile suggested anthems and summer dawns and blanc-mange all blent in one. And then he would gather up the landmarks of his affections, and put them back into the cigar-box. They were called "Tempest's scalps" in the regiment.

Archie had sat for "Sir Galahad" to one of the principal painters of the day. He might have sat for something very spiritual and elevating now. What historic heroes and saints have played the organ? He would have done beautifully for any one of them, or Dicksee might have worked him up into a pendant to his "Harmony," with an angel blowing instead of the footman.

And just at the critical moment when the organ was arriving at a final confession, and swelling towards a dominant seventh, the footman let the wind out of her. There was a discord, and a wheeze, and a death-rattle. Archie took off his hands with a shudder, and smiled a microscopic smile at the perspiring footman. Archie never, never, never swore; not even when he was alone, and when he cut himself shaving. He differed from his father in that. He smiled instead. Sometimes, if things went very wrong, the smile became a grin, but that was all.

"That will do, thank you!" he said, rising. "Well, John, how are you? Better? I did not wait dinner for you. I was too hungry, but I told them to keep the soup and things hot till you came in."

They had gone through the open double doors into the dining-hall. At the further end a table was laid for one.

"When did you arrive?" asked John.

"By the seven-ten. I walked up and found you were missing. It is distressing to see a man eat when one is not hungry one's self," continued

Archie plaintively as the servant brought in the "hot things" which he had been recently devastating. "No, thanks, I won't sit opposite you and watch you satisfying your country appetite. You don't mind my smoking in here, I suppose? No womankind to grumble as yet."

He lit his pipe, and began wandering slowly about the room, which was lit with candles in silver sconces at intervals along the panelled walls.

John wondered how much money he wanted, and ate his cutlets in silence. He had as few illusions about his fellow-creatures as the steward of a Channel steamer, and it did not occur to him that Archie could have any reason but one for coming to Overleigh out of the shooting season.

Archie was evidently pensive.

"It is a large sum," said John to himself.

Presently he stopped short before the fireplace, and contemplated the little silver figures standing in the niches of the highcarved mantelshelf. They had always stood there in John's childhood, and when he had come back from Russia in the spring he had looked for them in the plate-room, and had put them back himself: the quaint-frilled courtier beside the quaint-ruffed lady, and the little Cavalier in long boots beside the Abbess. The dresses were of Charles I. 's date, and there was a family legend to the effect that that victim of a progressive age had given them to his devoted adherent Amyas Tempest the night before his execution. It was extremely improbable that he had done anything of the kind, but, at any rate, there they were, each in his little niche. Archie lifted one down and examined it curiously.

"Never saw that before," he said, keeping his teeth on the pipe, which desecrated his profile.

"Everything was put away when I was not regularly living here," said John. "I dug out all the old things when I came home in the spring, and Mitty and I put them all back in their places."

"Barford had a sale the other day," continued Archie, speaking through his teeth. "He was let in for a lot of money by his training stables, and directly the old chap died he sold the library and half the pictures, and a lot of stuff out of the house. I went to see them at Christie's, and a very mouldy-looking assortment they were; but they fetched a pile of money. Barford and I looked in when the sale of the books was on, and you should have seen the roomful of Jews and the way they bid. One book, a regular old fossil, went for three hundred while we were there; it would have killed old Barford on the spot if he had been there, so it was just as well he was dead already. And there were two silver figures something like these, but not perfect. Barford said he had no use for them, and they fetched a hundred apiece. He says there's no place like home for raising a little money. Why, John, Gunningham can't hold a candle to Overleigh. There must be a mint of money in an old barrack stuffed full of gimcracks like this."

"Yes, but they belong to the house."

"Do they? Well, if I were in your place I should say they belonged to the owner. What is the use of having anything if you can't do what you like with it? If ever I wanted a hundred or two I would trot out one of those little silver Johnnies in no time if they were mine."

John did not answer. He was wondering what would have happened to the dear old stately place if he had died a month ago, and it had fallen into the hands of those two spendthrifts, Archie and his father. He could see them in possession whittling it away to nothing, throwing its substance from them with both hands. Easy-going, self-indulgent, weakly violent, unstable as water, he saw them both in one lightning-flash of prophetic imagination drinking in that very room, at that very table. The physical pain of certain thoughts is almost unbearable. He rose suddenly and went across to the deep bay window, on the stone sill of which Amyas Tempest and Tom Fairfax, his friend, who together had held Overleigh against the Roundheads, had cut their names. He looked out into the latticed darkness, and longed fiercely, passionately for a son.

Archie's light laugh recalled him to himself with a sense of shame. It is irritating to be goaded into violent emotion by one who is feeling nothing.

"A penny for your thoughts," said Sir Galahad.

There was something commonplace about the young warrior's manner of expressing himself in daily life which accorded ill with the refined beauty of his face.

"They would be dear at the price," said John, still looking out.

"Care killed a cat," said Archie.

He had a stock of small sayings of that calibre. Sometimes they fitted the occasion, and sometimes not.

There was a short silence.

"Quicksilver is lame," said Archie.

"What have you been doing with her?" asked John, facing round.

"Nothing in particular. I rode her in the Pierpoint steeplechase last week, and she came down at the last fence, and lost me fifty pounds. I came in third, but I should have been first to a dead certainty if she had stood up."

"Send her down here at once."

"Yes, and thanks awfully and all that sort of thing for lending her, don't you know. Very good of you, though of course you could not use her yourself when you were laid up. I am going back to town first thing tomorrow morning; only got a day's leave to run down here; thought I ought to tell you about her. I'll send her off the day after tomorrow if you like, but the truth is—"

A good deal of circumlocution, that favourite attire of certain truths, was necessary before the simple fact could be arrived at that Quicksilver had been used as security for the modest sum of four hundred and forty-five pounds, which it had been absolutely incumbent on Archie to raise at a moment's notice. Heaven only knew what would not have been involved if he had not had reluctant recourse to this obvious means of averting dishonour. When Colonel Tempest and Archie began to talk about their honour, which was invariably mixed up with debts of a dubious nature, and an overdrawn banking account, and an unpaid tailor, John always froze perceptibly. The Tempest honour was always having narrow escapes, according to them. It required constant support.

"I would not have done it if I could have helped it," explained Archie in an easy attitude on the window-seat. "Your mare, not mine. I knew that well enough. I felt that at the time; but I had to get the money somehow, and positively the poor old gee was the only security I had to give."

Archie was not in the least ashamed. It was always John who was ashamed on these occasions.

There was a long silence. Archie contemplated his nails.

"It's not the money I mind," said John at last, "you know that."

"I know it isn't, old chap. It's my morals you're afraid of; you said so in the spring."

"Well, I'm not going to hold forth on morals again, as it seems to have been of so little use. But look here, Archie, I've paid up a good many times, and I'm getting tired of it. I would rather build an infants' school or a home for cats, or something with a pretence of common sense, with the money in future. It does you no manner of good. You only chuck it away. You are the worse for having it, and so am I for being such a fool as to give it you. It's nonsense telling you suddenly that I won't go on paying when I've led you to expect I always shall because I always have. Of course you think, as I'm well off, that you can draw on me for ever and ever. Well, I'll pay up again this once. You promised me in April it should be the last time you would run up bills. Now it is my turn to say this is the last time I'll throw money away in paying them."

Archie raised his eyebrows. How very "close-fisted" John was becoming! And as a boy at school, and afterwards at college, he had been remarkably open-handed, even as a minor on a very moderate allowance. Archie did not understand it.

"I'll buy back my own horse," continued John, trying to swallow down a sense of intense irritation; "and if there is anything else—I suppose there is a new crop by this time—I'll settle them. You must start fair. And I'll go on allowing you three hundred a year, and when you want to marry I'll make a settlement on your wife, but, by— I'll never pay another sixpence for your debts as long as I live."

Archie smiled faintly, and stretched out his legs. John rarely "cut up rough" like this. He had an uneasy suspicion that the present promptly afforded assistance would hardly compensate for the opening vista of discomfort in the future. And John's tone jarred upon him. There was something fixed in it, and Archie's nebulous easy-going temperament had an invincible repugnance to anything unpliable. He had as little power to move John as a mist has to move a mountain. He had proved on many occasions how little amenable John was to persuasion, and each recurring occasion had filled him with momentary apprehension. He felt distinctly uncomfortable after the two had parted for the night, until a train of reasoning, the logic of which could not be questioned, soothed him into his usual trustful calm.

John, he said to himself, had been out of temper. He had eaten something that had disagreed with him. That was why he had flown out. How frightfully cross he himself was when he had indigestion! And he, Archie, would never have grudged John a few pounds now and again if their positions had been reversed. Therefore, it was not likely John would either. And John had always been fond of him. He had nursed him once at college through a tedious illness, unadorned on his side by Christian patience and fortitude. Of course John was fond of him. Everybody was fond of him. It had been an unlucky business about Quicksilver. No wonder John had been annoyed. He would have been annoyed himself

MARY CHOLMONDELEY

in his place. But (oh, all-embracing phrase!) *it would be all right*. He was eased of money difficulties for the moment, and John was not such a bad fellow after all. He would not really "turn against" him. He would be sure to come round in the future, as he had always done with clock-like regularity in the past.

Archie slept the sleep of the just, and went off in the best of spirits and the most expensive of light overcoats next morning with a cheque in his pocket.

John went back into the dining-hall after his departure to finish his breakfast, but apparently he was not hungry, for he forgot all about it. He went and stood in the bay window, as he had a habit of doing when in thought, and looked out. He did not see the purple pageant of the thunderstorm sweeping up across the moor and valley and already vibrating among the crests of the trees in the vivid sunshine below the castle wall. He was thinking intently of those two men, his next-of-kin.

Supposing he did not marry. Supposing he died childless. Overleigh and the other vast Tempest properties were entailed, in default of himself and his children, on Colonel Tempest and his children. Colonel Tempest and Archie came next behind him; one slip, and they would be in possession.

And John had almost slipped several times, had several times touched that narrow brink where two worlds meet. He had no fear of death, but nevertheless Death had assumed larger proportions in his mind and in his calculations than is usual with the young and the strong, simply because he had seen him very near more than once, and had ceased to ignore his reality. He might die. What then?

John had an attachment which had the intensity of a passion and the unreasoning faithfulness of an instinct for certain carved and pictured rooms and lichened walls and forests and valleys and moors. He loved Overleigh. His affections had been "planted under a north wall," and like some hardy tenacious ivy they clung to that wall. Overleigh meant much to him, had always meant much, more than was in the least consistent with the rather advanced tenets which he, in common with most young men of ability, had held at various times. Theories have fortunately little to do with the affections.

He could not bear to think of Overleigh passing out of his protecting love to the careless hands and selfish heedlessness of Colonel Tempest and Archie. There are persons for whom no income will suffice. John's nearest relations were of this time-honoured stamp. As has been well said, "In the midst of life they are in debt."

John saw Archie in imagination "trotting out the silver Johnnies." The miniatures, the pictures, the cameos, the old Tempest manuscripts, for which America made periodic bids, the older plate—all, all would go, would melt away from niche and wall and cabinet. Perhaps the books would go first of all; the library to which he in his turn was even now adding, as those who had gone before him had done.

How they had loved the place, those who had gone before! How they must have fought for it in the early days of ravages by Borderer and Scot! How Amyas the Cavalier must have sworn to avenge those Roundhead cannon-balls which crashed into his oak staircase, and had remained imbedded in the stubborn wood to this day! Had any one of them loved it, John wondered, with a greater love than his?

He turned from the blaze outside, and looked back into the great shadowed room, in the recesses of which a beautiful twilight ever lingered. The sunlight filtered richly but dimly through the time-worn splendour of its high windows of painted glass, touching here and there inlaid panel and carved wainscoting, and laying a faint mosaic of varied colour on the black polished floor.

It was a room which long association had invested with a kind of halo in John's eyes, far removed from the appreciative or ignorant admiration of the stranger, who saw in it only an unique Elizabethan relic.

Artists worshipped it whenever they got the chance, went wild over the Tudor fan vaulting of the ceiling with its long pendants, and the quaint inlaid frets on the oak chimney-piece; talked learnedly of the panels above the wainscot, on which a series of genealogical trees were painted representing each of the wapentakes into which Yorkshire was divided, having shields on them with armorial bearings of the gentry of the county entitled in Elizabeth's time to bear arms.

Strangers took note of these things, and spelt out the rather apocryphal marriages of the Tempests on the painted glass, or examined the date below the dial in the southern window with the name of the artist beneath it who had blazoned the arms.—*Bernard Diminckhoff fecit, 1585.*

John knew every detail by heart, and saw them never, as a man in love with a noble woman gradually ceases to see beauty or the absence of beauty in brow and lip and eyelid, in adoration of the face itself which means so much to him.

John's deep-set steady eyes absently followed the slow travelling of the coloured sunshine across the room. Overleigh had coloured his life as its painted glass was colouring the sunshine. It was bound up with his whole existence. The Tempest motto graven on the pane beside him, *Je le feray durant ma vie*, was graven on John's heart as indelibly. Mr. Tempest's dying words to him had never been forgotten. "It is an honour to be a Tempest. You are the head of the family. Do your duty by it." The words were sunk into the deep places of his mind. What the child had promised, the man was resolved to keep. His responsibility in the great position in which God had placed him, his duty, not only as a man, but as a Tempest, were the backbone of his religion—if those can be called religious who "trust high instincts more than all the creeds." The family motto had become a part of his life. It was perhaps the only oath of allegiance which John had ever taken. He turned towards the window again, against which his dark head had been resting.

The old thoughts and resolutions so inextricably intertwined with the fibre of pride of birth, the old hopes and aspirations, matured during three years' absence, temporarily dormant during these months of illness, returned upon him with the unerring swiftness of swallows to the eaves.

He pressed his hand upon the pane.

The thunderstorm wept hard against the glass.

The sable Tempest lion rampant on a field argent surmounted the scroll on which the motto was painted, legible still after three hundred years.

John said the words aloud.

Je le feray durant ma vie.

V

"There are many wonderful mixtures in the world which are all alike called love."

—GEORGE ELIOT

T hese are troublous times, granny," said Di to Mrs. Courtenay, coming into her grandmother's room on a hot afternoon early in September. "I can't get out, so you see I am reduced to coming and sitting with you."

"And why are the times troublous, and why don't you go out-of-doors again?"

"I have been to reconnoitre," said Di, wrathfully, "and the coast is not clear. He is sitting on the stairs again, as he did yesterday."

"Lord Hemsworth?"

"No, of course not. When does he ever do such things? The Infant."

"Oh dear!"

The Infant was Lord Hemsworth's younger brother.

"And it is becoming so expensive, granny. I keep on losing things. His complaint is complicated by kleptomania. He has got my two best evening handkerchiefs and my white fan already; and I can't find one of the gloves I wore at the picnic today. I dare not leave anything downstairs now. It is really very inconvenient."

"Poor boy!" said Mrs. Courtenay, reflectively. "How old *is* he?"

"Oh, he is quite sixteen, I believe. What with this anxiety, and the suspense as to how my primrose cotton will wash, which I am counting on to impress John with, I find life very wearing. Oh, granny, we ought not to have come here at all, according to my ideas; but if we ever do again, I do beg and pray it may not be in the holidays. I wish I had not been so kind to him when we first arrived. I only wanted to show Lord Hemsworth he need not be so unnecessarily elated at our coming here. I wish I had not spent so many hours in the workshop with the boy and the white rats. The white rats did it, granny. Interests in common are the really dangerous things, as you have often observed. Love me, love my rats."

"Poor boy!" said Mrs. Courtenay again. "Make it as easy as you can for him, Di. Don't wound his pride. We leave tomorrow, and the

Verelsts are coming today. That will create a diversion. I have never known Madeleine allow any man, or boy, or creeping child attend to any one but herself if she is present. She will do her best to relieve you of him. How she will patronize you, Di, if she is anything like what she used to be!"

And in truth when Madeleine drove up to the house half an hour later it was soon apparent that she was unaltered in essentials. Although she had been married several months she was still the bride; the bride in every fold of her pretty travelling gown, in her demure dignity and enjoyment of the situation.

It was her first visit to her cousin Lady Hemsworth since her marriage, and her eyes brightened with real pleasure when that lady mentioned that Di was in the house, whom she had not seen since her wedding day. She was conscious that she had some of her best gowns with her.

"I have always been so fond of Di," she said to Di's would-be mother-in-law. "She was one of my bridesmaids. You remember Di, Henry?" turning with a model gesture to her husband.

Sir Henry sucked his tea noisily off his moustache, and said he remembered Miss Tempest.

"Now do tell me," said Madeleine, as she unfastened her hat in her room, whither she had insisted on Di's accompanying her, "is there a large party in the house? I always hate a large party to meet a bride."

"There is really hardly any one," said Di. "I don't think you need be alarmed. The Forresters left yesterday. There are Mr. Rivers and a Captain Vivian, friends of Lord Hemsworth's, and Lord Hemsworth himself, and a Mrs. Clifford, a widow. That is all. Oh, I had forgotten Mr. Lumley, the comic man—he is here. You may remember him. He always comes into a room either polkaing or walking lame, and beats himself all over with a tambourine after dinner."

"How droll!" said Madeleine. "Henry would like that. I must have him to stay with us some time. One is so glad of really amusing people; they make a party go off so much better. He does not black himself, does he? That nice Mr. Carnegie, who imitated the pig being killed, always did. I am glad it is a small party," she continued, reverting to the previous topic, with a very moderate appearance of satisfaction. "It is very thoughtful of Lady Hemsworth not to have a crowd to meet me. I dislike so being stared at when I am sent out first; so embarrassing, every eye upon one. And I always flush up so. And now tell me, you dear thing, all about yourself. Fancy my not having seen you since my wedding. I don't know how we missed each other in London in June. I know I called twice, but Kensington is such miles away; and—and I have often longed to ask you how you thought the wedding went off."

"Perfectly."

"And you thought I looked well—well for me, I mean?"

"You looked particularly well."

"I thought it so unkind of mother to cry. I would not let her come into my room when I was dressing, or indeed all that morning, for fear of her breaking down; but I had to go with her in the carriage, and she held my hand and cried all the way. Poor mother always is so thoughtless. I did not cry myself, but I quite feared at one time I should flush. I was not flushed when I came in, was I?"

"Not in the least. You looked your best."

"Several of the papers said so," said Madeleine. "Remarks on personal appearance are so vulgar, I think. 'The lovely bride,' one paper called me. I dare say other girls don't mind that sort of thing being said, but it is just the kind of thing I dislike. And there was a drawing of me, in my wedding gown, in the *Lady's Pictorial*. They simply would have it. I had to stand, ready dressed, the day before, while they did it. And then my photograph was in one of the other papers. Did you see it? I don't think it is *quite* a nice idea, do you?—so public; but they wrote so urgently. They said a photograph would oblige, and I had to send one in the end. I sometimes think," she continued reflectively, "that I did not choose part of my trousseau altogether wisely. I *think*, with the summer before me, I might have ventured on rather lighter colours. But, you see, I had to decide on everything in Lent, when one's mind is turned to other things. I never wear any colour but violet in Lent. I never have since I was confirmed, and it puts one out for brighter colours. Things that look quite suitable after Easter seem so gaudy before. I am not sure what I shall wear tonight."

"Wear that mauve and silver," said Di, suddenly, and their eyes met.

Madeleine looked away again instantly, and broke into a little laugh.

"You dear thing," she said; "I wish I had your memory for clothes. I remember now, though I had almost forgotten it, that the mauve brocade was brought in the morning you came to hear about my engagement. And do you remember, you quixotic old darling, how you wanted me to break it off. You were quite excited about it."

"I had not seen the diamonds then," interposed Di, with a faint blush at the remembrance of her own useless emotion. "I am sure I never said

MARY CHOLMONDELEY

anything about breaking it off after I had seen the two tiaras, or even hinted at throwing over that rivière."

Madeleine looked puzzled. Whenever she did not quite understand what Di meant, she assumed the tone of gentle authority, which persons, conscious of a reserved front seat or possibly a leading part in the orchestra in the next world, naturally do assume in conversation with those whose future is less assured.

"I think marriage is too solemn a thing to make a joke of," she said softly. "And talking of marriage"—in a lowered tone—"you would hardly believe, Di, the difference it makes, the way it widens one's influence. With men now, such a responsibility. I always think a married woman can help young men so much. I find it so much easier now than before I was married to give conversation a graver turn, even at a ball. I feel I know what people really are almost at once. I have had such earnest talks in ball-rooms, Di, and at dinner parties. Haven't you?"

"No," said Di. "I distrust a man who talks seriously over a pink ice the first time I meet him. If he is genuine he is probably shallow, and the odds are he is not genuine, or he would not do it. I don't like religious flirtations, though I know they are the last new thing."

"You always take a low view, Di," said Madeleine, regretfully. "You always have, and I suppose you always will. It does not make me less fond of you; but I am often sorry, when we talk together, to notice how unrefined your ideas are. Your mind seems to run on flirtations. I see things very differently. You wanted me to throw over Henry, though I had given my solemn promise—"

"And it had been in the papers," interposed Di; "don't forget that. But"—she added, rising—"I *was* wrong. I ought never to have said a word on the subject; and there is the dressing-bell, so I will leave you to prepare for victory. I warn you, Mrs. Clifford has one gown, a Cresser, which is bad to beat—a lemon satin, with an emerald velvet train; but she may not put it on."

"I never vie with others in dress," said Madeleine. "I think it shows such a want of good taste. Did she wear it last night?"

"She did."

"Oh! Then she won't wear it again."

But Di had departed.

"In change unchanged," Di said to herself, as she uncoiled her hair in her own room. "I don't know what I expected of Madeleine, yet I thought that somehow she would be different. But she isn't. How is it that some people can do things that one would be ashamed one's self even to think of, and yet keep a good opinion of themselves afterwards, and *feel* superior to others? It is the feeling superior that I envy. It must make the world such an easy place to live in. People with a good opinion of themselves have such an immense pull in being able to do the most peculiar things without a qualm. It must be very pleasant to truly and honestly consider one's self better than others, and to believe that young men in white waistcoats hang upon one's words. Yes, Madeleine is not changed, and I shall be late for dinner if I moralize any longer," and Di brushed back her yellow hair, which was obliging enough to arrange itself in the most interesting little waves and ripples of its own accord, without any trouble on her part. Di's hair was perhaps the thing of all others that womankind envied her most. It had the brightness of colouring and easy fascination of a child's. Even the most wily and painstaking curling-tongs could only produce on other less-favoured heads a laboured imitation which was seen to be an imitation. Madeleine, as she sailed into the drawing-room in mauve and silver half an hour later, felt that her own rather colourless, elaborate fringe was not redeemed from mediocrity even by the diamonds mounting guard over it. The Infant would willingly have bartered his immortal soul for one lock off Di's shining head. The hope that one small lock might be conceded to a last wild appeal, possibly upon his knees, sustained him throughout the evening, and he needed support. He had a rooted conviction that if only his mother had allowed him a new evening coat this half, if he had only been more obviously in tails, Di might have smiled upon his devotion. He had been moderately fond of his elder brother till now, but Lord Hemsworth's cable-patterned shooting stockings and fair, well-defined moustache were in themselves enough to rouse the hatred of one whose own upper lip had only reached the stage when it suggested nothing so much as a reminiscence of treacle, and whose only pair of heather stockings tarried long at the wash. But the Infant had other grounds for nursing Cain-like sentiments towards his rival. Had not Lord Hemsworth repeatedly called him in the actual presence of the adored one by the nickname of "Trousers"! The Infant's sobriquet among those of his contemporaries who valued him was "Bags," but in ladies' society Lord Hemsworth was wont to soften the unrefinement of the name by modifying it to Trousers. The Infant writhed under the absolutely groundless suspicion that his brother already had or might at any moment confide the original to Di. And even if he did not, even if

MARY CHOLMONDELEY

the horrible appellation never did transpire, Lord Hemsworth's society term was almost as opprobrious. The name of Trousers was a death-blow to young romance. Sentiment withered in its presence. Years of devotion could not wipe out that odious word from her memory. He could see that it had set her against him. The mere sight of him was obviously painful to her sense of delicacy. She avoided him. She would marry Lord Hemsworth. In short, she would be the bride of another. Perhaps there was not within a radius of ten miles a more miserable creature than the Infant, as he stood that evening before dinner, with folded arms, alone, aloof, by a pillar, looking daggers at any one who spoke to Di.

After dinner things did not go much better. There were round games, in which he joined with Byronic gloom in order to sit near Di. But Mr. Lumley, the licensed buffoon of the party, dropped into his chair when he left it for a moment to get Di a footstool, and, when sternly requested to vacate it, only replied in fluent falsetto in the French tongue, "Je voudrais si je coudrais, mais je ne cannais pas."

The Infant controlled himself. He was outwardly calm, but there was murder in his eye.

Lord Hemsworth, sitting opposite shuffling the cards, looked up, and seeing the boy's white face, said, good-naturedly—

"Come, Lumley, move up one. That is Trousers' place."

"Oh, if Trousers wants it to press his suit," said Mr. Lumley, vaulting into the next place. "Anything to oblige a fellow-sufferer."

And Sir Henry neighed suddenly as his manner was when amused, and the Infant, clenching his hands under the table, felt that there was nothing left to live for in this world or the next save only revenge.

As the last evening came to an end even Lord Hemsworth's cheerful spirits flagged a little. He let the Infant press forward to light Di's candle, and hardly touched her hand after the Infant had released his spasmodic clutch upon it. His clear honest eyes met hers with the wistful *chien soumis* look in them which she had learned to dread. She knew well enough, though she would *not* have known it had she cared for him, that he had only remained silent during the last few days because he saw it was no good to speak. He had enough perception not to strike at cold or lukewarm iron.

"Why can't I like him?" she said to herself as she sat alone in her own room. "I would rather like him than any one else. I do like him better, much better than any one I know, and yet I don't care a bit about him.

When he is not there I always think I am going to care next time I see him. I wonder if I should mind if he fell in love with some one else? I dare say I should. I wish I could feel a little jealous. I tried to when he talked the whole of one afternoon to that lovely Lady Kitty;—what a little treasure that girl is! I would marry her if I were a man. But it was no good. I knew he only did it because he was vexed with me about—I forget what.

"Well, tomorrow I shall be at Overleigh. I shall really see it at last with my own eyes. Why, it is after twelve o'clock. It is tomorrow already. It certainly does not pay to have a date in one's mind. Ever since the end of July I have been waiting for September the third, and it has not hurried up in consequence. Anyhow, here it is at last."

VI

*"It's a deep mystery—the way the heart of man turns to one woman
out of all the rest he's seen i' the world, and makes it easier for him to
work seven year for her, like Jacob did for Rachel, sooner than have
any other woman for th' asking."*

—George Eliot

Life has its crystal days, its rare hours of a stainless beauty, and a joy
so pure that we may dare to call in the flowers to rejoice with us,
and the language of the birds ceases to be an unknown tongue. Our real
life as we look back seems to have been lived in those days that memory
holds so tenderly. But it is not so in reality. Fortitude, steadfastness, the
makings of character, come not of rainbow-dawns and quiet evenings,
and the facile attainment of small desires. More frequently they are the
outcome of "the sleepless nights that mould youth;" of hopes not dead,
but run to seed; of the inadequate loves and friendships that embitter
early life, and warn off the young soul from any more mistaking husks
for bread.

John had had many heavy days, and, latterly, many days and long-
drawn nights, when it had been uphill work to bear in silence, or bear
at all, the lessons of that expensive teacher physical pain. And now pain
was past and convalescence was past, and Fate smiled, and drew from
out her knotted medley of bright and sombre colours one thread of pure
untarnished gold for John, and worked it into the pattern of his life.

Di was at Overleigh. Tall lilies had been ranged in the hall to
welcome her on her arrival. The dogs had been introduced to her at tea
time. Lindo had allowed himself to be patted, and after sniffing her
dress attentively with the air of a connoisseur, had retired with dignity
to his chair. Fritz, on the contrary, the amber-eyed dachshund, all tail-
wagging, and smiles, and saliva, had made himself cheap at once, and
had even turned over on his back, inviting friction where he valued it
most, before he had known Di five minutes.

Di was really at Overleigh. Each morning John woke up incredulous
that such a thing could be, each morning listened for her light footfall
on the stairs, and saw her come into the dining-hall, an active living
presence, through the cedar and ebony doors. There were a few other

people in the house, the sort of chance collection which poor relations, arriving with great expectations and their best clothes, consider to be a party. There were his aunt, Miss Fane, and a young painter who was making studies for an Elizabethan interior, and some one else—no, more than one, two or three others, John never clearly remembered afterwards who, or whether they were male or female. Perhaps they were friends of his aunt's. Anyhow, Mrs. Courtenay, who had proposed herself at her own time, was apparently quite content. Di seemed content also, with the light-hearted joyous content of a life that has in it no regret, no story, no past.

John often wondered in these days whether there had ever been a time when he had known what Di was like, what she looked like to other people. He tried to recall her as he had seen her first at the Speaker's; but that photograph of memory of a tall handsome girl was not the least like Di. Di had become Di to John, not like anything or anybody; Di in a shady hat sitting on the low wall of the bowling-green; or Di riding with him through the forest, and up and away across the opal moors; or, better still, Di singing ballads in the pictured music-room in the evening, in her low small voice, that was not considered good enough for general society, but which, in John's opinion, was good enough for heaven itself.

The painter used to leave the others in the gallery and stroll in on these occasions. He was a gentle, elegant person, with the pensive, regretful air often observable in an imaginative man who has married young. He made a little sketch of Di. He said it would not interfere, as John feared it might, with the prosecution of his larger work.

Presently a wet morning came, and John took Di on an expedition to the dungeons with torches, and afterwards over the castle. He showed her the chapel, with its rose window and high altar, where the daughters of the house had been married, where her namesake, Diana, had been wed to Vernon of the Red Hand. He showed her the state-rooms with their tapestried walls and painted ceilings. Di extorted a plaintive music from the old spinet in the garret gallery where John's nurseries were. Mitty came out to listen, and then it was her turn. She invited Di into the nursery, which, in these later days, was resplendent with John's gifts, the pride of Mitty's heart, the envy of the elect ladies of the village. There were richly bound Bibles and church-services, and Russia leather writing-cases, and inlaid tea-caddies, and china stands and book-slides, and satin-lined workboxes bristling with cutlery, and photograph frames and tea-sets—in fact, there was everything. There, also, John's prizes were kept, for Mitty had taken charge of them for him since the first holidays, when he had rushed up to the nursery to dazzle her with the slim red volume, which he had not thought of showing to his father; to which as time went on many others were added, and even great volumes of Stuart Mill in calf and gold during the Oxford days.

Mitty showed them to Di, showed her John's little high chair by the fire, and his Noah's ark. She gave Di full particulars of all his most unromantic illnesses, and produced photographs, taken at her own expense, of her lamb in every stage of bullet-headed childhood; from an open-mouthed face and two clutching hands set in a lather of white lace, to a sturdy, frowning little boy in a black velvet suit leaning on a bat.

"There's the last," said Mitty, pointing with pride to a large steel engraving of John in his heaviest expression, in a heavy gilt frame. "That was done for the tenantry when Master John come of age." And Mitty, in spite of a desperate attempt on John's part to divert the conversation to other topics, went on to expatiate on that event until John fairly bolted, leaving her in delighted possession of a new and sympathetic listener.

"And all the steps was covered with red cloth," continued Mitty to her visitor, "and the crowd, Miss Dinah, you could have walked on their heads. And Mr. John come down into the hall, and Mr. Goodwin was with him, and he turns round to us, for we was all in the hall drawn up in two rows, from Mrs. Alcock to the scullery-maid, and he says, 'Where is Mrs. Emson?' Those were his very words, Miss Tempest, my dear; and I says, 'Here, sir!' for I was along of Mrs. Alcock. And he says to Parker, 'Open both the doors, Parker,' and then he says, quite quiet, as if it was just every day, 'I have not many relations here,' for there was not a soul of his own family, miss, and he did not ask his mother's folk, 'but,' he says, 'I have my two best friends here, and that is enough. Goodwin,' he says, 'will you stand on my right, and you must stand on the other side, Mitty.'"

"It took me here, miss," said Mitty, passing her hand over her waistband. "And me in my cap and everything. I was all in a tremble. I felt I could not go. But he just took me by the hand, and there we was, miss, us three on the steps, and all the servants agathered round behind, and a crowd such as never was in front. They trod down all the flower-beds to nothing. Eh dear! when we come out, you should have heard 'em cheer, and when they seed me by him, I heard 'em saying, 'Who's yon?' And they said, 'That's the old nuss as reared him from a babby,' and they shouted till they was fit to crack, and called out, 'Three cheers for the old nuss.' And Master John, he kept smilin' at me, and I could do nothin' but roar, and there was Mrs. Alcock, I could hear her crying behind, and Parker cried too, and he's not a man to show, isn't Parker. But we'd known 'im, miss, since he was born, and there was no one else there that did; only me and Parker, and Mrs. Alcock, and Charles, as had been footman in the family, and come down special from London at Master John's expense. And such a speech as my precious lamb did make before them all, saying it was a day he should remember all his life. Those were his very words. Eh! it was beautiful. And all the presents as the deputations brought, one after another, and the cannon fired off fit to break all the glass in the winders. And then in the evening a hox roasted whole in the courtyard, and a bonfire such as never was on Moat Hill. And when it got dark, you could see the bonfires burning at Carley and Gilling, and Wet Waste, and right away to Kenstone, all where his land is, bless him. Eh! dear me, Miss Tempest, why was not some of you there?"

"John!" said Di half an hour later, as he was showing her some miniatures in the ebony cabinet in the picture-gallery, which Cardinal Wolsey had given the Tempest of his day, "why were not some of us, Archie or father, at your coming of age?"

They were sitting in the deep window-seat, with the miniatures spread out between them.

"There was no question about their coming," said John. "Archie was going in for his examination for the army that week, and your father would not have come if he had been asked. I did invite our great-uncle, General Hugh, but he was ill. He died soon afterwards. There was no one else to ask. You and your father, and Archie and I are the only Tempests there are."

The miniatures were covered with dust. John's and Di's pocket-handkerchiefs had an interest in common, which gradually obliterated all difference between them.

"Why would not father have come if you had asked him?" said Di presently. "You are friends, aren't you?"

"I suppose we are," said John, "if by friends one only means that we are not enemies. But there is nothing more than civility between us. You seem wonderfully well up in ancient family history, Di. Don't you know the story of the last generation?"

"No," said Di. "I don't know anything for certain. Granny hardly ever mentions my mother even now. I know she is barely on speaking terms with father. I hardly ever see him. When she took me, it was on condition that father should have no claim on me."

"You did not know, then," said John slowly, "that your mother was engaged to my father at the very time that she ran away with his own brother, Colonel Tempest?"

Di shook her head. She coloured painfully. John looked at her in silence, and then pulled out another drawer.

"She was only seventeen," he said at last, with a gentleness that was new to Di. "She was just old enough to wreck her own life and my poor father's, but not old enough to be harshly judged. The heaviest blame was not with *her*. There is a miniature of her here. I suppose my father had it painted when she was engaged to him. I found it in the corner of his writing-table drawer, as if he had been in the habit of looking at it."

He opened the case, and put it into her hand.

Miniatures have generally a monotonous resemblance to one another in their pink-and-white complexions and red lips and pencilled eyebrows. This one possessed no marked peculiarity to distinguish it from those already lying on Di's knee and on the window-seat. It was a lovely face enough, oval, and pale and young, with dark hair, and still darker eyes. It had a look of shy innocent dignity, which gave it a certain individuality and charm. The miniature was set in diamonds, and at the top the name "Diana" followed the oval in diamonds too.

John and Di looked long at it together.

"Do you think he cared for her very deeply?" said Di at last.

"I am afraid he did."

"Always?"

"I think always. The miniature was in the drawer he used every day. I don't think he would have kept it there unless he had cared."

Di raised the lid of the case to close it, and as she did so a piece of yellow paper which had adhered to the faded satin lining of the lid became dislodged, and fell back over the miniature on which it had evidently been originally laid. On the reverse side, now uppermost, was written in a large firm hand the one word, "False."

John started.

"I never noticed that paper before," he said.

"It stuck to the lining of the lid," she replied.

"It must have been always there."

The soft rain whispered at the lattice. In the silence, one of the plants dropped a few faint petals on the polished floor.

"Then he never forgave her," said Di at last, turning her full deep glance upon her companion.

"He did not readily forgive."

"He must have been a hard man."

"I do not think he was hard at first. He became so."

"If he became so, he must have had it in him all the time. Trouble could not have brought it out, unless it had been in his nature to start with. Trouble only shows what spirit we are of. Even after she was dead he did not forgive her. He put the miniature where he could look at it; he must have often looked at it. And he left that bitter word always there. He might have taken it away when she died. He might have taken it away when he began to die himself."

"I am afraid," said John, "there were shadows on his life even to the very end."

"The shadow of an unforgiving spirit."

"Yes," said John gently, "but that is a deep one, Di. It numbs the heart. He took it down with him to the grave. If it is true that we can carry nothing away with us out of the world, I hope he left his bitterness of spirit behind."

Di did not answer.

"That very unforgiveness and bitterness were in him only the seamy side of constancy," said John at last. "He really loved your mother."

"If he had really loved her, he would have forgiven her."

"Not necessarily. A nobler nature would. But he had not a very noble nature. That is just the sad part of it."

There was a long silence. At last Di closed the case, and put it back in the drawer. She held the little slip of paper in her hand, and looked up at John rather wistfully.

He took it from her, and, walking down the gallery, dropped it into the wood fire burning at the further end. He came back and stood before her, and their grave eyes met. The growing intimacy between them seemed to have made a stride within the last half-hour, which left the conversation of yesterday miles behind.

"Thank you," she said.

MARY CHOLMONDELEY

VII

"Oh, the little more, and how much it is!
And the little less, and what worlds away!"

—R. Browning

Miss Fane, John's aunt, was one of those large, soft, fleecy persons who act as tea-cosies to the domestic affections, and whom the perspicacity of the nobler sex rarely allows to remain unmarried. That by some inexplicable mischance she had so remained was, of course, a blessing to her orphaned nephew which it would be hard to overrate. John was supposed to be fortunate indeed to have such an aunt. He had been told so from a child. She had certainly been kind to him in her way, and perhaps he owed her more than he was fully aware of; for it is difficult to feel an exalted degree of gratitude and affection towards a person who journeys through life with a snort and a plush reticule, who is ever seeking to eat some new thing, and who sleeps heavily in the morning over a lapful of magenta crochet-work.

On religious topics also little real sympathy existed between the aunt and nephew. Miss Fane was one of those fortunate individuals who can derive spiritual benefit and consolation from the conviction that they belong to a lost tribe, and that John Bull was originally the Bull of Bashan.

Very wonderful are the dispensations of Providence respecting the various forms in which religion appeals to different intellects. Miss Fane derived the same peace of mind and support from her bull, and what she called "its promises," as Madeleine did from the monster altar candles which she had just introduced into the church at her new home, candles which were really gas-burners—a pious fraud which it was to be hoped a Deity so partial to wax candles, especially in the daytime, would not detect.

Miss Fane had an uneasy feeling, as years went by, that, in spite of the floods of literature on the subject with which she kept him supplied, John appeared to make little real progress towards Anglo-Israelitism. Even the pamphlet which she had read aloud to him when he was ill, which proved beyond a doubt that the unicorn of Ezekiel was the prototype of the individual of that genus which now supports the royal arms,—even that pamphlet, all-conclusive as it was, appeared to have made no lasting impression on his mind.

But if the desire to proselytize was her weak point, good nature was her strong one. She was always ready, as on this occasion, to go to Overleigh or to John's house in London, if her presence was required. If she slept heavily amid his guests, it was only because "it was her nature to."

She slept more heavily than usual on this particular evening, for it was chilly; and the ladies had congregated in the music-room after dinner, where there was a fire, and a fire always reduced Miss Fane to a state of coma.

Mrs. Courtenay was bored almost to extinction—had been bored all day, and all yesterday—but nevertheless her fine countenance expressed a courteous interest in the rheumatic pains and Jäger underclothing of one of the elder ladies. She asked appropriate questions from time to time, bringing Miss Goodwin, who with her brother was dining at the Castle, into the conversation whenever she could.

Miss Goodwin, a gentle, placid woman of nine and twenty, clad in the violent colours betokening small means and the want of taste of richer relations, took but little part in the great Jäger question. Her pale eyes under their white eyelashes followed Di rather wistfully as the latter rose and left the room to fetch Mrs. Courtenay some wool. Between women of the same class, and even of the same age, there is sometimes an inequality as great as that between royalty and pauperism.

Soon afterwards the men came in. Miss Fane regained a precarious consciousness. The painter dropped into a low chair by Mrs. Courtenay, some one else into a seat by Mary Goodwin; Mr. Goodwin addressed himself indiscriminately to Miss Fane and the lady of the clandestine Jägers. John, after a glance round the room, and a short sojourn on the hearthrug, which proved too hot for him, seated himself on a strictly neutral settee away from the fire, and took up *Punch*. Immediately afterwards Di came back.

She gave Mrs. Courtenay her wool, and then, instead of returning to her former seat by the fire, gathered up her work, crossed the room, and sat down on the settee by John.

The blood rushed to his face. Her quiet unconcerned manner stung him to the quick. She spoke to him, but he did not answer. Indeed, he did not hear what she said. A moment before he had been wondering

MARY CHOLMONDELEY

what excuse he could make for getting up and going to her. He had been about to draw her attention to the cartoon in a two-days-old *Punch*, for persons in John's state of mind lose sight of the realities of life; and in the presence of half a dozen people, she could calmly make her way to him, and seat herself beside him, exactly as she might have done if he had been her brother. He felt himself becoming paler and paler. An entirely new idea was forcing itself upon him like a growing physical pain. But there was not time to think of it now. He wondered whether there was any noticeable difference in his face, and whether his voice would betray him to Di if he spoke. He need not have been afraid. Di did not know the meaning of a certain stolid look which John's countenance could occasionally take. She was perfectly unconscious of what was going on a couple of feet away from her, and picked up her stitches in a cheerful silence. Mary Goodwin saw that he was vexed, and, not being versed in the intricacies of love in its early stages, or, indeed, in any stages, wondered why his face fell when his beautiful cousin came to sit by him.

"Don't you sing?" she said, turning to Di.

"I whisper a little sometimes with the soft pedal down," said Di. "But not in public. There is a painful discrepancy between me and my voice. It is several sizes too small for me."

"Do whisper a little all the same," said the painter.

"John," said Di, "I am afraid you do not observe that I am being pressed to sing by two of your guests. Why don't you, in the language of the *Quiver*, conduct me to the instrument?"

The unreasoning, delighted pride with which John had until now listened to the smallest of Di's remarks, whether addressed to himself or others, had entirely left him.

"Do sing," he said, without looking at her; and he rose to light the candles on the piano.

And Di sang. John sat down by Mary, and actually allowed the painter to turn over.

It was a very small voice, low and clear, which, while it disarmed criticism, made one feel tenderly towards the singer. John, with his hand over his eyes, watched Di intently. She seemed to have suddenly receded from him to a great and impassable distance, at the very moment when he had thought they were drawing nearer to each other. He took new note of every line of form and feature. There was a growing tumult in his mind, a glimpse of breakers ahead. The atmosphere of peace and quietude of the familiar room, and the low voice singing in the listening silence, seemed to his newly awakened consciousness to veil some stern underlying reality, the features of which he could not see.

Mary Goodwin, who had the music in her which those who possess a lesser degree of it are often able more fluently to express, left John, and, going to the piano, began to turn over Di's music.

Presently she set up an old leather manuscript book before Di, who, after a moment's hesitation, began to sing—

> "Oh, broken heart of mine,
> Death lays his lips to thine;
> His draught of deadly wine
> He proffereth to thee!
> But listen! low and near,
> In thy close-shrouded ear,
> I whisper. Dost thou hear?
> 'Arise and work with me.'

> "The death-weights on thine eyes
> Shut out God's patient skies.
> Cast off thy shroud and rise!
> What dost thou mid the dead?
> Thine idle hands and cold
> Once more the plough must hold,
> Must labour as of old.
> Come forth, and earn thy bread."

The voice ceased. The accompaniment echoed the stern sadness of the last words, and then was suddenly silent.

What is it in a voice that so mightily stirs the fibre of emotion in us? It seemed to John that Di had taken his heart into the hollow of her slender hands.

"Thank you," said Mary Goodwin, after a pause; and one of the elder ladies felt it was an opportune moment to express her preference for cheerful songs.

Di had risen from the piano, and was gathering up her music. Involuntarily John crossed the room, and came and stood beside her. He did not know he had done so till he found himself at her side. Mary Goodwin turned to Miss Fane to say "Good night."

Di slowly put one piece of music on another, absently turning them right side upwards. He saw what was passing through her mind as clearly as if it had been reflected in a glass. He stood by her watching her bend over the piano. He was unable to speak to her or help her. Presently she looked slowly up at him. He had no conception until he tried how difficult it was to meet without flinching the quiet friendship of her eyes.

"John," she said, "my mother wrote that song. Do you remember what a happy, innocent kind of look the miniature had? She was seventeen then, and she was only four and twenty when she died. I don't know how to express it, but somehow the miniature seems a very long way off from the song. I am afraid there must have been a good deal of travelling between-whiles, and not over easy country."

John would have answered something, but the Goodwins were saying "Good night;" and shortly afterwards the others dispersed for the night. But John sat up late over the smoking-room fire, turning things over in his mind, and vainly endeavouring to nail shadows to the wall. It seemed to him as if, while straining towards a goal, he had suddenly discovered, by the merest accident, that he was walking in a circle.

VIII

"Vous me quittez, n'ayant pu voir
Mon âme à travers mon silence."

—Victor Hugo

It was Saturday morning. The few guests had departed by an early train. The painter cast a backward glance at Overleigh and the two figures standing together in the sunshine on the grey green steps which, with their wide hospitable balustrade, he had sketched so carefully. He was returning to the chastened joys of domestic life in London lodgings; to his pretty young jaded, fluffy wife, and fluffy, delicate child; to the Irish stew, and the warm drinking-water, and the blistered gravy of his home-life. Sordid surroundings have the sad power of making some lives sordid too. It requires a rare nobility of character to rise permanently above the dirty table-cloth, and ill-trimmed paraffin-lamp of poor circumstances. Poverty demoralizes. A smell of cooking, and, why I know not, but especially an aroma of boiled cabbage, can undermine the dignity of existence. A reminiscence of yesterday on the morning fork dims the ideals of youth.

As he drove away between the double row of beeches, with a hand on his boarded picture, the poor painter reflected that John was a fortunate kind of person. The dogcart was full of grapes and peaches and game. Perhaps the power to be generous is one of the most enviable attributes of riches.

"Poor fellow!" said John, as he and Di turned back into the cool gloom of the white stone hall.

"He has given granny the sketch of me," said Di. "He is a nice man, but after the first few days he hardly spoke to me, which I consider a bad sign in any one. It shows a want of discernment; don't you think so? Alas! we are going away this afternoon. I wish, John, you would try and look a little more moved at the prospect of losing us. It would be gratifying to think of you creeping on all-fours under a sofa after our departure, dissolved in tears."

John winced, but the reflections of the night before had led to certain conclusions, and he answered lightly—that is, lightly for him, for he had not an airy manner at the best of times—

"I am afraid I could not rise to tears. Would a shriek from the battlements do?"

"I should prefer tears," said Di, who was in a foolish mood this morning, in which high spirits take the form of nonsense, looking at her cousin, whose sedate and rather impenetrable face stirred the latent mischief in her. "Not idle tears, John, that 'I know not what they mean,' you know, but large solemn drops, full man's size, sixty to a teaspoonful. That's the measure by granny's medicine-glass."

She looked very provoking as she stood poising herself on her slender feet on the low edge of the hearthstone, with one hand holding the stone paw of the ragged old Tempest lion carved on the chimney-piece. John looked at her with amused irritation, and wished—there is a practical form of repartee eminently satisfactory to the masculine mind which an absurd conventionality forbids—wished, but what is the good of wishing?

"I must go and pack," said Di, with a sigh; "and see how granny is getting on. She is generally down before this. You won't go and get lost, will you, and only turn up at luncheon?"

"I will be about," said John. "If I am not in the library, look for me under the drawing-room sofa."

Di laughed, and went lightly away across the grey and white stone flags. There was a lamentable discrepancy between his feelings and hers which outraged John's sense of proportion. He went into the study and sat down there, staring at the shelves of embodied thought and speculation and aspiration with which at one time he had been content to live, which, now that he had begun to live, seemed entirely beside the mark.

Mrs. Courtenay was a person of courage and endurance, but even her powers had been sorely tried during the past week. She had been bored to the verge of distraction by the people of whom she had taken such a cordial leave the night before. There are persons who never, when out visiting, wish to retire to their rooms to rest, who never have letters to write, who never take up a book downstairs, who work for deep-sea fishermen, and are always ready for conversation. Such had been the departed. Miss Fane herself, for whom Mrs. Courtenay professed a certain friendship, was a person with whom she would have had nothing in common, whom she would hardly have tolerated, if it had not been for her nephew. But for him she was willing to sacrifice herself even further. She had seen undemonstrative men in love before now. Their actions had the same bald significance for her as a string of molehills for a mole-catcher. She was certain he was seriously attracted, and she was determined to give him a fair field, and as much favour as possible. That Di had not as yet the remotest suspicion of his intentions she regarded as little short of providential, considering the irritating and impracticable turn of that young lady's mind.

Di entered her grandmother's room, and found that conspirator sitting up in bed, looking with rueful interest at a boiled egg and untouched rack of toast on a tray before her. Mrs. Courtenay always breakfasted in bed, and could generally thank Providence for a very substantial meal.

"Take the tray away, Brown," said Mrs. Courtenay, with an effort.

"Why, you've not touched a single thing, ma'am," remarked Brown, reproachfully.

"I have drunk a little coffee," said Mrs. Courtenay, faintly.

"Granny, aren't you well?" asked Di.

Brown removed the tray, which Mrs. Courtenay's eyes followed regretfully from the room.

"I am not *very* well, my love," she replied, adjusting her spectacles, "but not positively ill. I had a threatening of one of those tiresome spasms in the night. I dare say it will pass off in an hour or two."

Di scrutinized her grandmother remorsefully.

"I never noticed you were feeling ill when I came in before breakfast," she said.

"My dear, you are generally the first to observe how I am," returned Mrs. Courtenay, hurriedly. "I was feeling better just then, but—and we are due at Carmyan today. It is very provoking."

Di looked perturbed.

"The others are gone," she said; "even the painter has just driven off. Do you think you will be able to travel by the afternoon, granny?"

"I am afraid *not*," said Mrs. Courtenay, closing her eyes; "but I think—I feel sure I could go tomorrow."

"Tomorrow is Sunday."

"Dear me! so it is," said Mrs. Courtenay, with mild surprise. "Today is Saturday. It certainly is unfortunate. But after all," she continued, "it could not have happened at a better place. Miss Fane is a good-natured person and will quite understand, and John is a relation. Perhaps you had better tell Miss Fane I am feeling unwell, and ask her to come here;

and before you go pull down the blinds half-way, and put that sheaf of her 'lost tribes' and 'unicorns' and 'stone ages' on the bed."

WHAT INDUCED JOHN TO SPEND the whole of Saturday afternoon and the greater part of a valuable evening at a small colliery town some twenty miles distant, it would be hard to say. The fact that some days ago he had arranged to go there after the departure of his guests did not account for it, for he had dismissed all thought of doing so directly he heard that Di and Mrs. Courtenay were staying on. It was not important. The following Saturday would do equally well to inspect a reading-room he was building, and the new shaft of one of his mines, about the safety of which he was not satisfied. Yet somehow or other, when the afternoon came, John went. Up to the last moment after luncheon he had intended to remain. Nevertheless, he went. The actions of persons under a certain influence cannot be predicted or accounted for. They can only be chronicled.

John did not return to Overleigh till after ten o'clock. He told himself most of the way home that Miss Fane and Di would be sure not to sit up later than ten. He made up his mind that he should only arrive after they had gone to bed. As he drove up through the semi-darkness he looked eagerly for Di's window. There was a light in it. He perceived it with sudden resentment. She *had* gone to bed, then. He should not see her till tomorrow. John had a vague impression that he was glad he had been away all day, that he had somehow done rather a clever thing. But apparently he was not much exhilarated by the achievement. It lost somewhat in its complete success.

And Mrs. Courtenay, who heard the wheels of his dogcart drive up just after Di had wished her "Good night," said aloud in the darkness the one word, "Idiot!"

IX

"Love, how it sells poor bliss
For proud despair!"

—Shelley

It was Sunday morning, and it was something more. There was a subtle change in the air, a mystery in the sunshine. Autumn and summer were met in tremulous wedlock. But the hand of the bride trembled in the bridegroom's. In the rapture of bridal there was a prophesy of parting and death. The birds knew it. In the songless silence the robin was practising his autumn reverie. Joy and sadness were blent together in the solemn beauty of transition.

The voice of the brook was sunk to a whisper today. Through the still air the tangled voices of the church bells came from the little grey church in the valley. A rival service was going on in the rookery on Moat Hill, in which the congregation joined with hoarse unanimity.

Miss Fane did not go to church in the morning, so John and Di went together down the steep path through the wood, across the park, over the village beck, and up the low hollowed steps into the churchyard. Overleigh was a primitive place.

The little congregation was sitting on the wall, or standing about among the tilted tombstones, according to custom, to see John and the clergyman come in. And then there was a general clump and clatter after them into church; the bells stopped, and the service began.

Di and John sat at a little distance from each other in the carved Tempest pew. The Tempests were an overbearing race. The little rough stone church with its round Norman arches was a memorial of their race.

"Lord, Thou hast been our Refuge from one generation to another," was graven in the stones of the wall just before Di's eyes. Beneath was a low arch surmounting the tomb of a knight in effigy. Beyond there were more tombs and arches. The building was thronged with the sculptured dead of one family—was a mortuary chapel in itself. Tattered flags hung where pious hands, red with infidel blood, had fastened them. With a simple confidence in their own importance, and the approval of their Creator, the Tempests had raised their memorials and hung their battered swords in the house of their God. The very sun himself smote, not through the gaudy figures of Scripture story, but through the painted arms of the Malbys; of the penniless, pious Malby who sold his land to his clutching Tempest brother-in-law in order to get out to the Crusades.

Had God really been their Refuge from all those bygone generations to this? Di wondered. In these latter days of millionaire cheesemongers who dwell *h*-less in the feudal castles of the poor, what wonder if the faith even of the strongest waxes cold?

She looked fixedly at John as he went to the reading-desk and stood up to read the First Lesson. It was difficult to believe the dead were not listening too; that the Knight Templar lying in armour, with his drawn sword beside him and broken hands joined, did not turn his head a little, pillowed so uncomfortably on his helmet, to hear John's low clear voice.

And as John read, a feeling of pride in him, not unmixed with awe, arose in Di's mind. All he did and said, even when in his gentlest mood—and Di had not as yet seen him in any other—had a hint of power in it; power restrained, perhaps, but existent. How strong his iron hand looked touching the book! She could more easily imagine it grasping a sword-hilt. He stood before her as the head of the race, his rugged profile and heavy jaw silhouetted in all their native strength and ugliness against the uncompromising light of the eastern window.

She looked at him, and was glad.

"He will do us honour," she said to herself.

Some one else was watching John too.

"I will arise and go to my Father," John read. And Mr. Goodwin closed his eyes, and prayed the old worn prayer—our prayers for others are mainly tacit reproaches to the Almighty—that God would touch John's heart.

Humanity has many sides, but perhaps none more incomprehensible than that represented by the patient middle-aged man leaning back in his corner and praying for John's soul; none more difficult to describe without an appearance of ridicule; for certain aspects of character, like some faces, lend themselves to caricature more readily than to a portrait.

Mr. Goodwin was one of that class of persons who belong so entirely to a class that it is difficult to individualize them; whose peculiar object in life it is to stick in clusters like limpets to existing, and especially to superseded, forms of religion. Their whole constitution and central ganglion consists of one adhesive organism. The quality of that to which they adhere does not appear to affect them, provided it is stationary. To their constitution movement is torture, uprootal is death. It would be impossible to chip Mr. Goodwin from his rock, and hold him up to the scrutiny of the reader, without distorting him to a caricature, which is an insult to our common nature. Unless he is in the full exercise of his adhesive muscle in company with large numbers of his kind, he is nothing. And even then he is not much.

Not much? Ah, yes, he is!

His class has played an important part in all crises of religious history. It was instrumental in the crucifixion of Christ. It called a new truth blasphemy as fiercely then as now. By its law truth, if new, must ever be put to death. But when Christianity took form, this class settled on it nevertheless; adhered to it as strictly as its forbears had done to the Jewish ritual. It was this class which resisted and would have burned out the Reformation, but when the Reformation gained bulk enough for it to stick to, it spread itself upon its surface in due course. As it still does today.

Let who will sweat and agonize for the sake of a new truth, or a newer and purer form of an old one. There will always be those who will stand aside and coldly regard, if they cannot crush, the struggle and the heartbreak of the pioneers, and then will enter into the fruit of their labours, and complacently point in later years to the advance of thought in their time, which they have done nothing to advance, but to which, when sanctioned by time and custom and the populace, they will *adhere*.

John shut the book, and Mr. Goodwin, taken up with his own mournful reflections, heard no more of the service until he was wakened by the shriek of the village choir—

> *"Before Jehovah's awful throne,*
> *Ye nations bow-wow-wow with sacred joy."*

When the clergyman had blessed his flock, and the flock had hurried with his blessing into the open air, Di and John remained behind to look at the nibbled old stone font, engraved with tangled signs, and unknown beasts with protruding unknown tongues, where little Tempests had whimpered and protested against a Christianity they did not understand. The aisle and chancel were paved with worn lettered stones, obliterated memorials of forgotten Tempests who had passed at midnight with flaring torches from their first home on the crag to their last in the valley. The walls bore record too. John had put up a tablet to his predecessor. It contained only the name, and date of birth and death, and underneath the single sentence—

"Until the day break, and the shadows flee away."

Di read the words in silence, and then turned the splendour of her deep glance upon him. Since when had the bare fact of meeting her eyes become so exceeding sharp and sweet, such an epoch in the day? John writhed inwardly under their gentle scrutiny.

"You are very loyal," she said.

He felt a sudden furious irritation against her which took him by surprise, and then turned to scornful anger against himself. He led the way out of the church into the sad September sunshine, and talked of indifferent subjects till they reached the Castle. And after luncheon John went to the library and stared at the shelves again, and Miss Fane ambled and grunted to church, and Di sat with her grandmother.

There are some acts of self-sacrifice for which the performers will never in this world obtain the credit they deserve. Mrs. Courtenay, who was addicted to standing proxy for Providence, and was not afraid to take upon herself responsibilities which belong to Omniscience alone, had not hesitated to perform such an act, in the belief that the cause justified the means. Indeed, in her eyes a good cause justified many sorts and conditions of means.

All Saturday and half Sunday she had repressed the pangs of a healthy appetite, and had partaken only of the mutton-broth and splintered toast of invalidism. With a not ill-grounded dread lest Di's quick eyes should detect a subterfuge, she had gone so far as to take "heart-drops" three times a day from the hand of her granddaughter, and had been careful to have recourse to her tin of arrowroot biscuits only in the strictest privacy. But now that Sunday afternoon had come, she felt that she could safely relax into convalescence. The blinds were drawn up, and she was established in an armchair by the window.

"You seem really better," said Di. "I should hardly have known you had had one of your attacks. You generally look so pale afterwards."

"It has been very slight," said Mrs. Courtenay, blushing faintly. "I took it in time. I shall be able to travel tomorrow. I suppose you and Miss Fane went to church this morning?"

"Miss Fane would not go, but John and I did."

Mrs. Courtenay closed her eyes. Virtue may be its own reward, but it is gratifying when it is not the only one.

"Granny," said Di, suddenly, "I never knew, till John told me, that my mother had been engaged to his father."

"What has John been raking up those old stories for?"

"I don't think he raked up anything. He seemed to think I knew all about it. He was showing me my mother's miniature which he had found among his father's papers. I always supposed that the reason you never would talk about her was because you had felt her death too much."

"I was glad when she died," said Mrs. Courtenay.

"Was she unhappy, then? Father speaks of her rather sadly when he does mention her, as if he had been devoted to her, but she had not cared much for him, and had felt aggrieved at his being poor. He once said he had many faults, but that was the one she could never forgive. And he told me that when she died he was away on business, and she did not leave so much as a note or a message for him."

"It is quite true; she did not," said Mrs. Courtenay, in a suppressed voice. "I have never talked to you about your mother, Di, because I knew if I did I should prejudice you against your father, and I have no right to do that."

"I think," said Di, "that now I know a little you had better tell me the rest, or I shall only imagine things were worse than the reality."

So Mrs. Courtenay told her; told her of the little daughter who had been born to her in the first desolation of her widowhood, round whom she had wrapped in its entirety the love that many women divide between husband and sons and daughters.

She told Di of young Mr. Tempest, then just coming forward in political life, between whom and herself a friendship had sprung up in the days when he had been secretary to her brother, then in the Ministry. The young man was constantly at her house. He was serious, earnest, diffident, ambitious. Di reached the age of seventeen. Mrs. Courtenay saw the probable result, and hoped for it. With some persons to hope for anything is to remove obstacles from the path of its achievement.

"And yet, Di," said Mrs. Courtenay, "I can't reproach myself. They *were* suited to each other. It is as clear to me now as it was then. She did not love him, but I knew she would; and she had seen no one else. And he worshipped her. I threw them together, but I did not press her to accept him. She did accept him, and we went down to Overleigh together. She had—this room. I remembered it directly I saw it again. The engagement had not been formally given out, and the wedding was not to have been till the following spring on account of her youth. I think Mr. Tempest and I were the two happiest people in the world. I felt such entire confidence in him, and I was thankful she should not run the gauntlet of all that a beautiful girl is exposed to in society. She was as innocent as a child of ten, and as unconscious of her beauty— which, poor child! was very great.

"And then he—your father—came to Overleigh. Ten days afterwards they went away together, and I—I who had never been parted from her for a night since her birth—I never saw her again, except once across a room at a party, until four years afterwards, when her first child was born. I went to her then. I tried not to go, for she did not send for me; but she was the only child I had ever had, and I remembered my own loneliness when she was born. And the pain of staying away became too great, and I went. And—she was quite changed. She was not the least like my child, except about the eyes; and she was taller. Mr. Tempest never forgave her, because he loved her; but I forgave her at last, because I loved her more than he did. I saw her often after that. She used to tell me when your father would be away—and he was much away—and then I went to her. I would not meet *him*. We never spoke of her married life. It did not bear talking about, for she had really loved him, and it took him a long time to break her of it. We talked of the baby, and servants, and the price of things, for she was very poor. She was loyal to her husband. She never spoke about him except once. I remember that day. It was one of the last before she died. I found her sitting by the fire reading 'Consuelo.' I sat down by her, and we remained a long time without speaking. Often we sat in silence together. You have not come to the places on the road, my dear, when somehow words are no use any more, and the only poor comfort left is to be with some one who understands and says nothing. When you do, you will find silence one degree more bearable than speech.

"At last she turned to the book, and pointed to a sentence in it. I can see the page now, and the tall French print. 'Le caractère de cet homme entraîne les actions de sa vie. Jamais tu ne le changeras.'

"'I think that is true,' she said. 'Some characters seem to be settled beforehand, like a weathercock with its leaded tail. They cannot really change, because they are always changing. Nothing teaches them. Happiness, trouble, love, and hate bring no experience. They swing round to every wind that blows on one pivot always—themselves. There was a time when I am afraid I tired God with one name. "Jamais tu ne le changeras." No, never. One changes one's self. That is all. And now, instead of reproaching others, I reproach myself—bitterly— bitterly.'

"And she never begged my pardon. She once said, when I found her very miserable, that it was right that one who had made others suffer should suffer too. But those were the only times she alluded to the past, and I never did. I did not go to her to reproach her. The kind of people who are cut by reproaches have generally reproached themselves more harshly than any one else can. She had, I know. It would have been better if she had been less reserved, and if she could have taken more interest in little things. But she did not seem able to. Some women, and they are the happy ones, can comfort themselves in a loveless marriage with pretty note-paper, and tying up the legs of chairs with blue ribbon. She could not do that, and I think she suffered more in consequence. Those little feminine instincts are not given us for nothing.

"She never gave in until she knew she was dying. Then she tried to speak, but she sank rapidly. She said something about you, and then smiled when her voice failed her, and gave up the attempt. I think she was so glad to go that she did not mind anything else much. They held the baby to her as a last chance, and made it cry. Oh, Di, how you cried! And she trembled very much just for a moment, and then did not seem to take any more notice, though they put its little hand against her face. I think the end came all the quicker. It seemed too good to be true at first. . .

"Don't cry, my dear. Young people don't know where trouble lies. They think it is in external calamity, and sickness and death. But one does not find it so. The only real troubles are those which we cause each other through the affections. Those whom we love chasten us. I never shed a single tear for her when she died. There had been too many during her life, for I loved her better than anything in the world except my husband, who died when he was twenty-five and I was twenty-two. You often remind me of him. You are a very dear child to me. She said she hoped you would make up a little to me; and you have—not a little. I have brought you up differently. I saw my mistake with her. I sheltered her too much. I hope I have not run into the opposite extreme with you. I have allowed you more liberty than is usual, and I have encouraged

MARY CHOLMONDELEY

you to look at life for yourself, and to think and act for yourself, and learn by your own experience. And now go and bathe your eyes, and see if you can find me Fitzgerald's 'Omar Khayyám.' I think I saw it last in the morning-room. John and I were talking about it on Friday. I dare say he will know where it is."

X

"Si tu ne m'aimes pas moi je t'aime."

It was the time of afternoon tea. Miss Fane rolled off the sofa, and with the hydraulic sniff that can temporarily suspend the laws of nature, proceeded to pour out tea. Presently John and the dogs came in, and Di, who had found Mrs. Courtenay's book without his assistance, followed. John had not the art of small-talk. Miss Fane, who was in the habit of attempting the simultaneous absorption of liquid and farinaceous nutriment with a perseverance not marked by success, was necessarily silent, save when a carroway seed took the wrong turn. She seldom spoke in the presence of food, any more than others do in church. Few things apart from the Bull of Bashan commanded Miss Fane's undivided homage, but food never failed to, though it was reserved for plovers' eggs and the roe of the sturgeon to stir the latent emotion of her nature to its depths.

The dogs did their tricks. Lindo contrived to swallow all his own and half Fritz's portion, but, fortunately for the cause of justice, during a muffin-scattering choke on Lindo's part, Fritz's long red tongue was able to glean together fragments of what he imagined he had lost sight of for ever.

Di inquired whether there were evening service.

"Evening service at seven," said Miss Fane; "supper at quarter past eight."

"Do not go to church again," said John. "Come for a walk with me."

Di readily agreed. It was very pleasant to her to be with John. She had begun to feel that he and she were near akin. He was her only first cousin. The nearness of their relationship, accounting as it did in her mind for a growing intimacy, prevented any suspicion of that intimacy having sprung from another source.

They walked together through the forest in the still opal light of the waning day. Through the enlacing fingers of the trees the western sun made ladders of light. Breast-high among the bracken they went, disturbing the deer; across the heather, under the whisper of the pines, down to the steel-white reeded pools below.

They sat down on the trunk of a fallen tree, and a faint air came across the water from the trees on the further side, with a message to the trees on this. Neither talked much. The lurking sadness in the air just touched and soothed the lurking sadness in Di's mind. She did not notice John's silence, for he was often silent. She wound a blade of grass round her finger, and then unwound it again. John watched her do it. He had noticed before, as a peculiarity of Di's, not observable in other women, that whatever she did was interesting. She asked some question about the lower pool gleaming before them through the trunks of the trees, and he answered absently the reverse of what was true.

"Then perhaps we had better be turning back," she said.

He rose, and they went back another way, climbing slowly up and up by a little winding track through steepest forest places. Many burrs left their native stems to accompany them on their way. They showed to great advantage on Di's primrose cotton gown. At last they reached the top of the rocky ridge, and she sat down, out of breath, under a group of silver firs, and, taking off her gloves, began idly to pick the burrs one by one off the folds of her gown.

There was no hurry. He sat down by her, and watched her hands. She put the burrs on a stone near her.

They were sitting on the topmost verge of the crag, and the forest fell away in a shimmer of green beneath their feet to the pools below, and then climbed the other side of the valley and melted into the purple of the Overleigh and Oulston moors. Far away, the steep ridge of Hambleton and the headland of Sutton Brow stood out against the evening sky. Some Tempest of bygone days had dared to perpetrate a Greek temple in a clearing among the silver firs where they were sitting, but time had effaced that desecration of one of God's high places by transforming it to a lichened ruin of scattered stones. It was on one of these scattered stones that Di was raising a little cairn of burrs.

"Forty-one," she said at last. "You have not even begun your toilet yet, John."

No answer.

The sun was going down unseen behind a bar of cloud. A purple light was on the hills. Their faces showed that they saw the glory, but the twilight deepened over all the nearer land. Slowly the sun passed below the leaden bar, and looked back once more in full heaven, and drowned the world in light. Then with dying strength he smote the leaden bar to one long line of quivering gold, and sank dimly, redly, to the enshrouding west. All colour died. The hills were gone. The land lay dark. But far across the sky, from north to south, the line of light remained.

Di had watched the sunset alone. John had not seen it. His eyes were fixed on her calm face with the western glow upon it. She did not even notice that he was looking at her. One of her ungloved hands lay on her knee, so near to him yet so immeasurably far away. Could he stretch across the gulf to touch it? His expressionless face took some meaning at last. He leaned a little towards her, and laid his hand on hers.

She started violently, and dropped her sunset thoughts like a surprised child its flowers. Even a less vain man than John might have been cut to the quick by the sudden horrified bewilderment of her face, and of the dazzled light-blinded eyes which turned to peer at him with such unseeing distress.

"Oh, John!" she said, "not you;" and she put her other hand quickly for one second on his.

"Yes," he said, "that is just it."

Her mouth quivered painfully.

"I thought," she said, "we were—surely we *are* friends."

"No," said John, mastering the insane emotion which had leapt within him at the touch of her hand. "We never were, and we never shall be. I will have nothing to do with any friendship of yours. I'm not a beggar to be shaken off with coppers. I want everything or nothing."

Her manner changed. Her self-possession came back.

"I am sorry it must be nothing," she said gently, and she tried quietly but firmly to withdraw her hand.

His grasp on it tightened ever so little, but in an unmistakable manner, and she instantly gave up the attempt.

A splendid colour mounted slowly to her face. She drew herself up. Her lightning-bright intrepid eyes met his without flinching. They looked hard at each other in the waning light. Once again they seemed to measure swords as at the moment when they first met. Each felt the other formidable. There was no slightest shred of disguise between them.

There was a breathless silence.

Di went through a frightful revulsion of mind. The sunset and the light along the sky seemed to have betrayed her. These pleasant days had been in league against her. And now, goaded by the grasp of his hand on hers, her mind made one headlong rush at the goal towards which these accomplices had been luring her. Where were they leading her? Glamour dropped dead. Marriage remained. To become this man's wife; to merge her life in his; to give up everything into the hand that still held hers, the pressure of which was like a claim! He had only laid his hand upon her hand, but it seemed to her that he had laid it upon her soul. Her whole being rose up against him in sudden passionate antagonism horrible to bear. And all the time she knew instinctively that he was stronger than she.

John saw and understood that mental struggle almost with compassion, yet with an exultant sense of power over her. One conviction of the soul ever remains unshaken, that whom we understand is ours to have and to hold.

He deliberately released her hand. She did not make the slightest movement at regaining possession of it.

John wrestled with his voice, and forced it back, harsh and unfamiliar, to do his bidding.

"Di," he said, "I believe in truth even between men and women. I know what you are feeling about me at this moment. Well, that, even that, is better than a mistake; and you were making one. You had not the faintest suspicion of what has been the one object of my life since the day I first met you. The fault was mine, not yours. You could not see what was not on the surface to be seen. You would have gone on for the remainder of your natural life liking me in a way I—I cannot tolerate, if I had not—done as I did. I have not the power like some men of showing their feelings. I can't say the little things and do the little things that come to others by instinct. My instinct is to keep things to myself. I always have—till now."

Silence again; a silence which seemed to grow in a moment to such colossal dimensions that it was hardly credible a voice would have power to break it.

The twilight had advanced suddenly upon them. The young pheasants crept and called among the bracken. The night-birds passed swift and silent as sudden thoughts.

Di struggled with an unreasoning, furious anger, which, like a fiery horse, took her whole strength to control.

"I love you," said John, "and I shall go on loving you; and it is better you should know it."

And as he spoke she became aware that her anger was but a little thing beside his.

"What is the good of telling me," she said, "what I—what you know I—don't wish to hear?"

"What good?" said John, fiercely, his face working. "Great God! do you imagine I have put myself through the torture of making myself intolerable to you for no purpose? Do you think that you can dismiss me with a few angry words? What good? The greatest good in the world, which I would turn heaven and earth to win; which please God I will win."

Di became as white as he. He was too strong, this man, with his set face, and clenched trembling hand. She was horribly frightened, but she kept a brave front. She turned towards him and would have spoken, but her lips only moved.

"You need not speak," he said more gently. "You cannot refuse what you have not been asked for. I ask nothing of you. Do you understand? *Nothing.* When I ask it will be time enough to refuse. It is getting late. Let us go home."

XI

*"Those who have called the world profane have succeeded
in making it so."*

—J. H. Thom

The dreams of youth and love so frequently fade unfulfilled into "the light of common day," that it is a pleasure to be able to record that Madeleine saw the greater part of hers realized. She was received with what she termed *éclat* in her new neighbourhood. She remarked with complacency that everybody made much too much of her; that she had been quite touched by the enthusiasm of her reception. It was an ascertained fact that she would open the hunt ball with the President—a point on which her maiden meditation had been much exercised. The Duchess of Southark was among the first to call upon her. If that lady's principal motive in doing so was curiosity to see what kind of wife Sir Henry, or, as he was called in his own county, "the Solicitor-General," had at length procured, Madeleine was comfortably unaware of the fact. After that single call, the duration of which was confined to nine minutes, Madeleine spoke of the duchess as "kindness and cordiality itself."

She was invited to stay at Alvery, and afterwards to fill her house for a fancy ball, in October, in honour of the coming of age of Lord Elver, the duke's eldest son and chief thorn in the flesh; a young man of great promise "when you got to know him," as Madeleine averred, in which case few shared that advantage with her.

Other invitations poured in. The neighbourhood was really surprised at the grace and beauty of the bride—*considering*. It was soon rumoured that she was a saint as well; that she read prayers every morning at Cantalupe, which the stablemen were expected to attend; and that she taught in the Sunday school. The ardent young vicar of the parish, who had hitherto languished unsupported and misunderstood at Sir Henry's door, in the flapping draperies that so well become the Church militant, was enthusiastic about her. She was what he called "a true woman." Those who use this expression best know what it means. Processions, monster candles, crucifixes, and other ingredients of the pharmacopoeia of religion, swam before his mental vision. The little illegal side-altar, to which his two "crosses," namely, the churchwardens, had objected, but without which his soul could not rest in peace, was reinstated after a conversation with Madeleine. A promise on that lady's part to embroider an altar-cloth for the same was noised abroad.

Sir Henry was jubilant at his wife's popularity, which lost nothing from her own comments on it. Although nearly six months had elapsed since his marriage, he was still in a state of blind adoration—an adoration so blind that none of the ordinary events by which disillusion begins had any power to affect him.

He was not conscious that once or twice during the season in London he had been duped; that the jealousy which had flamed up so suddenly against Archie Tempest had more grounds than the single note he found in his wife's pocket, when in a fit of clumsy fondness he had turned out all its contents on her knee, solely to cogitate and wonder over them. He had a habit which tried her more than his slow faculties had any idea of, of examining Madeleine's belongings. His admiring curiosity had no suspicion in it. He liked to look at them solely because they were hers.

One day, shortly after their arrival at Cantalupe, when he was sitting in stolid inconvenient sympathy in her room, whither she had vainly retreated from him on the plea of a headache, he occupied himself by opening the drawers of her dressing-table one after the other, investigating with aboriginal interest small boxes of hairpins, curling-irons, and that various assortment of feminine gear which the hairdresser elegantly designates as "toilet requisites." At last he peeped into a box where, carefully arranged side by side, were the dearest of curls on tortoiseshell combs which he had often seen on his wife's head, and some smaller much becrimped bodies which filled him with wondering dislike—hair caricatured—*frisettes*.

"What *are* you doing?" said Madeleine, faintly, lying on the sofa with her back to him, holding her salts to her nose. Oh, if he would only go away, this large dreadful man, and leave her half an hour in peace, without hearing him clear his throat and sniff! On the contrary, he came and sat down by her chuckling, holding the curls and frisettes in his thick hands. She dropped her smelling-bottle and looked at them in an outraged silence. Was there, then, no sanctity, no privacy, in married life? Was everything about her to be made common and profane? She hated Sir Henry at that moment. As long as he had remained an invoice accompanying the arrival of coveted possessions, she had felt only a vague uneasiness about him. Directly he became, after the wedding, a heavy bill demanding cash payment "to account rendered," she had found that the marriage market is not a very cheap one after all.

Sir Henry was not the least chagrined at a discovery which might have tried the devotion of a more romantic lover.

"Why, Maddy," he said, "you are much too young and pretty to wear this sort of toggery. Leave 'em to the old dowagers, my dear;" and he dropped them into the fire.

She saw them burn, but she made no sign. Presently, however, when he had left her, she began to cry feebly; for even feminine fortitude has its limits. She was in reality satisfied with her marriage on the whole, though she was wiping away a few natural tears at this moment. But in this class of union there is generally one item which is found almost intolerable, namely, the husband. He really was the only drawback in this case. The furniture, the house, the southern aspect of the reception-rooms, everything else, was satisfactory. The park was handsomer than she had expected. And she had not known there was a silver dinner-service. It had been a love match as far as that was concerned. If Henry himself had only been different, Madeleine often reflected! If he had not been so red, and if he had had curly hair, or any hair at all! But whose lot has not some secret sorrow?

So Madeleine cried a little, and then wiped her eyes, and fell to thinking of her gown for the fancy ball at Alvery next month. She called to mind Di's height and regal figure with a pang. Perhaps, after all, she had been unwise in asking her dear friend, whom it would be difficult to eclipse, for this particular ball. Madeleine was under the impression that she was "having Di" out of good nature. This was her tame caged motive, kept for the inspection of others, especially of Di. Nevertheless there were others which were none the less genuine because they did not wait to have salt put on their tails, and invariably flew away at the approach of strangers.

Madeleine had not remembered to be good-natured until a certain obstacle to the completion of her ball-party, as she intended it, had arisen. The subject of young men was one which she had approached with the utmost delicacy; for, according to Sir Henry, all young men— at least, all good-looking ones—were fools and oafs whom he was not going to have wounding *his* birds. She agreed with him entirely, but reminded him of the duchess's solemn injunction to bring a party of even numbers.

Sir Henry at last gave in so far as to propose an elderly colonel. Madeleine in turn suggested Lord Hemsworth, who was allowed to be "a good sort," and was invited.

"Then we ought to have Miss Di Tempest, if we have Hemsworth," said Sir Henry, blowing like a grampus, as his manner was in moments of inspiration. "I'm quite a matchmaker now I'm married myself. Ask her to meet him, Maddy. She's your special pal, ain't she?"

Madeleine felt that she required strength greater than her own to bear with a person who says "ain't" and "a good sort," and designates a lady-friend as a "pal."

She pressed the silver knob of her pencil to her lips. There was, she remarked, no one whom she would like to have so much as Di; but Mr. Lumley was her next suggestion, and Sir Henry slapped himself on the leg, and said he was the very thing.

"We want one other man," said Madeleine, reflectively, after a few more had passed through the needle's eye of Sir Henry's criticism. "Let me see. Oh, there's Captain Tempest. He dances well."

"I won't have him," said Sir Henry at once, his eyes assuming their most prawnlike expression. "You may have his cousin if you like, the owl with the jowl, as Lumley calls him—Tempest of Overleigh."

"He is sure to be asked to the house itself, being a relation," said Madeleine, dropping the subject of Archie instantly. She did not recur to it again. But after their return home from the visit to the Hemsworths', at which she had met Di, she told her husband she had invited Di for the fancy ball, as he had wished her to do.

"Me?" said Sir Henry, reddening. "Lord bless me, what do I want with her?" And it was some time before he could be made to recollect what he had said nearly a month ago about asking Di to meet Lord Hemsworth.

"You forget your own wishes more quickly than I do," she said, putting her hand in his.

He did, by Jove, he did; and he bent over the little hand and kissed it, while she noticed how red the back of his neck was. When he became unusually apoplectic in appearance, as at this moment, Madeleine always caught a glimpse of herself as a young widow, and the idea softened her towards him. If he were once really gone, without any possibility of return, she felt that she could have said, "Poor Henry!"

"The only awkward part about having asked Di," said Madeleine, after a pause, "is that Mrs. Courtenay does not allow her to visit alone."

"Well, my dear, ask Mrs. Courtenay. I like her. She has always been very civil to me."

She had indeed.

"I don't like her very much myself," said Madeleine. "She is so worldly; and I think she has made Di so. And she would be the only older person. You know you decided it should be a *young* party this time. It is very awkward Di not being able to come alone, at her age. She evidently wanted me to ask her brother to bring her, who, she almost told me, was anxious to meet Miss Crupps, the carpet heiress; but I did not quite like to ask him without your leave."

"Ask him by all means," said Sir Henry, entirely oblivious of his former refusal. "After that poor little girl, is he? Well, we'll sit out together, and watch the lovemaking, eh?"

Madeleine experienced a tremor wholly unmixed with compunction at gaining her point. She would have been aware, if she had read it in a book, that any one who had acted as she had done, had departed from the truth in suggesting that Di could not visit alone. She would have felt also that it was reprehensible in the extreme to invite to her house a man who had secretly, though not without provocation, made love to her since her marriage.

But just in the same way that what we regret as conceit in others we perceive to be a legitimate self-respect in ourselves, so Madeleine, as on previous occasions, "saw things very differently."

She was incapable of what she called "a low view." She had often "frankly" told herself that she took a deep interest in Archie. She had put his initials against some of her favourite passages in her morocco manual. She prayed for him on his birthday, and sometimes, when she woke up and looked at her luminous cross at night. She believed that she had a great influence for good over him which it was her duty to use. She was sincere in her wish to proselytize, but the sincerity of an insincere nature is like the kernel of a deaf nut; a mere shred of undeveloped fibre. What Madeleine wished to believe became a reality to her. Gratification of a very common form of vanity was a religious duty. She wrote to Archie with a clear conscience, and, when he accepted, had a box of autumn hats down from London.

XII

"Oh, Love's but a dance,
Where Time plays the fiddle!
See the couples advance,—
Oh, Love's but a dance!
A whisper, a glance,—
'Shall we twirl down the middle?'
Oh, Love's but a dance,
Where Time plays the fiddle!"

—Austin Dobson

It was the night of the fancy dress ball.

The carriages were already at the door, and could be heard crunching round and round upon the gravel. Sir Henry, all yeomanry red and gold, was having the bursting hooks and eyes at his throat altered in his wife's room. Something had to be done to his belt, too. At last he went blushing downstairs before the cluster of maids with his sword under his arm. The guests, who had gone up to dress after an early dinner, were reappearing by degrees. Lord Hemsworth, in claret-coloured coat and long Georgian waistcoat and tie-wig, came down, handsome and quiet as usual, with his young sister, whose imagination had stopped short at cotton-wool snowflakes on a tulle skirt. An impecunious young man in a red hunt coat rushed in, hooted on the stairs by Mr. Lumley for having come without a wedding garment. Madeleine sailed down in Watteau costume. Two married ladies followed in Elizabethan ones. Presently Archie made his appearance, a dream of beauty in white satin from head to foot, as the Earl of Leicester, his curling hair, fair to whiteness, looking like the wig which it was not. Every one, men and women alike, turned to look at him; and Mr. Lumley, following in harlequin costume, was quite overlooked, until he turned a somersault, saying, "Here we are again!" whereat Sir Henry instantly lost a hook and eye in a cackle of admiration.

"We ought to be starting," said Madeleine. "We are all down now."

"Not quite all," said Mr. Lumley, sinking on one knee, as Di came in crowned and sceptred, in a green and silver gown edged with ermine.

Lord Hemsworth drew in his breath. Madeleine's face fell.

"Good gracious, Di!" she said, with a very thin laugh. "This is dressing up indeed!"

The party, already late, got under way, Mr. Lumley, of course, calling in falsetto to each carriage in turn not to go without him, and then refusing to enter any vehicle in which, as he expressed it, Miss Tempest was not already an ornamental fixture.

"This is getting beyond a joke," said Lord Hemsworth, as a burst of song issued from the carriage leaving the door, and the lamp inside showed Di's crowned head, Sir Henry's violet complexion, and the gutta-percha face of the warbling Mr. Lumley.

Di sat very silent in her corner, and after a time, as the drive was a long one, the desultory conversation dropped, and Sir Henry fell into a nasal slumber, from which, as Madeleine was in another carriage, no one attempted to rouse him.

Di shut her eyes as a safeguard against being spoken to, and her mind went back to the subject which had been occupying much of her thoughts since the previous evening, namely, the fact that she should meet John at the ball. She knew he would be there, for she had seen him get out of the train at Alvery station the afternoon before.

As she had found on a previous occasion, when they had suddenly been confronted with each other at Doncaster races, to meet John had ceased to be easy to her—became more difficult every time.

Possibly John had found it as difficult to speak to Di as she had found it to receive him. But however that may have been, it would certainly have been impossible to divine that he was awaiting the arrival of any one tonight with the faintest degree of interest. He did not take his stand where it would be obvious that he could command a view of the door through which the guests entered. He had seen others do that on previous occasions, and had observed that the effect was not happy. Nevertheless, from the bay window where he was watching the dancing, the guests as they arrived were visible to him.

"He! he!" said Lord Frederick, joining him. "Such a row in the men's cloak-room! Young Talbot has come as Little Bo-Peep, and the men would not have him in their room; said it was improper, and tried to hustle him into the ladies' room. He is still swearing in his ulster in the passage. Why aren't you dancing?"

"I can't. My left arm is weak since I burned it in the spring."

"Well," rejoined Lord Frederick, who as a French marquis, with cane and snuff-box, was one of the best-dressed figures in the room, "you don't miss much. Onlookers see most of the game. Look at that fairy twirling with the little man in the kilt. Their skirts are just the same length. The worst part of this species of entertainment is that one cuts one's dearest friends. Some one asked me just now whether the 'Mauvaise Langue' was here tonight. Did not recognize the wolf in sheep's clothing. More arrivals. A Turk and a Norwegian peasant, and a man in a smock frock. And—now—what on earth is the creature in blue and red, with a female to match?"

"Otter-hounds," suggested John.

"Is it possible? Never saw it before. There goes Freemantle as a private in the Blues, saluting as he is introduced, instead of bowing. What a fund of humour the youth of the present day possess! Who is that bleached earwig he is dancing with?"

"I think it is Miss Crupps, the heiress."

"H'm! Might have known it. That is the sort of little pill that no one takes unless it is very much gilt. Here comes the Verelst party at last. Lady Verelst has put herself together well. I would not mind buying her at my valuation and selling her at her own. She hates me, that little painted saint. I always cultivate a genuine saint. I make a point of it. They may look deuced dowdy down here—they generally do, though I believe it is only their wings under their clothes; but they will probably form the aristocracy up yonder, and it is as well to know them beforehand. But Lady Verelst is a sham, and I hate shams. I am a sham myself. He! he! When last I met her she talked pious, and implied intimacy with the Almighty, till at last I told her that it was the vulgarest thing in life to be always dragging in your swell acquaintance. He! he! I shall go and speak to her directly she has done introducing her party. Mrs. Dundas—and—I don't know the other woman. Who is the girl in white?"

"Miss Everard."

"What! Hemsworth's sister? Then he will be here too, probably. I like Hemsworth. There's no more harm in that young man than there is in a tablet of Pears' soap. A crowned head next. Why, it's Di Tempest. By—she is handsomer every time I see her! If that girl knew how to advertise herself, she might become a professional beauty."

"Heaven forbid!" said John, involuntarily, watching Di with the intense concentration of one who has long pored over memory's dim portrait, and now corrects it by the original.

Lord Frederick did not see the look. For once something escaped him. He too was watching Di, who with the remainder of the Verelst party was being drifted towards them by a strong current of fresh arrivals in their wake.

The usual general recognition and non-recognition peculiar to fancy balls ensued, in which old acquaintances looked blankly at each other, gasped each other's names, and then shook hands effusively; amid which one small greeting between two people who had seen and recognized each other from the first instant took place, and was over in a moment.

"I cannot recognize any one," said Di, her head held a shade higher than usual, looking round the room, and saying to herself, "He would not have spoken to me if he could have helped it."

"Some of the people are unrecognizable," said John, with originality equal to hers, and stung by the conviction that she had tried to avoid shaking hands with him.

The music struck up suddenly as if it were a new idea.

"Are you engaged for this dance?" said Mr. Lumley, flying to her side.

"Yes," said Di with decision.

"So am I," said he, and was gone again.

"Dance?" said a *Sporting Times*, rushing up in turn, and shooting out the one word like a pea from a pop-gun.

"Thanks, I should like to, but I am not allowed," said Di. "My grandmother is very particular. If you had been the *Sunday at Home* I should have been charmed."

The "Pink 'un" expostulated vehemently, and said he would have come as the *Church Times* if he had only known; but Di remained firm.

John walked away, pricking himself with his little dagger, the sheath of which had somehow got lost, and watched the knot of men who gradually gathered round Di. Presently she moved away with Lord Frederick in the direction of Madeleine, who had installed herself at the further end of the room among the *fenders*, as our latter-day youth gracefully designates the tiaras of the chaperones.

John was seized upon and introduced to an elderly minister with an order, who told him he had known his father, and began to sound him as to his political views. John, who was inured to this form of address, answered somewhat vaguely, for at that moment Di began to dance. She had a partner worthy of her in the shape of a sedate young Russian, resplendent in the white-and-gold uniform of the imperial *Gardes à cheval*.

Lord Frederick gravitated back to John. No young man among the former's large acquaintance was given the benefit of his experience more liberally than John. Lord Frederick took an interest in him which was neither returned nor repelled.

"Elver is down at last," he said. "It seems he had to wait till his mother's maid could be spared to sew him into his clothes. It is a pity you are not dancing, John. You might dance with your cousin. She and Prince Blazinski made a splendid couple. What a crowd of moths round that candle! I hope you are not one of them. It is not the candle that gets singed. Another set of arrivals. Look at Carruthers coming in with a bouquet. Cox of the *Monarch* still, I suppose. He can't dance with it; no, he has given it to his father to hold. Supper at last. I must go and take some one in."

John took Miss Everard in to supper. In spite of her brother's and Di's efforts, she had not danced much. She did not find him so formidable as she expected, and before supper was over had told him all about her doves, and how the grey one sat on her shoulder, and how she loved poetry better than anything in the world, except "Donovan." John proved a sympathetic listener. He in his turn confided to her his difficulty in conveying soup over the edge of his ruff; and after providing her with a pink cream, judging with intuition unusual to his sex that a pink cream is ever more acceptable to young ladyhood than a white one, he took her back to the ball-room. The crowd had thinned. The kilt and the fairy and a few other couples were careering wildly in open space. John looked round in vain for Madeleine, to whom he could deliver up his snowflake, and catching sight of Mrs. Dundas on the chaperon's dais, made in her direction. Di, who was sitting with Mrs. Dundas, suddenly perceived them coming up the room together. What was it, what could it be, that indescribable feeling that went through her like a knife as she saw Miss Everard on John's arm, smiling at something he was saying to her? Had they been at supper together all this long time?

"What a striking face your cousin has!" said Mrs. Dundas. "I do not wonder that people ask who he is. I used to think him rather alarming, but Miss Everard does not seem to find him so."

"He can be alarming," said Di, lightly. "You should see him when he is discussing his country's weal, or welcoming his guests."

"Why did I say that?" she asked herself the moment the words were out of her mouth. "It's ill-natured and it's not true. Why did I say it?"

Mrs. Dundas laughed.

"It's the old story," she said. "One never sees the virtues of one's relations. Now, as he is not *my* first cousin, I am able to perceive that he is a very remarkable person, with a jaw that means business. There is tenacity and strength of purpose in his face. He would be a terrible person to oppose."

Di laughed, but she quailed inwardly.

"I am told he is immensely run after," continued Mrs. Dundas. "I dare say you know," in a whisper, "that the duchess wants him for Lady Alice, and they *say* he has given her encouragement, but I don't believe it. Anyhow, her mother is making her read up political economy and Bain, poor girl. It must be an appalling fate to marry a great intellect. I am thankful to say Charlie only had two ideas in his head; one was chemical manures, and the other was to marry me. Well, Miss Everard. Lady Verelst is at supper, but I will extend a wing over you till she returns. Here comes a crowd from the supper-room. Now, Miss Tempest, do go in. You owned you were hungry a minute ago, though you refused the tragic entreaties of the Turk and the stage villain."

"I was afraid," said Di; "for though the villain is my esteemed friend in private life, I know his wide hat or the turban of the infidel would catch in my crown and drag it from my head. I wish I had not come so regally. I enjoyed sewing penny rubies into my crown, and making the ermine out of an old black muff and some rabbit-fur; but—uneasy is the head that wears a crown."

"I am very harmless and inaggressive," said John, in his most level voice. "The only person I prick with my little dagger is myself. If you are hungry, I think you may safely go in to supper with me."

"Very well," said Di, rising and taking his offered arm. "I am too famished to refuse."

"She is taller than he is," said Miss Everard, as they went together down the rapidly filling room.

"No, my dear; it is only her crown. They are exactly the same height."

No one is more useful in everyday life than the man, seldom a rich man, who can command two sixpences, and can in an emergency produce a threepenny bit and some coppers. The capitalist with his halfcrown is nowhere—for the time.

In conversation, small change is everything. Who does not know the look of the clever man in society, conscious of a large banking account, but uncomfortably conscious also that, like Goldsmith, he has not a sixpence of ready money? And who has not envied the fool jingling his few halfpence on a tombstone or anywhere, to the satisfaction of himself and every one else?

Thrice-blessed is small-talk.

But between some persons it is an impossibility, though each may have a very respectable stock of his own. Like different coinages, they will not amalgamate. Di and John had not wanted any in talking to each other—till now. And now, in their hour of need, to the alarm of both, they found they were destitute. After a short mental struggle they succumbed into the abyss of the commonplace, the only neutral ground on which those who have once been open and sincere with each other can still meet—to the certain exasperation of both.

John was dutifully attentive. He procured a fresh bottle of champagne for her, and an unnibbled roll, and made suitable remarks at intervals; but her sense of irritation increased. Something in his manner annoyed her. And yet it was only the same courteous, rather expressionless manner that she remembered was habitual to him towards others. Now that it was gone she realized that there had once been a subtle difference in his voice and bearing to herself. She felt defrauded of she knew not what, and the wing of cold pheasant before her loomed larger and larger, till it seemed to stretch over the whole plate. Why on earth had she said she was hungry? And why had he brought her to the large table, where there was so much light and noise, and where she was elbowed by an enormous hairy Buffalo Bill, when she had seen as she came in that one of the little tables for two was at that instant vacant? She forgot that when she first caught sight of it she had said within herself that she would never forgive him if he had the bad taste to entrap her into a *tête-à-tête* by taking her there.

But he had shown at once that he had no such intention. Was this dignified, formal man, with his air of distinction, and his harsh immobile face, and his black velvet dress,—was this stranger really the John with whom she had been on such easy terms six weeks ago; the John who, pale and determined, had measured swords with her in the dusk of a September evening?

And as she sat beside him in the brilliant light, amid the Babel of tongues, a voice in her heart said suddenly, "That was not the end; that was only the beginning—only the beginning."

Her eyes met his, fixed inquiringly upon her. He was only offering her some grapes, but it appeared to her that he must have heard the words, and a sense of impotent terror seized her, as the terror of one who, wrestling for his life, finds at the first throw that he is overmatched.

MARY CHOLMONDELEY

She rose hastily, and asked to go back to the ball-room. He complied at once, but did not speak. They went, a grave and silent couple, through the hall and down the gallery.

"Have I annoyed you?" he said at last, as they neared the ball-room.

She did not answer.

"I mean, have I done anything more that has annoyed you?"

"Nothing more, thanks."

"I am glad," said John. "I feared I had. Of course, I would not have asked you to go in to supper with me if Mrs. Dundas had not obliged me. I intended to ask you to do so, when you could have made some excuse for refusing if you did not wish it. I was sorry to force your hand."

"You will never do that," said Di, to her own astonishment. It seemed to her that she was constrained by a power stronger than herself to defy him.

She felt him start.

"We will take another turn," he said instantly; and before she had the presence of mind to resist, they had turned and were walking slowly down the gallery again between the rows of life-size figures of knights and chargers in armour, which loomed gigantic in the feeble light. A wave of music broke in the distance, and the few couples sitting in recesses rose and passed them on their way back to the ball-room, leaving the gallery deserted.

A peering moon had laid a faint criss-cross whiteness on the floor.

The place took a new significance.

Each was at first too acutely conscious of being alone with the other to speak. She wondered if he could feel how her hand trembled on his arm, and he whether it was possible she did not hear the loud hammering of his heart. Either would have died rather than have betrayed their emotion to the other.

"You tell me I shall never force your hand," he repeated slowly at last. "No, indeed, I trust I never shall. But when, may I ask, have I shown any intention of doing so?"

Di had put herself so palpably and irretrievably in the wrong, that she had no refuge left but silence. She was horror-struck by his repetition of the words which her lips, but surely not she herself, had spoken.

"If you ever marry me," said John, "it will be of your own accord. If you don't, we shall both miss happiness—you as well as I, for we are meant for each other. Most people are so constituted that they can marry whom they please, but you and I have no choice. We have a claim upon each other. I recognize yours, with thankfulness. I did not know life held anything so good. You ignore mine, and wilfully turn away from it. I don't wonder. I am not a man whom any woman would choose, much less *you*. It is natural on your part to dislike me—at first. In the mean while you need not distress yourself by telling me so. I am under no delusion on that point."

His voice was firm and gentle. If it had been cold, Di's pride would have flamed up in a moment. As it was, its gentleness, under great and undeserved provocation, made her writhe with shame. She spoke impulsively.

"But I *am* distressed, I can't help being so, at having spoken so harshly; no—*worse* than harshly, so unpardonably."

"There is no question of pardon between you and me," said John, turning to look at her with the grave smile that seemed for a moment to bring back her old friend to her; but only for a moment. His eyes contradicted it. "I know you have never forgiven me for telling you that I loved you, but nevertheless you see I have not asked pardon yet, though I had not intended to annoy you by speaking of it again—at present."

"No," said Di, eagerly. "But that is just it. It was my own fault this time. I brought it on myself. But—but I can't help knowing—I feel directly I see you that you are still thinking of it. And then I become angry, and say dreadful things like—"

"Exactly," said John, nodding.

"Because I—not only because I am ill-tempered, but because though I do like being liked, still I don't want you or any one to make a mistake, or go on making it. It doesn't seem fair."

"Not if it really is a mistake."

"It is in this instance."

"Not on my part."

There was a short silence. Di felt as if she had walked up against a stone wall.

"John," she said with decision. "Believe me. I sometimes mean what I say, and I mean it now. I really and truly am a person who knows my own mind."

"So do I," said John.

Rather a longer silence.

"And—and oh, John! Don't you see how wretched, how foolish it is, our being on these absurd formal terms? Have you forgotten what friends we used to be? I have not. It makes me angry still when I think how you have taken yourself away for nothing, and how all the pleasure is gone out of meeting you or talking to you. I don't think you half knew how much I liked you."

"Di," said John, stopping short, and facing her with indignation in his eyes, "I desire that you will never again tell me you *like* me. I really cannot stand it. Let us go back to the ball-room."

XIII

*"Ah, man's pride
Or woman's—which is greatest?"*

—E. B. Browning

D i," said Archie, sauntering up to her on the terrace at Cantalupe, where she was sitting the morning after the ball, and planting himself in front of her, as he had a habit of doing before all women, so as to spare them the trouble of turning round to look at him, "I can't swallow little Crupps."

"No one wants you to," said Di. "If you don't like her, you had better leave her alone."

"Women are not meant to be let alone," said Archie, yawning, "except the ugly ones."

"Well, Miss Crupps is not pretty."

"No, but she is gilt up to the eyes. Poor eyes, too, and light eyelashes. I could not marry light eyelashes."

"I am glad to hear it."

"Oh! I know you don't care a straw whether I settle well or not. You never have cared. Women are all alike. There's not a woman in the world, or a man either, who cares a straw what becomes of me."

"Or you what becomes of them."

"John's just as bad as the rest," continued the victim of a worldly age. "And John and I were great chums in old days. But it is the way of the world."

Men who attract by a certain charm of manner which the character is unable to bear out, who make unconscious promises to the *hope* of others without ability to keep them, are ever those who complain most loudly of the fickleness of women, of the uncertainty of friendship, of their loveless lot.

Di did not answer. Any allusion to John, even the bare mention of his name, had become of moment to her. She never by any chance spoke of him, neither did she ever miss a word that was said about him in her presence; and often raged inwardly at the ruthless judgments and superficial criticisms that were freely passed upon him by his contemporaries, and especially his kinsfolk. From a very early date in this world's history, ability has been felt to be distressing in its own country, especially in the country. If a clever man would preserve unflawed the amulet of humility, let him at intervals visit among his country cousins. John had not many of these invaluable relations; but, happily for him, he had contemporaries who did just as well—men who, when he was mentioned with praise in their hearing, could always break in that they had known him at Eton, and relate how he had over-eaten himself at the sock-shop.

"One thing I am determined I won't do," continued Archie, "and that is marry poverty, like the poor old governor. He has often talked about it, and what a grind it was, with the tears in his eyes."

"What has turned your mind to marriage on this particular morning, of all others?"

"I don't know, unless it is the vision of little Crupps. I suppose I shall come to something of that kind some day. If it isn't her it will be something like her. One must live. You are on the look out for money, too, Di, so you need not be so disdainful. You can't marry a poor man."

"They don't often ask me," said Di. "I fancy I look more expensive to keep up than I really am."

"Ah! here comes Lady Verelst," said Archie, patronizingly. "I'd marry *her*, now, if she were a rich widow. I would indeed. She is putting up her red parasol. Quite right. She has not your complexion, Di, nor mine either."

Archie got up as Madeleine came towards them, and offered her his chair. Archie had several cheap effects. To offer a chair with a glance and a smile was one of them. Perhaps he could not help it if the glance suggested unbounded homage, if the smile conveyed an admiration as concentrated as Liebig's extract. His faithful, tender eyes could wear the sweetest, the saddest, or the most reproachful expression to order. Every slight passing feeling was magnified by the beauty of the face that reflected it into a great emotion. He felt almost nothing, but he appeared to feel a great deal. A man who possesses this talisman is very dangerous.

Poor Madeleine, confident of her appearance in her new Cresser garment, with its gold-flowered waistcoat, firmly believed, as Archie silently pushed forward the chair, that she had inspired—had been so unfortunate as to inspire—"une grande passion malheureuse." Almost all Archie's lovemaking, and that is saying a good deal, was speechless. He could look unutterable things, but he had not, as he himself expressed it, "the gift of the gab."

Madeleine was sorry for him, but she could not allow him to remain enraptured beside her in full view of Sir Henry's study windows.

"How delicious it is here!" she said, after dismissing him to the billiard-room. "I never lie in bed after a ball, do you, Di? I seem to crave for the sunshine and the face of nature after all the glitter and the worldliness of a ball-room."

"I don't find ball-rooms more worldly than other places—than this bench, for instance."

"Now, how strange that is of you, Di! This spot is quite sacred to *me*. I come and read here."

Madeleine had, by degrees, sanctified all the seats in the garden; had taken the impious chill even off the iron ones, by reading her little manuals on each in turn.

"It was here," continued Madeleine, "that I persuaded dear Fred to go into the Church. It was settled he was to be a clergyman ever since he had that slight stroke as a boy; but when he went to college he must have got into a bad set, for he said he did not think he had a vocation. And mother—you know what mother is—did not like to press it, and the whole thing was slipping through, when I had him to stay here, and talked to him very seriously, and explained that a living in the family *was* the call."

"Madeleine," said Di, rising precipitately, "it is getting late. I must fly and pack."

If she stayed another moment she knew she should inevitably say something that would scandalize Madeleine.

"And I did not say it," she said with modest triumph that evening, as she sat in her grandmother's room before going to bed; having rejoined her at Garstone, a relation's house, whither Mrs. Courtenay had preceded her. "I refrained even from bad words. Granny, you know everything: why is it that the people who shock me so dreadfully, like Madeleine, are just the very ones who are shocked at me? You are not. All the really good earnest people I know are not. But *they* are. What is the matter with them?"

"Oh, my dear, what is the matter with all insincere people? It is only one of the symptoms of an incurable disease."

"But the being shocked is genuine. They really feel it. There is something wrong somewhere, but I don't know where it is."

"It is not hard to find, Di," said Mrs. Courtenay, sadly; "and it is not worth growing hot about. You are only running a little tilt against religiosity. Most young persons do. But it is not worth powder and shot.

Keep your ammunition for a nobler enemy. There is plenty of sin in the world. Strike at that whenever you can, but don't pop away at shadows."

"Ah! but, granny, these people do such harm. They bring such discredit on religion. That is what enrages me."

"My dear, you are wrong; they bring discredit upon nothing but their own lamentable caricatures of holy things. These people are solemn warnings—danger-signals on the broad paths of religiosity, which, remember, are very easy walking. There's no life so easy. The religious life is hard enough, God knows. Providence put those people there to make their creed hideous, and they do it. Upon my word, I think your indignation against them is positively unpardonable."

Di was silent.

"You don't mind being disliked by these creatures, do you, Di?"

"Yes, granny, I think I do. I believe, if I only knew the truth about myself, I want every one to like me; and it ruffles me because they make round eyes, and don't like me when their superiors often do."

"Mere pride and love of admiration on your part, my dear. You have no business with them. To be liked and admired by certain persons is a stigma in itself. Look at the kind of mediocrity and feebleness they set on pedestals, and be thankful you don't fit into their mutual admiration societies. That 'like cleaves to like,' is a saying we seldom get to the bottom of. These unfortunates find blots, faults, evil, in everything, especially everything original, because they are sensitive to blots and faults. They commit themselves out of their own mouths. 'Those that seek shall find,' is especially true of the fault-finders. The truth and beauty which others receptive of truth and beauty perceive, escape them. Good nature sees good in others. The reverent impute reverence. This false reverence finds irreverence, as a mean nature takes for granted a low motive in its fellow. Oh dear me, Di! Have I expended on you for years the wisdom of a Socrates and a Solomon, that at one and twenty you should need to be taught your alphabet? Go to bed and pray for wisdom, instead of complaining of the lack of it in others."

Di had had but little leisure lately, and the unbounded leisure of her long visit at Garstone came as a relief.

"I shall have time to think here," she said to herself, as she looked out the first morning over the grey park and lake distorted by the little panes of old glass of her low window.

Two very old people lived at Garstone, who regarded their niece, Mrs. Courtenay, as still quite a young person, in spite of her tall granddaughter. Time seemed to have forgotten the dear old couple, and they in turn had forgotten it. It never mattered what time of day it was. Nothing depended on the hour. In the course of the morning the butler would open both the folding doors at the end of the long "parlour" leading to the chapel, and would announce, "Prayers are served." Long prayers they were. Long meals were served too, with long intervals between them, during which, in spite of a week of heavy rain, Di escaped regularly into the gardens and so away to the park. The house oppressed her. She was restless and ill at ease. She was never missed because she was never wanted; and she wandered for hours in the park, listening to the low cry of the deer, standing on the bridge over the artificial 1745 lake, or pacing mile on mile a sheltered path under the park wall. The thinking for which she had such ample opportunity did not come off. It shirked regularly. A certain vague trouble of soul was upon her, like the unrest of nature at the spring of the year. And day after day she watched the autumn leaves drop from the trees into the water, and there was a great silence in her heart, and underneath the silence a fear—or was it a hope? She knew not.

There was one subject to which Di's thoughts returned, and ever returned, in spite of herself. John was that subject. Gradually, as the days wore on, her shamed remorse at having wounded him gave place to the old animosity against him. She had never been angry with any of her numerous lovers before. She had, on the contrary, been rather sorry for them. But she was desperately angry with John. It seemed to her—why she would have been at a loss to explain—that he had taken a very great liberty in venturing to love her, and in daring to assert that they were suited to other.

She went through silent paroxysms of rage against him, sitting on a fallen tree among the bracken with clenched hands. Her sense of his growing power over her, over her thought, over her will, was intolerable. Why so fierce? why such a fool? she asked herself over and over again. He could not marry her against her will. Indeed, he had said he did not want to. Why, then, all this silly indignation about nothing? There was no answer until one day Mrs. Courtenay happened to mention to Mrs. Garstone, in her presence, the probability of John's eventually marrying Lady Alice Fane—"a very charming and suitable person," etc.

Then suddenly it became clear to Di that, though she would never marry him herself, the possibility of his marrying any one else was not to be borne for a moment. John, of course, was to—was to remain unmarried all his life. Her sense of the ludicrous showed her in a lightning-flash where she stood.

To discover a new world is all very well for people like Columbus, who want to find one. But to discover a new world by mistake when quite content with the old one, and to be swept towards it uncertain of your reception by the natives assembling on the beach, is another thing altogether. For the second time in her life Di was frightened.

"Then all these horrible feelings are being in love," she said to herself, with a sense of stupefaction. "This is what other people have felt for me, and I treated it as of little consequence. This is what I have read about, and sung about, and always rather wished to feel. I am in love with John. Oh, I hope to God he will never find it out!"

Probably no man will ever understand the agonies of humiliation, of furious unreasoning antagonism, which a proud woman goes through when she becomes aware that she is falling in love. Pride and love go as ill together in the beginning as they go exceeding well together later on. To be loved is incense at first, until the sense of justice—fortunately rare in women—is aroused. "Shall I take all, and give nothing?"

Pride, often a very tender pride for the lover himself, asks that question. Directly it is asked the battle begins.

"I will not give less than all. How *can* I give all?" The very young are spared the conflict, because the future husband is regarded only as the favoured ball-partner, the perpetual admirer of a new existence. But women who know something of life—of the great demands of marriage—of the absolute sacrifice of individual existence which it involves—when they begin to tremble beneath the sway of a deep human passion suffer much, fear greatly until the perfect love comes that casts out fear.

Some natures, and very lovable they are, give all, counting not the cost. Others, a very few, count the cost and then give all.

Di was one of these.

XIV

*"Austerity in women is sometimes the accompaniment of a rare power
of loving. And when it is so their attachment is strong as death;
their fidelity as resisting as the diamond."*

—AMIEL

The newspapers arrived at tea-time at Garstone. Every afternoon Mrs. Garstone and Mrs. Courtenay drove out along the straight high-road to D— to fetch the papers and post the letters; four miles in and four miles out; the grey pair one day and the bays the next, in the old yellow chariot. It was the rule of the house. And after tea and rusks, and a poached egg under a cover for Mr. Garstone, that gentleman read the papers aloud in a voice that trembled and halted like the spinnet in the southern parlour.

"Is Parliament prorogued yet?" Mrs. Garstone asked regularly every afternoon.

Mr. Garstone, without answering, struck his key-note at the births, and quavered slowly through the marriages and deaths. Before he had arrived on this particular afternoon at the fact that Princess Beatrice had walked with Prince Henry of Battenberg, Mrs. Garstone was already nodding between her little rows of white curls. Mrs. Courtenay was awake, but she looked too solemnly attentive to continue in one stay.

"The remains of the Dean of Gloucester," continued Mr. Garstone, "will be interred at Gloucester Cathedral on Friday next."

The information was received, like most sedatives, without comment.

Latest intelligence. Colliery explosion at Snarley.

"Di, has not John coal-pits at Snarley?" asked Mrs. Courtenay, becoming suddenly wide awake.

"Yes," said Di.

"Explosion of fire-damp," continued Mr. Garstone, slower than ever. "No particulars known. Great loss of life apprehended. Mr. Tempest of Overleigh, to whom the mine belonged, instantly left Godalmington Court, where he was the guest of Lord Carradock, and proceeded at once to the spot, where he organized a rescue party led by himself. Mr. Tempest was the first to descend the shaft. The gravest anxiety was felt respecting the fate of the rescuing party. Vast crowds assembled at the pit's mouth. No further news obtainable up to date of going to press."

Mrs. Courtenay looked at Di.

"He must be mad to have gone down himself," she said agitatedly. "What could he possibly do there?"

"His duty," said Di; and she got up and left the room. How could any one exist in that hot close atmosphere? She was suffocating.

The hall was cold enough. She shivered as she crossed it, and went up the white shallow stairs to her own room, where a newly lit fire was spluttering. She knelt down before it and pushed a burning stick further between the bars, blackening her fingers. It would catch the paper at the side now.—John had gone down the shaft.—Yes, it would catch. The paper stretched itself and flared up. She went and stood by the window.

"John has gone down," she said, half aloud. Her heart was quite numb. Only her body seemed to care. Her limbs trembled, and she sat down on the narrow window seat, her hands clutching the dragon hasp of the window, her eyes looking absently out.

There was a fire in the west. Upon the dreaming land the dreaming mist lay pale. The sentinel trees stood motionless and dark, each folded in his mantle of grey. Only the water waked and knew its God. And far across the sleeping land, in the long lines of flooded meadow, the fire trembled on the upturned face of the water, like the reflection of the divine glory in a passionate human soul.

It passed. The light throbbed and died, but Di did not stir. And as she sat motionless, her mind slipped sharp and keen out of its lethargy and restlessness, like a sword from its scabbard.

"Now, at this moment, is he alive or dead?"

And at the thought of death, that holiest minister who waits on life, all the rebellious anger, all the nameless fierce resentment against her lover—because he *was* her lover—fell from her like a garment, died down like Peter's lies at the glance of Christ.

The evening deepened its mourning for the dead day. One star shook in the empty sky, above the shadow and the mist.

"Love the gift is Love the debt." Di perceived that at last. A great shame fell upon her for the divided feelings, the unconscious struggle with her own heart, of the last few weeks. It appeared to her now ignoble, as all elementary phases of feeling, all sheaths of deep affections must appear, in the moment when that which they enfolded and protected grows beyond the narrow confines which it no longer needs.

If he is dead? Di twisted her hands.

Who, one of two that have loved and stood apart has escaped that pang, if death intervene? A moment ago and the world was full of messengers waiting to speed between them at the slightest bidding. A penny stamp could do it. But there was no bidding. A moment more and all communication is cut off. No Armada can cross that sea.

"Perhaps he is dying; and I sit here," she said. "I would give my life for him, and I cannot do a hand's turn." And she rocked herself to and fro.

For the first time in her life Di dashed herself blindly against one of God's boundaries; and the shock that a first realization of our helplessness always brings, struck her like a blow. She could do nothing.

Many impulsive people, under the intolerable pressure of their own impotence, make a feverish pretence of action, and turn stones and pebbles, as they cannot turn heaven and earth; but Di was not impulsive.

And the gong sounded, first far away in the western wing, and then at the foot of the staircase.

Many things fail us in this world; youth, love, friendship, take to themselves wings; but meals are not among our migratory joys. Amid the shifting quicksands of life they stand fast as milestones.

Di dressed and went downstairs. It seemed years since she had last seen the "parlour," and old Mr. Garstone standing alone before the fire.

He did not appear aged.

"It's later than it was," he remarked; and she had a dim recollection that in some misty bygone time he invariably used to say those particular words every evening, and that she used to smile and nod and say, "Yes, Uncle George."

And so she smiled now, and repeated like a parrot, "Yes, Uncle George."

And he said, "Yes, Diana, yes."

Breakfast was later than usual next morning. It always is when one has lain awake all night. But it ended at last, and Di was at last at liberty to rush up to her room, pull on an old waterproof and felt hat, and dart out unobserved into the rain.

The white mist closed in upon her, and directly she was out of sight of the house she began to run. There were no aimless wanderings and pacings today. Oh, the relief of rapid movement after the long inertia of the night, the joy of feeling the rain sweeping against her face! She did not know the way to D—, but she could not miss it. It was only four miles off. It was eleven now. The morning papers would be in by this time. If she walked hard she would be back by luncheon-time.

And, in truth, a few minutes before two Di emerged from her room in the neatest and driest of blue serge gowns. Only her hair, which curled more crisply than usual, showed that she had been out in the damp. She had come home dead beat and wet to the skin, but she had hardly known it. A new climbing agitated joy pulsated in her heart, in the presence of which cold and fatigue could not exist; in the presence of which no other feeling can exist—for the time.

"Are you glad John is out of danger?" said Mrs. Courtenay that evening as they went upstairs together, after Mr. Garstone had read of John's narrow escape—John had been one of the few among the rescuing party who had returned.

"Very glad," said Di; and she was on the point of telling her grandmother of her expedition to D— that morning, when a sudden novel sensation of shyness seized her, and she stopped short.

Mrs. Courtenay sighed as she settled herself for her nap before dinner.

"Has she inherited her father's heartlessness as well as his yellow hair?" she asked herself.

Mrs. Courtenay had lived long enough to know how few and far between are those among our fellow-creatures whose hearts are not entirely engrossed by the function of their own circulation. Youth believes in universal warmth of heart. It is as common as rhubarb in April. Later on we discern that easily touched feelings, youth's dearest toys, are but toys; shaped stones that look like bread. Later on we discern how fragile is the woof of sentiment to bear the wear and tear of life. Later still, when sorrow chills us, we learn on how few amid the many hearths where we are welcome guests a fire burns to which we may stretch our cold hands and find warmth and comfort.

END OF VOLUME II

VOLUME III

I

"Time and chance are but a tide."

—Burns

Between aspiration and achievement there is no great gulf fixed. God does not mock His children by putting a lying spirit in the mouth of their prophetic instincts. Only the faith of concentrated endeavour, only the stern years which must hold fast the burden of a great hope, only the patience strong and meek which is content to bow beneath "the fatigue of a long and distant purpose;" only these stepping-stones, and no gulf impassable by human feet, divide aspiration from achievement.

To aspire is to listen to the word of command. To achieve is to obey, and to continue to obey, that voice. It is given to all to aspire. Few allow themselves to achieve. John had begun to see that.

If he meant to achieve anything, it was time he put his hand to the plough. He had listened and learned long enough.

"My time has come," he said to himself, as he sat alone in the library at Overleigh on the first day of the new year. "I am twenty-eight. I have been 'promising' long enough. The time of promise is past. I must perform, or the time of performance will pass me by."

He knit his heavy brows.

"I must act," he said to himself, "and I cannot act. I must work, and I cannot work."

John was conscious of having had—he still had—high ambitions, deep enthusiasms. Yet lo! all his life seemed to hinge on the question whether Di would become his wife. Who has not experienced, almost with a sense of traitorship to his own nature, how the noblest influences at work upon it may be caught up into the loom of an all-absorbing personal passion, adding a new beauty and dignity to the fabric, but nevertheless changing for the time the pattern of the life?

John's whole heart was set on one object. There is a Rubicon in the feelings to pass which is to cut off retreat. John had long passed it.

"I cannot do two things at the same time," he said. "I will ask Mrs. Courtenay and Di here for the hunt ball, and settle matters one way or the other with Di. After that, whether I succeed or fail, I will throw myself heart and soul into the career Lord— prophesies for me. The general election comes on in the spring. I will stand then."

John wrote a letter to the minister who had such a high opinion of him—or perhaps of his position—preserved a copy, pigeon-holed it, and put it from his mind. His thoughts reverted to Di as a matter of course. He had seen her several times since the fancy ball. Each particular of those meetings was noted down in the unwritten diary which contains all that is of interest in our lives, which no friend need be entreated to burn at our departure.

He was aware that a subtle change had come about between him and Di; that they had touched new ground. If he had been in love before—which, of course, he ought to have been—he would have understood what that change meant. As it was, he did not. No doubt he would be wiser next time.

Yet even John, creeping mole-like through self-made labyrinths of conjecture one inch below the surface, asked himself whether it was credible that Di was actually beginning to care for him. When he knew for certain she did not, there seemed no reason that she should not; now that he was insane enough to imagine she might, he was aware of a thousand deficiencies in himself which made it impossible. And yet—

So he wrote another letter, this time to Mrs. Courtenay, inviting her and Di to the hunt ball in his neighbourhood, at the end of January.

And his invitation was accepted. And one if not two persons, perhaps even a third old enough to know better, began the unprofitable task of counting days.

It was an iron winter. It affected Fritz's health deleteriously. His short legs raised him but little above the surface of the earth, and he was subject to chills and cramps owing to the constant contact of the under portion of his long ginger person with the snow. Not that there was much snow. One steel and iron frost succeeded another. Lindo, on the contrary, found the cold slight compared with the two winters which he had passed in Russia with John. His wool had been allowed to grow, to the great relief of Mitty, who could not "abide" the "bare-backed state" which the exigencies of fashion required of him during the summer.

It was a winter not to be forgotten, a winter such as the oldest people at Overleigh could hardly recall. As the days in the new year lengthened, the frost strengthened, as the saying goes. The village beck at Overleigh froze. By-and-by the great rivers froze. Carts went over the Thames. Some one, fonder of driving than of horses, drove a four-in-hand on the ice at Oxford. The long lake below Overleigh Castle, which had formerly supplied the moat, was frozen feet thick. The little islands and the boathouse were lapped in ice. It became barely possible, as the days went on, to keep one end open for the swans and ducks. The herons came to divide the open space with them. The great frost of 18—was not one that would be quickly forgotten.

John kept open house, for the ice at Overleigh was the best in the neighbourhood, and all the neighbours within distance thronged to it. Mothers drove over with their daughters; for skating is a healthy pursuit, and those that can't skate can learn.

The most inaccessible hunting men, rendered desperate like the herons by the frost, turned up regularly at Overleigh to play hockey, or emulate John's figure-skating, which by reason of long practice in Russia was "bad to beat."

John was a conspicuous figure on the ice, in his furred Russian coat lined with sable paws, in which he had skated at the ice carnivals at St. Petersburg.

Mitty, with bright winter-apple cheeks and a splendid new beaver muff, would come down to watch her darling wheel and sweep.

"If the frost holds I will have an ice carnival when Di is here," John said to himself; and after that he watched the glass carefully.

The day of Di's arrival drew near, came, and actually Di with it. She was positively in the house. Archie came the same day, but not with her. Archie had invariably shown such a marked propensity for travelling by any train except that previously agreed upon, when he was depended on to escort his sister, that after a long course of irritation Mrs. Courtenay had ceased to allow him to chaperon Di, to the disgust of that gentleman, who was very proud of his ornamental sister when she was not in the way, and who complained bitterly at not being considered good enough to take her out. So Mrs. Courtenay, who had accepted for the sake of appearances, but who had never had the faintest intention of leaving her own fireside in such inhuman weather, discovered a tendency to bronchitis, and failed at the last moment, confiding Di to the charge of Miss Fane, who good-naturedly came down from London to assist John in entertaining his guests.

And still the following day the frost held. The hunt ball had dwindled to nothing in comparison with the ice carnival at Overleigh the night following the ball. The whole neighbourhood was ringing with it. Such a thing had never taken place within the memory of man at Overleigh. The neighbours, the tenantry, cottagers and all, were invited. The hockey-players rejoiced in the rumour that there would be hockey by torchlight, with goals lit up by flambeaux and a phosphorescent bung. Would the frost hold? That was the burning topic of the day.

There was a large house-party at Overleigh, a throng of people who in Di's imagination existed only during certain hours of the day, and melted into the walls at other times. They came and went, and skated and laughed, and wore beautiful furs, especially Lady Alice Fane, but they had no independent existence of their own. The only real people among the crowd of dancing skating shadows were herself and John, with whom all that first day she had hardly exchanged a word—to her relief, was it, or her disappointment?

After tea she went up with Miss Fane to the low entresol room which had been set apart for that lady's use, to help her to rearrange the men's button-holes, which John had pronounced to be too large. As soon as Di took them in hand, Miss Fane of course discovered, as was the case, that she was doing them far better than she could herself, and presently trotted off on the pretext of seeing to some older lady who did not want seeing to, and did not return.

Di was not sorry. She rearranged the bunches of lilies of the valley at leisure, glad of the quiet interval after a long and unprofitable day.

Presently the person of whom she happened to be thinking happened to come in. He would have been an idiot if he had not, though I regret to be obliged to chronicle that he had had doubts on the subject.

"I thought I should find Aunt Loo here," he said, rather guiltily, for falsehood sat ungracefully upon him. And he looked round the apartment as if she might be concealed in a corner.

"She was here a moment ago," said Di, and she began to sort the flowers all over again.

"The frost shows no signs of giving."

"I am glad."

After the frost John found nothing further of equal originality to say, and presently he sat down, neither near to her nor very far away, with his chin in his hands, watching her wire her flowers. The shaded light dealt gently with the folds of Di's amber tea-gown, and touched the lowest ripple of her yellow hair. She dropped a single lily, and he picked it up for her, and laid it on her knee. It was a day of little things; the little things Love glorifies. He did not know that his attitude was that of a lover—did not realize the inference he would assuredly have drawn if he had seen another man sit as he was sitting then. He had forgotten all about that. He thought of nothing; neither thought of anything in the blind unspeakable happiness and comfort of being near each other, and at peace with each other.

Afterwards, long afterwards, John remembered that hour with the feeling as of a Paradise lost, that had been only half realized at the time. He wondered how he had borne such happiness so easily; why no voice from heaven had warned him to speak then, or hereafter for ever hold his peace. And yet at the time it had seemed only the dawning of a coming day, the herald of a more sure and perfect joy to be. The prophetic conviction had been at the moment too deep for doubt that there would be many times like that.

"Many times," each thought, lying awake through the short winter night after the ball.

John had discovered that to be alternately absolutely certain of two opposite conclusions, without being able to remain in either, is to be in a state of doubt. He found he could bear that blister as ill as most men.

"I will speak to her the morning after the carnival," he said, "when all this tribe of people have gone. What is the day going to be like?"

He got up and unbarred his shutter, and looked out. The late grey morning was shivering up the sky. The stars were white with cold. The frost had wrought an ice fairyland on the lattice. While that fragile web held against the pane, the frost that wrapped the whole country would hold also.

II

"A funeral morn is lit in heaven's hollow,
And pale the star-lights follow."

—Christina Rossetti

Towards nine o'clock in the evening carriage after carriage began to drive up to Overleigh in the moonlight. When Di came down, the white stone hall and the music-room were already crowded with guests, among whom she recognized Lord Hemsworth, Mr. Lumley, and Miss Crupps, who had been staying at houses in the neighbourhood for the hunt ball the night before, and had come on with their respective parties, to the not unmixed gratification of John.

"Here we are again," said Mr. Lumley, flying up to her. "No favouritism, I beg, Miss Tempest. Tempest shall carry one skate, and I will take the other. Hemsworth must make himself happy with the button-hook. Great heavens! Tempest, whose funeral have you been ordering?"

For at that moment the alarm-bell of the Castle began to toll.

"It is unnecessary to hide in the curtains," said John. "That bell is only rung in case of fire. It is the signal for lighting up."

And, headed by a band of torches, the whole party went streaming out of the wide archway, a gay crowd of laughing expectant people, into the gardens, where vari-coloured lines of lights gleamed terrace below terrace along the stone balustrades, and Neptune reined in his dolphins in the midst of his fountain, in a shower of golden spray.

The path down to the lake through the wood was lit by strings of Chinese lanterns in the branches. The little bridge over the frozen brook was outlined with miniature rose-coloured lights, in which the miracles wrought by the hoar-frost on each transfigured reed and twig glowed flame-colour to their inmost tracery against the darkness of the overhanging trees.

Di walked with John in fairyland.

"Beauty and the beast," said some one, probably Mr. Lumley. But only the "beast" heard, and he did not care.

There was a chorus of exclamations as they all emerged from the wood into the open.

The moon was shining in a clear sky, but its light was lost in the glare of the bonfires, leaping red and blue and intensest green on the further bank of the lake, round which a vast crowd was already assembled. The islands shone, complete circles of coloured light like jewels in a silver shield. The whole lake of glass blazed. The bonfires flung great staggering shadows across the hanging woods.

John and Di looked back.

High overhead Overleigh hung in mid air in a thin veil of mist, a castle built in light. Every window and archer's loophole, from battlement to basement, the long lines of mullioned lattice of the picture-gallery and the garret gallery above, throbbed with light. The dining-hall gleamed through its double glass. The rose window of the chapel was a rose of fire.

"They have forgotten my window," said John; and Di saw that the lowest portion of the western tower was dark. Her own oriel window, and Archie's next it, shone bravely.

Mitty was watching from the nursery window. In the fierce wavering light she could see John, conspicuous in his Russian coat and peaked Russian cap, advance across the ice, escorted by torches, to the ever-increasing multitude upon the further bank. The enthusiastic cheering of the crowd when it caught sight of him came up to her, as she sat with a cheek pressed against the lattice, and she wept for joy.

Di's heart quickened as she heard it. Her pride, which had at first steeled her against John, had deserted to his side. It centred in him now. She was proud of him. Lord Hemsworth, on his knees before her, fastening her skates, asked her some question relating to a strap, and, looking up as she did not answer, marvelled at the splendid colour in her cheek, and the flash in the eyes looking beyond him over his head. At a signal from John the band began to play, and some few among the crowd to dance on the sanded portion of the ice set apart for them; but far the greater number gathered in dense masses to watch the "musical ride" on skates which the house-party at Overleigh had been practising the previous day, which John led with Lady Alice, circling in and out round groups of torches, and ending with a grand chain, in which Mr. Lumley and Miss Crupps collapsed together, to the delight of the spectators and of Mr. Lumley himself, who said he should tell his mamma.

And still the crowd increased.

As John was watching the hockey-players contorted like prawns, wheeling fast and furious between their flaming goals, which dripped liquid fire on to the ice, the local policeman came up to him.

"There's over two thousand people here tonight, sir," he said.

"The more the better," said John.

"Yes, sir, and I've been about among 'em, me and Jones, and there's a sight of people here, sir, as are no tenants of yours, and roughish characters some of 'em."

"Sure to be," said John. "If there is any horseplay, treat it short and sharp. I'll back you up. I've a dozen men down here from the house to help to keep order. But there will be no need. Trust Yorkshiremen to keep amused and in a good temper."

And, in truth, the great concourse of John's guests was enjoying itself to the utmost, dancing, sliding, clutching, falling one on the top of the other, with perfect good humour, shouting with laughter, men, women, and children all together.

As the night advanced an ox was roasted whole on the ice, and a cauldron of beer was boiled. There was a tent on the bank in which a colossal supper had been prepared for all. Behind it great brick fire-places had been built, round which the people sat in hundreds, drinking, singing, heating beer and soup. They were tactful, these rough Yorkshiremen; not one came across to the further bank set apart for "t' quality," where another supper, not half so decorously conducted, was in full swing by the boathouse. John skated down there after presiding at the tent.

Perhaps negus and mutton-broth were never handed about under such dangerous circumstances. The best *Consommé à la Royale* watered the earth. The men tottered on their skates over the frozen ground, bearing soup to the coveys of girls sitting on the bank in nests of fur rugs.

Mr. Lumley and Miss Crupps had supper together in one of the boats, Mr. Lumley continually vociferating, "Not at home," when called upon, and retaliating with Genoese pastry, until he was dislodged with oars, when he emerged wielding the drumstick of a chicken, and a free fight ensued between him and little Mr. Dawnay, armed with a soup-ladle, which ended in Mr. Lumley's being forced on to his knees among the mince-pies, and disarmed.

John looked round for Di, but she was the centre of a group of girls, and he felt aggrieved that she had not kept a vacant seat for him beside her, which of course she could easily have done. Presently, when the fireworks began, every one made a move towards the lower part of the lake in twos and threes, and then his opportunity came.

He held out his hand to help her to her feet, and they skated down the ice together. Every one was skating hand in hand, but surely no two hands trembled one in the other as theirs did.

The evening was growing late. A low mist was creeping vague and billowy across the land, making the tops of the trees look like islands in a ghostly sea. The bonfires, burning down red and redder into throbbing hearts of fire, gleamed blurred and weird. The rockets rushed into the air and dropped in coloured flame, flushing the haze. The moon peered in and out.

And to John and Di it seemed as if they two were sweeping on winged feet among a thousand phantasmagoria, in the midst of which they were the only realities. In other words, they were in love.

"Come down to the other end of the lake, and let us look at the fireworks from there," said John; and they wheeled away from the crowd and the music and the noise, past all the people and the lighted islands and the boathouse, and the swinging lamps along the banks, away to the deserted end of the lake. A great stillness seemed to have retreated there under shadow of the overhanging trees. The little island left in darkness for the waterfowl, with its laurels bending frozen into the ice, had no part or lot in the distant jargon of sound, and the medley of rising, falling, skimming lights. There was no sound save the ringing of their skates, and a little crackling of the ice among the grass at the edge.

They skated round the island, and then slackened and stood still to look at the scene in the distance.

One of the bonfires just replenished leapt one instant lurid high, only to fall the next in a whirlwind of sparks, and cover the lake with a rush of smoke. Figures dashed in and out, one moment in the full glare of light, the next flying like shadows through the smoke.

"It is like a dream," said Di. "If it is one, I hope I shan't wake up just yet."

To John it was not so wild and incredible a dream as that her hand was still in his. She had not withdrawn it. No, his senses did not deceive him. He looked at it, gloved in his bare one. He held it still. He could not wait another moment. He must have it to keep always. Surely, surely fate had not thrown them together for nothing, beneath this veiled moon, among the silver trees!

"Di," he said below his breath.

"There is some one on the bank watching us," said Di, suddenly.

John turned, and in the uncertain light saw a man's figure come deliberately out of the shadow of the trees to the bank above the ice.

John gave a sharp exclamation.

"What has he got in his hand?" said Di.

He did not answer. He dropped her hand and moved suddenly away from her. The figure slowly raised one arm. There was a click and a snap.

"Missed fire," said John, making a rush for the edge. But he turned immediately. He remembered his skates. Di screamed piercingly. In the distance came the crackling of fireworks, and the murmur of the delighted crowd. Would no one hear?

The figure on the bank did not stir; only a little steel edge of light rose slowly again.

There was a sharp report, a momentary puff of light in smoke, and John staggered, and began scratching and scraping the ice with his skates. Di raised shrieks that shook the stars, and rushed towards him.

And the cruel moon came creeping out, making all things visible.

"Go back," he gasped hoarsely. "Keep away from me. He will fire again."

And he did so; for as she rushed up to John, and in spite of the strength with which he pushed her from him, caught him in her arms and held him tightly to her, there was a second report, and the muff hopped and ripped in her hand.

She screamed again. Surely some one would come! She could hear the ringing of skates and voices. Torches were wheeling towards her. Lanterns were running along the edge. Good God! how slow they were!

"Go back—go back!" gasped John, and his head fell forward on her breast. He seemed slipping out of her arms, but she upheld him clasped convulsively to her with the strength of despair.

"Where?" shouted voices, half-way up the lake.

She tried to shriek again, but only a harsh guttural sound escaped her lips.

The man had not gone away. She had her back to him, but she heard him run a few steps along the frost-bitten bank, and she knew it was to make his work sure.

John became a dead weight upon her. She struggled fiercely with him, but he dragged her heavily to her knees, and fell from her grasp, exposing himself to full view. There was a click.

With a wild cry she flung herself down upon his body, covering him with her own, her face pressed against his.

MARY CHOLMONDELEY

"We will die together! We will die together!" she gasped.

She heard a low curse from the bank. And suddenly there was a turmoil of voices, and a rushing and flaring of lights all round her, and then a sharp cry like the fire-engines clearing the London streets.

"I must get him to the side," she said to herself, and she beat her hands feebly on the ice.

Away in the distance, in some other world, the band struck up, "He's a fine old English gentleman."

Her hands touched something wet and warm.

"The thaw has come at last," she thought, and consciousness and feeling ebbed away together.

III

"And dawn, sore trembling still and grey with fear,
Looked hardly forth, a face of heavier cheer
Than one which grief or dread yet half enshrouds."

—SWINBURNE

W hen Di came to herself, it was to find that she was sitting on the bank supported by Miss Crupps' trembling arm, with her head on Miss Crupps' shoulder. Some one, bending over her—could it be Lord Hemsworth with that blanched face and bare head?—was wiping her face with the gentleness of a woman.

"Have I had a fall?" she asked dizzily. "I don't remember. I thought it was—Miss Crupps who fell."

"Yes, you have had a fall," said Lord Hemsworth, hurriedly; "but you will be all right directly. Don't be all night with that brandy, Lumley."

Di suddenly perceived Mr. Lumley close at hand, trying to jerk something out of a little silver lamp into a tumbler. She had seen that lamp before. It had been handed round with lighted brandy in it with the mince-pies. No one drank it by itself. Evidently there was something wrong.

"I don't understand," she said, beginning to look about her. A confused gleam of remembrance was dawning in her eyes which terrified Lord Hemsworth.

"Drink this," he said quickly, pressing the tumbler against her lip.

Her teeth chattered against the rim. Miss Crupps was weeping silently. Di pushed away the glass and stared wildly about her.

What was this great crowd of eyes kept back by a chain of men? What was that man in a red uniform with a trumpet, craning forward to see? There was a sound of women crying. How dark it was! Where was the moon gone to?

"What is it?" she whispered hoarsely, stretching out her hands to Lord Hemsworth, and looking at him with an agony of appeal. "What has happened?"

But he only took her hands and held them hard in his. If he could have died to spare her that next moment he would have done it.

"When I say three," said a distinct voice near at hand. "Gently, men. One, two, *three*. That's it."

Di turned sharply in the direction of the voice. There was a knot of people on the ice at a little distance. One was kneeling down. Another knelt too, holding a lantern ringed with mist. As she looked, the others raised something between them in a fur rug, something heavy, and began to move slowly to the bank.

Her face took a rigid look. She remembered. She rose suddenly to her feet with a voiceless cry, and would have fallen forward on her face had not Lord Hemsworth caught her in his arms. He held her closely to him, and put his shaking blood-stained hand over her eyes. Miss Crupps sobbed aloud. Mr. Lumley sat down by her, telling her not to cry, and assuring her that it would all be all right; but when he was not comic he was not up to much.

There was no need to keep the crowd off any longer. Their whole interest centred in John, and they broke away in murmuring masses along the bank, and down the ice, in the wake of the little band with the lantern.

Now that the lantern had gone, the place was wrapped in a white darkness. The other lights had apparently gone out, except the red end of a torch on the bank. The mist was covering the valley.

"Is he dead? Is he dead?" gasped Di, clinging convulsively to the friend who had loved her so long and so faithfully.

"No, Di, no," said Lord Hemsworth, speaking as if to a child; "not dead, only hurt. And the doctor is there. He was on the ice when it happened. He was with you both almost as soon as I was. I am going to take off your skates. Can you walk a little with my help? Yes? It will be better to be going gently home. Put your hands in your muff. Here it is. You must put in the other hand as well. The bank is steep here. Lean on me." And Lord Hemsworth helped her up the bank, and guided her stumbling feet towards the dwindling constellation of lights at the further end of the lake.

A party of men passed them in the drifting mist. One of them turned back. It was Archie, his face streaming with perspiration.

"Did you get him?" asked Lord Hemsworth.

"Get him? Not a chance," said Archie. "He stood on the bank till Dawnay and I were within ten yards of him, and then laughed and ran quietly away. He knew we could not follow on our skates, though we made a rush for him, and by the time we had got them off he was out of sight, of course. I expect he has doubled back, and is watching among the crowd now."

"Would you know him again?"

"No; he was masked. He would never have let me come so close to him if he had not been. I say, how is John?"

Lord Hemsworth glared at Archie, but the latter was of the species that never takes a hint, like his father before him, who was always deeply affronted if people resented his want of tact. He called it "touchiness" on their part. The "touchiness" of the world in general affords tactless persons a perennial source of offended astonishment.

"What are you frowning at me about?" said Archie, in an injured voice. "What has become of John? Hullo! what's that? Why, it's the omnibus. They have been uncommonly quick about getting it down. My word, the horses are giving trouble! They can't get them past the bonfires."

"Go on and say Miss Tempest and Miss Crupps are coming," said Lord Hemsworth, "and keep places for them."

He knew the omnibus had not been sent for for them, but he did not want Di to realize for whom it was required. Archie hurried on. Miss Crupps and Mr. Lumley passed at a little distance.

"You are deceiving me," gasped Di. "You mean it kindly, but you are deceiving me. He is dead. Did not Archie say he was dead? It is no good keeping it from me."

Lord Hemsworth tried to soothe her in vain.

"The man on the bank shot twice," she went on incoherently. "I tried to get between, but it was no good; and I screamed, but you were all so long in coming. I never knew people so slow. You were too late, too late, too late!"

Lord Hemsworth was experiencing that unbearable wrench at the heart which goes by the easy name of emotion. He was reading his death-warrant in every random word Di said. It appeared to him that he had always known that John loved Di; and yet until this evening he had never thought of it, and certainly never dreamed for a moment that she cared for him. He had not imagined that Di could care for any one. The ease with which any man can marry any woman nowadays, the readiness of women to give their affection to any one, irrespective of age, character, and antecedents, has awakened in men's minds a profound and too well grounded disbelief in women's love. The average woman of the present day is, as men are well aware, in love with marriage, and in order to attain to that state a preference for one person rather than another is quickly seen to be prejudicial; for though love conduces to happy marriages, love conduces also to the catastrophe of single life, and is but a blind leader of the blind at best.

Lord Hemsworth loved Di, but that was different. The fact that she, being human, might be equally attached to himself or to some other man had never struck him. It struck him now, and for a few minutes he was speechless.

It was only a very great compassion and tenderness that was able to wrestle with and vanquish the intolerable pain of the moment.

"See, Di," he said gently, through his white lips. "Look at that great tear and hole through your muff. I saw it directly I picked it up. A bullet did that; do you understand?—a bullet that perhaps would have hit Tempest but for you. But you saved him from it. Perhaps he is better now, and afraid *you* are hurt. There is the carriage coming to us; let us go on to meet it."

And in truth the great Overleigh omnibus, with men at the horses' heads, was lurching across the uneven turf to meet them.

"Where is John?" asked Di of Archie, peering at the empty carriage.

"The doctor would not have him lifted in, after all," said Archie. "They went on on foot. We may as well go up in it;" and he helped in Lady Alice Fane and Miss Crupps, who came up at the moment. Lord Hemsworth followed Di and sat down by her. He was determined she should be spared all questioning. Mr. Lumley and Mr. Dawnay got in too, and sat silently staring straight in front of them. No one spoke. Archie stood on the step; and the long lumbering vehicle turned and got slowly under way—the same in which such a merry party had driven to the ball the night before.

As they reached the courtyard a confused mass of people became visible within it—the guests of the evening; the girls standing about in silent groups, muffled to the eyes, for the cold had become intense; the men hurrying to and fro, getting out their own horses and helping the coachmen to harness them. Through the darkness came the uplifted voices of Lindo and Fritz in hysterics at being debarred from taking part in the festivities. Carriages were beginning to drive off. There was no leave-taking.

"There is our omnibus," said Mr. Lumley to Miss Crupps. "That is Montagu lighting the lamps. They will be looking for us." And they got out and rejoined their party, nodding silently to the others, who drove on to the hall door, Lord Hemsworth with them: he seemed quite oblivious of the fact that he was not staying at Overleigh.

The hall was brilliantly lighted. Every carved lion and griffin on the grand staircase held its lamp. The house-party was standing about in the hall. They looked at the remainder as they came in, but no one spoke. Miss Fane was blinking in their midst. The other elder ladies who had stayed up at the Castle whispered with their daughters. A blaze of light and silver came through the opened folding doors of the dining-hall, where supper for a large number had been prepared.

"Any news?" asked Lord Hemsworth, as he guided Di to an armchair.

Miss Fane shook her head.

"They won't let me in," she said. "They have taken him to his room, and they won't let any one in."

"Who is with him?" said Di, in a loud hoarse voice that made every one look at her.

She did not see what every one else did, namely, that the neck and breast of her grey coat was drenched with blood—not hers.

"The doctor and his sister are with him. They were both on the ice at the time. I think Lord Elver is there too, and his valet."

Lord Hemsworth went into the dining-hall and came back with a glass of champagne and a roll.

"Bring things out to the people," he said to the bewildered servants; "they won't come in here for them." And they followed with trays of wine and soup.

Without making her conspicuous, he was thus able to force Di to drink and eat. She remembered afterwards his wearying pertinacity till she had finished what he brought her.

The men, most of whom were exhausted by the pursuit of the assassin, or by carrying John up the steep ascent, drank large quantities of spirits. Archie, quite worn out, fell heavily asleep in an oak chair. The women were beginning to disappear in two and threes. Every one was dead beat.

It was Lord Hemsworth who took the onus of giving directions, who told the servants to put out the lights from all the windows. Miss Fane was of no more use than a sheep waked at midnight for an opinion on New Zealand lamb would have been. She stood about and ate sandwiches because they were handed to her, although she and the other chaperons had just partaken of roast turkey; went at intervals into the picture-gallery, at the end of which John's room was, and came back shaking her head.

It was Lord Hemsworth who helped Di to her room, while Miss Fane accompanied them upstairs. Di's room was still brilliantly lighted. Lord Hemsworth lingered on the threshold.

"You will promise me to take off that damp gown at once," he said.

Somehow there seemed nothing peculiar in the authoritative attitude which he had assumed towards Di. She and Miss Fane took it as a matter of course.

"Yes, change all her things," said Miss Fane. "Quite right—quite right."

"Where is your maid? Can you get her?" asked Lord Hemsworth, uneasily.

"I have no maid," said Di, trying and failing to unfasten her grey furred coat.

He winced as he saw her touch it, and then, an idea seeming to strike him, closed the door and went downstairs again.

The servants had put out the lamps in the windows of the picture-gallery, leaving, with unusual forethought, one or two burning in the long expanse in case of need.

In the shadow at the further end, near John's room, a bent figure was sitting, silently rocking itself to and fro. It had been there whenever he had ventured into the gallery. It was there still.

It was Mitty—Mitty in her best violet silk that would stand of itself, and her black satin apron, and her gold brooch with the mosaic of the Coliseum that John had brought her from Rome. She raised her wet face out of her apron as the young man touched her gently on the shoulder.

"They won't let me in to him, sir," said Mitty, the round tears running down her cheeks, and hopping on to her violet silk. "Me that nursed him since he was a baby. He was put into my arms, sir, when he was born. I took him from the month, and they won't let me in."

"They will presently," said Lord Hemsworth. "He will be asking for you, you'll see; and then how vexed he will be if he sees you have been crying!"

"And the warming-pan, sir," gasped Mitty, shaken with silent sobs, pointing to that article laid on the settee. "I got it ready myself. I was as quick as quick. And a bit of brown sugar in it to keep off the pain. And they said they did not want it—as if I didn't know what he'd like! He'll want his old Mitty, and he won't know they are keeping me away from him."

"Some one wants you very much," said Lord Hemsworth. "Poor Miss Tempest. And she has no maid with her. She is not fit to be left to herself. Won't you go and see to her, Mitty?"

But Mitty shook her head.

"He may ask for me," she said.

"I will stay here and come for you the first minute he asks," said Lord Hemsworth, moving the rejected warming-pan, and sitting down beside her on the hot settee. "Poor Miss Tempest! And she tried so hard to save him. Won't you go to her? She has only Miss Fane with her."

"Miss Fane!" said Mitty, evidently with the recollection of a long-standing feud. "Much good she'd do a body; doesn't know chalk from cheese. She didn't even know when Master John had got the measles, though the spots was out all over him. 'It's only nettle-rash, nurse,' she says to me. And the same when he had them little ulsters in his throat. Miss Fane indeed!"

And after a little more persuasion Mitty consented to go if he promised to come for her if John asked for her.

Lord Hemsworth gave a sigh of relief as Mitty went reluctantly away. He was in mortal anxiety about Di. He had a nervous misgiving, increased by his feeling of masculine helplessness to do anything further for her, lest she should fall ill or faint alone in that gaily lighted room; for, of course, Miss Fane would not have remained. As, indeed, was the case. She was yawning herself out of the room when Mitty appeared.

"That's it—that's it," she said, evidently relieved. "Get to bed, Di. No use sitting up. We shall hear in the morning;" and she departed to her own room.

Di turned her white exhausted face slowly towards the old woman, and vainly tried to frame a question. Mitty's maternal instinct was aroused by the sight of her lamb's "Miss Dinah" sitting in her mist-damped clothes, which steamed where the warmth of the fire reached them. She had made no effort to take off her walking things, but she was passive under Mitty's hands, as the latter unfastened them and wrapped her in her warm dressing-gown.

"I can't go to bed, Mitty," said Di, hoarsely, holding her gown. "Don't make me. Let me come and sit in the nursery with you. We shall be nearer there, and then I shall hear. There is no one to come and tell me here."

The girl clung convulsively to the old woman, and the two went together to the nursery, and Mitty, after putting her guest into the

MARY CHOLMONDELEY

rocking-chair by the fire, went down once more to ask for news. But there was no news. John was still unconscious, and the doctor would say nothing. Presently Mitty came tearfully back, and sat down on the other side of the fire. Lord Hemsworth, who was sitting up with Archie, had promised to come to the nursery the moment there was any change.

The nursery still bore traces of the little party that had broken up so disastrously, for Mitty had invited the *élite* of the village ladies to view the carnival from the nursery windows. The "rock" buns for which Mitty was celebrated, and one of Mrs. Alcock's best cakes, were still on the table, and Mitty's fluted silver teapot with a little nest of clean cups round it. Presently she got up, and, opening the corner cupboard, began to put them away; but the impulse of tidying was forgotten as she caught sight of John's robin mug on the top shelf. She took it down, and stood holding it in her old withered hands.

"I give it him myself," she said, "on his birthday when he was five years old; twenty-four years ago come June. I thought some of his mother's family would have remembered his birthday if his father didn't. I thought something would have come by post. But there wasn't so much as a letter. And Mrs. Alcock give him the tin plate with the soldier on it, but I never let him eat off it. And we had Barker's little nephew to tea as he was learning to shoemaykle, but nobody took no notice of his birthday except me and Mrs. Alcock. And when he went to school I kep' his mug and his toys. He never had a many toys, but what there was I have 'em. And his clothes, my dear, everything since he was born, from his little cambric shirts, I have 'em all, put away; with a bit of camphor to his velvet suit as I took him to York to be measured for, on purpose to make him look pretty to his papa when he come home from abroad. But he never took a bit of notice of him— never." Mitty sat down by the fire, still holding the mug. "And a lace collar he had with it—real lace, the best as money could buy. I might spend what I liked on him; but no one ever took no notice of him, not even in his first sailor's; and he with his pretty ways and his grave talk! Mrs. Alcock and me has often cried over the things he'd say. There's his crib still in the night-nursery by my bed. I could not sleep without it was there; and the little blankets and sheets and piller-slips as belong, all put away, and not a iron mould upon 'em. Eh, dear miss, many's the time I've got 'em out and aired 'em, thinking maybe the day 'ud come when he would have a babby of his own, and I should hold it in my old arms before I died. And even if I was gone they'd be all ready, and the bassinet only wanting muslin to it. And now—oh, my lamb, my lamb! And they won't let his old Mitty go to him." And Mitty's grief broke into a paroxysm of sobbing.

Di looked at the old woman rocking herself backwards and forwards, and, rising unsteadily, she went and knelt down by her, putting her arms round her in silence. She had no comfort to give in words. It seemed as if her strong young heart were breaking; but she realized that Mitty's anguish for a love knit up into so many faithful years was greater than hers.

As she knelt, a step came along the creaking garret gallery with its uneven flooring.

It was Lord Hemsworth.

He stood in the doorway with the wan light of the morning behind him. His face looked pinched and aged.

"He is better," he said. "He has recovered consciousness, and has spoken. The other doctor has arrived, and they think all will go well."

And the two women who loved John clung and sobbed together.

Lord Hemsworth looked fixedly at Di and went out.

IV

"Toute passion nuisible attire, comme le gouffre, par le vertige. La faiblesse de volonté amène la faiblesse de tête, et l'abîme, malgré son horreur, fascine alors comme un asile."

—AMIEL

People said that John had a charmed life. The divergence of an eighth of an inch, of a hundredth part of an inch, of a hair's-breadth and the little bead that passed right through his neck would have pierced the jugular artery, and John would have added one more to the long list of names in Overleigh Church. As it was, when once the direction of the bullet had been ascertained, he was pronounced to be in little danger. He rallied steadily, and without relapse.

People said that he bore a charmed life, and they began to say something more, namely, that it was an object to somebody that it should be wiped out. Men are not shot at for nothing. John was not an Irish landlord. Some one evidently bore him a grudge. Society instantly formed several more or less descreditable reasons to account for John's being the object of some one's revenge. Half-forgotten rumours of Archie's doings were revived with John's name affixed to them. Decidedly there had been some "entanglement," and John had brought his fate upon himself. Colonel Tempest, just returned from foreign travel, heard the matter discussed at his club. His opinion was asked as to the truth of the reports, but he only shrugged his shoulders, and it was supposed that he could not deny them. Di's, Lady Alice Fane's, and Miss Crupps' names were all equally associated with John's in the different versions of the accident.

Colonel Tempest did not go to see his daughter. She had been telegraphed for the morning after the ice carnival by Mrs. Courtenay, who had actually developed with the thaw the bronchitis which she had dreaded throughout the frost. Di and Archie, whose leave was up, returned to town together for once.

Archie had experienced a distinct though shamed pang of disappointment when John's state was pronounced to be favourable.

All night long, as he had sat waking and dozing beside the gallery fire opposite Lord Hemsworth's motionless, wakeful figure, visions of wealth passed in spite of himself before his mind; visions of four-in-hands, and screaming champagne suppers, and smashing things he could afford to pay for, and running his own horses on the turf. He did not want John to die. He had been dreadfully shocked when he had first caught sight of the stony upturned face almost beneath his feet, and had strained every nerve in his body to overtake the murderer. He did not want John to go where he, Archie, would have been terrified to go himself. But—he wanted the things John had, which his father had often told him should by rights have been his, and they could not both have them at one and the same time.

He could not understand his father's fervent "Thank God!" when he assured him that John was out of danger.

"A miss is as good as a mile," said Archie, with his smallest grin. He was desperately short of money again by this time, and he had no one to apply to. He knew enough of John to be aware that nothing was to be expected from that quarter. Twenty-four hours ago he had thought—how could he help it?—that perhaps there would be no further trouble on that irksome, wearisome subject; for lack of money, and the annoyance entailed by procuring it, was the thorn in Archie's flesh. But now the annoyance was still there, beginning as it were all over again, owing to—John. Madeleine would lend him money, he knew, but he would be a cad to take it. He could not think of such a thing, he said to himself, as he turned it over in his mind.

The ice carnival and John's escape were a nine days' wonder. In ten days it was forgotten for a *cause célèbre* by every one except Colonel Tempest.

Colonel Tempest had had a fairly pleasant time abroad. While his small stock of ready money lasted, the remainder of the five hundred subtracted from the sum he had returned to John after his interview with Larkin, he had really almost enjoyed himself. He had picked up a few old companions of the hanger-on species at Baden and Homburg, and had given them dinners—he was always open-handed. He had the natural predilection for the society of his social inferiors which generally accompanies a predilection for being deferred to, and regarded as a person of importance. He was under the impression that he was the most liberal-minded of men in the choice of his companions, and without the social prejudices of his class. He had won a little at "baccarat." His health also had improved. On his return in December to the lodgings which he had left in such a panic in July, he told himself that he had been in a morbid state of health, that he had taken things too much to heart, that he had been over-sensitive; that there was no need to be afraid. Five months had elapsed. It would be all right.

And it had been all right for about a month, and then—

If the distressing theory that virtue is its own reward has any truth, surely sin is its own punishment.

The old monotonous pains took Colonel Tempest.

It is a popular axiom among persons in robust health that others labouring long under a painful disease become accustomed to it. It is perhaps as true as all axioms, however freely laid down by persons in one state respecting the feelings of others in a state of which they are ignorant, can be.

The continual dropping of water wears away the stone. The stone ought, of course, to put up an umbrella—any one can see that—or shift its position. But it seldom does so.

There was a continual dropping of a slowly diluted torture on the crumbling sandstone of Colonel Tempest's heart. The few months of intermission only rendered more acute the agony of the inevitable recommencement.

As he felt in July after the fire in John's lodgings, so he felt now; just the same again, all over again, only worse. The porous sandstone was wearing down.

He wandered like a ghost in the snowy places in the Park—for snow had followed the thaw—or paced for hours by the Serpentine, staring at the water. Once in a path across the Park he suddenly caught sight of John walking slowly in the direction of Kensington. The young man passed within a couple of yards of him without seeing him, his head bent, and his eyes upon the ground.

"It is his ghost," said Colonel Tempest to himself, clutching the railing, and looking back at the receding figure with an access of shuddering horror.

Another figure passed, a heavy man in an ulster.

"He is being followed," thought Colonel Tempest. "It is Swayne, and he is following him."

He rushed panting after the second figure, and overtook it at a meeting of the ways.

"Swayne!" he gasped; "for mercy's sake, Swayne, don't—"

A benevolent elderly face turned and peered at him in the twilight, and Colonel Tempest remembered that Swayne was dead.

"My name is Smith," said the man, and after waiting a moment passed on.

In a flash of memory Colonel Tempest saw Swayne's huddled figure crouching in the disordered bed, and the check trousers over a chair, and the candle on the window-sill bent double by the heat. That had been the manner of Swayne's departure. How had he come to forget he was dead, and that John was laid up at Overleigh?

"I am going mad," he said to himself. "That will be the end. I shall go mad and tell everything."

The new idea haunted him. He could not shake it off. There was nothing in the wide world to turn to for a change of thought. If he fell asleep at night he was waked by the sound of his own voice, to find himself sitting up in bed talking loudly of he knew not what. Once he heard himself call Swayne's and John's names aloud into the listening darkness, and broke into a cold sweat at the thought that he might have been heard in the next room. Perhaps the other lodger, the young man with the red hair, cramming for the army, knew everything by this time. Perhaps the lodging-house people had been listening at the door, and would give him in charge in the morning. Did he not at that very moment hear furtive steps and whispering on the landing? He rushed out to see the thin tabby cat, the walking funeral of the beetles and mice of the establishment, slip noiselessly downstairs, and he returned to his room shivering from head to foot, to toss and shudder until the morning, and then furtively eye the landlady and her daughter in curl-papers.

More days passed. Colonel Tempest had had doubts at first, but gradually he became convinced that the people in the house knew. He was sure of it by the look in their faces if he passed them on the stairs. It was merely a question of time. They were waiting to make certain before they informed against him. Perhaps they had written to John. There was no news of John, except a rumour in the *World* that he was to stand at the coming general election.

Colonel Tempest became the prey of an *idée fixe*. When John came forward on the hustings he would be shot at and killed. He became as certain of it as if it had already happened. At times he believed it *had* happened—that he had been present and had seen him fall forward; and it was he, Colonel Tempest, who had shot him, and had been taken red-handed with one of his old regimental pistols smoking in his hand.

Colonel Tempest had those pistols somewhere. One day he got them out and looked at them, and spent a long time rubbing them up.

They used to hang crosswise under a photograph of himself in uniform in his wife's little drawing-room. He recollected, with the bitterness that accompanies the remembrance of the waste of lavished affections, how he had sat with his wife and child a whole wet afternoon polishing up those pistols, while another man in his place would have gone off to his club. (Colonel Tempest always knew what that other man would have done.) And Di had been gentle and affectionate, and had had a colour for once, and had played with her creeping child like a cat with its kitten. And they had had tea together afterwards, sitting on the sofa with the child asleep between them. Ah! if she had only been always like that, he thought, as he remembered the cloud that, owing to her uncertain temper, had gradually settled on his home-life.

An intense bitterness was springing afresh in Colonel Tempest's mind against his dead wife, against his dead brother, against Swayne, against his children who never came near him (Di was nursing Mrs. Courtenay in bronchitis, but that was of no account), against the world in general which did not care what became of him. No one cared.

"They will be sorry some day," he said to himself.

And still the waking nightmare remained of seeing John fall, and of finding he had shot him himself.

More days passed.

And gradually, among the tottering *débris* of a life undermined from its youth, one other thought began, mole-like, to delve and creep in the darkness.

Truly the way of transgressors is hard.

No one cared what he suffered, what he went through. This was the constant refrain of these latter days. He had paroxysms of angry tears of self-pity with his head in his hands, his heart rent to think of himself sitting bowed with anguish by his solitary fireside. Love holds the casting vote in the destinies of most of us. There is only one love which wrings the heart beyond human endurance—the love of self.

And yet more days. The sun gave no light by day, neither the moon by night.

To THE SEVERE COLD OF January a mild February had succeeded. March was close at hand. The hope and yearning of the spring was in the air already. Already in Kensington Gardens the silly birds had begun to sing, and the snowdrops and the little regiments of crocuses had come up in double file to listen.

On this particular afternoon a pale London sun was shining like a new shilling in the sky, striking as many sparks as he could out of the Round Pond. There was quite a regatta at that Cowes of nursery shipping. The mild wind was just strong enough to take sailing-vessels across. The big man-of-war belonging to the big melancholy man who seemed open to an offer, the yachts and the little fishing-smacks, everything with a sail, got over sooner or later. The tiny hollow boats with seats were being towed along the edge in leading-reins. A wooden doll with joints took advantage of its absence of costume to drop out of the boat in which it was being conveyed, and take a swim in the open. But it was recovered. An old gentleman with spectacles hooked it out with the end of his umbrella in a moment, quite pleased to be of use. The little boys shouted, the little girls tossed their manes, and careered round the pool on slender black legs. Solemn babies looked on from perambulators.

The big man started the big man-of-war again, and the whole fleet came behind in its wake.

Colonel Tempest was sitting on a seat near the landing-place, where the ship-owners had run to clutch their property a moment ago. His hand was clenched on something he held under his overcoat.

"When the big ship touches the edge," he said to himself.

They came slowly across the pool in a flock. Every little boy shrieked to every other little boy of his acquaintance to observe how his particular craft was going. The big man alone was perfectly apathetic, though his priceless possession was the first, of course. He began walking slowly round. Half the children were at the landing before him, calling to their boats, and stretching out their hands towards them.

The big one touched land.

"Not this time," said Colonel Tempest to himself; "next time."

How often he had said that already! How often his hand had failed him when the moment which he and that other self had agreed upon had arrived! How often he had gone guiltily back to the rooms to which he had not intended to return, and had lain down once more in the bed which had become an accomplice to the torture of every hour of darkness!

Between the horror of returning once again, and the horror of the step into another darkness, his soul oscillated with the feeble violence of despair.

He remembered the going back of yesterday.

"I will not go back again," he said to himself, with the passion of a spoilt child. "I will not—I will not."

"It is time to go home, Master Georgie," said a nursery-maid.

"Just once more, Bessie," pleaded the boy. "Just one *single* once more."

"Well, then, it must be the last time, mind," said the good-natured arbiter of fate, turning the perambulator, and pushing it along the edge, while the occupant of the same added to the hilarity of the occasion by beating a much-chewed musical rattle against the wheel.

"*The last time.* " The chance words seized upon Colonel Tempest's shuddering panic-stricken mind, and held it as in a vice.

"Next time," he said over and over again to himself. "Next time shall really be the last time—really the last, the very last."

The boats were coming across again, straggling wide of each other; how quick, yet what an eternity in coming! The top-heavy boat with the red sail would be the first. It had been started long before the others. The wind caught it near the edge. It would turn over. No, it righted itself. It neared, it bobbed in the ripple at the brink; it touched.

Colonel Tempest's mind had become quite numb. He only knew that for some imperative reason which he had forgotten he must pull the trigger. He half pulled it; then again more decidedly.

There was a report. It stunned him back to a kind of consciousness of what he had done, but he felt nothing.

There was a great silence, and then a shrieking of terrified children, and a glimpse of agitated people close at hand, and others running towards him.

The man with the big boat under his arm said, "By gum!"

Colonel Tempest looked at him. He felt nothing. Had he failed?

The smoke came curling out at his collar, and something dropped from his nerveless hand and lay gleaming on the grass. There was a sound of many waters in his ears.

"He might have spared the children," said a man's voice, tremulous with indignation.

"That is always the way. No one thinks of *me*," thought Colonel Tempest. And the Round Pond and the growing crowd, and the child nearest him with its convulsed face, all turned slowly before his eyes, slid up, and disappeared.

V

"Vous avez bien froid, la belle;
Comment vous appelez-vous?
Les amours et les yeux doux
De nos cercueils sont les clous.
Je suis la morte, dit-elle.
Cueillez la branche de houx."

—Victor Hugo

As John lay impatiently patient upon his bed in the round oak-panelled room at Overleigh during the weeks that followed his accident, his thoughts by day, and by night, varied no more than the notes of a chaffinch in the trees outside.

"Oh, let the solid earth
Not fail beneath my feet,
Before I too have found
What some have found so sweet!"

That was the one constant refrain. The solid earth had nearly failed beneath his feet, nearly—nearly. If the world might but cohere together and not fly off into space; if body and soul might but hold together till he had seen Di once more, till he knew for certain from her own lips that she loved him! Unloved by any woman until now, wistfully ignorant of woman's tenderness, even of its first alphabet learned at a mother's knee, unread in all its later language,—in these days of convalescence a passionate craving was upon him to drink deep of that untasted cup which "some have found so sweet."

He had Mitty, and Mitty at least was radiantly happy during these weeks, with John fast in bed, and in a condition to dispense with other nursing than hers. She sat with him by the hour together, mending his socks and shirts, for she would not suffer any one to touch his clothes except herself, and discoursing to him about Di—a subject which she soon perceived never failed to interest him.

"Miss Dinah," Mitty would say for the twentieth time, but without wearying her audience—"now, there's a fine upstanding lady for my lamb."

"Lady Alice Fane is very pretty, too," John would remark, with the happy knack of self-concealment peculiar to the ostrich and the sterner sex.

"Hoots!" Mitty replied. "She's nothing beside Miss Dinah. If you have Lady Fane with her silly ways, and so snappy to her maid, you'll repent every hair of your head. You take Miss Dinah, my dear, as is only waiting to be asked. She wants you, my precious," Mitty never failed to add. "I tell you it's as plain as the nose on your face" (a simile the force of which could not fail to strike him). "It's not that Lord Hemstitch, for all his pretty looks. It's *you*."

And John told himself he was a fool, and then secretly felt under the pillow for a certain pencilled note which Di had left with the doctor on her hurried departure to London the morning after the ice carnival. It had been given to him when he was able to read letters. It was a short note. There was very little in it, and a great deal left out. It did not even go over the page. But nevertheless John was so very foolish as to keep it under his pillow, and when he was promoted to his clothes it followed into his pocket. Even the envelope had a certain value in his eyes. Had not her hand touched it, and written his name upon it?

Lindo and Fritz, who had been consumed with ennui during John's illness, were almost as excited as their master when he hobbled, on Mitty's arm, into the morning-room for luncheon. Lindo was aweary of sediments of beef-tea and sticks of toast. Fritz, who had had a plethora of whites of poached eggs, sniffed anxiously at the luncheon-tray with its roast pheasant.

There were tricks and Albert biscuits after luncheon, succeeded by heavy snoring on the hearthrug.

John was almost as delighted as they were to leave his sick-room. It was the first step towards going to London. When should he wring permission from his doctor to go up on "urgent business"? Five days, seven days? Surely in a week at latest he would see Di again. He made a little journey round the room to show himself how robust he was becoming, and wound up the old watches lying in the *blue du roi* Sèvres tray, making them repeat one after the other, because Di had once done so. Would Di make this her sitting-room? It was warm and sunny. Perhaps she would like the outlook across the bowling-green and low ivy-coloured balustrade away to the moors. It had been his mother's sitting-room. His poor mother. He looked up at the pretty vacant face that hung over the fireplace. He had looked at it so often that it had ceased to make any definite impression on him.

He wondered vaguely whether the happy or the unhappy hours had preponderated in this room in which she was wont to sit, the very furniture of which remained the same as in her quickly finished day. And then he wondered whether, if she had lived, Di would have liked her; for it was still early in the afternoon, and he had positively nothing to do.

He tried to write a few necessary letters in the absence of Mitty, who was busy washing his handkerchiefs, but he soon gave up the attempt. The exertion made his head ache, as he had been warned it would, so he propelled himself across the room to his low chair by the window.

What should he do till teatime? If only he had asked Mitty for a bit of wash-leather he might have polished up the brass slave-collar in the Satsuma dish. He took it up and turned it in his hands. It was a heavy collar enough, with the owner's name engraved thereon. "Roger Tempest, 1698."

"It must have galled him," said John to himself; and he took up the gag next, and put it into his mouth, and then had considerable difficulty in getting it out again. What on earth should he do with himself till teatime?

One of the bits of Venetian glass standing in the central niche of the lac cabinet at his elbow had lost its handle. He got up to examine it, and, thinking the handle might have been put aside within, pushed back the glass in the centre of the niche, which, as in so many of its species, shut off a small enclosed space between the tiers of drawers. The glass door and its little pillars opened inwards, but not without difficulty. It was clogged with dust. The handle of the Venetian glass was not inside. There was nothing inside but a little old, old, very old, glue-bottle, standing on an envelope, and a broken china cup beside it, with the broken bits in it. The hand that had put them away so carefully to mend, on a day that never came, was dust. They remained. John took out the cup. It matched one that stood in the picture-gallery. The pieces seemed to be all there. He began to fit them together with the pleased interest of a child. He had really found something to do at last. At the bottom of the cup was a key. It was a very small key, with a large head, matching the twisted handles of the drawers.

This was becoming interesting. John put down the cup, and fitted the key into the lock of one of the drawers. Yes, it was the right one. He

MARY CHOLMONDELEY

became quite excited. Half the cabinets in the house were locked, and would not open; of some he had found the keys by diligent search, but the keys of others had never turned up. Here was evidently one.

The key turned with difficulty, but still it did turn, and the drawer opened. The dust had crept over everything—over all the faded silks and bobbins and feminine gear, of which it was half full. John disturbed it, and then sneezed till he thought he should kill himself. But he survived to find among the tangle of work a tiny white garment half made, with the rusted needle still in it. He took it out. What was it? Dolls' clothing? And then he realized that it was a little shirt, and that his mother had probably been making it for him and had not had time to finish it. John held the baby's shirt that he ought to have worn in a very reverent hand, and looked back at the picture. That bit of unfinished work, begun for him, seemed to bring her nearer to him than she had ever been before. Yes, it was hers. There was her ivory workbox, with her initials in silver and turquoise on it, and her small gold thimble had rolled into a corner of the drawer. John put back the little remnant of a love that had never reached him into the drawer with a clumsy gentleness, and locked it up. "I will show it Di some day," he said.

The other drawers bore record. There were small relics of girlhood— ball cards, cotillon ribbons, a mug with "Marion Fane" inscribed in gold on it, a slim book on confirmation. "One of darling Spot's curls" was wrapped in tissue-paper. John did not even know who Spot was, except that from the appearance of the lock he had probably been a black retriever. Her childish little possessions touched John's heart. He looked at each one, and put it tenderly back.

Some of the drawers were empty. In some were smart note-paper with faded networks of silver and blue initials on them. In another was an ornamental purse with money in it and a few unpaid bills. John wondered what his mother would have been like now if she had lived. Her sister, Miss Fane, had a weakness for gorgeous note-paper and smart work-baskets which he had often regarded with astonishment. It had never struck him that his mother might have had the same tastes.

He opened another drawer. More fancy-work, a ball of silk half wound on a card, a roll of vari-coloured embroidery, and, thrust in among them, a half-opened packet of letters. The torn cover which still surrounded them was addressed to Mrs. Tempest, Overleigh Castle, Yorkshire.

Inside the cover was a loose sheet which fell apart from the packet, tied up separately. On it was written, in a large cramped hand that John knew well—

"I dare say you are wise in your generation to prefer to break with me. 'Tout lasse,' and then naturally 'on se range.' I return your letters as you wish it, and as you have been kind enough to burn mine already, I will ask you to commit this last effusion to the flames."

The paper was without date or signature.

John opened the packet, which contained many letters, all in one handwriting, which he recognized as his mother's. He read them one by one, and, as he read, the pity in his face gave place to a white indignation. Poor foolish, foolish letters, to be read after a lapse of eight and twenty years. John realized how very silly his poor mother had been; how worldly wise and selfish some one else had been.

"We ought to have been married, darling," said one of the later letters, dated from Overleigh, evidently after her marriage with Mr. Tempest. "I see now we ought. You said you were too poor, and you could not bear to see me poor; but I would not have minded that one bit—did not I tell you so a hundred times? I would have learnt to cook and mend clothes and everything if only I might have been with you. It is much worse now, feeling my heart is breaking and yours too, and Fate keeping us apart. And you must not write to me any more now I am married, or me to you. It is not right. Mother would be vexed if she knew; I am quite sure she would. So this is the very last to my dearest darling Freddie, from poor Marion."

Alas! there were many, many more from "poor Marion" after the very last; little vacillating, feeble, gilt-edged notes, with every other word under-dashed; some short and hurried, some long and reproachful; sad landmarks of each step of a blindfold wandering on the brink of the abyss, clinging to the hand that was pushing her over.

The last letter was a very long one.

"You have no heart," wrote the pointed, slanting handwriting. "You do not care what I suffer. I do not believe now you ever cared. You say it would be an act of folly to tell my husband, but you know I was always silly. But it is not necessary. I am sure he knows. I feel it. He says nothing, but I know he knows. Oh, if I were only dead and in my grave, and if only the baby might die too, as I hope it will, as I pray to God it

will! If I die and it lives, I don't know what will happen to
it. Remember, if he casts it off, it is your child. Oh, Freddie,
surely it can't be all quite a mistake. You were fond of me
once, before you made me wicked, and when I am dead you
won't feel so angry and impatient with me as you do now.
And if the child lives and has no friend, you will remember
it is yours, won't you? I am so miserable that I think God will
surely let me die. And the child may come any day now. Last
night I felt so ill that I dared not put off any longer, and this
morning I burned all your letters to me, every one, even the
first about the white violets. Do you remember that letter? It
is so long ago now; no, you have forgotten. It is only I who
remember, because it was only I who cared. And I burned the
locket you gave me with your hair in it. It felt like dying to
burn it. Everything is all quite gone. But I can't rest until you
have sent me back my letters. I can't trust you to burn them. I
know what trusting to you means. Send them all back to me,
and I will burn them myself. Only be quick, be quick; there is
so little time. If they come when I am ill, some one else may
read them. I hope if I live I shall never see your face again; and
if I die, I hope God will keep you away from me. Oh! I don't
mean it, Freddie, I don't mean it; only I am so miserable that
I don't know what I write. God forgive you. I would too if I
thought you cared whether I did or not. God forgive us both.

—M.

John looked back at the cover of the packet. The Overleigh
postmark was blurred but legible. June the 8th, and the year—. *It was
his birthday.*

Her lover had sent back her letters, then, with those few harsh lines
telling her she was wise in her generation. Even the last he had returned.
And they had reached her on the morning of the day her child was born.
Had it been a sunny day, with no fire on the hearth before which Lindo
and Fritz now lay stretched, into which she could have dropped that
packet? Had she not had time even to burn them? She had glanced at
them, evidently. Had she been interrupted, and had she thrust them for
the moment with her work into that drawer?

Futile inquiry. He should never know. And she had had her wish.
She had been allowed to die, to hide herself away in the grave. John's

heart swelled with sorrowing pity as at the sight of a child's suffering. She had been very little more. She should have her other wish, too.

He gathered up the letters, and, stepping over the dogs, dropped them into the heart of the fire. They were in the safe keeping of the flames at last. They reached their destination at last, but, a little late—twenty-eight years too late.

And suddenly, as he watched them burn, like a thunderbolt falling and tearing up the ground on which he stood, came the thought, "Then I am illegitimate."

THE MINUTE-HAND OF THE CLOCK on the mantelpiece had made a complete circuit since John had dropped the letters into the fire, yet he had not stirred from the armchair into which he had staggered the moment afterwards.

His fixed eyes looked straight in front of him. His lips moved at intervals.

"I am illegitimate," he said to himself, over and over again.

But no, it was a nightmare, an hallucination of illness. How many delusions he had had during the last few weeks! He should wake up presently and find he had been torturing himself for nothing. If only Mitty would come back! He should laugh at himself presently.

In the mean while, and as it were in spite of himself, certain facts were taking a new significance, were arranging themselves into an unexpected, horrible sequence. Link joined itself to link, and lengthened to a chain.

He remembered his father's evident dislike of him; he remembered how Colonel Tempest had contested the succession when he died. As he had lost the case, John had supposed, when he came to an age to suppose anything, that the slander was without foundation, especially as Mr. Tempest had recognized him as his son. He had known of its existence, of course, but, like the rest of the world, had half forgotten it. That Lord Frederick Fane (evidently the Freddie of the letters) was even his supposed father, had never crossed his mind. If he was like the Fanes, why should he not be so? He might as naturally resemble his mother's as his father's family. He recalled Colonel Tempest's inveterate dislike of him, Archie's thankless reception of anything and everything he did for him.

"I believe," said John, in astonished recollection of divers passages between himself and them—"I believe they think I know all the time, and am deliberately keeping them out."

That, then, was the reason why Mr. Tempest had not discarded him. To recognize him as his son was his surest means of striking at the hated brother who came next in the entail.

"I was made use of," said John, grinding his teeth.

It was no use fighting against it. This hideous, profane incredibility was the truth. Even without the letters to read over again he knew it was true.

"Remember, if he casts it out, it is your child." The long-dead lips still spoke. His mother had pronounced his doom herself.

"I am illegitimate," said John to himself. And he remembered Di and hid his face in his hands, while his mother simpered at him from the wall. The solid earth had failed beneath his feet.

Let us beware how we sin, inasmuch as by God's decree we do not pay. We could almost conceive a right to do as we will, if we could keep the penalty to ourselves, and pay to the uttermost farthing. But not from us is the inevitable payment required. The young, the innocent, the unborn, smart for us, are made bankrupt for us; from them is exacted the deficit which we have left behind. The sins of the fathers are visited on the children heavily—heavily.

VI

"What name doth Joy most borrow
When life is fair?
'Tomorrow.'"

—George Eliot

On her hurried return to London the morning after the ice carnival, Di found Mrs. Courtenay in that condition of illness, not necessarily dangerous, in which the linseed poultice and the steam-kettle and the complexion of the beef-tea are the objects of an all-absorbing interest, to the exclusion of every other subject.

Di was glad not to be questioned upon the one subject that was never absent from her thoughts. As Mrs. Courtenay became convalescent she was able to leave her for an hour or two, and pace in the quieter parts of Kensington Gardens. Happiness, like sorrow, is easier to bear out-of-doors, and Di had a lurking feeling that would hardly bear being put into words, but was none the worse company for that, that the crocuses and the first bird-note in the trees and the pale sky knew her secret and rejoiced with her.

John would come to her. He was getting well, and the first day he could he would come to her, and tell her once more that he loved her. And she? Impossible, incredible as it seemed, she should tell him that she loved him too. Imagination stopped short there. Everything after that was a complete blank. They would be engaged? They would be married? Other people who loved did so. Words, mere words, applicable to "other people," but not to her and John. Could such impossible happiness ever come about? Never, never. She must be mad to think of such a thing. It could not be. Yet it was so; it was coming, it was sure, this new, incomprehensible, dreaded happiness, of which, now that it was almost within her trembling hand, she hardly dared to think.

"Di," said Mrs. Courtenay one afternoon, as she came in from her walk, "there is a paragraph in the paper about John. He is going to contest—at the general election, in opposition to the present Radical member. Did he say anything about it while you were at Overleigh? It must have been arranged some time ago."

"No, granny, he did not mention it."

"I am glad he is taking part in politics at last. It is time. I may not live to see it, but he will make his mark."

"I am sure he will," said Di.

Mrs. Courtenay looked in some perplexity at her granddaughter. It seemed to her, from Di's account, that she had taken John's accident very placidly. She had not forgotten the girl's apparent callousness when his life had been endangered in the mine. It was very provoking to Mrs. Courtenay that this beautiful creature, whom she had taken out for nearly four years, seemed to have too much heart to be willing to marry without love, and too little to fall genuinely in love.

Mrs. Courtenay had gone to considerable expense in providing her with a new and becoming morning-gown for that visit, and Di had managed to lose one of the lace handkerchiefs she had lent her, and had come back unengaged after all. Mrs. Courtenay, who had taken care to accept the invitation for her without consulting her, and had ordered the gown in spite of Di's remonstrances, felt keenly that if Di had refused John, she had gone to that social gathering under false pretences.

"Di," she said, "I seldom ask questions, but I have been wondering during the last few days whether you have anything to tell me or not."

Considering that this was not a question, it was certainly couched in a form conducive to eliciting information.

"I have, and I have not," said Di. "Of course I know what you expected, but it did not happen."

"You mean John did not propose to you?"

"No, granny."

Mrs. Courtenay was silent. She was prepared to be seriously annoyed with Di, and it seemed John was in fault after all. There is no relaxation for a natural irritability in being angry with a person a hundred miles off.

"I think he meant to," said Di, turning pink.

Mrs. Courtenay saw the change of colour with surprise.

"My dear," she said, "do you care for him?"

"Yes," said Di, looking straight at her grandmother.

"I am very thankful," said Mrs. Courtenay. "I have nothing left to wish for."

"I believe I have sometimes done you an injustice," she said tremulously, after wiping her spectacles. "I thought you valued your own freedom and independence too much to marry. It is difficult to advise the young to give their love if they don't want to. Yet, as one grows old, one sees that the very best things we women have lose all their virtue if we keep them to ourselves. Our love if we withhold it, our freedom if we retain it,—what are they later on in life but dead seed in our hands? Our best is ours only to give. Our part is to give it to some one who is worthy of it. I think John is worthy. I wish he had managed to speak, and that it were all settled."

"It is really settled," said Di. "Now and then I feel frightened, and think I may have made a mistake, but I know all the time that is foolish. I am certain he cares for me, and I am quite sure he knows I care for him. Granny"—blushing furiously—"I often wish now that I had not said quite so many idiotic things about love and marriage before I knew anything about them. Do you remember how I used to favour you with my views about them?"

"I don't think they were exactly idiotic. Only the elect hesitate to pronounce opinions on subjects of which they are ignorant. I have heard extremely intelligent men say things quite as silly about housekeeping, and the rearing of infants. You, like them, spoke according to your lights, which were small. I don't know about charming men. There are not any nowadays. But it is always

'. . . a pity when charming women
Talk of things that they don't understand.'"

"We should not have many subjects of conversation if we did not," said Di.

And the old woman and the young one embraced each other with tears in their eyes.

VII

"Oh, well for him whose will is strong!"

—Tennyson

There come times in our lives when the mind lies broken on the revolving wheel of our thought. "I am illegitimate." That was the one thought which made John's bed for him at night, which followed him throughout the spectral day until it brought him back to the spectral night again.

It was a quiver in which were many poisoned arrows. Because the first that struck him was well-nigh unbearable, the others did not fail to reach their mark.

If he were nameless and penniless, he could not marry Di. That was the first arrow. Such marriages are possible only in books and in that sacred profession which, in spite of numerous instances to the contrary, believes that "the Lord will provide." Di would not be allowed to marry him, even if she were willing to do so. And after a time—a long time, perhaps—she would marry some one else, possibly Lord Hemsworth.

John writhed. He had set his heart on this woman. He had bent her strong will to love him as a proud woman only can. She had been hard to win, but she was his as much as if they were already married; his by right, as the living Galatea was by right the sculptor's, who gave her marble heart the throbbing life and love of his own.

"She is mine—I cannot give her up," he said aloud.

There was no voice, nor any that answered.

Strange how the ploughshare turns up little tags and ends of forgotten rubbish buried by the mould of a few years' dust.

One utterance of Archie's, absolutely forgotten till now, was continually recurring to John's mind. Its barbed point rankled.

"There must be a mint of money in an old barrack stuffed full of gimcracks like this. If ever I wanted a hundred or two, I would trot out one of those little silver Johnnies in no time if they were mine."

And he would. If the thought of what Colonel Tempest and Archie would achieve after his own death had stung John as Archie said that, how should he bear to stand by and *see* them do it? The books, the pictures, the family manuscripts which he was even then arranging, the jewels, the renowned diamond necklace that the Spanish government had offered to buy from his grandfather, which he had hoped one day to clasp on Di's neck—all the possessions of the past but almost regal state of a great name, which he had kept with such a reverent hand—he should live to see them cast right and left, lost, sold, squandered, stolen. Archie would give the diamonds to the first actress who asked for them. Colonel Tempest would be equally "open-handed."

As the days went on, John shut his eyes to the pictures in the gallery as he passed through it. A mute suspense and reproach seemed to hang about the whole place. The Velasquez and the Titian peered at him. Tempest of the Red Hand clutched his sword-hilt uneasily. Mieris' old Dutch-woman seemed to have lost her interest in selling her marvellous string of onions to the little boy. Ribalta's Spanish Jesuit fingered the red cross of Santiago embroidered on his breast, and looked askance at John.

John turned back many times from the library door. The new books which he had had bound in exact reproduction of a beautiful old missal of the Tempest collection, and for the arrival of which he had been eagerly waiting, remained untouched in their packing-cases. He could not look at them.

Once he went into the dining-hall, unused when he was alone, and opened one of the ponderous shutters. The rich light pierced the solemn gloom, catching the silver sconces on the wall and the silver figures standing in the carved niches above the fireplace.

"You will not give us up," they seemed to say; and the little cavalier turned to his lady with a shake of his head.

As John closed the shutter his eyes fell on the Tempest motto on the pane, "Je le feray durant ma vie;" and it stabbed him like a knife.

He went out into the open air like one pursued, and paced in the dead forest waiting for the spring. All he had held so sacred meant nothing then—nothing, nothing, nothing. The Tempest motto, round which he had bound his life, round which his most solemn convictions and aspirations had grown up, had nothing to do with him. He had been mocked. He, a nameless bastard, the offspring of a mere common intrigue, had been fooled into believing that he was John Tempest, the head of one of the greatest families in England; that Overleigh belonged to him and he to it as entirely as—nay, more than—his own hands and feet and eyes.

It was as if he had been acting a serious part to the best of his ability on a stage with many others, and suddenly they had all dropped their masks and were grinning at him with satyr faces in grotesque attitudes, and he found that he alone had mistaken a screaming farce, of which he was the butt, for a drama of which he had imagined himself one of the principal figures.

John laughed a harsh wild laugh under the solemn overarching trees. Everything, himself included, had undergone a hideous distortion. His whole life was dislocated. His faith in God and man wavered. The keystone of his existence was gone from the arch, and the stones struck him as they fell round him. The confusion was so great that for the first few days he was incapable of action, incapable of reflection, incapable of anything.

Mitty! That thought came next. That stung. He had nothing in the wide world which he could call his own; no roof for Mitty, no fire to warm her by. He was absolutely without means. His mother's small fortune he had sunk in an annuity for Mr. Goodwin. What would become of Mitty? How would she survive being uprooted from her little nest in the garret gallery? How would she bear to see her lamb turned adrift upon the world? Mitty was growing old, and her faithful love for him would make the last years sorrowful which were so happy now. Oh, if he could only wait till Mitty died!

John had not wept a tear for himself, but he hid his face against the trunk of one of the trees that were not his, and sobbed aloud at the thought of Mitty.

And next day came a letter from Archie, saying that Colonel Tempest was at death's door in one of the London hospitals, owing to having accidentally shot himself with a revolver. John sent money, much more than was actually necessary, and drew breath. Nothing could be done until Colonel Tempest was either convalescent or dead. He was reprieved from telling Mitty anything for the moment.

And as the spring was just beginning to whisper to the sleeping earth, and the buds of the horse-chestnut to grow white and woolly beneath the nursery windows, as John had seen them many and many a time—how or why I know not, but with the waking of the year Mitty began to fail.

She had never been ill in John's recollection. She had had "a bone in her leg" occasionally, but excepting that mysterious ailment and a touch of rheumatism in later years, Mitty had always been quite well. She was not actually ill now, but—

It was useless to tell her not to "do" her nurseries herself, and to positively forbid her to wash his socks and handkerchiefs. Mitty worked exactly the same; and John with an ache at his heart came indoors every day in time for nursery tea, and Mitty made him buttered toast, and was happy beyond words; but I think her eyesight must have begun to fail her, or she would have seen how grey and haggard the face of her "lamb" became as the days went by.

WHO SHALL SAY WHEN A thought begins? Long before we see it, it was there, but our eyes were holden. "L'amour commence par l'ombre." So do many things besides love.

The letters were destroyed. When did John think of that first, or rather, when did he first hear it whispered? Why was his mind always going back to that?

He would not have burned them if he had taken time to consider, but the first impulse to do with them as their writer had herself intended, had been acted upon before he had even thought of their bearing upon himself and others.

At any rate they were gone—quite gone—sprinkled to the four winds of heaven.

There was no other proof.

And his—no, not his father—Mr. Tempest, who knew all about him, had intended him to be his heir. He had left him his name and his place, with a solemn charge to do his duty by them.

"I have done it," said John to himself, "as those two would never have done. Shall I let all go to rack and ruin now? If I was not born a Tempest I have become one. I *am* one, and if I marry one my children will be Tempests, and those two fools will not be suffered to pull Overleigh stone from stone, and drag a great name into the dust; as they would, as they assuredly would."

Had not Mr. Tempest foreseen this when he exacted that solemn promise from John on his death-bed to uphold the honour of the family? Could he break that promise? And through the vain sophistries, upsetting them all, a mad cry rang, "Di loves me! She loves me at last! I cannot give her up!"

The challenge was thrown out into the darkness. No one took it up.

A fierce restlessness laid hold on John. He rushed up to London several times to hear how Colonel Tempest was going on. Each time he told himself that he was going to see Di. But although the first time he went to Colonel Tempest's lodgings the servant informed him that Di was with her father, he did not ask to see her. Each time he came back without having dared to go to the little house in Kensington. He could not meet those grave clear eyes with the new gentleness in them that went to his head like wine. He knew they would make him forget everything, everything except that he loved her, and would sell his very soul for her.

Time stopped. In all this enormous interval the buds of the horse-chestnut had not yet burst to green. It was ages since he had seen the first primrose, and yet today, as he walked in the woods on the day after his return from another futile journey to London, they were all out in the forest still.

And something stirred within him that had not deigned to take notice of all his feverish asseverations and wanderings, that had not rebuked him, that had not even listened when he had said repeatedly that he could not give up Di.

By an invisible hand the challenge was taken up, and John knew the time of conflict was at hand.

He walked on and on, not knowing where he went, past the forest and the meadowland, and away over the rolling moors, with only Lindo for his companion.

At last his newly returned strength failing him, he threw himself down in the dry windswept heather. He had not outstripped his thoughts. This was the appointed place. He knew it even as he flung himself down. His hour was come.

It was an April afternoon, pale and bleak. The late frost had come back, and had silenced the birds. One only deeply in love, somewhere near at hand, but invisible, repeated plaintively over and over again a small bird-name in the silence of the shrinking spring.

And John's heart said over and over again one little word—

"Di, Di, Di!"

There are some sacrifices which partake of the nature of self-mutilation. That is why principle often falls before the onslaught of a deep human passion, which is nothing but the rebellion of human nature brought to bay, against the execution upon itself of that dread command of the spiritual nature, "If thy right hand offend thee, cut it off."

To give up certain affections is with some natures to give up all possibility of the quickening into life of that latent maturer self that craves for existence in each one of us. It is to take, for better for worse, a more meagre form of life, destitute, not of happiness perhaps, but of those common joys and sorrows which most of all bind us in sympathy with our fellow-men. What marriage in itself is to the majority, the love of one fellow-creature, and one only, is to the few. To a few, happily a very few, there is only one hand that can minister among the pressure of the crowd. There was none other woman in the world for John, save only Di. Sayings common to vulgarity, profaned by every breach of promise case, can yet be true sometimes.

"Di, Di, Di!" said John.

He tried to recall her face, but he could not. When they were together he had not seen her; he had only felt her presence, only trembled at each slight movement of her hands. He always watched them when he was talking to her. He knew every movement of those strong, slender hands by heart. She had a little way of opening and shutting her left hand as she talked. He smiled even now as he thought of it. And she had a certain wave in her hair just above the ear, that was not the same over the other ear. But her face—no, he could not see her face.

He tried again. They were sitting once again, he and she, not very near, nor very far apart, in the low entresol room at Overleigh. He could see her now. She was arranging the lilies of the valley, and he was saying to himself, as he watched her with his chin in his hands, "This is only the beginning. There will be many times like this, only dearer and sweeter than this."

Many times! That deep conviction had proved as false as all the rest—as false as everything else which he had trusted.

And all in a moment as he looked, as he remembered, was it endurance, was it principle, that seemed to snap?

He set his teeth and ground his heel into the earth. Agony had come upon him. Passion, writhing in torment, rose gigantic without warning and seized him in a Titan grip. It was a duel to the death.

John sat motionless in the solitude of the heather. The bird was silent. On either hand the level moors met the level sky. Lindo walked in and out in semi and total eclipse near at hand, now emerging life-size upon a hillock, now visible only as an erect travelling tail amid the heather. The sun came faintly out. There was a little speech of bees, a little quivering among the poised spears of the tall bleached grasses against the sky.

Time passed.

John's was not the easy faith which believes that in another world what has been given up in this will be restored a thousandfold. The hope of future reward had no more power to move him than the fear of future punishment. The heaven of rewards of which those speak who have authority, would be no heaven at all to many; a place from which the noblest would turn away. Love worthy of the name, even down here, gives all, asking nothing back.

John did not try to define even to himself the faith by which he had lived so far; but as the veiled sun stooped near and nearer to the west, he began to see, as clearly as he saw the sword-grass shaking against the sky, that he was about to remain true to it, or be false to it for ever.

Perhaps that faith was more than anything else a stern allegiance to the Giver of that law within the heart which independent natures ever recognize as the only true authority; which John had early elected to obey, which he had obeyed with ease, till now. He had been condemned by many as a freethinker; for to be obedient to the divine prompting has ever been stigmatized as lawlessness by those who are obedient to a written code. John had no code.

Yet God, who made (if the tourists who cheaply move in flocks on beaten highways could only believe it) those solitary, isolated natures, knew what He was about. And to those to whom little human guidance is vouchsafed He adds courage, and that self-reliance which comes only of a deep-rooted faith in a God who will not keep silence, who will not leave the traveller journeying towards Him unpiloted upon a lonely shore, or ultimately suffer His least holy one to see corruption.

John looked wildly round him. Even nature seemed to have turned against him. It spoke of peace when there was no peace. For nature has no power to mitigate the bitterness of that cup of self-surrender which even Christ Himself, beneath the kindred stars of still Gethsemane, prayed might pass from Him.

John hid his convulsed face in his hands.

The crises of life have their hour of loneliness and prostration, their agony and bloody sweat. That cup which may not pass, how ennobling it is to read of in the lives of others, how interesting to theorize upon in our own; how appalling in actual experience, when it is in our hands to drink or to refuse; refusing for ever with it, if we accept it not, the hand of Him who offers it!

THE SOLEMN WORLD OF GREY earth and sky waited. The light in the west waited. How much longer were they to wait? How much longer would this bowed figure sway itself to and fro?

"I will do it!" said John suddenly, and with a harsh inarticulate cry he flung himself down on his face among the heather, clutching the soft earth; for the Hand of the God whom he would not deny was heavy on him.

VIII

"The dead abide with us! Though stark and cold
Earth seems to grip them, they are with us still.
They have forged our chains of being for good or ill."

—Mathilde Blind

John was late. Mitty looked out several times to see if he were coming, and then put down the tea-cake to the fire.

At last his step came slowly along the garret gallery, and Lindo, who approved of nursery tea, walked in first, his dignity somewhat impaired by a brier hanging from his back flounce.

John saw the firelight through the open door, and the figure in the low chair waiting for him. She had heard him coming, and was getting stiffly up to make the tea.

"Mitty, you should not wait for me," he said, sitting down in his own place by the fire.

Would they let her keep the brass kettle and her silver teapot? Yes, no doubt they would; but somebody would have to ask. He supposed he should be that somebody. Everything she possessed had been bought by himself with other people's money.

He let the tea last as long as possible. If Lindo had more than his share of tea-cake, no one was the wiser. At last Mitty cleared away, and sat down in the rocking-chair.

"Don't light the candles, Mitty."

"Why not, my dear? I can't be settin' with my hands before me, and holes in your socks a shame to be seen."

John came and sat down on the floor beside her, and leaned his head against her.

"Never mind the socks just now. There is something I want to talk to you about."

He looked at the fire through the bars of the high nursery fender, and something in its glimmer, seen from so near the floor through the remembered pattern of the wires which he had lost sight of for twenty years, suddenly recalled the times when he had sat on the hearthrug, as he was sitting now, with his head against Mitty's knee, confiding to her what he would do when he was a man.

"Do you remember, Mitty," he said, "how I used to tell you that when I grew up you should ride in a carriage, and have a gold brooch, and a clock that played a tune?"

"I remember, my darling; and how, next time Charles went into York, you give him all you had, and half a crown it was, to buy me a brooch, and the silly staring fool went and spent it, and brought back that great thing with the mock stones in. And you was as pleased as pleased. Eh! I was angry with Charles for taking your bits of money, and all he said was, 'Well, Mrs. Emson, I went to a many shops, and I give five shillin's for it so as to get a big un.'"

"I remember it," said John. "It was about the size of a small poultice. And so Charles paid half. Good old Charles! I seem to have been much deceived in my youth."

His deep-set eyes watched the fire, watched the semblance of a little castle in the heart of the glow. Mitty was quite happy with her darling's head against her knee.

"When the castle falls in I will tell her," said John to himself.

But the fire had settled itself. The castle held. At last Mitty put out her hand, and gave it a poke; not with the brass poker, of course, but with a little black slave which did that polished aristocrat's work for it.

"Mitty," said John, "I am not so rich now as when I was in pinafores; and even then, you see, the brooch was not bought with my own money. Charles gave half. I have never given you anything that was paid for with my own money. I have been spending other people's all my life."

"Why, bless your dear heart!" said Mitty; "and who gave me my silver teapot, I should like to know, and the ivory workbox, and that very kettle a-staring you in the face, and the Wedgwood tea-things, and—and everything, if it was not you?"

John did not answer. His face twitched.

The bars of the fender were blurred. The brass kettle, instead of staring him in the face, melted quite away.

Mitty stroked his head and face.

"Cryin'!" she said—"my lamby cryin'!"

"Not for myself, Mitty."

"Who for, then? For that Miss Dinah?"

"No, Mitty, for you. This is no home for you and me." He took her hard hand and rubbed his cheek against it. "It belongs to Colonel Tempest. I am not my father's son, Mitty."

MARY CHOLMONDELEY

"Well, my precious," said Mitty, soothingly, in no wise discomposed by what John feared would have quite overwhelmed her, "and if your poor mammy did say as much to me when she was light-headed, when her pains was on her, there's no call to fret about that, seeing it's a long time ago, and her dead and all. Poor thing! I can see her now, with her pretty eyes and her little hands, and she'd put her head against me and say, 'Nursey' (Nursey I was to her), 'I'm not fit neither to live nor to die.' Many and many's the night I've roared to think of her after she was gone, when you was asleep in your crib. But there's no need for you to fret, my deary."

John's heart contracted. Mitty knew also. Oh, if he might but have started life knowing what even Mitty knew!

"They'd no business to marry her to Mr. Tempest," continued Mitty, shaking her head, "and she, poor thing, idolizing that black Lord Fane, as was her first cousin. It wasn't likely, after that, she'd settle to Mr. Tempest, who was as light as tow. It was against nature. She never took a bit of interest in him, nor him in her neither, that I could see. A hard man he was, too—a hard man. She sent for him when she was dying. She would not see him while there was any chance. 'Forgive me,' she says; she says it over and over, me holding her up. 'I wouldn't ask it if I was staying, but I'm doing the best I can by dying. It's not much to make up, but it's the best I can. And,' she says, 'don't think, Jack, as all women are bad like me. There's a many good ones as 'ull make you happy yet when I'm gone.' I can see him now, standing by her, looking past her out of the window with his face like a flint. 'I've known two false ones,' he says; and he went away without another word. And she says after a bit to me, 'I've always been frightened at the very thought of dying, but it's living I'm frightened of now.' Eh! Master John, your poor mammy! She did repent. And Mr. Tempest sent for me to the library after the funeral, and he says, 'Promise me, nurse, that you'll never repeat what your mistress said to me when she was not herself.' And he looked hard at me, and I promised. And I've never breathed it to any living soul, not to one I haven't, from that day to this."

"I found it out three weeks ago," said John. "And as I am not Mr. Tempest's son, everything I have belongs by right to Colonel Tempest, the next heir, not to me. Overleigh is not mine. It never was mine."

But Mitty could not be made to understand what his mother's frailty had to do with John. When at last she grasped the idea that John would make known the fact that he was not his father's son, she was simply incredulous that her lamb could do such a thing—could bring shame upon his own mother. No, whatever else he might do, he would never do that. Why, Mrs. Alcock would know; and friends as she was with Mrs. Alcock, and had been for years, such a word had never passed her lips. And the people in the village, and the trades-people, and Jones and Evans from York, who were putting up the new curtains,—everybody would know. Mitty became quite agitated. Surely, surely, he'd never tell against his poor mother in her grave.

"Mitty," said John, forcing himself to repeat what it had been difficult enough to say once, "don't you see that I can't stay here and keep what is not mine? Nothing is mine if I am not Mr. Tempest's son. I ought never to have been called so. We must go away."

But Mitty was perplexed.

"Not to that great weary house in London," she said anxiously, "with every spot of water to carry up from the bottom?"

"That is not mine either," said John in despair, rising to his feet and standing before her. "Oh, Mitty, try and understand. Nothing is mine—nothing, nothing, nothing; not even the clothes I have on. I am a beggar."

Mitty looked at him in a dazed way. She could not understand, but she could believe. Her chin began to tremble.

It was almost a relief to see at last the tears which he had dreaded from the first. "My lamb a beggar," she said over and over again; and she cried a little, but not much. Mitty was getting old, and she was not able to realize a change—a change so incomprehensible as this.

"But we need not be unhappy," said John, kneeling down by her, and putting his arms round her. "We shall be together still. Wherever I go you will go with me. I don't know yet where it will be, but we shall have a little home together somewhere, just you and I; and you'll do my socks and handkerchiefs, won't you, Mitty? and"—John controlled his voice, but he hid his face in her lap that she might not see it—"we'll be so happy together." At the moment I think John would have given up heaven itself to make that hour smooth to Mitty. "And your cakes, Mitty," he went on hoarsely. "They are better than any one else's. You shall have a little kitchen, and you will make the cakes yourself, won't you? and the"—his voice stumbled heavily—"the rock buns."

"My precious," said Mitty, sobbing, "don't you fret yourself! I can make a many things besides them; Albert puddings and moulds, and them little

MARY CHOLMONDELEY

cheese straws, and a sight of things. There's a deal of work in my old hands yet. It's only the spring as has took the starch out of me. I always feel a sinking in the spring. Lord, my darling, the times and times again I've been settin' here just dithering with a mossel of crotchet, or idling over a bit of reading, and wishing you was having a set of nightshirts to make!"

Love had found out the way. John had appealed to the right instinct. Mitty was already busying herself with a future in which she should minister to her child's comfort, and John saw, with a relief that was half a pang, that the calamity of his life held hardly any place in the heart that loved him so much.

"I've a sight of things," continued Mitty, wiping her eyes. "Books and pictures and cushions put away. My precious shall not go short. And there's two pair of linen sheets as I bought with my own money, and piller-slips to match, and six silver teaspoons and one dessert. My lamb shall have things comfortable about him."

She fell to communing with herself. John did not speak.

"I'll leave my places tidy," said Mitty. "Tidy I didn't find 'em, but tidy I'll leave 'em. I can't go till after the spring cleaning, Master John. I'll never trust that Fanny to do the scrubbing unless I'm behind her. I caught her washing round the mats instead of under only last week."

John felt unable to enter into the question of the spring cleaning. There was another silence.

At last Mitty said defiantly, "And I shall take your morroccy shoes, and your little chair as I give you myself. I don't care what anybody says, I shall take 'em. And the old horse and the Noey's ark."

"It will be all right," said John, getting slowly to his feet. "Nobody will want to have them, or anything of mine;" and he kissed her, and went out.

He went to the library and sat down by the fire.

The resolution and aspiration of a few hours ago—where were they now? He felt broken in body and soul.

Lindo came in, nibbled John's elbow, and scrutinized the fire. John scratched him absently on the top of his back between the tufts.

"Lindo," he said, "the world is a hard place to live in."

But Lindo, bulging with an unusual allowance of tea-cake, and winnowing the air with an appreciative hind leg, did not think so.

IX

*"Et souvent au moment où l'on croyait tenir
Une espérance, on voit que c'est un souvenir."*

—VICTOR HUGO

When Colonel Tempest lay in a precarious condition owing to the unexpected explosion of a revolver which he was taking to his gun-maker, and which he believed to be unloaded—when this fatality occurred, Mrs. Courtenay somewhat relaxed the stringency of her usual demeanour to him, and allowed his daughter to be with him constantly in the hospital to which he was first conveyed, and afterwards in his rooms in Brook Street when he was sufficiently convalescent to be conveyed thither.

Colonel Tempest was a trying patient; in one sense he was not a patient at all; melting into querulous tears when denied a sardine on toast for which his soul thirsted, the application of which would infallibly have separated his soul from his body; and bemoaning continually, when consciousness was vouchsafed to him, the neglect of his children and the callousness of his friends. Di bore it with equanimity. It is only true accusations which one feels obliged to contradict. She did not love her father, and his continual appeals to her pity and filial devotion touched her but little. Colonel Tempest confided to his nurse in the night-watches that he was the parent of heartless children, and when Di took her place in the daytime, reviled the nurse's greed, who, whether he was suffering or not, could eat a large meal in the middle of the night.

"I hate nurses," he would say. "Your poor mother had such a horrid nurse when Archie was born. I could not bear her, always making difficulties and restrictions, and locking the door, and then complaining to the doctor because I rattled the lock. I urged your mother to part with her whenever she was not in the room. But she only cried, and said she could not do without her, and that she was kind to her. That was your mother all over. She always sided against me. I must say she knew the value of tears, did your poor mother. She cried herself into hysterics when I rang the front door bell at four in the morning because I had gone out without a latch-key. I suppose she expected me to sit all night on the step. And first the nurse and then the doctor spoke to me about agitating her, and said it was doing her harm; so I just walked straight out of the house, and never set foot in it again for a month till they had both cleared out. They overreached themselves that time."

Archie, who looked in once a day for the space of ten seconds, came in for the largest share of Colonel Tempest's reproaches.

"I don't like sick people," that young gentleman was wont to remark. "Don't understand 'em. No use. Nursing not in my line. Better out of the way."

So, with the consideration of his kind, he was so good as to keep out of it, while Colonel Tempest wept salt tears into his already too salt beef-tea (it was always too salt or not salt enough), and remarked with bitterness that he could have fancied a sardine, and that other people's sons nursed their parents when they were at death's door. Young Grandcourt had never left *his* father's bedside for three weeks when he had pneumonia; but Archie, it seemed, was different.

"My children are not much comfort to me," he told the doctor as regularly as he put out his tongue.

"John might have come," he said one day to Di. "He got out of it by sending a cheque, but I think he might have taken the trouble just to come and see whether I was alive or dead."

"John is ill himself," said Di.

"John is always ill," said Colonel Tempest, fretfully, with the half-memory of convalescence—"always ailing and coddling himself; and yet he has twice my physique. John grows coarse-looking—very coarse. I fancy he is a large eater. I remember he was ill in the summer. I went to see him. I was always sitting with him; and there did not seem to be much the matter with him. I think he gives way."

"Perhaps it is a family failing," said Di, who was beginning to discover what a continual bottling up and corking down of effervescent irritation is comprised under the name of patience.

How many weeks was it after Di's return to London when a cloud no larger than a man's hand arose on the clear horizon of that secret happiness which no amount of querulousness on Colonel Tempest's part could effectually dim? It was a very small cloud. It took the shape of a card with John's name on it, who had come to Brook Street to inquire after his uncle.

"He is in London. He will call this afternoon," said Di to herself; and as Colonel Tempest happened to be too sleepy to wish to be read to, she left him early in the afternoon, and hurried home. And she and

Mrs. Courtenay sat indoors all that afternoon, though they had been lent a carriage, and they waited to make tea till after the time; and whenever the door bell rang, Mrs. Courtenay's hands shook quite as much as Di's. And aimless, foolish persons called, but John did not call.

"He is ill," said Mrs. Courtenay in the dusk, "or he has been prevented coming. There is some reason. He will write."

"Yes," said Di, "he will come when he can." But nevertheless a little shiver of doubt crept into her heart for the first time. "If I had been in his place," she said to herself, "I should have come ill or well, and I should *not* have been prevented."

She put the thought aside instantly as unreasonable, but the shy dread she had previously felt of meeting him changed to a restless longing just to see him, just to be reassured.

To be loved by one we love is, after all, so incredible a revelation that it is not wonderful that human nature seeks after a sign. Only a great self-esteem finds love easy to believe in.

The days passed, and linked themselves to weeks. Was it fancy, or did Mrs. Courtenay become graver day by day? and Di remembered with misgiving a certain note which she had written to John the morning she left Overleigh. The little cloud grew.

ONE AFTERNOON DI CAME IN rather later than usual, and after a glance round the room, which had become habitual to her, sat down by her grandmother, and poured out tea.

"Any callers, granny?"

"One—Archie."

Di sighed. Coming home had always the possibility in it of finding some one sitting in the drawing-room, or a note on the hall table. Yet neither possibility happened.

"Archie came to say that the doctor thinks your father does not gain ground, and that he might be moved to the seaside with advantage. He wanted to know whether you could go with him. He can't get leave himself for more than a couple of days. I said I would allow you to do so, if he took your father down himself, and got him settled. He can do that in two days, and he ought to take his share. He has left everything to you so far. He mentioned," continued Mrs. Courtenay with an effort, "that he had met John at the Carlton yesterday, and that he was all right, and able to go about again as usual. He went back to Overleigh today."

There was a long silence.

"What do you think, granny?" said Di at last.

"How long is it since you were at Overleigh?"

"Two months."

"When you were there did you allow John to see that you had changed your mind, or were you friendly with him, as you used to be? Nothing discourages men so much as that."

"No; I tried to be, but I could not. I don't know what I was, except very uncomfortable."

"Had he any real opportunity of speaking to you without interruption?"

Di remembered the half-hour in the entresol sitting-room. It had never occurred to her till that moment that certainly, if he had wished to do so, he could have spoken to her then.

"Yes," she said, "he had; and," she added, "I am sure he knew I liked him. If he did not know it then, I am quite sure he knows it now. I wrote a note."

"What kind of note?"

"Oh, granny, that is just it. I don't know what kind it was. It seemed natural at the time. I can't remember exactly what I said. I've tried to, often. It was written in such a hurry, for you telegraphed for me, and I had been up all night waiting to hear whether he was to live or die, and it was so dreadful to have to go away without a word."

Mrs. Courtenay leaned back in her chair. She seemed tired.

"Tell me what you think," said Di again.

"I think," said Mrs. Courtenay, "that if John had been seriously attached to you, he would either have come, or have answered your letter by this time. I am afraid we have made a mistake."

Di did not answer. The world was crumbling down around her.

"I may be making one now," said Mrs. Courtenay; "but it appears to me he has had every opportunity given him, and he has made no use of them. Men worth their salt *make* their opportunities, but if they don't even take them when they are ready-made to their hand, they cannot be in earnest. Women don't realize what a hateful position a man is in who is deeply in love, and who has no knowledge of whether it is returned or not. He won't remain in it any longer than he can help."

"John is not in that position," said Di, colouring painfully. "Granny, why don't you reproach me for writing that letter?"

"Because, my dear, though I regret it more than I can say, I should have done the same in your place."

"And—and what would you do *now* in my place?"

"This," said Mrs. Courtenay. "You cannot dismiss the subject from your mind, but whenever it comes into your thoughts, hold steadily before you the one fact that he is certainly aware you are attached to him, and he has not acted on that knowledge."

"They say men don't care for anything when once they know they can have it," said Di hoarsely, pride wringing the words out of her. "Perhaps John is like that. He knows I—am only waiting to be asked."

"Fools say many things," returned Mrs. Courtenay. "That is about as true as that women don't care for their children when they get them. A few unnatural ones don't; the others do. I have seen much trouble caused by love affairs. After middle life most people decry them, especially those who have had superficial ones themselves; for there is seldom any love at all in the mutual attraction of two young people, and the elders know very well that if it is judiciously checked it can also be judiciously replaced by something else. But a real love which comes to nothing is more like the death of an only child than anything else. It *is* a death. The great thing is to regard it so. I have known women go on year after year waiting, as we have been doing during the last two months, refusing to believe in its death; believing, instead, in some misunderstanding; building up theories to account for alienation; clinging to the idea that things might have turned out differently if only So-and-so had been more tactful, if they had not refused a certain invitation, if something they had said which might yet be explained had not been misconstrued. And all the time there is no misunderstanding, no need of explanation. The position is simple enough. No man is daunted by such things except in women's imaginations. What men want they will try to obtain, unless there is some positive bar, such as poverty. And if they don't try, remember the inference is *sure*, that they don't really want it."

Di did not answer. Her face had taken a set look, which for the first time reminded Mrs. Courtenay of her mother. She had often seen the other Diana look like that.

"My child," she said, stretching out her soft old hand, and laying it on the cold clenched one, "a death even of what is dearest to us, and a funeral and a headstone to mark the place, hard as it is, is as nothing compared to the death in life of an existence which is always dragging about a corpse. I have seen that not once nor twice. I want to save you from that."

Di laid her face for a moment on the kind hand.

"I will bury my dead," she said.

X

I t seems a pity that our human destinies are too often so constituted that with our own hands we may annul in one hour—our hour of weakness—the long, slow work of our strength; annul the self-conquest and the renunciation of our best years. We ought to be thankful when the gate of the irrevocable closes behind us, and the power to defeat ourselves is at last taken from us. For he who has once solemnly and with conviction renounced, and then, for no new cause, has taken to himself again that which he renounced, has broken the mainspring of his life.

John went early the following morning to London, for he had business with three men, and he could not rest till he had seen them, and had shut that gate upon himself for ever.

So early had he started that it was barely midday when he reached Lord Frederick's chambers. The valet told him that his lordship was still in bed, and could see no one; but John went up to his bedroom, and knocked at the door.

"It is I—John Tempest," he said, and went in.

Lord Frederick was sitting up in bed, sallow and shrunk like a mummy, in a blue watered-silk dressing-gown. His thin hair was brushed up into a crest on the top of his head. The bed was littered with newspapers and letters. There was a tray before him, and he was in the act of chipping an egg as John came in.

He raised his eyebrows and looked first with surprised displeasure, and then with attention, at his visitor.

"Good morning," he said; and he went on tapping his egg. "Ah," he said, shaking his head, "hard-boiled again!"

John looked at him as a plague-stricken man might look at the carcase of some obscene animal found rotting in his water-spring.

Lord Frederick's varied experiences had made him familiar with the premonitory symptoms of those outbursts of anger and distress which he designated under the all-embracing term of "scenes." He felt idly curious to know what this man with his fierce white face had to say to him.

"Oblige me by sitting down," he said; "you are in my light."

"I have been reading my mother's letters to you," said John, still standing in the middle of the room, and stammering in his speech. He had not reckoned for the blind paroxysm of rage which had sprung up at the mere sight of Lord Frederick, and was spinning him like a leaf in a whirlwind.

"Indeed!" said Lord Frederick, raising his eyebrows, and carefully taking the shell off his egg. "I don't care about reading old letters myself, especially the private correspondence of other people; but tastes differ. You do, it seems. I had imagined the particular letters you allude to had been burnt."

"My mother intended to burn them."

"It would certainly have been wiser to do so, but probably for that reason they remained undestroyed. From time immemorial womankind has shown a marked repugnance to the dictates of common sense."

"I have burnt them."

"Just so," said Lord Frederick, helping himself to salt. "I commend your prudence. Had you burnt them unread, I should have been able to commend your sense of honour also."

"What do you know about honour?" said John.

The two men looked hard at each other.

"That remark," said Lord Frederick, joining the ends of his fingers and half shutting his eyes, "is a direct insult. To insult a man with whom you are not in a position to quarrel is, in my opinion, John, an error of judgment. We will consider it one, and as such I will let it pass. The letters, I presume, contained nothing of which you were not already aware?"

"Only the fact that I am your illegitimate son."

"I deplore your coarseness of expression. You certainly have not inherited it from me. But, my dear Galahad, it is impossible that even your youth and innocence should not have known of my *tendresse* for your mother."

"Is that the last new name for adultery?" said John huskily, advancing a step nearer the bed. His face was livid. His eyes burned. He held his hands clenched lest they should rush out and wrench away all semblance of life and humanity from that figure in the watered-silk dressing-gown.

Lord Frederick lay back on his pillows, and looked at him steadily. He was without fear, but it appeared to him that he was about to die. The laws of his country, of conscience and of principle, all the protection that envelops life, seemed to have receded from him, to have slipped away into the next room, or downstairs with the valet. They would come back, no doubt, in time, but they might be a little late, as far as he was concerned.

"He has strong hands, like mine," he said to himself, his pale, unflinching eyes fixed upon his son's; while a remembrance slid through his mind of how once, years ago, he had choked the life out of a mastiff which had turned on him, and how long the heavy brute had taken to die.

"Do not spill the coffee," he said quietly, after a moment.

John started violently, and wheeled away from him like a man regaining consciousness on the brink of an abyss. Lord Frederick put out his lean hand, and went on with his breakfast.

There was a long silence.

"John," said Lord Frederick at last, not without a certain dignity, "the world is as it is. We did not make it, and we are not responsible for it. If there is any one who set it going, it is his own look out. Reproach *him*, if you can find him. All we have to do is to live in it. And we can't live in it, I tell you we can't exist in it, with any comfort until we realize that it is rotten to the core."

John was leaning against the window-sill shaking like a reed. It seemed to him that for one awful moment he had been in hell.

"I do not pretend to be better than other men," continued Lord Frederick. "Men and women are men and women; and if you persist in thinking them angels, especially the latter, you will pay for your mistake."

"I am paying," said John.

"Possibly. You seem to have sustained a shock. It is incredible to me that you did not know beforehand what the letters told you. Wedding-rings don't make a greater resemblance between father and son than there is between you and me."

Lord Frederick looked at the stooping figure of the young man, leaning spent and motionless against the window, his arms hanging by his sides. He held what he called his prudishness in contempt, but he respected an element in him which he would have termed "grit."

"You are stronger built than I am, John," he said, with a touch of pride, "and wider in the chest. Come, bygones are bygones. Shake hands."

"I can't," said John. "I don't know that I could on my account, but anyhow not on *hers*."

"H'm! And so this was the information which you rushed in without leave to spring upon me?"

"It was, together with the fact that of course I withdraw in favour of Colonel Tempest, the heir at law. I am going on to him from here."

Lord Frederick reared himself slowly in his bed, his brown hands clutching the bedclothes like eagles' talons.

"You are going to own your—"

"*My* shame—yes; not yours. You need not be alarmed. Your name shall not be brought in. If I take the name of Fane, it will only be because it was my mother's."

"But you said you had burned the letters."

"I have. I don't see what difference that makes. The fact that they are burnt does not alter the fact that I am—nobody, and he is the legal heir."

"And you mean to tell him so?"

"I do."

"To commit suicide?"

"Social suicide—yes."

"Fool!" said Lord Frederick, in a voice which lost none of its force because it was barely above a whisper.

John did not answer.

"Leave the room," said the outraged parent, turning his face to the wall, the bedclothes and the tray trembling exceedingly. "I will have nothing more to do with you. You need not come to me when you are penniless. Do you hear? I disown you. Leave me. I will never speak to you again."

"I hope to God you never will," said John; and he took up his hat and went out.

He had settled his account with the first of the three people whom he had come to London to see. From Lord Frederick's chambers he went straight to Colonel Tempest's lodgings in Brook Street. But Colonel Tempest had that morning departed with his son to Brighton, and John, momentarily thrown off his line of action by that simple occurrence, stared blankly at the landlady, and then went to his club and sat down to write to him. There was no question of waiting. Like a man walking across Niagara on a tight rope, it was no time to think, to hesitate, to look round. John kept his eyes riveted to one point, and shut his ears to the roar of the torrent below him, in which a moment's giddiness would engulf him.

It was afternoon by this time. As he sat writing at a table in one of the bay windows, a familiar voice spoke to him. It was Lord Hemsworth. They had not met since the night of the ice carnival. Lord Hemsworth's face had quite lost its boyish expression.

"I hope you are better, Tempest," he said, with obvious constraint, looking narrowly at him. Could Di's accepted lover wear so grey and stern a look as this?

John replied that he was well; and then, with sudden recollection of Mitty's account of Lord Hemsworth's conduct during that memorable night, began to thank him, and stopped short.

The room was empty.

"It was on *her* account," said Lord Hemsworth.

John did not answer. It was that conviction which had pulled him up.

Lord Hemsworth waited some time for John to speak, and then he said—

"You know about me, Tempest, and why I was on the ice that night. Well, I have kept out of the way for three months under the belief that—I should hear any day that—I am not such a fool as to pit myself against you—I don't want to be a nuisance to—But it's three months. For God's sake tell me; are you on or are you not?"

"I am not," said John.

"Then I will try my luck," said the other.

He went out, and John knew that he had gone to try it there and then; and sat motionless, with his hand across his mouth and his unfinished letter before him, until the servant came to close the shutters.

XI

"We live together years and years,
And leave unsounded still
Each other's springs of hopes and fears,
Each other's depths of will."

—Lord Houghton

B ut still more bewildering is the way in which we live years and years
with ourselves in an entire ignorance of the powers that lie dormant
beneath the surface of character. The day comes when vital forces of
which we know nothing arise within us, and break like glass the even
tenor of our lives. The quiet hours, the regulated thoughts, the peaceful
aspiration after things but little set above us, where are they? The angel
with the sword drives us out of our Eden to shiver in the wilderness of an
entirely changed existence, unrecognizable by ourselves, though perhaps
lived in the same external groove, the same divisions of time, among the
same faces as before.

Day succeeded day in Di's life, each day adding one more stone to the
prison in which it seemed as if an inexorable hand were walling her up.

"I will not give in. I will turn my mind to other things," she said to
herself. And—there were no other things. All lesser lights were blown
out. The heart, when it is swept into the grasp of a great love, is ruthlessly
torn from the hundred minute ties and interests that heretofore held it
to life. The little fibres and tendrils of affections which have gradually
grown round certain objects are snapped off from the roots. They cease
to exist. The pang of love is that there is no escape from it. It has the
same tension as sleeplessness.

Di struggled and was not defeated; but some victories are as sad as
defeats. During the struggle she lost something—what was it—that
had been to many her greatest charm? Women were unanimous in
deploring how she had "gone off." There was a thinness in her cheek,
and a blue line under her deep eyes. Her beauty remained, but it was
not the same beauty. Mrs. Courtenay noticed with a pang that she was
growing like her mother.

Easter came, and with it the wedding of Miss Crupps and the
Honourable Augustus Lumley, youngest son of Lord Mortgage. Miss

Crupps' young heart had long inclined towards Mr. Lumley; but on the occasion of seeing him blacked as a Christy Minstrel, she had finally succumbed into a state of giggling admiration, which plainly showed the state of her affections. So he cut the word "yes" out of a newspaper, and told her that was what she was to say to him, and amid a series of delighted cackles they were engaged. Di went to the wedding, looking so pale that it was whispered that Mr. Lumley and his tambourine had won her heart as well as that of his adoring bride.

On a sunny afternoon shortly afterwards, Di was sitting alone indoors, her grandmother having gone out driving with a friend. She told herself that she ought to go out, but she remained sitting with her hands in her lap. Every duty, every tiny decision, every small household matter, had become of late an intolerable burden. Even to put a handful of flowers into water required an effort of will which it was irksome to make.

She had stayed in to make an alteration in the gown she was to wear that night at the Speaker's. As she looked at the card to make sure it was the right evening, she remembered that it was at the Speaker's she had first met John, just a year ago. One year. How absurd! Five, ten, fifteen! She tried to recollect what her life could have been like before he had come into it; but it seemed to start from that point, and to have had no significance before.

"I must go out," she said again; and at that moment the door bell rang, and although Mrs. Courtenay was out, some one was admitted. The door opened, and Lord Hemsworth was announced.

There is, but men are fortunately not in a position to be aware of it, a lamentable uniformity in their manner of opening up certain subjects. Di knew in a moment from previous experience what he had come for. He wondered, as he stumbled through a labyrinth of platitudes about the weather, how he could broach the subject without alarming her. He did not know that he had done so by his manner of coming into the room, and that he had been refused before he had finished shaking hands.

Di was horribly sorry for him while he talked about—whatever he did talk about. Neither noticed what it was at the time, or remembered it afterwards. She was grateful to him for not alluding even in the most distant manner to their last meeting. She remembered that she had clung to him, and that he had called her by her Christian name, but she was too callous to be ashamed at the recollection. It was as nothing compared to another humiliation which had come upon her a little later.

"It is no good beating about the bush," said Lord Hemsworth at last, after he had beaten it till there was, so to speak, nothing left of it. "I have come up to London for one thing, and I have come here for one thing, which is—to ask you to marry me. Don't speak—don't say anything just for a moment," he continued hurriedly, raising his hand as if to ward off a rebuff. "For God's sake don't stop me. I've kept it in so long I must say it, and you must hear me."

She let him say it. And he got it out with stumbling and difficulty and long gaps between—got out in shaking commonplaces a tithe of the love he had for her. And all the time Di thought if it might only have been some one else who was uttering those halting words! (I wonder how many men have proposed and been accepted while the woman has said to herself, "If it had only been some one else!")

Despair at his inability to express himself, and at her silence, seized him: as if it mattered a pin how he expressed himself if she had been willing to listen.

"If you understood," he said over and over again, with the monotonous reiteration of a piano-tuner, "you would not refuse me. I know you are going to, but if only you understood you would not. You would not have the heart. It's—it's just everything to me." And Lord Hemsworth—oh, bathos of modern life!—looked into his hat.

"Lord Hemsworth," said Di, "have I ever given you any encouragement?"

"None," he replied. "People might think you had, but you never did. I knew better. I never misunderstood you. I know you don't care a straw about me; but—oh, Di, you have not your equal in the world. There's no woman to compare with you. I don't see how you could care for any one like me. Of course you don't. I would not expect it. But if—if you would only marry me—I would be content with very little. I've looked at it all round. I would be content with—very little."

There was a long silence.

What woman whose love has been slighted can easily reject a great devotion?

"I think," said Di, after several false starts to speak, "that if I only considered myself I would marry you; but there is the happiness of one other person to think of—*yours*."

"I can't have any apart from you."

"You would have none with me. If it is miserable to care for any one who is indifferent, it would be a thousand times more miserable to be married to that person."

"Not if it were you."

"Yes, if it were I."

"I would take the risk," said Lord Hemsworth, who held, in common with most men, the rooted conviction that a woman will become attached to any husband, however little she cares for her lover. It is precisely this conviction which makes the average marriages of the present day such mediocre affairs; which serves to place worldly or facile women, or those whose affections have never been called out, at the head of so many homes; as the mothers of the new generation from which we hope so much.

"I would take any risk," repeated Lord Hemsworth, doggedly. "I would rather be unhappy with you than happy with any one else."

"You think so now," said Di; "but the time would come when you would see that I had cut you off from the best thing in the world—from the love of a woman who would care for you as much as you do for me."

"I don't want her. I want you."

"I cannot marry you."

Lord Hemsworth clutched blindly at the arms of the chair.

"I would wait any time."

Di shook her head.

"Any time," he stammered. "Go away for a year, and—come back."

"It would be no good."

Then he lost his head.

"So long as you don't care for any one else," he said incoherently. "I thought at the carnival—that is why I have kept out of the way— but I met Tempest today at the Carlton, and—I asked him straight out, and he said there was nothing between you and him. I suppose you have refused him, like the rest of us. Oh, my God, Di, they say you have no heart! But it isn't true, is it? Don't refuse me. Don't make me live without you. I've tried for three months"—and Lord Hemsworth's face worked—"and if you knew what it was like, you wouldn't send me back to it."

Every vestige of colour had faded from Di's face at the mention of John.

"I don't care enough for you to marry you," she said, pitiless in her great pity. "I wish I did, but—I don't."

"Do you care for any one else?"

Di saw that nothing short of the truth would wrest his persistence from its object.

"Yes, I do," she said passionately, trembling from head to foot. "For some one who does not care for me. You and I are both in the same position. Do you see now how useless it is to talk of this any longer?"

Both had risen to their feet. Lord Hemsworth looked at Di's white convulsed face, and his own became as ashen. He saw at last that he had no more chance of marrying her than if she were lying at his feet in her coffin. Constancy, which can compass many things, avails nought sometimes.

"I beg your pardon," he said, holding out his hand to go.

"I think I ought to beg yours," she said brokenly, while their hands clasped tightly each in each. "I never meant to make you as—unhappy as—as I am myself, but yet I have."

They looked at each other with tears in their eyes.

"It does not matter," said Lord Hemsworth, hoarsely. "I shall be all right—it's you—I think of. Don't stand—mustn't stand—you're too tired. Good-bye."

DI FLUNG HERSELF DOWN ON her face on the sofa as the door closed. She had forgotten Lord Hemsworth's existence the moment after he had left the room. *John had told him that there was nothing between her and himself.* John had told him that. John had said that. A cry escaped her, and she strangled it in the cushion.

Hope does not always die when we imagine it does. It is subject to long trances. The hope which she had thought dead was only giving up the ghost now. "Chaque espérance est un oeuf d'où peut sortir un serpent au lieu d'une colombe." Out of that frail shell of a cherished hope lying broken before her the serpent had crept at last. It moved, it grew before her eyes.

"Slighted love is sair to bide."

XII

"We met, hand to hand,
We clasped hands close and fast,
As close as oak and ivy stand;
But it is past."

—Christina Rossetti

"Half false, half fair, all feeble."

—Swinburne

When John roused himself from the long stupor into which he had fallen after Lord Hemsworth's departure, he put his finished letter to Colonel Tempest into an envelope, and then remembered with annoyance that he did not know how to address it. When the landlady in Brook Street had told him that Colonel and Captain Tempest had gone to Brighton that morning, he had been too much taken aback at the moment to think of asking for their address. He was too much exhausted in mind and body to go back to the lodgings for it immediately. He wrote a second letter, this time to his lawyer, and then, conscious of the state of his body by the shaking hand and clumsy, tardy brain which made of a short and explicit statement so lengthy an affair, he mechanically changed his clothes, dined, and sat watching the smoke of his cigar.

Presently, with food and rest, the apathy into which exhaustion had plunged him lifted, and the restlessness of a tortured mind returned. He had only as yet seen one of the three men whom he had come to London to interview, namely, Lord Frederick. Colonel Tempest, the second, was out of town; but probably the third, Lord—, the minister, was not. It was close on ten o'clock. He should probably find him in his private room in the House.

John flung away his cigar, and was in a few minutes spinning towards the Houses of Parliament in a hansom. He had not thought much about it till now, but as he turned in at the gates the lines of the great buildings suddenly brought back to him the remembrance of his own ambition, and of the splendid career that had seemed to be opening before him when last he had passed those gates; which had fallen at a single touch like a house of cards—a house built with Fortune's cards.

There was a *queue* of carriages at the Speaker's entrance. A party was evidently going on there. John went to the House and inquired for Lord—. He was not there. Perhaps he was at the Speaker's reception. John remembered, or thought he remembered, that he had a card for it, and went on there. His mind was set on finding Lord—.

HISTORY REPEATS ITSELF, AND SO does our little private history. Only when the same thing happens it finds us changed, and we look back at what we were last time, and remember our old young self with wonder. Was that indeed I?

Possibly to some an evening party may appear a small event, but to Di, as she stood in the same crowd as last year, in the same pictured rooms, it seemed to her that her whole life had turned on the pivot of that one evening a year ago.

The lights glared too much now. The babel dazed her. Noises had become sharp swords of late. Every one talked too loud. She chatted and smiled, and vaguely wondered that her friends recognized her. "I am not the same person," she said to herself, "but no one seems to see any difference."

Presently she found herself near the same arched window where she had stood with John last year. She moved for a moment to it and looked out. There was a mist across the river. The lights struggled through blurred and feeble. It had been clear last year. She turned and went on talking, of she knew not what, to a very young man at her elbow, who was making laborious efforts to get on with her.

Her eyes looked back from the recess across the sea of faces and fringes, and bald and close-cropped heads. The men who were not John, but yet had a momentary resemblance to him, were the only people she distinctly saw. Tall fair men were beginning to complain of her unrecognizing manner.

Yes, history repeats itself.

Among the crowd in the distance she suddenly saw him. John's rugged profile and square head were easy to recognize. *He had said there was nothing between them.* Their last meeting rushed back upon her with a scathing recollection of how she had held him in her arms and pressed her face to his. Shame scorched her inmost soul.

She turned towards her companion with fuller attention than what she had previously accorded him.

MARY CHOLMONDELEY

As John walked through the rooms scanning the crowd, the possibility of meeting Di did not strike him. With a frightful clutch of the heart he caught sight of her. A man who instantly aroused his animosity was talking eagerly to her. Something in her appearance startled him. Was it the colour of her gown that made her look so pale, the intense light that gave her calm dignified face that peculiar worn expression? She had a faint fixed smile as she talked that John did not recognize, and that, why he knew not, cut him to the quick.

Was this Di? Could this be Di?

He knew she had seen him. He hesitated a moment and then went towards her. She received him without any change of countenance. The fixed smile was still on her lips as he spoke to her, but the lips had whitened. Their eyes met for a moment. Oh! what had happened to Di's lovely eyes that used to be so grave and gay?

He stammered something—said he was looking for some one—and passed on. She turned to speak to some one else as he did so. He strangled the nameless emotion which was choking him, and made his way into the next room. He had a vague consciousness of being spoken to, and of making herculean efforts to grind out answers, and then of pouncing on the secretary of the man he was looking for, who told him his chief had suddenly and unexpectedly started for Paris that afternoon on affairs of importance.

John mechanically noted down his address in Paris and left the house.

The necessity of remembering where his feet were taking him recalled him somewhat to himself. He pulled himself together, and slackened his pace.

"I will go to Paris by the night express," he said to himself, the feverish longing for action increasing upon him as this new obstacle met him. He dared not remain in London. He knew for a certainty that if he did he should go and see Di. Neither could he write to Lord— all that he must tell him, or put into black and white the favour he had to ask of him—the first favour John had ever needed to ask, namely, to be helped by means of Lord—'s interest to some post in which he could for the moment support himself and Mitty.

As he turned up St. James's Street, he remembered with irritation that he had not yet procured Colonel Tempest's and Archie's address. While he hesitated whether to go on, late as it was, to Brook Street for it, he remembered that he could probably obtain it much nearer at hand, namely, at Archie's rooms in Piccadilly. Archie, who was a person of much pink and monogrammed correspondence, would probably have left his address behind him, stuck in the glass of the mantelpiece, as his manner was. The latch-key he had lent John in the autumn, when John had made use of his rooms, was still on his chain. He had forgotten to return it. He let himself in, went upstairs to the second floor, and opened the door of the little sitting-room.

"Here you are at last," said a woman's voice.

He went in quickly and shut the door behind him.

A small woman in shimmering evening dress, with diamonds in her hair, came towards him, and stopped short with a little scream.

It was Madeleine.

He looked at her in silence, standing with his back to the door. The smouldering fire in his eyes seemed to burn her, for she shrank away to the further end of the room. John observed that there was a fire and lamps, and knit his brows.

Some persons are unable to perceive when explanations are useless. Madeleine began one—something about Archie's difficulties, money, etc.; but John cut her short.

"You are not accountable to me for your actions," he said. "Keep your explanations for your husband."

He looked again with perplexity at the fire and the lamps. He knew Archie had gone that morning on three days' leave to Brighton with his father.

"Let me go," she said, whimpering. "I won't stay here to be thought ill of, to have evil imputed to me."

"You will answer one question first," said John.

"You impute evil to me—I know you do," said Madeleine, beginning to cry; "but it is your own coarse mind that sees wickedness in everything."

"Possibly," said John. "When do you expect Archie?"

"Any moment. I wish he was here, that he might tell you—"

"Thank you, that will do. You can go now."

He opened the door. She drew a long cloak over her shoulders and passed him without speaking, looking like what she was—one of that class whose very existence she professed to ignore, but whose ranks she had virtually joined when she announced her engagement to Sir Henry in the *Morning Post*. Perhaps, inasmuch as that, untempted, she had sold herself for diamonds and position, instead of, under strong temptation, for the bare necessities of life like her poorer sisters, she was more degraded than they; but fortunately for her, and many others in our midst, society upheld her.

John looked after her and then followed her. There was not a soul on the common staircase or in the hall. He passed out just behind her, and they were in the street together.

"Take my arm," he said, and she took it mechanically.

He signalled a four-wheeler and helped her into it.

"Where do you wish to go?" he said.

"I don't know," she said feebly, apparently too much scared to remember what her arrangements had been.

John considered a moment.

"Where is Sir Henry?"

"Dining at Woolwich."

"Can't you go home?"

"No, no. It is much too early. I'm dressed for—I said I was going to—, and I have left there already, and the carriage is waiting there still."

"You must go back there," said John. "Get your carriage and go home in it."

He gave the cabman the address and paid him. Then he returned to the cab door.

"Lady Verelst," he said less sternly, "believe me—Archie is not worth it."

"You don't understand," she tried to say, with an assumption of injured dignity. "It was only that I—"

"He is not worth it," said John with emphasis; and he shut to the door of the cab, and watched it drive away. Then he went back to Archie's room, and sat down to consider. A faint odour of scent hung about the room. He got up and flung open the window. Years afterwards, if a woman used that particular scent, the same loathing disgust returned upon him.

"He took three days' leave to nurse his father at Brighton, with the intention of coming back here tonight," John said to himself. "He will be here directly." And he made up his mind what he would do.

And in truth a few minutes later a hansom rattled to the door, and Archie came in, breathless with haste. He looked eagerly round the room, and then, as he caught sight of the unexpected occupant, his face crimsoned, and he grinned nervously.

"She is gone," said John, without moving.

"Gone? Who? I don't know what you mean."

"No, of course not. What made you so late?"

"Train broke down outside London."

"I came here to get your address at Brighton, because I have news for you. You are there at this moment, aren't you, looking after your father?"

Archie did not answer. He only grinned and showed his teeth. John was aware that though he stood quietly enough by the table, turning over some loose silver in his pocket, he was in a state of blind fury. He also knew that if he waited a little it would pass. Something in John's moral and physical strength had always the power to quell Archie's fits of passion.

"I had no intention of prying on you," said John, after an interval. "I wanted your address at Brighton, and I could not wait till tomorrow for it. I am going to Paris tonight on business, and—as it is yours as much as mine—you will go with me."

Archie never indulged in those flowers of speech with which some adorn their conversation. But there are exceptions to every rule, and he made one now. He culled, so to speak, one large bouquet of the choicest epithets and presented it to John.

"He knew not what to say, and so he swore." That is why men swear often, and women seldom.

"I shall not leave you in London with that woman," said John, calmly. "You will go to her if I do."

"I shall do as I think fit," stammered Archie, striking the table with his slender white hand.

"There you err," said John. "You will start with me in half an hour for Paris."

XIII

"There's not a crime
But takes its proper change out still in crime
If once rung on the counter of this world."

—E. B. BROWNING

There is in Paris, just out of the Rue du Bac, a certain old-fashioned hotel, the name of which I forget, with a little *cour* in the middle of the rambling old building, and a thin fountain perennially plashing therein, adorned by a few pigeons and feathers on the brink. It had been a very fashionable hotel in the days when Madame Mohl held her *salon* near at hand. But the old order changes. It was superseded now. Why John often went there I don't know. He probably did not know himself, unless it was for the sake of quiet. Anyhow, he and Archie arrived there together that morning; for it is needless to say that, having determined to get Archie at any cost out of London, John had carried his point, as he had done on previous occasions, to the disgust of the sulky young man, who had proved anything but a pleasant travelling companion, and who, late in the afternoon, was still invisible behind the white curtains in one of the two little bedrooms that opened out of the sitting-room in which John was walking up and down.

He had put several questions to Archie respecting the state of his father's health, and that gentleman had assured him he was all right, quite able to look after himself; no need for him to remain with him.

"Of course not," said John, "or you would not have left him. But is he able to attend to business?"

"Rather," said Archie, with the emphasis of ignorance.

As long as Archie was in the next room, out of harm's way, John did not want his company. He knew that when he did appear he had to tell him that for eight and twenty years he had lived on Colonel Tempest's substance; and then he must post the letter lying ready written on the table to Colonel Tempest, only needing the address.

After that life was a blank. Archie would rush home, of course. John did not know where he should go, except that it would not be with Archie. Back to Overleigh? No. And with a sudden choking sensation he realized that he should not see Overleigh again. He wondered what

Mitty was doing at that moment, and whether the horse-chestnut against the nursery window would ever burst to leaf. Here in Paris they were out. He had noticed them as he returned from an interview with Lord—. That gentleman had been much pressed for time, but had nevertheless accorded him a quarter of an hour. He was genuinely perturbed by the disclosure the young man made to him, deplored the event as it affected John, but after the first moment was obviously more concerned about the seat, and the loss of the Tempest support, than the wreck of John's career. After a decorous interval, Lord— had put a few questions to him about Colonel Tempest, his age, political views, etc. John perceived with what intentions those questions were put, and they made it the harder for him to ask the great man to help him to a livelihood.

As John spoke, and the elder man's eye sought his watch, John experienced for the first time the truth of the saying that the highest price that can be paid for anything is to have to ask for it. If it had not been for Mitty he could not have forced himself to do it.

"But my dear—er—Tempest," said Lord—, "surely we need not anticipate that—er—your uncle—er—that Colonel Tempest will fail to make a suitable provision for one—who—who—"

"He may offer to do so," replied John; "but if he did, I should not take it. He is not the kind of man from whom it is possible to accept money."

"Still, under the circumstances, the extraordinary combination of circumstances, I should advise you to—my time is so circumscribed—I should certainly advise you to—you see, Tempest, with every feeling of regard for yourself and your father—ahem—Mr. Tempest before you, it is difficult for a person situated as I am at the present moment, to offer you, on the eve of the general election, any position at all adequate to your undeniably great abilities."

"We shall not hear much more of my great abilities now that I am penniless," said John, with bitterness. "If I can get any kind of employment by which I can support myself and an old servant, I shall be thankful."

Lord— promised to do his best. He felt obliged to add that he could do but little, but he would do what he could. John might rest assured of that. In the meantime— He looked anxiously at the watch on the table. John understood, and took his leave. Lord— pressed him warmly by the hand, commended his conduct, once more deplored the turn

MARY CHOLMONDELEY

events had taken, which he should consider as strictly private until they had been publicly announced, and assured him he would keep him in his mind, and communicate with him immediately should any vacancy occur that, etc., etc.

John retraced his steps wearily to the hotel. The loss of his career had stung him yesterday. How to keep Mitty in comfort seemed of far greater importance today—how to provide a home for her with a little kitchen in it. John wondered whether he and Mitty could live on a hundred a year. He knew a good deal about the ways and means of the working classes, but of how the poor of his own class lived he knew nothing.

But even the thought of Mitty could not hold him long. His mind ever went back to Di with an agony of despair and rapture. During these three interminable months during which he had not seen her, he had pictured her to himself as taking life as usual, wondering perhaps sometimes—yes, certainly wondering—why he did not come; but it had never struck him that she would be unhappy. When he saw her he had suddenly realized that the same emotions which had rent his soul had left their imprint on her face. Could women really love like men? Could Di actually, after her own fashion, feel towards him one tithe of the love he felt for her? John recognized with an exaltation, which for the moment transfigured as by fire the empty desolation of his heart, that the change which had been wrought in Di was his own work. Her cheek had grown pale for him, her eyes had wept for him, her very beauty had become dimmed for his sake.

"I shall go mad," said John, starting to his feet. "Why is that damned letter still unposted?"

Purpose was melting within him. The irrevocable step even now had not been taken. Lord— and his own lawyer would say nothing if at the eleventh hour he drew back. He must act finally this instant, or he would never act at all.

He went into the next room, where Archie was languidly shaving himself in a pink silk *peignoir*, and obtained from him Colonel Tempest's address. He addressed the letter, and took his hat and stick.

"I will post it myself this instant," he said to himself.

He went quickly downstairs and across the little court, scattering the pigeons. His face looked worn and ravaged in the vivid sunshine.

He passed under the archway into the street, and as he did so two well-dressed men came out of a *café* on the opposite side. Before he had gone many steps one of them crossed the road, and raised his hat, holding out a card.

"Mr. Tempest of Overleigh, I think," he said respectfully.

John stopped and looked at the man. He did not know him. The decisive moment had come even before posting the letter.

"Now or never," whispered conscience.

"My name is Fane," he said, and passed on.

The man fell back at once and rejoined his companion.

"I told you so," he said. "That man is a deal too old, and he said his name was Fane. It's the other one in the tow wig, as I said from the first. That ain't real hair. It's the wig as alters him."

John posted his letter, saw it slide past recall, and then walked back to the hotel, found Archie in the sitting-room reading the playbills for the evening, and told him.

Perhaps nothing is more characteristic of our fellow-creatures than the manner in which they bear unexpected reverses of fortune. Archie had some of the callousness of feeling for others which accompanies lack of imagination. He had never put himself in the place of others. He was not likely to begin now. He had no intention of hurting John by setting his iron heel on his face. He had no idea people minded being trodden on. And, indeed, as John stood by the window with his hands clasped behind his back, he was as indifferent as he appeared to be to anything that Archie, pacing up and down the room with flashing eyes, could say. He had at last closed the iron gates of the irrevocable behind himself, and he was at first too much stunned by the clang even to hear what the excited young man was talking about. Perhaps it was just as well.

"By Jove!" Archie was saying, as John's attention came slowly back. "To think of the old governor at Overleigh, poor old chap! He has missed it all his best years, but I hope he'll live to enjoy it yet. I do indeed." Archie felt he could afford to be generous. "And Di, John, dear old Di, shall come and queen it at Overleigh. And she shall have a suitable fortune. I'll make father do the right thing by Di. He won't want to do more than he can help, because she has never been much of a daughter to him; but he shall. And when it's known, she'll marry off quick enough; and I'll see it gets about. And don't you be down-hearted, John. We'll do the right thing by you. You know you never cared for the money when you had it. You were always a bit of a screw, to yourself as well as to others—I will say that for you; but—let me see—you allowed me three hundred a year. Don't you wish now it had been four? for you shall have the same, if the old guv. agrees. And I dare say I shall be a bit freer with a ten-pound note now and then than ever you were to me."

"There will be no necessity for this reckless generosity," said John, wondering why he did not writhe, as a man might who watches a knife cut into his benumbed limb. It gave him no pain.

"And you shall have a hunter," continued Archie. "By Jove, what hunting *I* shall have! I shall get the governor to add another wing to the stables; and I will keep Quicksilver for you, John. You mustn't turn rusty because the luck has come to us at last. You know I knew all along I ought to have been the heir, and I put up with your being there, and never raised a dust."

"I think I can promise I shall not raise a dust," said John, dispassionately, watching the knife turn in his flesh.

"And—and," continued Archie—"why, I need not marry money now. I can take my pick." New vistas seemed to open at every turn. His weak mouth fell ajar. "My word, John, times are changed. And—my debts; I can pay them off."

"And run up more," said John. "It is an ill wind that blows nobody any good."

"I don't call it much of an ill wind," said Archie, chuckling; "not much of an ill wind."

In spite of himself, John laughed aloud at the *naïveté* of Archie's remark. That it was an ill wind to John had not even crossed his mind.

It would cross Di's, John thought. She would do him justice. But, alas! from the few who will do us justice we always want so much more, something infinitely greater than justice—at least, John did.

The early *table d'hôte* dinner broke in on Archie's soliloquy, and, much to John's relief, that favoured young gentleman discovered that a lady of his acquaintance was dancing at one of the theatres that evening, and he determined to go and see her. He could not persuade John to accompany him, even though he offered, with the utmost generosity, to introduce him to her.

"Well, if you won't, you won't," said Archie, seeing his persuasions did nought avail, and much preferring to go by himself. "If you would rather sit over the fire in the dumps, that's your affair, not mine. Ta-ta. I expect you will have turned in before I'm back. By-the-by, can you lend me five thick 'uns?"

John was on the point of refusing when he remembered that the actual money he had with him was more Archie's than his.

"Thank'ee," said Archie. "You part easier than you used to do. I expect it'll be the last time I shall borrow of you—eh, John? It will be the other way about in future."

"Will it?" said John, as he put back his pocket-book.

Archie laughed and went out.

Oh! it is good to be young and handsome and admired. The dancers pirouetted in the intense electric light, and the music played on every chord of Archie's light pleasure-loving soul. And he clapped and applauded with the rest, his pulse leaping high and higher. A sense of triumph possessed him. His one thorn in the flesh was gone for ever. He rode on the top of the wave. He had had all else before, and now the one thing that was lacking to him had come. He was rich, rich, rich. There was much goods laid up for many years of pleasure.

Archie touched the zenith.

It was very late, or rather it was very early, when he walked home through the deserted streets. A great mental exaltation was still upon him, but his body was exhausted, and the cool night air and the silence, after the babel of tongues, and the shrieking choruses, and the flaring lights of the last few hours, were pleasant to his aching eyes and head.

The dawn stretched like a drawn sword behind the city. The Seine lay, a long line of winding mist under its many bridges. The ruins of the scorched Tuileries pushed up against the sky. Archie leant a moment on the parapet, and looked down to the Seine below whispering in its shroud. He took off his hat and pushed back the light curling hair from his forehead, laughing softly to himself.

An invisible boat, with a red blur coming down-stream, was making a low continuous warning sound.

A hand came suddenly over his shoulder, and was pressed upon his mouth, and at the same instant something exceeding sharp and swift, pointed with death, pierced his back, once and again. Archie saw his hat drop over the parapet into the mist.

He tried to struggle, but in vain. He was choking.

"It is a dream," he said. "I shall wake. I have dreamt it before."

He looked wildly round him.

The steadfast dawn was witness from afar. There was the boat still passing down-stream. There was the city before him, with its spires piercing the mist. *Was* it a dream?

The hot blood rushed up into his mouth. The drenched hand released its pressure.

"I shall wake," he said, and he fell forward on his face.

XIV

"The earth buildeth on the earth castles and towers;
The earth sayeth to the earth, 'All shall be ours;'
The earth walketh on the earth, glistering like gold;
The earth goeth to the earth sooner than it wold."

John was late next morning. He had not slept for many nights, and the heavy slumber of entire exhaustion fell on him towards dawn. It was nearly midday when he re-entered the sitting-room where he had sat up so late the night before.

He went to Archie's room to see whether he had come in; but it was empty.

He was impatient to be gone, to get away from that marble-topped side-table, and the horsehair chairs, and the gilt clock on the mantelpiece. At least, he thought he wished to get away from these things; but it was from himself that he really wanted to get away— from this miserable tortured self that was all that was left of him in this his hour of weakness and prostration; the hour which inevitably succeeds all great exertions of strength. How could he drag this wretched creature about with him? He abhorred himself; the thought of being with himself was intolerable. It seems hard that the nobler side of human nature, which can cheer and urge its weaker brother up such steep paths of duty and self-sacrifice, should desert us when the summit is achieved, leaving the weaker to wail unreproved over its bleeding feet and rent garments till we madden at the sound.

An overwhelming sense of loneliness fell on John as he sat waiting for Archie to come in. He had no strong, earnest, steadfast self to bear him company. He felt deserted, lost.

Who has not experienced it, that fierce depression and loathing of all life, which, though at the time we know it not, is only the writing and fainting of the starved human affections! The very ordinary sources from which the sharpest suffering springs, shows us later on how narrow are the limits within which our common human nature works, and from which yet irradiate such diversities of pain.

Alphonse disturbed him at last to ask whether he and "Monsieur" would dine at *table d'hôte*. "Monsieur," with a glance at Archie's door, had not yet come in.

John said they would both dine; and then, roused somewhat by the interruption, an idea struck him. Had Archie, in the excitement of the moment, gone back to England without telling him?

He went to the room, but there were no evidences of departure. On the bed the clothes were thrown which Archie had worn on the previous day. The gold watch John had given him was on the dressing-table. He had evidently left it there on purpose, not caring, perhaps, to risk taking it with him. All the paraphernalia of a man who studies his appearance were strewed on the table. There was his little moustache-brush, and phial of *brilliantine* to burnish it. John knew that he would never have left *that* behind. Archie had evidently intended to return.

In the mean while hour succeeded hour, but he did not come. That Archie should have been out all night was not surprising, but that he should be still out now in his evening clothes in the daytime, began to be incomprehensible. After a few premonitory tremors of misgiving, which, man-like, he laughed at himself for entertaining, John took alarm.

Evening fell, and still no Archie. And then a hideous night followed, in which John forgot everything in heaven above or earth beneath except Archie. The police were informed. The actress at whose house he had supped after the play was interviewed, but could only vociferate between her sobs that he had left her house with the remainder of her party in the early hours of the morning, and she had not seen him since.

Directly the office opened, John telegraphed to his colonel to know if he had returned to London. The answer came, "Absent without leave."

John remembered that he had only three days' leave, and that the third day was up yesterday. Archie would not have forgotten that.

A nightmare of a day passed. John had been out during the greater part of it, rushing back at intervals in the hope, that was no longer anything but a masked despair, of finding Archie in his rooms on his return.

In the dusk of the afternoon he came back once more, and peered for the twentieth time into the littered bedroom, which the frightened servants had left exactly as Archie had left it. He was standing in the doorway looking into the empty room, where a certain horror was beginning to gather round the familiar objects with which it was strewed, when a voice spoke to him.

It was the superintendent of police to whom he had gone long ago—the night before—when first the horror began. Alphonse, who had shown him up, was watching through the doorway.

The man said something in French. John did not hear him, but it did not matter much. He knew. They went downstairs together. Alphonse brought him his hat and stick. The other waiters were gathered in a little knot at the *table d'hôte* door. A fiacre was waiting under the archway. John and the superintendent got into it, and it drove off at once without waiting for directions. They were lighting the lamps in the streets. The dusk was falling, falling like the shadow of death. They drove deeper and ever deeper into it.

Time ceased to be.

"Nous voiçi, Monsieur," said the man, gravely, as they pulled up before a building, the long low outline of which was dimly visible.

John knew it was the Morgue.

He followed his guide down a white-washed passage into a long room. There was a cluster of people at the further end, towards which the man was leading him, and in the dusk there was a subdued whispering, and a sound of trickling water.

As they reached the further end, some one turned on the electric light, and it fell full on a man's figure on one of the slabs. A little crowd of people were peering through the glass screen at the toy which the Seine had tired of and cast aside.

"Ah! qu'il est beau," said a high woman's voice.

John shaded his eyes and looked.

The face was turned away, but John knew the hair, fair to whiteness in that brilliant light, as he had often seen it in London ball-rooms.

They let him through the glass screen which kept off the crowd, and, oblivious of the many eyes watching him, John bent over the slab and touched the clenched marble hand with the signet-ring on it which he had given him when they were at Oxford together.

Yes, it was Archie.

The dead face was set in the nervous grin with which he had been wont in life to meet the inevitable and the distasteful.

The blue pencillings of dissolution had touched to inexorable distinctness the thin lines of dissipation in the cheek and at the corners of the mouth. The death of the body had overtaken the creeping death of the soul. Their landmarks met.

MARY CHOLMONDELEY

The poor beautiful effeminate face, devoid of all that makes death bearable, stared up at the electric light.

An impotent overwhelming compassion, as for some ephemeral irresponsible being of another creation, who knows not how to guide itself in this grim world of law, and has wandered blindfold within the sweep of a vast machinery of which it knew nothing, wrung John's heart. He hid his face in his hands.

XV

*"For human bliss and woe in the frail thread
Of human life are all so closely twined,
That till the shears of fate the texture shred,
The close succession cannot be disjoined,
Nor dare we, from our hour, judge that which comes behind."*

—Sir Walter Scott

Di had seen her father and Archie off on their journey to Brighton, and, having arranged to replace her brother in three days' time, was surprised when a hasty note, the morning after their departure, informed her that Archie had been recalled to London *on business*, and that she must go to her father at once.

Mrs. Courtenay was incensed. Archie had shirked before, and now he had shirked again. But Colonel Tempest remained in far too precarious a condition for her to refuse to allow her granddaughter to go, as she would certainly otherwise have done. So Di went off the morning after the Speaker's party.

She had told Mrs. Courtenay that she had met John there.

"In one way I am glad to have met him," she said firmly, her proud lip quivering. "Any uncertainty I may have been weak enough to feel is at an end, and it was time the end should come. For, in spite of all you said, I had had a lingering idea that if we met—. And now we *have* met—and he had evidently no wish to see me again."

Mrs. Courtenay looked fixedly at the beautiful pallid face, and wondered that she had ever wished Di had a heart.

"This pain will pass," she said gently. "You have always believed me, Di; believe me now. Take courage and wait. You have had an untroubled life till now. That has passed. Trouble has come. It is part of life. It will pass too; not the feeling, perhaps, but the suffering."

"Good-bye, my child," she said a little later, kissing the girl's cold cheek with a tenderness which Di was powerless to return. "Take care of yourself. Go out every day; the sea air will do you good. And tell your father I cannot spare you more than a fortnight."

Di would have given anything to show her grandmother that she was thankful—oh, how thankful in this grey world!—for her sympathy and love, but she had no words. She kissed Mrs. Courtenay, and went down to the cab.

Mrs. Courtenay remained motionless until she heard it drive away. Then she let two tears run down from below her spectacles, and wiped them away. No more followed them. The old cannot give way like the young. Mrs. Courtenay had once said that nothing had power to touch her very nearly; but she was still vulnerable on one point. Her old heart, worn with so many troubles, ached for her granddaughter.

"Thank God," she said to herself, "that in the next world there will be neither marrying nor giving in marriage. Perhaps God Almighty sees it's a mistake."

Di found Colonel Tempest wrapped up in a *duvet* in an armchair by the window of his sitting-room, in a state of equal indignation against his children for deserting him, and against the rain for blurring the seaview from the window. With his nurse, it is hardly necessary to add, he was not on speaking terms—a fact which seemed to cause that patient, apathetic person very little annoyance, she being, as she told Di, "accustomed to gentlemen."

Di soothed him as best she could, took his tray from the nurse at the door, so that he might be spared as much as possible the sight of the most hideous woman in the world, rang for lights, and drew a curtain before the untactful rain, while he declaimed alternately on the enormity of Archie's behaviour, and on the callousness of Mrs. Courtenay in endeavouring to keep his daughter, his only daughter, away from him. Colonel Tempest and Archie detested Mrs. Courtenay. However much the father and son might disagree and bicker on most subjects, they could always sing a little duet together in perfect harmony about her.

Colonel Tempest began a feeble solo on that theme to Di when he had finished with Archie; but Di visibly froze, and somehow the subject, often as it was started, always dropped. Di, as Colonel Tempest frequently informed her, did not care to hear the truth about her grandmother. If she knew all that *he* did about her, and what her behaviour had been to *him*, she would not be so fond of her as she evidently was.

Earlier in his illness Di had been obliged to exercise patience with her father, but she needed none now. That is the one small compensation for deep trouble. It numbs the power of feeling small irritations. It is when it begins to lift somewhat that the small irritations fit themselves out with new stings. Di had not reached that stage yet. The doctor who came daily to see her father looked narrowly at her, and ordered her to go out-of-doors as much as possible, in wet weather or fine.

"I sometimes take a little nap after luncheon," said Colonel Tempest with dignity. "You might go out then, Di."

"Miss Tempest will in any case go out morning and afternoon," said the doctor with decision.

Colonel Tempest had before had his doubts whether the doctor understood his case, but now they were confirmed. He wished to change doctors, and a painful scene ensued between him and Di, in the course of which a hole was kicked in the *duvet*, and a cup of broth was upset. But it is an ascertained fact that women are not amenable to reason. Di sewed up the hole in the *duvet*, rubbed the carpet, and remained, as Colonel Tempest hysterically informed her, "as obstinate as her mother before her."

On the second morning after her arrival at Brighton she was sitting with Colonel Tempest, reading the papers to him, when the waiter brought in the letters. There were none for her, two for her father. One was a foreign letter with a blue French stamp. She took them to him where he lay on the sofa.

Colonel Tempest looked at them.

"Nothing from Archie again," he said. "He does not care even to write and ask whether I am alive or dead."

"Archie is not a good hand at writing," said Di, echoing, for the sake of saying something, the time-honoured masculine plea for exemption from the tedium of domestic correspondence.

"This is John's hand," said Colonel Tempest. "A Paris postmark. How these rich men do rush about!"

Di had actually not known it was John's writing. She had never seen it, to her knowledge, but nevertheless it appeared to her extraordinary that she had not at once divined that it was his. She was not anxious to hear her father's comments on John's letter, or the threadbare remark, sacred to the poor relation, that when the rich one *was* sitting down to draw a cheque he might just as well have written it for double the amount. He would never have known the difference. The poor relation always knows exactly how much the rich one can afford to give. So Di told her father she was going out, and left the room.

It stung her, as she laced her boots, to think that John had probably sent another cheque to cover their expenses at the hotel,

MARY CHOLMONDELEY

and that the fried soles and semolina-pudding which she had ordered for luncheon would be paid for by him. It exasperated her still more to know that whatever John sent, Colonel Tempest would pronounce to be mean.

Before she had finished lacing her boots, however, the sitting-room door was opened, and Di heard her father calling wildly to her.

Colonel Tempest was not allowed to move, except with great precaution, owing to the slow healing of the obstinate internal injury caused by that unlucky pistol-shot.

She rushed headlong downstairs.

"Father!" she cried, horrified to find him standing on the landing. "Father, come back at once!" And she put her arms round him, and supported him back to the sofa.

He was trembling from head to foot. She saw that something had happened, but he was not in a state to be questioned. She administered what restoratives she had at hand, and presently the constantly moving lips got out the words, "Read it;" and Colonel Tempest pointed to a letter on the floor.

"Read it," repeated Colonel Tempest, lying back on his cushions, and recovering from his momentary collapse. "Read it."

Di picked up the letter and sat down by the window. She was suddenly too tired to stand. Her father was talking wildly, but she did not hear him; was calling to her to read it aloud, but she did not hear him. She saw only John's strong, small handwriting.

It was a business letter, couched in the most matter-of-fact terms. John stated his case—expressed a formal regret that the facts he mentioned had not come to light at Mr. Tempest's death, mentioned that the accumulation of income during his minority had fortunately remained untouched, that he had desired his lawyer to communicate with Colonel Tempest, and signed himself "John Fane." He had written the word "Tempest," and had then struck it through.

Di pressed her forehead against the glass on which the rain was beating.

Was the emotion which was shattering her joy or sorrow, or both?

She knew it was joy. In a lightning-flash of comprehension she realized that it was this awful calamity which had kept John silent, which had held him back from coming to her, from asking her to marry him. He loved her still! Love, dead and buried, had risen out of his grave. The impossible had happened. John loved her still.

"I cannot bear it," she said; and for a moment the long yellow waves, and her father's impatient voice, and even John's letter, were alike blotted out, unheard.

Colonel Tempest considered Di's apathy, after she had read the letter, unfeeling and unsympathetic in the extreme, and he did not hesitate to tell her so. But when she presently turned her averted face towards him he was already off on another tack, his excitement, which seemed to increase rather than diminish, tossing him as a wave tosses a spar.

"Twenty years," he said tremulously. "Think of it, Di—not that you seem to care! Twenty years have I toiled and moiled in poverty, twenty years have I and my children been ground down while that nameless interloper has spent our money right and left. Oh, my God! I've got it at last. I've got my own at last. But who will give me back those twenty years?" and Colonel Tempest's voice broke into a sob.

Other consequences of that letter began to dawn on Di's awakening consciousness.

"Then John," she said, bewildered. "Oh, father, what will become of John?"

"John," said Colonel Tempest, bitterly, "is now just where I was twenty years ago—disinherited, penniless. He has kept me out all these years, and now at last Providence gives me my own."

It is to be hoped that Providence is not really responsible for all the shady transactions for which we offer up our best thanks.

"I dare say he has put by," continued Colonel Tempest. "He has had time enough."

"You have not read the letter carefully," said Di. "He only discovered all this less than three months ago, and you have been ill for more than two."

Colonel Tempest did not hear her. He had ceased for the last twenty years to hear anything he did not want to.

"Fifty thousand a year," he went on; "not a penny less. And the New River shares have gone up since Jack's day. And there was a large sum which rolled up during the minority. John is right there. There must be over a hundred thousand. You shall have that, Di. Archie will kick, but you shall have it. Eight thousand pounds John settled on you a year ago. That was the amount of *his* generosity to my poor girl. You shall not have a penny less than a hundred thousand. Not during my lifetime, of course; but when I die—" he added hastily.

Di could articulate nothing.

"I shall pay my own debts and Archie's in a moment," he continued, not noticing whether she answered or not. "If you want a new gown, Di, you may send the bill to me. I don't believe I owe a thousand, and Archie not so much, poor lad, though John was always pulling a long face over his debts. How deuced mean John was from first to last! Well, do as you would be done by. I'll do for him alone what he thought enough for the two of you. I'll never give him cause to say I'm close-fisted. He shall have your eight thousand, and he shall have three hundred a year, the same that he allowed Archie, as well."

"He won't take it."

"Won't take it!" said Colonel Tempest, contemptuously. "That's all you know about the world, Di. I tell you he'll have to take it. I tell you he has not a sixpence in the world at this moment, to say nothing of owing me twenty years' income."

Colonel Tempest rambled on of how Archie should leave the army and live at Overleigh, of how Di should live there too, and Mrs. Courtenay might go to the devil. Presently he fell to wondering what state the shooting was in, and how many pheasants John was breeding at that moment. Every instant it became more unbearable, till at last Di sent for the nurse, made an excuse of posting her letters, and slipped out of the room.

She went out to her old friends, the yellow waves, and, too exhausted to walk, sat down under the lee of one of the high wooden rivets between which the sea licks the pebbly shore into grooves.

Gradually the tension of her mind relaxed. Di sat and watched the waves until they washed away the high invalid voice vibrating in some acute recess of her brain; washed away the hideous thought that they were rich because John was penniless and dishonoured; washed away everything except the one fact that his silence was accounted for, and that he loved her after all.

Di looked out across the rain-trodden sea. If it was raining, she did not know it. What did anything in this wide world matter so long as John loved her? Poverty was nothing. Marriage was nothing either. What did it matter if they could not marry so long as they loved each other?

Once in a lifetime it is vouchsafed alike to the worldly and to the pure, to the earnest and to the frivolous, to discern that vision—which has been ever life's greatest reality or life's greatest illusion according to the character of the beholder—that to love and to be loved is enough.

A wet glint came across the sea, exquisite and evanescent as the gleam across Di's heart.

"It is enough!" said Di; and her soul was flooded with a solemn joy a thousand times deeper than when she had first discovered her love for John, and his for her, and a brilliant future was before her.

Sorrow with his pick mines the heart. But he is a cunning workman. He deepens the channels whereby happiness may enter, and hollows out new chambers for joy to abide in, when he is gone.

XVI

"Though the mills of God grind slowly, yet they grind exceeding small."

—Longfellow

The doctor was sitting with Colonel Tempest on Di's return to the hotel, and Di perceived that her father, who was still in a very excited state, had been telling him about his sudden change of fortune.

The doctor courteously offered his congratulations, and on leaving made a pretext of inquiring after Di's health in order to see her alone.

"Colonel Tempest has been telling me of his unexpected access of wealth," he said. "In his present condition of nervous prostration, and tendency to cerebral excitement, the information should most certainly have been withheld from him. His brain is not in a state to bear the strain which such an event might have put upon it, has put upon it. Were such a thing to occur again in his enfeebled condition, I cannot answer for the consequences."

"It was absolutely unforeseen," said Di. "None of us had the remotest suspicion. He has been in the habit of reading his letters for the past month."

"They must be kept from him for the present," replied the doctor. "Let them be brought to you in future, and use your own discretion about showing them to him after you have read them yourself. Your father must be guarded from all agitation."

This was more easily said than done. Nothing could turn Colonel Tempest's shattered, restless mind from hopping like a grasshopper on that one subject for the remainder of the day. The bit of cork in his medicine, which at another time would have elicited a torrent of indignation, excited only a momentary attention. He talked without ceasing—hinted darkly at danger to John which that young man's creditable though tardy action had averted, alluded to passages in his own life which nothing would induce him to divulge, and then lighting on a sentimental vein, discoursed of a happy old age (the old age of fiction), in which he should see Archie's and Di's children playing in the gallery at Overleigh. And the old name—

Di had not realized, until her parent descanted upon the subject in a way that set her teeth on edge, how hideous, how vulgar, is the seamy side of pride of birth. When Colonel Tempest began to dwell on "the goodness and the grace that on his birth had smiled," shall we blame Di if she put on the clock half an hour, and rang for the nurse?

Things were not much better next morning. Di gave strict orders that all letters and telegrams should be brought to her room. Colonel Tempest fidgeted because he had not heard from the lawyer in whose hands John had placed the transfer of the property. The letter was in Di's pocket, but she dared not give it to him, for though it contained nothing to agitate him, she knew that the fact that she had opened it would raise a whirlwind.

"And Archie," said Colonel Tempest, querulously—"I ought to have heard from him too. If John told him the same day that he wrote to me, we ought to have heard from Archie this morning. I should have imagined that though Archie did not give his father a thought when he was poor, he might have thought him worthy of a little consideration *now*."

"If that is the motive you would have given him if he had written, it is just as well he has not," said Di; but she wondered at his silence nevertheless.

But she did not wonder long.

She left her father busily writing to an imaginary lawyer, for he had neither the name nor address of John's, and on the landing met a servant bringing a telegram to her room. She took it upstairs, and though it was addressed to her father, opened it. She had no apprehension of evil. The old are afraid of telegrams, but the young have made them common, and have worn out their prestige.

The telegram was from John, merely stating that Archie had been taken seriously ill.

Di's heart gave a leap of thankfulness that her father had been spared this further shock. But Archie. Seriously ill. She was indignant at John's vague statement. What did seriously ill mean? Why could not he say what was the matter? And how could she keep the fact of his illness from her father? Ought she to go at once to Archie? Seriously ill. How like a man to send a telegram of that kind! She would telegraph at once to John for particulars, and go or stay according as the doctor thought she could or could not safely leave her father. Di put on her walking things, and ran out to the post-office round the corner, where she despatched a peremptory telegram to John; and then, seeing there was no one else to advise her, hurried to the doctor's house close at hand. For a wonder he was in. For a greater still, his last patient walked out as she walked in. The doctor, with the quickness of his kind, saw the difficulty, and caught up his hat to come with her.

"You shall go to your brother if you can," was the only statement to which he would commit himself during the two minutes' walk in the rain; the two minutes which sealed Colonel Tempest's fate.

NO ONE KNEW EXACTLY HOW it happened. Perhaps the hall porter had gone to his dinner, and the little boy who took his place for half an hour brought up the telegram to the person to whom it was addressed. No one knew afterwards how it had happened. It did happen, that was all.

Colonel Tempest had the pink paper in his hand as the doctor and Di entered the room. He was laughing softly to himself.

"Archie is dead," he said, chuckling. "That is what John would like me to believe. But I know better. It is John that is dead. It is John who had to be snuffed out. Swayne said so, and he knew. And John says it's Archie, and he will write. Ha, ha! We know better, eh, doctor? eh, Di? John's dead. Eight and twenty years old he was; but he's dead at last. He won't write any more. He won't spend my money any more. He won't keep me out any more."

Colonel Tempest dropped on his knees. The only prayer he knew rose to his lips. "For what we are going to receive, the Lord make us truly thankful."

FOR AN AWFUL DAY AND night the fierce flame of delirium leaped and fell, and ever leaped again. With set face Di stood hour after hour in the blast of the furnace, till doctor and nurse marvelled at her courage and endurance.

On the evening of the second day John came. He had written to tell Colonel Tempest of his coming, but the letter had not been opened.

The doctor, thinking he was Di's brother, brought him into the sick-room, too crowded with fearful images for his presence to be noticed by the sick man.

"John is dead," the high-pitched terrible voice was saying. "Blundering fools. First there was the railway, but Goodwin saved him; damn his officiousness. And then there was the fire. They nearly had him that time. How grey he looked! Burnt to ashes. Bandaged up to the eyes. But he got better. And then the carnival. They muffed it again. Oh, Lord, how slow they were! But"—the voice sank to a frightful whisper—"they got him in Paris. I don't know how they did it—it's a secret; but they trapped him at last."

Suddenly the glassy eyes looked with horrified momentary recognition at John.

"Risen from the dead," continued the voice. "I knew he would get up again. I always said he would; and he has. You can't kill John. There's no grave deep enough to hold him. Look at him with his head out now, and the earth upon his hair. We ought to have put a monument over him to keep him down. He's getting up. I tell you I did not do it. The grave's not big enough. Swayne dug it for him when he was a little boy—a little boy at school."

Di turned her colourless face to John, and smiled at him, as one on the rack might smile at a friend to show that the anguish is not unbearable. She felt no surprise at seeing him. She was past surprise. She had forgotten that she had ever doubted his love.

In silence he took the hand she held out towards him, and kept it in a strong gentle clasp that was more comfort than any words.

Hour after hour they watched and ministered together, and hour by hour the lamp of life flared grimly low and lower. And after he had told everything—everything, everything that he had concealed in life—after John and Di had heard, in awed compassion and forgiveness, every word of the guilty secret which he had kept under lock and key so many years, at last the tide of remembrance ebbed away and life with it.

Did he know them in the quiet hours that followed? Did he recognize them? They bent over him. They spoke to him gently, tenderly. Did he understand? They never knew.

And so, in the grey of an April morning, poor Colonel Tempest, unconscious of death, which had had so many terrors for him in life, drifted tranquilly upon its tide from the human compassion that watched by him here, to the Infinite Pity beyond.

Conclusion

"Where there are twa seeking there will be a finding."

After John had taken Di back to London he returned to Brighton, and from thence to Overleigh, to arrange for the double funeral. He had not remembered to mention that he was coming, and in the dusk of a wet afternoon he walked up by the way of the wood, and let himself in at the little postern in the wall. He had not thought he should return to Overleigh again, yet here he was once more in the dim gallery, with its faint scent of *pot-pourri*, his hand as he passed stirring it from long habit. The pictures craned through the twilight to look at him. He stole quietly upstairs and along the garret gallery. The nursery door was open. A glow of light fell on Mitty's figure. What was she doing?

John stopped short and looked at her, and, with a sudden recollection as of some previous existence, understood.

Mitty was packing. Two large white grocery boxes were already closed and corded in one corner. John saw "Best Cubes" printed on them, and it dawned upon his slow masculine consciousness that those boxes were part of Mitty's luggage.

Mitty was standing in the middle of the room, holding at arm's length a little red flannel dressing-gown, which knocked twenty years off John's age as he looked.

"I shall take it," she said, half aloud. "It's wore as thin as thin behind; that and the open socks as I've mended and better-be-mended;" and she thrust them both hastily, as if for fear she should repent, into a tin box, out of which the battered head of John's old horse protruded.

If there was one thing certain in this world, it was that the Noah's ark would not go in unless the horse came out. Mitty tried many ways, and was contemplating them with arms akimbo when John came in.

She showed no surprise at seeing him, and with astonishment John realized that it was only six days since he had left Overleigh. It was actually not yet a week since that far-distant afternoon, separated from the present by such a chasm, when he had lain on his face in the heather, and the deep passions of youth had rent him and let him go. Here at Overleigh time stopped. He came back twenty years older, and the almanac on his writing-table marked six days.

John made the necessary arrangements for the funeral to take place at midnight, according to the Tempest custom, which he knew Colonel Tempest would have been the last to waive. He wrote to tell Di what he had settled, together with the hour and the date. He dared not advise her not to be present, but he remembered the vast concourse of people who had assembled at his father's funeral to see the torchlight procession, and he hoped she would not come.

But Mrs. Courtenay wrote back that her granddaughter was fixed in her determination to be present, that she had reluctantly consented to it, and would accompany her herself. She added in a postscript that no doubt John would arrange for them to stay the night at Overleigh, and they should return to London the next day.

THE NIGHT OF THE FUNERAL was exceeding dark and still; so still that many, watching from a distance on Moat-hill, heard the voice saying, "I am the resurrection and the life, saith the Lord: he that believeth in Me, though he were dead, yet shall he live."

And again—

"We brought nothing into this world, and it is certain we can carry nothing out."

The night was so calm that the torches burned upright and unwavering, casting a steadfast light on church and graveyard and tilted tombstones, on the crowded darkness outside, and on the worn faces of a man and woman who stood together between two open graves.

JOHN AND DI EXCHANGED NO word as they drove home. There were lights and a fire in the music-room, and she went in there, and began absently to take off her hat and long crêpe veil. Mrs. Courtenay had gone to bed.

John followed Di with a candle in his hand. He offered it to her, but she did not take it.

"It is good-bye as well as good night," he said, holding out his hand. "I must leave here very early tomorrow."

Di took no notice of his outstretched hand. She was looking into the fire.

"You must rest," he said gently, trying to recall her to herself.

A swift tremor passed over her face.

"You are right," she said, in a low voice. "I will rest—when I have had five minutes' talk with you."

John shut the door, and came back to the fireside. He believed he knew what was coming, and his face hardened. It was bitter to him that Di thought it worth while to speak to him on the subject. She ought to have known him better.

She faced him with difficulty, but without hesitation. They looked each other in the eyes.

"You are going to London early to see your lawyer," she said, "on the subject that you wrote to father about."

"I am."

"That is why I must speak to you tonight. I dare not wait." Her eyes fell before the stern intentness of his. Her voice faltered a moment, and then went on. "John, don't go. It is not necessary. Don't grieve me by leaving Overleigh, or—changing your name."

A great bitterness welled up in John's heart against the woman he loved—the bitterness which sooner or later few men escape, of realizing how feeble is a woman's perception of what is honourable or dishonourable in a man.

"Ah, Di," he said, "you are very generous. But do not let us speak of it again. Such a thing could not be."

He took her hand, but she withdrew it instantly.

"John," she said with dignity, "you misunderstand me. It would be a poor kind of generosity in me to offer what it is impossible for you to accept. You wound me by thinking I could do such a thing. I only meant to ask you to keep your present name and home for a little while, until—they both will become yours again by right—the day when—you marry me."

A beautiful colour had mounted to Di's face. John's became white as death.

"Do you love me?" he said hoarsely, shaking from head to foot.

"Yes," she replied, trembling as much as he.

He held her in his arms. The steadfast heart that understood and loved him beat against his own.

"Di!" he stammered—"Di!"

And they wept and clung together like two children.

Postscript.

Mitty's packing was never finished—why, she did not understand. But John, who helped her to rearrange her things, understood, and that was enough for her. For many springs and spring cleanings the horse-chestnut buds peered in at the nursery windows and found her still within. I think the wishes of Mitty's heart all came to pass, and that she loved "Miss Dinah;" but nevertheless I believe that, to the end of life, she never quite ceased to regret the little kitchen that John had spoken of, where she would have made "rock buns" for her lamb, and waited on him "hand and foot."

PRINTED BY WILLIAM CLOWES AND SONS, LIMITED
LONDON AND BECCLES
D. & Co.

MARY CHOLMONDELEY

A Note About the Author

Mary Cholmondeley (1859–1925) was an English novelist. Born in Shropshire, Cholmondeley was raised in a devoutly religious family. When she wasn't helping her mother at home or her father in his work as a Reverend, she devoted herself to writing stories. Her first novel, The Danvers Jewels (1887), initially appeared in serial form in Temple Bar, earning Cholmondeley a reputation as a popular British storyteller. Red Pottage (1899), considered her masterpiece, was a bestselling novel in England and the United States and has been recognized as a pioneering work of satire that considers such themes as religious hypocrisy and female sexuality.

A Note from the Publisher

Spanning many genres, from non-fiction essays to literature classics to children's books and lyric poetry, Mint Edition books showcase the master works of our time in a modern new package. The text is freshly typeset, is clean and easy to read, and features a new note about the author in each volume. Many books also include exclusive new introductory material. Every book boasts a striking new cover, which makes it as appropriate for collecting as it is for gift giving. Mint Edition books are only printed when a reader orders them, so natural resources are not wasted. We're proud that our books are never manufactured in excess and exist only in the exact quantity they need to be read and enjoyed.

bookfinity™

Discover more of your favorite classics with Bookfinity™.

- Track your reading with custom book lists.
- Get great book recommendations for your personalized Reader Type.
- Add reviews for your favorite books.
- AND MUCH MORE!

Visit **bookfinity.com** and take the fun Reader Type quiz to get started.

Enjoy our classic and modern companion pairings!